THE NIGHT IS A TIME
FOR LISTENING

THE NIGHT IS A TIME FOR LISTENING

A NOVEL BY

ELLIOT WEST

PANTHEON BOOKS, NEW YORK

For my mother and father,
Stella and Harry,
With Love

THE NIGHT IS
A TIME FOR
LISTENING

CHAPTER ONE

1

He had been told to stand at three P.M. in the entrance to Breite
Strasse facing Marx-Engels Platz, where a taxi would pick him
up. Not just any taxi—a very special one, whose driver wouldn't
need to be given instructions but merely told: "My face is frozen
stiff." The vehicle would be a medium Mercedes, color black,
registration number 663425; the driver would be wearing a blue
cap with white piping above the visor, and a dark blue half-
coat. A yellow scarf would be around his neck and hanging out
in front. Such particulars seemed ludicrous when coldly recited.
They were not. The possibility of error in these matters hovered
habitually like a bird of evil intent. Darsoss found the baroque
procedure as logical as making sure his trousers were zipped
up before leaving the house. Anyhow, they wanted to see him.
This was either a good sign, a bad sign, or no sign at all. He
couldn't be certain of anything as he stood there at the appointed
time, but the sensation of action was more than welcome and
he was exhilarated by the thought of what might be in store.
The bitter cold of Berlin gave meaning and authenticity to his
identification speech. The driver replied as he was supposed to:
"It is our worst winter in history." Which in fact it was. And
things then began as scheduled. A copy of the *Tageblatt* lay
on the back seat. It reported the events of the day before at

Nuremberg. A number of former leaders including Ribbentrop, Rosenberg, and Keitel had been hanged. Darsoss glanced down at the newspaper. British football scores were of equal interest to him.

Within twenty minutes he was transferred to another car, a Mercedes 300, along the Autobahn leading to Bernau. This was done no more to confuse possible followers than simply to adhere to blueprint in even the smallest of matters. The taxi driver was obviously a rank and file Party member blindly obeying a set of simple instructions. The second driver, a gray-faced German in his fifties, thin, silent, prewar in quality, was undoubtedly the cutout. There was no need for the taxi driver to know more than just that little bit. Darsoss' observations were all automatic; Russian security measures couldn't have differed too greatly from those under which he himself had once operated.

The second leg of the journey took place without conversation, lasted another twenty minutes, and ended in the front room of a small two-story frame house one hundred yards from the main road. Here Darsoss saw for the first time S. Kalinin, a bespectacled man in his early thirties, bushy-haired and clever-looking, wearing a baggy civilian suit and smoking a cigarette. Despite a broad, jovial mouth and soft, watery blue eyes rather closely spaced, Kalinin gave the impression he was someone who could not be easily fooled.

"Shall we go immediately to the purpose of this meeting?" he said, gesturing his visitor to a choice of any seat, his English accented but long-learned and spoken in a lively tone.

Darsoss looked around with a certain appearance of indifference, but obviously familiar with all the possible surprises: the hidden devices for listening, for recording, for photographing; the sudden attack by a couple of oversized simpletons against whom you would have no chance. He did not sit down, and Kalinin said: "The letter you sent to our people in News and Information is very puzzling. We don't know quite what to make of it."

Darsoss waited, wanted to hear more. He was meagerly rewarded.

"We require clarification," Kalinin said. "Surely you wouldn't mind."

Darsoss looked directly at him. "Providing we don't kid each other right from the start," he said.

4

"Meaning?"

"Meaning that you begin by admitting the substance of my letter to you is true," Darsoss said. "That in your sector you have Otto Vorst, formerly of RSHA under Walter Schellenberg; that he is now alive, kicking, and in the employ of the Soviet Occupation Command. Without that we'll go nowhere."

"And if it is true?" Kalinin said, watching Darsoss light a cigarette. Before Darsoss could speak, he added in a warning voice touched with admiration: "You know, Mr. Darsoss, you've done a very extreme thing—perhaps even rash."

Darsoss shrugged. "I don't think it is," he said offhandedly. He was accounted for in every way, even down to the ampule sewn into the point of his shirt collar, easily bitten in half and instantly effective. "If anything happens to me, there's the automatic release of an explanatory letter I've left in the American sector. With it goes the article I've written about Otto Vorst, about how the Soviet Occupation Command is employing Nazis—not just everyday hacks, but inspired murderers like Vorst. Fully documented." He spoke quietly and evenly with a faint New York City accent, the air of indifference covering his inability to relax fully, his deep anger, his nerve ends thin and worn as the soles of old walking shoes. "I don't expect such a thing, of course," he said with not quite discernible sarcasm. "But better safe than sorry."

Kalinin nodded. "A good saying," he said. "Of course, I am not a policeman, you must understand. I am basically a journalist. So things of this nature come to my attention only when they are related to news or information with political and social relevancy."

Darsoss removed the photostat from an inside pocket. "Let's skip the baby steps," he said, and tossed the photostat on a small table next to the sofa. Kalinin went to it with an eye on Darsoss. "That's a letter written by Vorst just five days ago. To his daughter in the American sector. Naturally the original is not with me."

Kalinin examined the photostat and the impact was immediate, his face still, his eyes fixed. "You can keep that one," Darsoss said. "You might like to show it around."

Kalinin looked up. "You intercepted it," he observed.

"I stole it. But then you know how journalists are. Anything for an interesting story."

"Is that what you are?"

"Like yourself," Darsoss said. He dragged on his cigarette and gestured toward the photostat in Kalinin's hand. "I'd say that it pretty much tells the story, wouldn't you? Alive, in good health, and employed. No need to worry. Soon we'll be reunited. Touching, isn't it?"

Kalinin remained unruffled. "How do you know this is genuine?" he asked.

"That's his handwriting," Darsoss said. "I've seen it before. Anyhow, my mind is made up."

"Of course we do not wish a contretemps, whatever the basis," Kalinin said as if referring to a proposition on the blackboard in a classroom, making a steeple of his fingers. "But your interest in this matter is still not clear to me."

"Let's say I don't like the idea of Nazis at large."

Kalinin shrugged and said pleasantly: "Well, go to your side. You've plenty to choose from there."

"Oh, yes," Darsoss admitted. "But this is the one you and I are talking about now."

Kalinin gave a deferential nod; it was all so academic. He might well have said: "*Touché*," but instead he said, "A sound point. How can I refuse to recognize it?"

"You can if you want to. And I can send my story into *Time* before the sun sets."

"This is, of course, blackmail."

"Yes, it is."

Kalinin smiled a little less broadly than when Darsoss had first arrived. "All right. What do you want?" he asked.

"A private and exclusive interview with Vorst."

"An interview?" Kalinin said. "What you actually mean is you wish that he be released to you, but not simply to interview him." As if he had gained something in the scramble for a foothold he added: "No one would go to this extreme simply for that."

Darsoss stood very still and said nothing. He had no real gauge yet of how strong his hand was, if indeed it was strong at all. Kalinin was obviously not ready to deal; the probing phase was under way. There would be skips and by-passes and enormous amounts of negative psychology before it was done. Kalinin seemed suddenly to change course. "That aside for the moment," he said, as if his suspicions were too obvious to state directly, "what will you do if you are thwarted?"

"I've told you," Darsoss answered.

"And otherwise you will . . . shut up?"

"Exactly."

"I see," Kalinin said. "Then I'm afraid I must tell you to proceed with what you have planned."

"You don't mean that," Darsoss said, insolently unimpressed.

Kalinin ignored him. "He is much too valuable to us, let us be frank," he said. "If that is to be used as an attack on the Soviet Occupation Command, we must be prepared to counter the calumny." He lit one cigarette from another. "And we can," he continued as he crushed out the tiny butt in an ashtray. "He has proved to be an extraordinary material witness against a score of others whose cases were not so complete as his admittedly was. His background provides a limitless use in the war we must continue to wage against the far-from-dead fascist elements in our midst."

"So now he's one of us. Isn't that nice?"

Kalinin might have been momentarily embarrassed but he was a man trained for rapid recovery. "I'm afraid my hands are tied," he said with sincerity, to be made of whatever one might wish.

"Then you want me to go ahead."

"Not at all. But it is rather beyond our control as you have arranged things, is it not?" He stopped short in the middle of a sudden move away from Darsoss. He shrugged and said, "Part of our answer is that you have done exactly the same. At the moment you are using General Reinhard Gehlen. The former chief of the German High Command Section Foreign Armies East. Who among us is pure?"

"There are many people the Soviet Union would like to impress with its purity," Darsoss said. "A story like this makes you look worse than the capitalists."

"Don't be patronizing, please," Kalinin said.

Darsoss shrugged a little. "Do I walk back?" he said.

"Not at all," Kalinin said, perhaps too cordially, and went to the front window where he motioned to the driver sitting behind the wheel of the car. "He will take you."

Darsoss was still not convinced, but he was vaguely depressed by how things had gone. He suspected that he had failed to throw too much of a scare into anybody. "You went to quite a lot of bother," he said quietly, as if it didn't, after all, matter that much to him.

"Not so much," Kalinin said. "We had to know what you had in mind." He smiled. "Now we know. But after all you are asking us to come out of everything with absolutely no gain to ourselves." He shook his head. "Of course that wouldn't do."

"I'd as soon file the story," Darsoss said. It was the best thing to say at the moment.

As if Darsoss had not spoken at all, Kalinin said: "You do not have that powerful a position, really. I mean, for sake of argument, if you had *some* sort of exchange. If you were doing some sort of service for us, let us say. Well, then. Perhaps that would be different. Perhaps then an arrangement could be made. I mean, normally we can be bargained with just like anyone else, but we cannot be blackmailed."

Darsoss acted as if he had either not understood what was being said or just didn't care, and began walking toward the door. "Could you—" came Kalinin's voice with a cautiously experimental sound, "let us say, conceive of such a possibility?"

Darsoss stopped in his tracks at the entrance hall doorway. "What possibility?" he said.

"The possibility of—working for us?"

Kalinin came to where Darsoss was standing, and Darsoss said: "What kind of work?"

Kalinin said: "I don't know. Actually I don't know that such a thing could be arranged at all." He smiled. "It was a hypothetical question."

Darsoss walked back to the table where the ashtray was and put out his cigarette. "I'd just as soon file the story," he said. "I think there's prestige in it."

"In my country prestige comes only through decent achievement," Kalinin said. "Evidently it can be attained through slander in yours. Be that as it may, allow me to suggest that you allow a grace period to yourself as well as to us."

"Why?"

"Perhaps something can be worked out."

"On whose terms?"

"On whatever terms come closest to the desires of all concerned."

8

Darsoss said nothing, and Kalinin said: "I am not going to probe your motives in the matter at this moment—but obviously they are very powerful. Who knows? Perhaps a *quid pro quo* could be arranged, one that you would find preferable to failing in your quest."

Darsoss walked to the door once again. "I make no promises," he said.

"Then you've moved from your original position," Kalinin said. "Perhaps some good will come of it. But I too make no promises."

Neither man said good-bye to the other. They had not sat down; they had not removed their overcoats. The signs had been clear to both. As he walked from the house to the waiting car, Darsoss knew that he stood outside a heavy door with a huge brass knocker and that soon he would enter the forbidden interior. He could have repeated the conversation verbatim, of course. But he could also have repeated certain conversations he had had with his father twenty years before. There was little he could not recall to mind; nearly fresh in his memory was the day his mother sprained her ankle in the vestibule of the apartment building where they lived on Île St. Louis in Paris. Since Darsoss was but fourteen months old at the time of the incident, it was perhaps not so startling that he could now remember every nuance, every pause, every clearing of the throat in a conversation that had taken place just five minutes before.

2

It was not yet five o'clock when he was back in Dahlem. Faces froze and marrow turned to ice in the bone. He would not be sorry to get into his room in Frau Nessermann's flat, cold as it was, a few blocks away from the OMGUS building. As he walked toward it from the Thiel Platz U-bahn, a Kommandatura jeep churned past him through a muddy mélange of ice and snow, dusk deepening, street lamps not yet lit. The four soldiers rode in silence. This seemed to mark the nature of the quadripartite patrol but not the meetings between their superiors. Already crevasses had formed, the fruits of victory a bit too spotted. The arguments between Clay and Sokolovsky grew

9

more intense with each passing day, the question of what was right and true having long before begun to play a subordinate role in the exchanges.

Darsoss crossed the street, giving the soldiers only a passing glance. He didn't care about any of it; he was a passer-by. Germany was like one of those creatures in a zombie film: it was not alive, it was not dead. Hangings had taken place and so its head was neutralized, but its body awaited the wooing of transfixed, vaguely horrified lovers. Darsoss felt separate and apart from all of it. He had only one devotion. Like an Orthodox Jew he held to it with endless zeal, oblivious to pain and outrage. He could only hope the bargain with the Russians would not be too hard.

When he arrived at the building and entered the flat, he found Frau Nessermann burning the legs of a small table in the kitchen stove, standing close to it for warmth. In German she said: "Someone is waiting for you. I let her in, I thought you would want me to."

Darsoss stood in the kitchen doorway for a moment and gathered in the trailing ends of this unexpected information. He finally said: "Thank you, *gnädige Frau,*" and walked off down the carpeted hallway to the door of his room. Only one person could have been awaiting him. He wondered how in the world she had discovered his billet. He had gone to great pains to keep it from her.

When he opened the door, she turned, the look on her face so suited to a former *Blitzmädel:* rage, hauteur, arrogance. In a moment it would all crumble; pure petulance would be the best she would have to offer. He looked at her somewhat blankly. She was about twenty-one, blue-eyed, pink-cheeked, and despite a longish upper lip was not bad-looking. He would have killed her without a thought or a moment's hesitation. Easily, eagerly, and in an expert fashion.

"Herr Manfred," she said with heavy mockery. " 'Call me Frederich, my dear,' " she then mimicked. " 'Otherwise you make me feel old and decayed.' You bastard. An American spy."

Darsoss looked at her, deeply satisfied that he had been able to establish an avuncular relationship with her, that he had not been required to go any further than he had; a man of thirty-eight was, fortunately, quite ancient in her eyes. "You didn't do too badly," he said, throwing his hat on the bed. "Too good, as a matter of fact, but I'll overlook it." He had dropped the perfect Ruhr accent he had affected for all these past weeks. Now it was the flat, unadorned German certain foreigners used. "It seems that someone has been talking to you. Who?"

"Never mind," she said. "A friend. You rotten liar."

"Such language," he said. "Especially from a person with two names—the one she uses and her real one, the name she doesn't tell anyone."

"And with good reason," the former *Blitzmädel* snapped.

"We all have our reasons, *nicht wahr?*" He rapped his knuckles on the cold steam pipe. "Sometimes the janitor is luckier finding fuel than at other times," he said. "But not today." Then: "You won't mind terribly if I lie down, will you? I've had a long day."

"I don't care what you do," she said, her angry eyes following his every move. "Where is my letter?"

"Letter?"

"You are a thief too."

"Lower your voice."

"I'll deny everything."

"I think you're confused."

"Not any longer," she said. "I know your name, where you live, who you are—everything about you."

"Fine. Why not forget the whole thing?"

"Forget the whole thing?" she said, incredulous.

She stopped dead. Darsoss sat down heavily. He felt almost sorry for her, but not quite. He was sure no other women but these would have behaved with such venality, under the circumstances. Reasons ceased to matter at a certain point and results were what you dealt with. "I have a carton of cigarettes for you," he said, because even if it were possible to insult her, he would have had no reluctance to do so; but chiefly because he was tired and wanted her out of the way with as little fuss as possible.

"Here?" she asked.

"Yes, here."

He got up and pulled his Valpak from beneath the bed, unlocked it, and put a carton of Lucky Strikes in her hands. "Here. Now go." For her the world was a place of deception and barter. It hadn't toughened her (toughness implied understanding and dignity) but had left her hard and without the shred of a decent instinct. You had only to look at her to know.

"What are you going to do?" she asked, the steam gone out of her attack.

Darsoss trained his eyes on her. "What did they tell you? Whoever it was told you I was an American spy."

"Nothing," she said impatiently. "Just that; and that your name was Darsoss, not Manfred. That you were using me. I couldn't believe it. Then I found my letter missing . . ."

Darsoss made no comment, continued to look at her.

"Give it back to me . . . please. I must have it."

"Why? Assuming I had it."

"For . . . sentimental reasons."

"Oh? Sentimental enough to trade back those cigarettes for it?"

She didn't answer and he said: "No, I guess no one in Berlin could be that sentimental."

"Why have you done all this? *Why* did you steal my letter? *Why* did you pose as a German? What is it you're after?"

"First let's talk about a deal," he said. "Two cartons of cigarettes—any brand—for telling me how you found out about me . . . No?"

The look in her eyes was unmistakable; there was no chance of such a trade. Perhaps fear governed her, perhaps the urge to get back at him; her position was immediately clear in either case.

"You seem worried about it," she said, turning sly and enjoying a small torment.

"Not a bit," he said with a complacent shrug. "It makes no difference now anyhow." But someone, for some reason, had dogged his footsteps, had tried to upset his house of cards before he could finish the delicate structure. They had missed, but they had tried. "You were misinformed, by the way. I'm a newsman—a journalist, not a spy." He could, of course, expect no public defense of his name from her, but he felt constrained to voice the denial; it didn't do to face that accusation in silence anywhere at any time, least of all here and now. "I was looking for an inside story on the postwar *Blitzmädel*," he said. "I wanted to see you and hear you as you were. That was why I posed as a kindly old fart with American PX connections. It

12

made my viewpoint more authentic. If you like I'll even mention you by name when I write it."

Without warning he took her by the arm and steered her firmly to the door. "Now I've had all I want of you," he said, as if he suddenly remembered who she was, as if it were a sacred duty to treat her with contempt. "On your way."

She grew wide-eyed. "You *are* dreck," she said. "I hope you are killed." Her rage seemed to strangle her. But she left without returning the carton of cigarettes. The gesture would have been too much to expect. It wouldn't have helped matters anyway.

Darsoss smiled cheerlessly. She knew what was going on. An upstanding and loyal German like her father would have to be in danger from a man like Darsoss, as he had now been revealed to her. But not one direct exchange on the subject had taken place between them; open acknowledgments were hard to come by in such matters as these. No one ever wants to admit what is actually going on. Not before it is absolutely necessary to do so.

Darsoss poured a double shot of Scotch into a glass and took a swallow. It was only vaguely satisfying. Nothing got any closer than the fringes—not since that day, that day of pitiless confirmation, that day so wanting in mercy. The greatest individual agonies came at times like these, on days of great rejoicing for the many. How the first day of spring did mock the man whom cancer would kill before the season was out. Darsoss had known that same cruelty as he had stood there in the Paris office of the MI6 major, hearing the good public school accent weighed down by grievous detail. "I'm terribly sorry . . . It's dead certain . . . I only wish it weren't . . . You're welcome to the report . . . All the affidavits and clearances are there . . . Everything cross-checked. But you shouldn't . . . dwell on it too long, if I may say so . . ."

It had been that way; the dreadful fragments had buried themselves deeply in his flesh. And there followed the curious sensation of wandering the streets through gentle storms of confetti and streamers, the roar and peal of exultant voices everywhere, strangers exchanging kisses in Place de la Concorde, people jostling and pushing each other jubilantly. Joy, after all, found countless forms and endless expression on the day a war ended. Darsoss had walked through all of it grimly and somberly and forsaken-looking, accepting an unfelt kiss here, a push there, an embrace farther along, with the eyes of a man who was perhaps seeing an endless field of dead after a battle without pity, remembering only his murdered wife and the man he must find and kill before he could ever again rest. Nothing from that day to this—nineteen months later in the dreary netherworld of Berlin and Frau Nessermann's flat—had abated. But now there was the new element of the Russians. He had followed the twists and turns to their doorstep. They would have to do something about it. He wouldn't need to wait too much longer to discover just what it would be.

He finished the drink and lay down on the iron-posted bed, a weak lamplight breaking the early evening gloom, his hands clasped behind his head, his eyes trained on the riveleted ceiling plaster. Time and substance were like water colors run together in his mind. Paris, Berlin, Zurich, Lausanne, and Madrid; a snowy forest in Hesse, the view from a hotel window in a small town overlooking the Aegean Sea, a face of sheer cliff in the Carpathians, miles of train track, of air space, of hope and of loss; of a fragment here and a false lead there—how many places he had been; how many cobbled streets he had walked; dirty tables at which he had sat, unfriendly faces he had looked into, lies he had been told, empty threats he had made, cold alleyways he had waited in. All the old skills and ancient memories, so perfect and so harrowing, and the hatred that passed for vocation had revived themselves again and again. That was why he had been able to go back to it the next day and the next day and the day after that, as surely as other men went to their jobs in offices or factories or grocery stores. The annuity, paid for with backbreaking effort, was finally going to mature. Everything pointed to it.

As he sat alone at a certain table in the restaurant off Gelferstrasse a short time later, the signs continued. The waiter, a doughy-faced nondescript in his forties set a plate of soup before Darsoss and leaned down to say: "Everything goes well tonight, Mein Herr?"

Darsoss had half expected this. "Just fine," he answered.

"Good," the waiter said. Then: "In your inside coat pocket." After saying that much, the waiter left Darsoss to himself. The very same thing had taken place the night before.

First, on the previous afternoon, there had been the telephone advertisement in English: "May we suggest that as an American

you acquaint yourself with German cuisine?" The name and
the location of the restaurant were then mentioned and an additional suggestion casually made. "Eight o'clock is best, at a
table next to the window with a reserved card. You might begin
by ordering *Eisbein*. If you are told there is no more *Eisbein*,
you will then do well to ask for a portion of *Königsberger Klops*."
This was the procedure through which he had received the
rendezvous instructions for his first meeting with Kalinin. And
now, on the following night, the procedure was repeating itself.
They were wasting no time. Darsoss sensed accomplishment
but also the need to be cautious. Not for his own skin; personal
safety had long ceased to concern him. But through the too
hasty reaction, or through the betrayal of anxiety at the last
moment—through any of a score of unnamed and well-hidden
wrong moves, he could lose the chance he was so desperately
seeking.

With no relish at all he brought the food to his mouth. He
ate very little as a rule; his wiry body, neither large nor small,
seemed to subsist in its quick, nervous way on cigarettes and
coffee. He contained himself long enough to establish the appearance of a man who had come to a restaurant for dinner and
for no other reason. Then he paid his check and departed.

When he reached his room he opened the envelope that had
been placed in his coat pocket. As he suspected, it contained
rendezvous instructions to be carried out the next day. A solely
verbal identification would be made. It was distinctive enough.
Darsoss absorbed it in the time required to read it, and then
he burned the slip of paper it was written on in Frau Nessermann's kitchen stove. The lady had evidently received a dinner
invitation and was not at home.

He watched the flame consume the instructions, and from
the same match he lit a cigarette and examined the present
and the future with faraway eyes. Then the dreadful past in-
truded. It was never far from his heart and mind, his black
dominion where all the brave missions receded and vanished
in the shadows; all except the one that had counted more than
anything he had yet undertaken in his life: the mission to find
and bring a woman out from behind the enemy lines where
she was trapped. The woman had been his wife. The mission
had failed. There was no doing away with it, no coming to
terms. Recollection was almost as vivid as actual experience

and frequently more painful. Perhaps more so at night when one could go nowhere but to an uncomfortable and lonely bed to remember and to listen. Often it was better to walk through the streets. In a very short while, Darsoss had left Frau Nessermann's flat to do just that, to walk through cold and dimly lit streets and to try to unwind. It wasn't easy; the wear and tear had been too great. Sometimes he was sure he could feel the blood moving in his veins; he was that highly pitched and on edge.

By the time he found himself near the Club he was cold enough to be driven indoors. All the accredited newspaper, magazine, and radio correspondents spent considerable off-time in its precincts. Others also. Berlin was filled with shadowy people whose functions were veiled, whose connections were mysterious, whose objectives couldn't be clearly defined. Vernon, for example, fit this description, though Darsoss knew exactly what it concealed.

He was about thirty-five, good-looking and easygoing, a graduate of the University of Wisconsin who knew of fifteen different ways of killing a man within two or three seconds using only the hands. He left the bar where he had been sitting and carrying a glass of beer in his hand, came toward Darsoss. "I didn't know you were in Berlin," he said.

Darsoss didn't believe him but said: "I've been in and out. How are you?"

"Fine," Vernon said, as if he meant it. Nothing tragic ever had or ever could happen to him. "I've been wondering about you a lot," he said as they sat down at a table.

"I was on an assignment," Darsoss said.

"Sure, sure, I know all about that assignment," Vernon said. "How was Madrid?"

You had to like Vernon, but you might not have wanted to. "Are you people tailing me?" Darsoss asked softly, looking right into Vernon's round face with its even features and boyish blue eyes.

"Of course not," Vernon said. "But we knew about Vorst's brother in the German embassy. You got the information from us, I knew that."

"I don't remember discussing it with you," Darsoss said.

"You didn't," Vernon admitted casually. "Anyhow, you had to follow it up. That's not so hard to figure out, is it?"

16

Darsoss gently raked his thumbnail along his chapped lower lip. With his other hand he beckoned the bar waiter.

"How did you make out?" Vernon said. Darsoss didn't answer and Vernon said: "I mean, you're still at it, Marco. Only a blind man couldn't see that."

"All right," said Darsoss. He lit a cigarette and asked the waiter to bring a straight Scotch.

"You know he could have slipped through the net," Vernon pointed out. "Christ—a whole bunch of them did. He could also have died anonymously and unaccounted for in any one of a thousand different ways for a thousand different reasons."

Darsoss gave his former comrade-in-arms a smile meant to be nasty. He was beginning to put things together. "I don't think he's dead," he said.

Vernon looked at him with some surprise and said, "So you *did* come up with something in Spain."

The waiter delivered the Scotch and Darsoss swallowed part of it. "The brother wasn't available," he said. "But some of his belongings were."

Vernon began to listen with the complete absorption but apparent detachment of the vocational information-gatherer as Darsoss said: "Among them I found a photograph of Vorst and two bitches who might easily have been his wife and daughter. They turned out to be. There was also a letter to the brother's former address in Madrid, written in September of last year, a letter from Vorst saying he was all right but in need of money. There was no return address, but the Germans are so neat and methodical, the letter was still in its envelope. The envelope carried a Dahlem post-office validation." Darsoss took a deep pull on his cigarette and crushed out the butt.

Vernon was silent and continued to watch the other man steadily. Darsoss' eyes clouded with a memory he couldn't make peace with. Then he looked back at Vernon. "I decided to focus on the two women in order to get to Vorst. I had an idea they were out in the open somewhere—probably in the American sector of Berlin. Maybe they had even mailed the letter for Vorst to the brother. I could identify either of them from the picture. I came back here and began to check wherever indigenous personnel were employed—everything from secretaries to *Trümmerfrauen*, army and civilian billets alike. I got to the daughter. It took about three weeks. Suddenly—there she was."

"Where?"

"In Pommler's," Darsoss said. "It's a GI hangout, as you know. She looked like a ready-made *Schatzi*. So I made Pommler's a major target."

"You were lucky," Vernon said. "What about the mother?"

"Nothing. I haven't seen her yet."

"How did you contact the girl?"

Darsoss gave him a sidelong look and said: "Do you think I'd be telling you about it if I thought for a minute you didn't already know most of it?"

"Now, what makes you say that?"

"Because somebody tipped off the girl," Darsoss said. "Told her where I live, that I was an American spy, everything. And I think it was you people."

Vernon said calmly: "If you were a slot machine, Marco, you'd light up with a tilt sign."

"You people have been onto the girl," Darsoss went on simply, "and you didn't want anyone getting too close."

"Come on."

"One reason comes to mind immediately. Vorst can talk about who is and who isn't a Nazi among some of the people employed by MG. It could be embarrassing. I might have been getting too close for comfort."

"You keep tilting, Marco."

"Do I?" Darsoss realized that perhaps the theory was not altogether logical, but he nevertheless suspected that AMG had warned Luzzi Vorst against him. The position was now a matter of strategy. "You've got my opinion," he said.

"It's for the birds. We want Vorst as much as you do. He's on everybody's *Fahndungsbuch*, not just yours."

"It doesn't make much difference now anyway," Darsoss said. "The girl flicked me off like a piece of lint. I'm right back where I began." He looked off with an air of disgust and regret.

"Maybe it was the Russians," Vernon said. "Why pick on us?"

Darsoss wanted to avoid the subject of the Russians. The main thing now was to give Vernon the impression that he, Vernon, had succeeded in breaking something up, if indeed he had tried, and that Darsoss was presently off the track. More than that; that Darsoss was perhaps too old before his time and

18

too weary to care any longer. On the chance that they had been tailing him, Darsoss was attempting to plant the idea that there was no longer any reason to do so. A close surveillance by CIC or any other MG unit could break the back of all his hopes and desires, edged with poison and solitude though they may have been. "Anyhow, I'm sure he's not dead," Darsoss said in a tired voice but with dead certainty. "Just way out of my reach."

"Had you gotten close?" Vernon asked.

"Not close enough," Darsoss said. He finished his Scotch and dragged on his cigarette.

"That's too bad."

"Do you mean that?"

"Why shouldn't I? I don't mean to offend you, but we have been buddies. Or if you prefer a less emotional word—friends. I mean, I do understand. I do sympathize."

Darsoss gave him an acceptant look. "Sure," he said just above a whisper. "I know you do."

There was a moment's silence, Vernon staring reflectively as he began to pack his pipe. Suddenly he seemed to recall something past and he grinned. "Listen, do something for me, will you?" he said and stuck the pipe stem between his teeth.

"What?" Darsoss asked and beckoned the waiter and indicated his empty glass.

"The old trick," Vernon said as he drew a pen and small note pad from inside his jacket.

Vernon bent his head to write something down. Darsoss knew him to have been close to death himself, and witness to the deaths of others. Vernon had been fundamentally untouched by what he had experienced. This was Darsoss' opinion; no envy attached to it.

Vernon now tore what he had written from the pad and extended it to Darsoss. Not longer than thirty seconds had elapsed when Darsoss handed the slip back to Vernon and accepted a blank one in exchange. With Vernon's pen, Darsoss then began to write. He finished a series of tight, rapid jottings, and handed them back to Vernon. Vernon compared the two slips of note paper. "It's all done with the mirrors inside your head," he said in a soft tone of deep respect, perhaps even awe. After all, in the space of half a minute Darsoss had studied a column of fifteen separate and nonsequential numbers accounting for some forty-odd digits, and then had been able to write them down from memory exactly as they had been presented to him.

Darsoss was scarcely gratified by the feat. Memory so deep and rare was like an affliction. It provided tricks in the parlor and anguish in the silence of the night.

"I wanted to see if there had been any damage," Vernon said frankly, a look of satisfaction on his face. "There hasn't been a bit, has there? You're as good as you ever were."

"You're a sneak," Darsoss said quietly and directly. This had been a form of examination, under the circumstances; of cold, clinical fingers probing without consent. "You *belong* in spy work."

"I hate to see you wasting yourself, Marco," Vernon said with that hopeful solemnity people often affect with others who would be so much better off if only they would see the light. "It makes me sad," he said.

"Don't you have a girl?" Darsoss said.

"From time to time," Vernon said, indulgent, unoffended, so in control, so suited to withstanding pressure.

Darsoss gave a slow, knowing shake of the head and then said: "Let me tell you something. I'm convinced you gave me the finger. But now I see a new motive—one I hadn't considered before."

"This should be good."

"It is," Darsoss said. "You did it to save me from myself. Kind of like pals at boarding school. Frank, Chet, and Chip all make the varsity. But only because Chet and Chip got Frank away from that fast girl in town, because she was in with the gamblers. At first Frank was sore. But later on he thanked them." He finished the Scotch in one swallow and put down the glass.

Vernon spoke with the pipe stem between his teeth. "Are you still in that flat in back of OMGUS?" he asked.

"Yes. As if you didn't know," Darsoss said. He looked at his watch. "I'm all in. I think I'll hit the sack."

"Okay. So long, Marco. If you run into Chet and Chip, say hello for me, will you?"

Darsoss left Vernon sitting there lighting his pipe, the beer in front of him. He hoped he had appeared sufficiently betrayed and weary. As he walked toward his address through nearly deserted streets spread with snow, he *felt* betrayed and weary. And old. And chilled to the bone suddenly. Again he was hounded by recollection; recollection of the touch, the scent, and the sound of Anne; of the things she and Darsoss had said to each other, of the places they had visited, of the five years they had been married. Of how good and how kind, of how tender she had been. Pain came in the memories of pleasure, pleasure now dead. It neutralized all other things, all other feelings but the faith born of so long a time alone with but one deadly idea. He wouldn't have had it any other way.

3

Next day the snow had been partially removed, but surfaces of ice were everywhere. Vehicles, for all their caution, skidded in helpless configurations at certain intersections or in areas where no amount of caution would help. Despite the biting cold, the clearing of rubble from the streets continued unabated. Workers with their precious first-class ration cards went at the debris in the once-beautiful Tiergarten, where deluded men had entrenched themselves with the hope of stemming the approach of foreign armies. Everywhere there were bricks, rubble, twisted steel. Darsoss walked from the Zoo station, accustomed to the destruction. Almost nowhere did two buildings stand side by side and intact, and the Kurfürstendamm was a shambles. But soon everything would recover its old glitter, the graceless opulence of the thirties which the fun-loving Germans were so fond of.

In the lobby of the AmZoo, one of the few untouched buildings, and something of a beehive even now because of its size and clinging prewar atmosphere, Darsoss bought a copy of the *Herald Tribune* and sat down on one of the divans in the lounge. Perhaps eight or ten others, all German civilians, were scattered here and there, some vaguely well dressed, one or two of the men looking old-fashioned and natty, one particular woman almost stylish. Bastards, Darsoss thought to himself, and then began to read the paper. It was eleven A.M. By eleven-fifteen the contact arrived.

A man like the Baron in *Grand Hotel*, though older, about fifty, moustached, conspicuously handsome if somewhat worn

21

down, better days behind him, sat down next to Darsoss. At first Darsoss didn't buy him; not even when he said in German: "Didn't we meet in Biarritz before the war?"

Darsoss waited, but not for too long. "At the Bristol Hotel?" he said.

"No," said the other in a thoughtful, melodious tone. "I believe it was that little place on rue Gambetta."

They exchanged a smile of mutual discovery. "So it was," Darsoss said. "How have you been?"

The man nodded and said: "If you'd really be interested in finding out, I suggest that tonight at about—oh, say, half-past eight, you pay a visit to Eichenstrasse fifteen in Pankow."

"I'm not altogether sure I'm not being tailed," Darsoss said.

"That's all right," the Baron said. "If you're followed to that address it won't matter."

Darsoss looked at him, wondered if he were really a part of the Russian *apparat*, could scarcely believe he was.

"It's *une maison de joie*," the man said after a pause. 'Very suitable, under the circumstances."

"The hell it is," Darsoss said. "It's not natural behavior on my part. Anybody who knows my habits knows that."

"That's interesting," the man said. "Perhaps you have a different view of yourself than other people have."

"It's possible," Darsoss said. "I'm just mentioning it so you can pass it along to the psychology department."

"In any case," said the Baron, continuing on in the unhurried, conversational tone, "I am not empowered to make decisions. You know what to do better than I. But I think that no man is so out of place going to a house under any and all circumstances. Any man might. Kings have been known to. Also their generals. Even poets and scholars."

"You make a good case," Darsoss said.

"The point is," the other man went on, "if you've given everyone the impression you're above such a thing and then are seen going into one, they will sooner think of you as a hypocrite than as a political intriguer."

The logic was sound. Darsoss said nothing, inhaled on the cigarette he was holding, and wondered again how this man had come to service for the Russians. His accent was good, shaped by a good deal of travel. He was a strange specimen, impossible to place in time and motive, a man who might have rejected the Nazis merely because they were vulgar. Certainly his dedication to the cause of communism was unlikely.

"All right," Darsoss said. "What else?"

"You have the address?"

"Eichenstrasse fifteen, Pankow."

"Correct. Once there you will ask to see Frau Moller. When you do, tell her you have just arrived from Hamburg and would like a girl with red hair and breasts like teacups. Have you got that?"

"Yes."

"Good. Now, is anyone watching us at this moment?"

"Not likely."

"It doesn't matter."

"It could matter to me."

"You've nothing to worry about," the man assured him.

"How do you know?"

"Because everything has been well thought out by rather thorough people. Everything including the likelihood of your visit to Eichenstrasse fifteen. You're not a homo, are you?"

"No. Are you?"

"Not so far. I think our meeting and conversation has looked fine. Artistic, really. You're a good actor."

"So are you."

Both men stood up and shook hands with cordial smiles. "It was very nice to run into you this way," the Baron said. "It's not likely we'll see each other again."

"Does it matter?"

"Not in the least. *Lebewohl*."

The rest of the day was divided between the Club, where he passed time partly in solitude and partly in the company of the New York *Times* man and an INS reporter; an afternoon press conference with General Clay, among twenty-five other reporters; and his room. His reputation as a man with the capacity and preference for solitude was well established. Few people sought him out. He had no room for any of them, though few knew or could guess exactly why, and he issued no invitations either in word or deed. Perhaps his habits were not so easy to pin down, after all, and his visit to Eichenstrasse 15 may not have astonished anyone in the least, assuming anyone of importance would have been interested even to begin with.

Frau Moller was small, thin, fifty, and wore a pince-nez. She had to have been in good standing, at the very least, with the Nazis. "Red hair and breasts like teacups, indeed, you handsome devil," she said in a peculiarly dead voice. "I have just the one for you."

Darsoss stood near a wall of thick velvet drapes probably covering windows to an inner court. The madame, so classic in her way, pressed a button on her desk. Almost immediately an inner door opened and a tall woman of twenty-five, with red hair and wearing a scant lamé dress, entered. Her breasts were abundant and hardly concealed. Not really teacup, in any sense. The *gnädige Frau* said: "Yvonne, this is Herr Schmidt. He asked especially for you."

The other woman smiled faintly and didn't speak. Darsoss nodded to Frau Moller and in a moment was following Yvonne in silence along a thickly carpeted corridor. The walls were brocaded and there was a heavy scent everywhere, meant to encourage if not to inflame. Faint laughter came and went from behind one of the closed doors. It was all very predictable, the atmosphere so very standard. Darsoss walked along, his hand on the grip of a Czechoslovakian P-38 automatic deep in his overcoat pocket.

Yvonne led him to a closed door, smiled, opened it, and ushered him into a dim, not too large but high-ceilinged room, an anteroom of some kind. She drew aside a curtain and beckoned him to go through to still another room. He gripped the automatic, his finger loose but ready in the trigger guard. He proceeded only as far as the threshold of a room designed and decorated for but a single purpose and circumstance. Here were the total deceit and cheap trappings necessary when a man pays money for sexual intercourse with a woman who can scarcely feel what is being done to her but pretends it is a heavenly experience.

At the foot of a dais on which there was a large canopied bed, on a brocaded, armless chair turned back to front, sat S. Kalinin. No one else was present. Darsoss didn't move from the threshold. "Come in," Kalinin said. "I'm not a red-haired girl with breasts like teacups, but . . ." He shrugged.

Darsoss remained stock-still. "I want that mirror covered," he said, nodding toward the front wall of the room.

"My word of honor," Kalinin said in a tone of grave and breathless offense, "it is a normal, ordinary mirror. I don't wish to go into its chief significance, but surely you can understand why it is where it is."

"I know its face value," Darsoss said. "But you wouldn't expect me to trust that, would you?"

"Never mind," Kalinin said with irritation, and got up and came to where Darsoss was standing. "This will do as well."

The anteroom with only an uncomfortable-looking chaise longue became the alternative. Darsoss' hand relaxed and left the gun grip. Kalinin brought the brocaded chair with him and said: "Do you think someone is trying to frame you?"

"Probably not. But under the circumstances I'm happier in a room without mirrors."

"This is a safe house, my friend," said the Russian in a sincere voice.

"There's probably a doctor right on the premises," Darsoss said. "But I'm a very cautious person."

"All right, no matter. Let us sit down."

"I haven't long to wait, my friend," Darsoss said, in an effort to seize the initiative.

Kalinin was quite prepared for anything. "Mr. Darsoss, let us put this matter in its proper perspective. It is you who want something and have only one channel in which to seek it—not the Soviet Occupation Command. You said yesterday, let us not kid one another, and I am absolutely in accord. By all means, let us not kid one another. You have overestimated our interest in your information. At the same time, you revealed a more than casual interest of your own. Since your first suggestion has left us, shall we say cold?—perhaps you will not object to a countersuggestion."

Darsoss' mouth thinned into a sardonic line; there had always been the chance of countersuggestions, hadn't there? He said nothing, but had the familiar sensation of operating from an off-balance position.

"Your request is one thing," Kalinin said. "But the exchange is absurd."

"Did you think so right from the start?"

Kalinin gave a slight shrug. "Perhaps," he said. "So now we will take off our masks and come close enough to face reality. Warts and all."

"Why don't we simply forget the whole thing?" Darsoss bluffed. "I'll simply file the story."

25

"That would be your option," Kalinin granted. "No harm has been done up till now." He stood up. "Go right ahead and expose us," he said with a wide, confident smile. "If that is what you want. But no. You would never have come to us had it been; you'd have done it. Of course. It's obvious. So what are we left with now?" He shrugged. "The basis of a possible bargain. Without mincing words, you can have what you are after—and we are prepared to guarantee it—in return for certain services. That is simple enough, isn't it? I indicated in our previous meeting that this was the area I would explore in your behalf. I have done so and a beginning is made. It is entirely in your hands. You needn't bother to answer now. You should first determine in your own mind whether there is a basis for discussion in depth on such a matter. Frankly, I do not believe this decision should be a hasty one." He inhaled on his long-ashed cigarette and then messily stubbed it out on the brass door handle and put the crumpled butt in his pocket, probably more as a matter of security than tidiness.

Darsoss stood up from the chaise. "Forget it," he said.

Kalinin gave his shrug, by now characteristic of him in Darsoss' mind, so acceptant in appearance but so concealing of a mind ready with an alternate means to any desired objective. "It is, of course, up to you," he said. "It is possible that even as you overestimated our interest in your information, we in turn are overestimating your interest in Otto Vorst."

"These things happen," Darsoss said.

"Yes," Kalinin agreed, with open skepticism in his eyes. "Of course I am astounded by how potent you thought your discovery was. These accusations are being exchanged daily between our two countries. This is really not that special."

Darsoss felt very restless and overanxious suddenly. He was on the verge of saying: "What is it you have in mind?" but held himself in check for the moment. He smiled philosophically and said nothing.

"Anyhow," Kalinin went on, "should you wish to say anything further on the subject or ask questions of me, you will need a standard procedure." He paused and when Darsoss made no move of any kind, Kalinin took it as a sign to go further. "Tell me, do you have a briefcase or attaché valise of some kind?"

Darsoss couldn't allow himself a quick response, didn't want to appear to be a stationary target for this obvious recruitment effort. But he finally answered: "Yes." After all, that obligated him to nothing.

"What color?"

"Black."

"Zipper?"

"Yes."

"Good," Kalinin said, almost as if congratulations were in order. "There is a public notice board in Unter den Linden," he went on, then gave its exact location. "Every day at three o'clock you can make contact in front of it merely by unzipping the case and looking inside. Then zip it closed. Then remove your hat and readjust it on your head. That is all. A man carrying a *brown* attaché case will approach you and say: 'Didn't we meet in New York before the war?' and you will reply: 'Yes. You are Herr Schmidt, aren't you?' Then he will do the rest." Kalinin paused and then added: "If by the end of forty-eight hours you have not done this, I'll assume there will be no further contact between us."

Darsoss remained silent, and Kalinin went to the door to leave. "I think it would be best if you remain here for at least half an hour longer," he said. "It wouldn't be too good if you were seen leaving so soon after arriving. Not—natural." Then: "Yes. Well, *au revoir.*"

Darsoss, no longer concerned with the mirror, found an ashtray in the next room. But he returned to the anteroom to smoke three cigarettes in the twenty minutes after Kalinin had left him. Then, escorted to the main lounge by Yvonne, he bid Frau Moller farewell and walked out into the cold, darkened street in front of Eichenstrasse 15. The presence of women, wanton and frankly erotic, the calculated distribution of certain sights, sounds, and scents had made no impression on him. He might well have been coming from an army briefing room, or a meat storage building.

He sat for some time in a bar on Hohenzollerndamm where he drank part of a glass of foul-tasting beer and smoked several cigarettes. It was in the British sector and yet not too far from his billet. When someone began to sing "*Hörst Du mein Heimliches Rufen,*" he got up and left. German tenderness made him want to puke.

Vernon was waiting for him in his room, seated in a hard-backed chair Frau Nessermann had already condemned for fuel. He was wearing both his hat and coat. "Your landlady allowed me into the sitting room but I came in here because the door was unlocked," Vernon said, as if this thoroughly explained everything.

"No reason to lock it," Darsoss said, transferring the automatic from his coat pocket to the table, first adjusting the safety catch. "Anything valuable I carry with me."

"Or keep hidden somewhere else," Vernon said.

"I don't own very much," Darsoss said.

"Do you carry that with you everywhere?" Vernon asked, gesturing at the pistol.

"In case I'm attacked by teen-agers," Darsoss said, opening his coat and sitting down on the bed.

"You don't seem surprised to see me," Vernon said.

"I knew somebody was in here."

"How? Do you mark your door?"

"Every time I leave," Darsoss said. He allowed himself a smile. "I'm full of corny tricks." He held up a half-inch-long nail. "Every time you close that door—no matter how softly—this rolls off the outside molding over the doorway." He tossed it on the bed. "It won't move unless it's disturbed."

"You took me out," Vernon said. "If we were playing for keeps I wouldn't be smiling right now, would I?"

"Maybe not. Were you hoping to give me a shock?"

"No," Vernon said with cheerful emphasis, and then changed tone. "At least not the kind you mean."

Darsoss lit a cigarette. "What kind?" he asked casually.

"The Russians have your man," Vernon told him. "I did some digging after I saw you yesterday. They have him under lock and key. Not in Germany, probably Russia."

This was at variance with Darsoss' intelligence in the matter and he didn't know quite what to make of it. He knew, in any case, that the information must appear to startle him somewhat, and he said: "The *Russians* have him? How do you know?"

"It's a good source," Vernon assured him.

Darsoss looked off into space, perplexed and defeated. "The Russians," he repeated, as if feeling the impact of the news more and more.

"The chances are they bagged him recently," Vernon said.

"They probably pressed him into service for a while and so they kept quiet about it. Anyhow, that closes the book on Vorst."

A very lengthy silence ensued. Vernon remained seated on the hard-backed chair and began to scrape the bowl of his pipe. The crusts went into the palm of his hand, and then into the ashtray within his reach. Darsoss stood next to a single window looking toward the crumbled back of another apartment building fifty yards away. Only the scraping of the bowl and the knocking of the bowl against the palm of Vernon's hand broke the silence of many long moments. Finally Vernon said: "It's better than having him scot-free, isn't it?"

"No," Darsoss said. "Because I would have gotten him sooner or later."

Vernon was silent for another moment or two and then he stood up and said in a soft, reasoning tone: "Leave Yorst's punishment to them. That's got to make sense to you."

Darsoss glanced toward Vernon and said: "I don't have too much choice in the matter, do I?"

"No, that's right. You don't," Vernon said. "It could be the best thing that's happened to you in a long, long time."

Darsoss turned and looked Vernon directly in the eyes. "Why don't you go back to your law practice?" he asked. "Not to change the subject, but I can't help wondering."

"Change it, by all means," Vernon said. "The reason I don't return to my practice is that I have a job here that appeals to me far more."

"Just wondering."

"I think it's an important job," Vernon said. "I'm not interested right now in the personal squabbles of husbands and wives or relatives contesting a will; there's still a war going on."

"Is there?"

Vernon gave him a look almost of forbearance. "The Russians are trying to sabotage the Four Power Administration of Germany, and they're going to succeed," he said. "That should be war enough for anyone, Marco."

"I was just wondering," Darsoss said in a noncommittal tone of voice.

"As a matter of fact," Vernon continued, "there's a need for all sorts of people with all sorts of skills, now as before."

"I suppose that's true," Darsoss said.

Vernon took the proper pause before saying: "No one fits in more perfectly than you do."

Darsoss was now certain that Vernon, at least, knew nothing of his contact with the Russians; the chances of any surveillance now were nil. All to the good. "No, not any more," Darsoss said with a slow shake of the head. "What I need is . . . a monastery—one that specializes in making wine. I could take a vow of silence and stay partially drunk for the rest of my life without anyone being the wiser." He grinned faintly as if he only half meant it; it didn't pay to go too far with the impression of failure and loss of hope. Rather than dulling the interest of others, such a condition could serve to alert them.

Vernon put a fraternal hand on Darsoss' arm, said: "That's what you think at the moment," and moved to the door. "You've too much guts for that. Nobody knows that better than I do. Get some sleep."

Vernon was then gone without another word. Darsoss wondered how he had ever felt any respect for him when they were in tandem during the war. The answer was that that particular war provided an enemy who gave not only unity but affection and brotherhood to people without another particle of common ground.

Darsoss lay awake for several hours in the dark, everything going at breakneck speed in his mind, thoughts and feelings colliding again and again. He thought deeply about the Russian position and about his own. There seemed to be some question as to whether Vorst was their employee or their prisoner. Did it matter? It was hard to know one way or the other. Finally, in sheer exhaustion he dropped off and then experienced his usual fitful sleep. Tigers stalked his dreams, and Anne was always dead before he could get there.

4

At the public notice board in Unter den Linden, a short and stocky man of thirty with fair skin pinched with cold kept the rendezvous. Darsoss had waited until a day and a half later to make the step. They had been quite prepared to ignore him indefinitely. For the moment, the terms were theirs.

"Do you know Pommler's?" the man asked in German.

"Yes," Darsoss said, and then added: "Am I to go there?"

"Yes."

"It is not a good spot."

"That is something I don't know about. Do you want this or not?"

"Go ahead."

"A blond woman wearing a green dress with red flowers printed on it will come up to you and say her name is Verna. You will ask her if she is from Berlin, and she will say, no she is originally from Bremen. After that the instructions will come from her."

"When?"

"Tonight. Between nine-thirty and ten. She'll get to you."

"How?"

"She has already seen you."

"I don't like the arrangement," Darsoss said.

"It's too cold to stand here and argue," the other said. "You have the time, the place, and the identification."

The man, second rate from the look of him, perhaps uncertain of his role in the *apparat*, touched the brim of his hat and walked away. He was a different cut from the man of two days before, the Baron with his casually worldly airs. This one had only the virtue of an appearance so inconspicuous and undistinguished that he was totally forgettable after a first brief look. An important factor in this sort of work.

Darsoss had frequented Pommler's often while searching for Luzzi Vorst; maybe he would be recognized. But all his uneasiness vanished when he arrived at the appointed time to find the place desperately crowded, filled with push and jostle, with noise and smoke, as he had never seen it before. It seemed almost staged. Darsoss was put in mind of the not-quite-convincing gaiety and commotion found in the New Year's Eve scene in certain movies. A four-piece band fought the din with "*Hörst Du mein Heimliches Rufen,*" and there were people trying to dance to its all-too-familiar strains. Darsoss had time to order one beer and smoke a cigarette before Verna was carrying out her instructions.

She was quite thin and flat-chested, but tall, and somehow managed to be faintly pretty despite protruding teeth. She was about thirty. The obligatory posturings took place and soon she and Darsoss were seated against the rear wall at a table large enough to accommodate two drinks and four elbows. An ever-shifting wall of noisy people shielded them from view from the front of the place.

Darsoss looked at her in silence. She smiled with pursed lips. "What now?" he asked.

"Well, you should be very much interested in soon leaving with me through the door behind you. In the meantime, pretend you find me attractive."

"There's no need to pretend," he said. "You've quite stolen my heart away."

"Really, darling? How wonderful."

"If only there were some way I could prove just what you mean to me."

She kept smiling, but something flickered in her eyes, recognition and response. "You know, I seem to get something that is not quite pleasant in your voice," she said.

This was a bright one. "Not pleasant?" he said.

"Am I wrong?"

"Well, what do you mean, my dear?"

"You know—sarcastic. Personal."

"I deserve no thanks, my dear. I can't help being personal with you."

She looked at him directly and said: "You know, not all of us were the way you might think."

"Of course not, sweetheart," he said tenderly. "*None* of you were. When do we leave this place?"

"Whenever you like. Since you find me so irresistible."

"Now, my sweet innocent, now."

Within a minute they were in the street behind Pommler's where a taxicab drew immediately into the curb. "Get in," Verna said.

Once in the back seat neither of them spoke and the cab pulled out without instructions. The driver made a few twists and turns that led onto Potsdammer Strasse, and Darsoss knew the Russian sector was once again his destination. Thirty minutes of unyielding silence ended when in the icebound suburb of Karlshorst a high iron fence loomed just ahead, and the woman said: "We're here."

They drew closer and Darsoss could see the fence and the

gateway which was blocked by the striped bar familiar to frontiers and various other forbidden areas in Europe. A sentry box always went with such a barrier.

As the cab was waved through, Darsoss caught sight of a bulky German cop walking a police dog and carrying a Russian submachine gun: part of the twenty-four-hour patrol outside this place, this huge compound sealed off by the Russian Occupation Command within the Russian sector itself. Here were apartment buildings, stores, and administrative structures; there was no apparent need for any of the thousands of inhabitants to have contact beyond the fence and the three boundaries of barbed wire adjoining it. Darsoss had half expected that this would be where it would all finally take shape.

The cab stopped in one of the darkened streets not too far inside the gate. "This is where we say *auf Wiedersehen*," Verna told him.

Darsoss knew what to expect by now. He nodded, said: "It was a lovely evening," and got out of the cab.

The cab circled away toward the gate, and a second vehicle slid alongside the curb, the rear door opening instantly. "Get in, please," said a voice in English.

Darsoss seated himself next to a sturdily built, Slavic-looking man in civilian clothes. Nothing more was said and the car drove several large city blocks to a three-story building surrounded by a wooden fence and an inner gate, sentries everywhere. The car drove through the various checkpoints. Within a few minutes, Darsoss had been led from the car and escorted into the building, which looked very much like a converted hospital. And then, once again, he was alone with S. Kalinin. This time in an office in the Inspection Building of the place designated as Military Unit, Field Post Number 62076. Darsoss had once seen the ID card of one of its employees. Kalinin himself undoubtedly carried one bearing the same innocuous legend. It was a place of card files, dossiers, and code books; of records filled with cold statistical recitations of anguish, fear, and injustice. It was a police building; one could feel it immediately, even without one's own shadowy experience to fall back on.

"Sit down, sit down."

"You must have a strange idea of what I'm like," Darsoss

said. "I don't bother with women; and yet twice in three days you've had me acting like someone who can't keep his pants buttoned."

Kalinin looked at him impassively. "We were careful," he said. "Believe me, you were well protected."

Darsoss didn't reply, didn't sit down, and began to smoke.

"I assume you wish to confer," Kalinin said. "All right. Without mincing words, there is use for you in our present work structure."

"I've gathered that," Darsoss said.

"Shall we begin?"

"Begin what? You've never really made yourself clear."

"What did you expect? A photostatic copy of all our military installations signed by Stalin? And how clear have you made yourself? Rather less than candid, I should imagine."

Darsoss waited. Kalinin seemed far less good-humored than on the previous occasions. "The fact is, my friend, no one ever wants to show everything all at once, does he?" Kalinin said. "I think each of us can understand the other in that respect. One might liken these circumstances to a search for something that can be recognized only after it is found."

"Very nice."

"Have we reached that point? That is the question. I would say yes. You shouldn't have come here otherwise. It's a very long journey. I don't think a man like you would make it casually."

Darsoss said nothing. Kalinin took from the silence the signal he apparently most wanted. He picked up his desk phone, dialed one digit and waited a moment. Then he began to speak in a voluble but liquid-sounding Russian, and Darsoss regretted his ignorance of the language. After a moment or two of conversation with an unseen authority, Kalinin hung up the phone. "If you'd care to accompany me," he said, getting up from his desk. "We are awaited."

"Where?" Darsoss asked.

"In an upstairs office," Kalinin said, and then grinned amiably. "It's perfectly safe. I go there frequently myself, and I have never been known not to return here each time."

In an office on the third floor a different sort of man awaited Darsoss. At his desk sat a man with a hard bald head like a blunt weapon, his neck thick and jammed into a tight tunic collar, his eyes almond-shaped obsidian, a cigarette clamped gently between teeth which now formed an accidental smile. On his shoulders were the majority insignia of the Red Army. Darsoss knew he was in the presence of the business end of Russian Security. This was the long arm of Bureau Number One of MGB—the guns, knives, and blackmail section.

Major Kholenko began without preliminary. "We know what your interest in Otto Vorst is based upon," he said in good English that, unlike Kalinin's, had probably been practiced in an English-speaking country.

Darsoss lit a cigarette and tried to look unconcerned.

"We know," Kholenko went on, his eyes scanning the material before him, "that you were married and that your wife, a French citizen, was arrested in Paris in January of nineteen-forty-four and interrogated by the Intelligence and Security Branch of the SS; that during the course of that interrogation she died." He looked up with eyes that were not cruel but simply cold. "That the interrogation was conducted by Otto Vorst; that you, naturally enough, would like to . . . have a moment or two alone with him. You've been trying to locate him since the end of the war. Isn't that so? You have no other interest in him but vengeance, isn't that so?"

Darsoss glanced behind him to where Kalinin stood next to a glass-encased secretarial section above which there was a large portrait of Stalin. Kalinin's face was never blank, but now it was in strict repose.

Major Kholenko's voice, almost upper-class English, was now murmuring the particulars of a lifetime. "Marco Darsoss, born Paris nineteen-ten; mixed parentage of French, Italian, English, and Greek origins. Emigrated to the United States nineteen-twenty-two, naturalized citizenship. Political Science, Columbia University Bachelor's Degree nineteen-thirty-one. Fluent in French, German, Italian, as well as English. A basic knowledge of Greek. Occupation: journalist. European residence from nineteen-thirty-five to the onset of World War Two; marriage nineteen-thirty-seven in Savoie to Anne Levi, French citizen, religion Jewish. Service in Office of Strategic Services, penetration and illegal residence in both Germany and German-occupied France, code name Baker . . ." Major Kholenko trailed off, so quickly and easily having accounted for pleasure, for pain, for tedium. He looked up once again. "I think you should be impressed with just how much we do know about you," he said, "so that all the game-playing is laid to rest immediately. There is no use in telling us that you are interested in Vorst either academically or from a police point of view; it would do no good."

Darsoss leaned forward from his chair and stubbed out his cigarette in an ashtray on the desk. "That dossier must have caused you endless toil," he said. "I'll bet there are things in it that even I don't know."

"Perhaps," Kholenko said, and crushed out his own cigarette. "We have a record of your first inquiry of Lieutenant Borodkin last year," he went on. "We did not have Vorst in custody at the time, as you were then told. But your query prompted a review of what we knew concerning his SD activities. Among many other things, your wife's arrest came to light. The connection was easily established. Your comings and goings have been noted since then."

Darsoss nodded with a sour smile of acknowledgment. They had allowed his hunger to build, the obsession to grow with time; they had known all along, had waited until now. "Very good indeed," he said in a mock complimentary tone. "And now comes the bargain. Vorst in exchange for what?"

Kholenko glanced away as if to disassociate himself from any emotional engagements with the man seated before him. Almost haughtily he said: "Otto Vorst has served several purposes and can serve yet another. His availability for . . . an interview . . . can be arranged. Under certain conditions."

"I thought he was of such great importance in your ceaseless war on fascism," Darsoss said, ready to probe Vorst's doubtful status.

"Otto Vorst," Kholenko said without the slightest hesitation, "was arrested two days ago and removed to Lubyanka Prison, where he will await trial on the charges finally documented and authenticated by the People's Tribunal."

Vernon's information had been up to date. The Russians had used Vorst and were continuing to use him. Kholenko further corroborated this when he said: "The waiting period for his trial could be quite extended." He paused and then said: "Of course it would depend on many things."

"What you're saying is that you'll keep him on ice for me if we make a deal," Darsoss said. "Shall I translate that?"

"Not necessary."

"You waited for me to get to you, didn't you?" Darsoss said. "You kept Vorst out of trouble until then, and then you shipped him home where there's no chance of slip-ups. Very good. But what if I hadn't found the daughter and discovered the letter written by Vorst?"

"We waited for nothing," Kholenko said. "We have merely taken advantage of various accidents. And through them we've all stumbled on a convenient situation. You've shown enormous determination, a willingness to do . . . almost anything." He paused, then said: "A willingness we are prepared to reward."

"You must want something very badly," Darsoss said.

"Your services," Kholenko admitted. "We are eager for them. But even without them we will survive. I think just to keep things in perspective, we must regard you as the buyer and ourselves as the seller. In a seller's market."

Darsoss took this in and then said: "When do I get the interview?"

"Are you ready to begin?" Kholenko asked.

"I'm ready to listen. But it has to be good."

"It is a single mission," Kholenko said, concealing any eagerness he might have felt. "Duration, flexible. A matter of several months, perhaps."

"What about Vorst?"

"We will guarantee that."

"How?"

"The guarantee is actually woven into the mission itself," Kholenko said. "When the time comes you will see how impossible it would be for us not to fulfill the promise."

"I can't give you an answer on that little."

"A step at a time."

"I'd have to know what the thing is all about."

"Right at the moment, that is impossible," Kholenko said. "Only that you are well suited to the mission and that you would have to leave Berlin—more than this I cannot tell you."

"Why? Don't you know?"

"That's possible. But irrelevant. I'm beginning to think we've misunderstood each other. Perhaps your willingness and determination are not as great as we thought."

"I can't be responsible for what you may or may not think," Darsoss said, fighting for that delicate balance between one's own will and total submission to another. "But I want to make it clear that certain things are out of the question."

"Such as?"

"I'll supply no names; I'll commit no acts of violence or sabotage; I'll be no part of frame-ups, regardless of how small."

Kholenko smiled dryly. "Anything else?" he asked.

"I don't know. It depends on what you ask of me."

"We will not be able to bargain back and forth endlessly," Kholenko said. "And I've no intentions of it."

Kalinin suddenly cleared his throat and stepped forward. "May I suggest that we take a recess and use the time to ponder," he said. "We've come a good distance."

Kholenko was silent for a moment, then, as if he were only vaguely concerned with the whole thing, he said: "I've no objections."

"Good," Kalinin said. "I have my flat nearby, Mr. Darsoss. Why not spend the night? That is, unless we *have* misunderstood you."

"You haven't." He knew they had to check with someone higher up. The Center possibly. Or the Resident Director of the net he was to be woven into. "But why don't I go to my own flat?"

"Because your absence there will not be noted, and the need for a rendezvous is eliminated if you remain here until the matter is settled," Kalinin explained.

Darsoss said: "Good enough," and looked toward Kholenko. They exchanged a curt nod, no words. Kalinin said to Kholenko: "We will speak later." Darsoss noted the fact that he had said nothing in Russian upon departing. Kalinin was a good psychologist.

In his flat a few buildings away, Kalinin's importance to the *apparat* was completely revealed when he said to Darsoss: "My wife is undoubtedly asleep, but I will be delighted to brew a cup of tea for you." It had to have been enormous; wives were simply not standard on a Soviet foreign assignment.

"No thanks," Darsoss said.

Kalinin ushered him into a darkened living room where he switched on a table lamp and said: "Make yourself comfortable."

"What comes next?"

"Very simple," Kalinin said. "You will spend the next few hours here and then you will leave."

"What does that mean?"

"A final vet is taking place," Kalinin told him evenly. "Your various stipulations are being confirmed." He paused, then shrugged. "Or denied," he added.

He gestured Darsoss to the divan and he took a chair directly opposite.

"What is the guarantee you're talking about?" Darsoss asked as he lit a cigarette.

"Aren't we ahead of ourselves?"

"No. That's a stepping stone," Darsoss said. "That's what this whole thing is about, as far as I'm concerned. You know that. We can't proceed without it."

"That is the point; you won't *need* to proceed without it. I do not know the details, but that much I am certain of. Why, after all, should we wish to deceive you?"

"There must be a few reasons, at least."

"Are any apparent?"

"I'm not sure. I haven't looked carefully."

"I think you are anything but careless, Mr. Darsoss," Kalinin said, lighting his own cigarette and looking through the dim light at the other man. "You know exactly what is what."

"You flatter me."

"Do I? Why do you think . . . ?" Kalinin stopped and smiled.

"What?" Darsoss asked. "That you're trying to recruit me?" He shrugged. "Who knows? Maybe precisely because you think I *am* careless. Not everyone used by an intelligence organization is brave, brilliant, and well balanced. How many times has MGB or some other outfit played on the weakness of an agent and assigned him to something where his very carelessness would pay dividends? Someone filled with false information which he could be counted on to divulge to an unsuspecting enemy."

"Make your judgment when you have more facts. You'll find it is different from the suspicions you are now voicing."

"All right. What do we do? Just sit here?"

"Why don't you lie down?" Kalinin said. "Come," he said, rising. "Let me show you to a small room in the rear of the flat."

Darsoss followed Kalinin along a narrow hallway to the room with its small daybed and ancient armoire. "I hope you will find it comfortable," Kalinin said.

"Quit worrying about my comfort," Darsoss said. "It makes me nervous."

Kalinin smiled. "We will talk later," he said, and then departed.

Darsoss lay down on the narrow bed, probably once used by a servant, his overcoat serving as a blanket. He was sure there was no chance of sleeping, and for what seemed like a very long while he smoked cigarettes in the dark. He felt like someone facing a carefully arranged life-and-death situation. You had to live by yourself in those final moments before you were called upon. It was the only way.

Suddenly Kalinin's hand was on his arm, awakening him. A cold, gray dawn had arrived.

"Your terms are acceptable," Kalinin said when he could see that Darsoss was fully awake. "As soon as possible you are to proceed to London. But we will talk of that presently. There is a bathroom at the end of the hallway. I'm sure you will wish to use it. We can then have coffee and discuss various details."

Darsoss nodded. He felt broken into small pieces of frosted glass. He said nothing. It was six A.M.

The two men sat in the kitchen together ten minutes later, coffee and *Brötchen* before them. "My wife is not yet awake," Kalinin said. "I prepared this myself."

"It's very nice. What about London?"

"As I say, your terms are acceptable. There will be no need for violence or sabotage or transmission of names. Nothing to steal, nothing to carry."

"What must I do? Become Prime Minister of England?"

Kalinin smiled faintly. "I do not know yet what you will actually do. I may never know. In any case, you must first go to London and await instructions."

"How?"

"Simply by behaving exactly as you would behave ordinarily in London," Kalinin said. "There is to be no clandestine activity. You will go as a free-lance journalist—your present occupation—and do nothing abnormal. Avoid no old contacts— this is especially important—and take up residence anywhere in the city. But not a flat; a hotel—the kind you would normally choose. So that you will be left free to move quickly without attracting attention."

Darsoss nodded and said nothing.

"Only one segment of this operation has been allotted to each of the persons involved. For my own part, I know only that Center requested an agent of certain qualifications to be sent to London. You meet every requirement." He shrugged. "So each directive will be issued as the mission progresses."

"London has been alerted to my arrival, I gather," Darsoss said.

"We can be sure of that," Kalinin said. "Part of your value lies in your mobility, your acceptability as you are. You will be very much out in the open. You will have a code name. Johnson. But its use will probably be quite limited. You will be contacted with this identification speech: 'Last week my auto broke down on the road between Dunster and Minehead. I had to wait two hours for the garage to come for me.' "

"And what do I say?"

"Nothing. The contact is a friend of yours. He knows you already. That is why it is imperative that you get in touch with all your friends and acquaintances when you arrive—the ones you would normally see."

Darsoss was a bit surprised by this new factor, perhaps even shocked. One of his friends was a Soviet spy. "When do I get what I'm after?" he said.

"Before the mission is done. Really, you will be able to soon verify this for yourself. It is safe to trust our assurances until then, isn't it? I mean, what can we possibly do if you are not immediately satisfied on this point? Shoot you? We could, but we are sure you wouldn't care."

Darsoss took some coffee and inhaled on his cigarette. "And what guarantee do you have?" he asked.

"Your passion," Kalinin said. "Obviously."

There was a moment of silence before Kalinin said quietly, "It is interesting to me to observe such a . . . steadfast devotion to personal vengeance."

Darsoss looked up from staring into his coffee cup. His eyes began to glitter. He could feel a burning sensation in back of them. "He drowned her," he said in a quiet, choked voice. Then he said no more.

Kalinin appeared somewhat startled, but surely not because he didn't know of such things. "In the tank," he said in an

41

appalled whisper of recognition. "Yes . . ." The words could hardly have failed to evoke the image of dreadful human struggle, of strangulation, of a futile effort to remain afloat, to stay alive. Each man considered it in his own way, both with fixed eyes that seemed vividly confronted by outrage.

"You can go up and down," Darsoss said, "many more than three times."

Kalinin nodded. "I know," he said.

"Many more, if it's spaced properly—if somebody's an expert," Darsoss said. "A question, a pause. Then a push on the harness . . . What it must feel like to want breath and not have it—to choke for it, to feel your lungs bursting. What it must feel like."

"Yes," Kalinin said grimly. "So you want to do it that way to him . . ."

Darsoss broke his fixed stare, inhaled on his cigarette and ground it out. He said nothing.

Kalinin had to have been a hardened Party man, his mysteriously flexible position in the logistics of Darsoss' recruitment attesting to wide past experience. Yet he seemed moved beyond normal expectations. "Oh, my friend," he said, "what a terrible thing . . ."

There was sympathy in the eyes and sadness in the voice. Darsoss looked at him. It was all genuine, as genuine as the gothic cruelty and the coldly mechanistic attitudes of which the man was probably also capable. "We had better arrange your return to Dahlem," he said, coming back to the realities after a moment or two. "Wait a day or two, then book a flight."

"What about my flat?" Darsoss asked.

"Keep it, by all means. You will be returning to Berlin in due course. Oh, yes, and disbursement of your funds will be provided for in London. You will have dollars, of course, in an account in the Bank of America."

"I've no interest in payment," Darsoss said.

"Yes, but we have," Kalinin said. "No person serves without payment. It is a strictly enforced rule."

"I can donate it."

"As you wish. As long as it is not to the Communist Party."

"No need to worry."

"Or any other left-wing group."

"I've no politics, comrade."

In a few hours Darsoss was back in Dahlem. In two days he was boarding a BEA DC-3 at Tempelhof Airport: the 9 A.M. Flight 7, Berlin to London, nonstop.

5

As the plane moved out toward the North Sea, Darsoss sat in his seat and smoked one of the sixty cigarettes he would have smoked before the day was out. All the old ideas stood embarrassed and empty like the twisted ribbing of Berlin's bombed-out buildings. The hopelessness of the human situation obtained at all points of contact; the Russians and the Americans in Berlin merely served to spotlight the dominance of human avarice, stupidity, and weakness. Darsoss had thought these things through many times. He did not except himself. He was conscious of what he was: a man who lived on the thought of murder. How carefully the Russians had selected him. They were always on the lookout for certain people: the warped, the misguided, and the empty-handed. The Baron, Frau Moller, Verna, Yvonne, the contact at the public notice board, the waiter on Gelferstrasse—none of them were whole and in working order. Darsoss knew. After all, he was one of them.

Now he sat and thought endlessly about the people he knew in London. Someone among them would be his contact. This was obviously part of Darsoss' qualifications. But contact to what? He would soon find out. He continued to smoke as he waited for London to appear through the fog below.

CHAPTER TWO

1

A new airfield had replaced bombed-out Croyden with shacks and barracks and crude improvisations. The plane touched down. A wheel skidded on the runway, and Darsoss gripped the arm of his seat as if to strangle it. An eternal moment passed before he let out his breath, spared the last-minute mishap, unrelated and idiotic. Then he displayed his passport, nodded to his luggage, and proceeded to a hotel in Kensington High Street to which he had been partial in other times, and checked in easily because it was not nearly fully occupied.

He hung out his Valpak, removed his overcoat, and lit a cigarette. London was exhausted and gray and the smell of convalescence was everywhere. People went about their business, on the whole patient with the disrepair and all that had happened to them. But disappointment seemed acute in certain eyes, and there was indifference in some of the voices. No victory was ever clear-cut, of course. In a way, that was why he was here.

In a small red address book were seventeen names with either London or other United Kingdom addresses. Darsoss examined it. Richard Eilers, Waterloo Road, Smethwick, Staffs, brought to mind a dim and brief moment in Cornwall ten years before. Whatever details attached to this entry were attributable to a memory that gleamed with impressions like spackling on a dark, endless surface. Everywhere in the midst of painful and mean-ingful recollection were trivia: cheap song lyrics of thirty years ago; a chance remark made by a now-gone schoolmate; the design on a packet of ten-cent cigarettes no longer manufac-tured. That he remembered Eilers as a middle-aged public-school master of English history on holiday with his wife, Celia; that he remembered Eilers' lisp, the wen on his left eyelid, the touch of engine grease on the sleeve of his blue blazer, and the brown brogues and close-cropped fingernails that characterized the man's wife, as well as the exchange of addresses over a beer in the King's Arms in the village of Boscastle, in no way made the people or the incident important. Certainly he would never be moved to telephone Mr. Eilers. More than half the names in his book meant as little to him. Which then among the remainder was that of a British traitor? One could hardly avoid playing such a guessing game, under the circumstances.

He had to start somewhere. Miles Lawson, if not a close friend, had been a good companion on numerous occasions going back twelve years. He was cool, calm, and politically conservative, though he might have voted Labor once or twice. George Greavy was a mystery-story writer Darsoss had met in Spain and was so leftish he was not likely to be of use to the Russians; a Popular Front background didn't make one an especially good candidate for Russian Intelligence Service. Alex Dinsdale, another newspaperman, like Miles Lawson, was worth a call, certainly, but was an overt malcontent in so many ways that he could be considered too obtrusive to be a spy. Jack Mordram made Darsoss think of that faraway time of a slum-bering England and the protest marches and rallies meant to awaken her. He hadn't seen Mordram since then. None of this served to condemn Miles Lawson, of course. He merely became Darsoss' first contact in London. If he had been expecting Darsoss' telephone call, he managed to conceal it.

"Well, this is something," he said with an air of surprise. "How long are you here for?"

"Uncertain at the moment," Darsoss replied, looking out at the rain. "Are you busy at lunchtime?"

"Luckily, no. What about The Gate at half past twelve?"

Darsoss knew the place well. It was in Fleet Street nearby to Consolidated Press Services, Limited, where Miles Lawson was employed as an editor. It was typical of the neighborhood at lunchtime: a crowded scene smelling of dampness, dominated by the sight of tightly rolled umbrellas, and bowler hats perched here and hanging there, dark-suited men from everywhere in the city taking their midday recess of lager and sandwiches.

Miles Lawson, once an RAF Squadron Leader, grounded early in the war as overage at thirty-two, always an expert and energetic reporter, had lost the sky-blue gleam in eyes that once looked with cordial disdain in the face of death; and the silky blond hair had darkened and thinned a bit. Any other fissures or erosion didn't show. But there was something wrong. He sat on a bench next to Darsoss, beer and sandwiches on the low table in front of them. "You've had rotten luck, old boy, no doubt about it," he was saying. "I mean, what does one say to a man whose wife . . . ?"

Darsoss inhaled on his cigarette and didn't like what he heard. The sympathy was somehow a mere matter of words; Lawson's solicitude and comradely attitudes were unconvincing. From the moment they had met there was something not quite right with Lawson's handshake, with his smile, with the tone of his voice. It was not the bright and totally good-humored Lawson of other times. Darsoss would normally have felt disappointment. Now he was merely sour with suspicion. There was the feeling of being the leper or someone disfigured to whom one owed civility and tolerance but not more. Darsoss' bad impression was strong, though maybe he was letting his nerves get the better of him. Not unlikely.

"Nothing," he said quietly, acting well, but very much waiting to catch that threatening scent from which the foraging animal runs. "Nothing. But I appreciate your sympathy."

He smiled because it seemed normal to do so. He looked into the young-old face of the man he was with. What was there? Did the eyes hide knowledge of secret disgrace? The details of something unspeakable, the life-and-death secret; the discovery, made somehow, that Darsoss was a Soviet agent? Darsoss still feared the mishap before contact. He hadn't expected to. He fought hard to push it down.

"Just more than one can begin to understand," Miles Lawson intoned solemnly, turning to his drink. "Or bear, I suppose . . ." He had a sensitive mouth; it did all sorts of things quickly and easily: accused, regretted, held doubt.

"I thought you knew," Darsoss said.

"No, I didn't," Lawson replied, and took some of the contents in the glass. "Was no attempt made to get her out? Forgive me, perhaps you'd rather not discuss it. But I can't help asking."

Darsoss' uneasiness turned to resentment. "Of course, every attempt was made," he said. "What did you think? That she'd been abandoned like a piece of equipment?"

"Sorry, didn't mean anything like that. I suppose I was just wondering how close it had been. God-awful thing to happen. Really."

"Yes, you can put it that way," Darsoss said. "Carry on."

"Oh, now, look here," Lawson said. "You can't expect someone to choose all the right words, you know. For one thing, there aren't any. And I was actually getting at something else, frankly."

Darsoss was set for whatever it was.

"You were in Intelligence, weren't you?" Lawson went on after a brief pause. "OSS?"

Darsoss' expression remained unchanged and he said nothing.

"I always suspected it from the time we bumped into each other that night in Charing Cross Road," Lawson said, "over three years ago now."

"Why do you ask that?" Darsoss said, looking right at him.

"Not meaning to pry," Lawson assured him. "It's not the sort of thing you ask a chap—not point-blank, certainly. But I suddenly realize you were carrying a terrible burden with you at the time. Your wife was behind their lines right then. That very night. Of course. You disappeared so quickly, and now it makes sense."

"Does it?"

"Yes. You needn't answer, but was it you who went in after her?"

"Yes," Darsoss said without hesitation. Then: "You *really* didn't know about it until now, did you?"

"Why does that surprise you?"

"I suppose because we always assume others know more about us than they do," said Darsoss.

Lawson's smile was almost malevolent, the young-old face brushed by an off-white shadow. "Sometimes we think they know nothing," he said. "And then we find out they know more than we dream they do."

"That can be embarrassing," Darsoss said.

"Decidedly," Lawson said. "Depending on what it is." He paused. "Anyhow, I hope I didn't stir up old ashes."

"It's all right."

"You must tell me about your assignment, by the way."

"It's not an assignment," Darsoss said. "I've been stringing."

"Oh, I see."

"I'm trying to contrast postwar London with postwar Berlin in a series of separate pieces centering on art, politics, and sex."

"That covers everything, doesn't it?"

"It should keep me busy," Darsoss said. "If they work out, I'll make a book out of them. I'm interested enough to try, anyhow," he continued, warming to the subject as if it were his actual and main purpose; he was a very good actor. "I'm tired of running down stories. That's for kids."

"Yes," Lawson agreed. Then he looked at his wrist watch. "Where are you off to now?"

"I'm easing into the atmosphere."

"Yes, it's fairly grim. We're not really so much a hardy island race as grimly resigned inmates." Lawson didn't appear at all amused by what he had said. He began to rise. "I'm back to the office now, are you walking that way?"

"Is there a barbershop you use exclusively?"

"A haircutter? Oh, no. It's all the same to me. Try in Wardour Street. You're at the DeVere, you say?"

"No, the Kensington Gardens."

"Good. I'll ring you."

A minute later they had parted on the crowded sidewalk amidst a sea of umbrellas and the endless sound of scuffling shoes and galoshes, a fine rain continuing to fall as it had done since Darsoss' arrival a few hours before. Darsoss' sense of solitariness was as intense as ever.

As he sat in a men's hairdressing place in the Strand, a barber shears clicking in his ears, he continued to think about his old friend. And he realized his fears and suspicions had been unreasoning. Lawson had simply grown less ebullient than he had always been, his public-school accent still cheery but vaguely pained. The man's normal aging process had happened to put the glint of suspicion in once-candid eyes and a telling grain of disbelief in the voice. It was like a sneer on the face of a dog. The effect could perhaps be there if one really wished to accept it. But why would one?

2

In the next few days Darsoss addressed himself to living the part of a person who had not been sent to London by Russian Intelligence. He strolled through streets and parks, in foul weather mostly, went to the cinema, and wrote a letter to his New York bank requesting a draft transference to the London branch of Bank of America. Dinsdale was out of London; Greavy was recovering from the flu and had plans for departing for the Riviera within forty-eight hours. Tom Phillips, American chief of World Dispatch Wire Service, would be available for dinner next week, perhaps.

By eleven A.M. on the fourth day, no revelations had yet taken place. Darsoss hadn't particularly expected that any would have so quickly. Certain situations demanded a look to the left and a look to the right and once over the shoulder before a decisive move could be made, and this was surely one of them. It presented a good opportunity to behave as a free-lance journalist might if he were that and nothing else; not one who was watching and waiting and listening in every waking moment. To that end he remained in his room overlooking Kensington Gardens, so gray and cold and forlorn; and he began to write, and actually became absorbed in doing so, because people were hardly ever simply this or simply that; they were two or three things at once. Darsoss was fastened to an idea that had nothing to do with contacting another Soviet agent or with the slow death of Otto Vorst. He was putting it onto a sheet of paper in his typewriter with conviction as unexpected and sourceless as a single moment of high fever. "Old hatreds gain strength with every passing day; they must die young or they do not die at all. They survive the people who serve them, the national boundary lines which they create. They begin wars and are deepened by the time the war is done. One need only walk where the bombed-out ruin abides behind St. Paul's, or near the twisted remains of the Gedachtniskirche, to understand hatred in its deepest, most religious sense . . ."

He stopped suddenly. His nerves were like the birds fluttering beneath the pie crust. The motions could be very tough. He tore the sheet out of the roller and crumpled it up just seconds before the phone began to ring. The caller was Alex Dinsdale, a man gratified by all the disillusioning discoveries he had made. "Of course you'll meet me for a toddy, won't you?" he said. "I'd have got to you sooner but my editor had me off on something in Liverpool. Can't discuss it and anyway you wouldn't care. Can you be at The Blue Boar at six? Do you know it?"

"Yes. Next to Consolidated."

"Right."

"Are you with a newspaper, Alex?"

"Yes, the *Compass*."

"What were you doing in Liverpool? Looking through keyholes?"

"I know, old boy, but I've lost all that snobbishness about high-minded journalism and all of that twaddle. Besides, it's a living. Shall we save it until later?"

"By all means."

"Awfully glad to hear from you, old Greek."

Darsoss hung up and considered Dinsdale's parting words. Dinsdale was by nature a bit expansive, but the intimacy seemed strained. The affection had been forced; it was covering up something. Everything was covering up something else. Even the hall porter's good morning had appeared suspicious, hadn't it? And as soon as he saw Dinsdale, Darsoss' suspicions, all hopeful, increased.

The high dome and the vaguely worried eyes, the superior expression of intelligence somehow at odds with nervous and mistrusting fingers—Alex Dinsdale surely had something on his mind and soon would reveal it. More than just the dissertation he had slipped into after an initial exchange of particulars. "Two women have divorced me already and I've no intention of trying a third," he was saying as they stood in the bar among many others, whiskey before each of them. "Life is basically altogether too difficult and to be married is to double it. Even worse. The headaches progress geometrically. One and one don't make two, they make four, if you know what I mean."

Darsoss didn't want to prolong the matter with disagreement. "Yes, I know," he said.

Dinsdale was a man for whom whiskey provided the excuse to confess, to expose everything, to speak of all the youthful hopes, all the shattered dreams. Maybe Darsoss was now about to discover that it was a cover-up for what he had always been: a clever, cold-blooded Soviet agent. Anybody could be, when you came right down to it.

"It's all a sadistic prank, really . . ."

Darsoss watched him take a drink and said nothing. Let him play it out in his own way and get to it finally, if there was anything to get to; or drum up his courage if by some chance the thing had made him edgy.

"By the time you're forty-four, Marco, you've forgotten most of your disappointments—or at least you've become incapable of suffering further ones. And I suppose that's an achievement in itself."

Darsoss shifted his weight. "You sound as if you expected more than you got," he said.

"Didn't you?"

"Not personally," Darsoss said. "I'm not a bitter type."

"You're a *very* bitter type. You're straight bitterness, un-adulterated—neat and unspoiled by compromise."

"How do you know?" Darsoss asked, even and calm.

"Everything points to it," Dinsdale said. "You're quite sensitive, love. You've had rotten things happen. So have I. I recognize the signs."

"Do you?"

"Of course. That's why I can speak freely to you," Dinsdale said, and finished his whiskey. "Another here, please," he told the barmaid, and then turned back to Darsoss. "We haven't seen each other in years, but I know more about you than you think."

Darsoss looked over his shoulder, and then quietly and with a faint smile he said: "I'd like to hear about it."

Dinsdale's glass was refilled. "You're bound to," he said, and took a sip. "I think you're at a crossroads. You're where I was five years ago."

"Where is that?" Darsoss said. This had to be it—the link between Darsoss and whatever awaited him.

Dinsdale's mouth opened. "Hello, I hope I'm not intruding," Miles Lawson said.

Dinsdale's mouth remained partially ajar. Darsoss crushed

out his cigarette. Lawson had placed himself alongside of Darsoss. "Do be frank, and I'll just buzz off. How are you, Alex?" he said.

Darsoss could easily have pushed Lawson into the path of an oncoming truck. He saw Dinsdale stiffen. "Of course not," Darsoss said. "What would you like?"

"Gin and French," Lawson told the barmaid. "I'm staying in the city for dinner. Normally I'm on my way home. How are you, Alex?"

"Well. And you?"

"Coming along. Well, what a coincidence."

"Yes."

"I've meant to call you, Marco, but things have been rather feverish lately," Lawson said.

Darsoss felt as if he were having a frustration dream: something happens to forestall you just as the apple, whatever it may be, is within reach. "That's all right, Miles. I've been tied up myself."

"How's that very interesting project going?"

"Fine," Darsoss answered without thinking. "That is, it could be worse."

There seemed to be on Lawson's face a cold and searching look. Darsoss knew exactly what to make of it this time; there would be no more pouncing on shadows: Lawson had simply developed certain characteristics one associates with skepticism and mistrust—the unconvinced expression in unwavering eyes; the absence of accord in the voice when saying: "Oh, yes."

Dinsdale said: "I must spend a penny, if you'll excuse me."

Darsoss watched him go toward the back of the place. He felt like someone who had just missed a connection and now would need to spend overnight in a station waiting room. He stifled his anger with a casually lit cigarette.

"He's so damned maudlin, isn't he?" Lawson said. "Drinks like hell constantly."

"You fall out over something?" Darsoss said.

"No, no," Lawson was quick to reply. "Just a matter of drift. He was unhappy, I think, when I was getting married."

"Was he? Why?"

"Because he was getting divorced. Marriage is his sworn enemy. And women."

Darsoss nodded to the barmaid for a refill, and inhaled deeply on his cigarette. Shadows he had seen before appeared in Lawson's eyes, then quickly vanished. A new, on-the-spot tone was in Lawson's voice as he said: "Anyhow, the hell with all that. I wonder could you come to dinner tomorrow night. I told Norma I would ask you. I know it's terribly short notice . . ."

"Not at all. I can make it."

"Jolly good. I've told Norma all about you—or at least enough to make you interesting. She's a Yorkshire girl. You'll like her, I think. I do. We get on together. She's not pretty, but passion's not the end and all. I'm old for it, really."

"Where are you located?"

"Fifty-seven Ashcroft Gardens. But it's best that you call just before you come and I'll give you exact directions."

"About seven?"

"Yes, that's fine. I would ordinarily chauffeur you, but I'm afraid I can't tomorrow," Lawson said, then paused to drink. "Last week my auto broke down on the road between Dunster and Minehead. I had to wait two hours for the garage to come for me."

The little game was over. Darsoss was mildly surprised; he had been betting on Dinsdale. But it didn't matter; the ground was broken, the foundation in, and the cornerstone laid. He looked at Lawson, the strange mannerisms and the sly eyes not so puzzling any longer.

"Now what happens?" Darsoss said, after only a brief pause.

"You're all business, aren't you?" Lawson said, as if he had had a nasty premonition verified.

"Aren't you?" Darsoss asked, calm and patient.

"Someone presses a button and I move," Lawson said.

"Is that all?"

"Totally. I've a cutout between myself and a control I've never seen. Or if I have, I'm not aware of it."

"What does the cutout tell you?"

"Why are you so bloody full of questions?" Lawson said, smiling the way people do when they are saying one thing and wish to appear as if they are saying something else. "This is not an interrogation, you know."

"Calm yourself."

"The fact is we've been put together for purposes certainly

not known to me. As a guess I would say they researched one of us and found the other in his background. I hope the duration is brief."

A strange frost had fallen between the two men. "Here comes old pisshead now," Lawson said. "I'm going to hop it. Don't bother to say good-bye for me." He downed the gin and French in a gulp, said: "You will forgive me, of course," and was gone.

By the time Dinsdale was back at his side, Darsoss' sense of amenity had vanished. Everything was once again what it seemed to be. The chambermaid, the sybaritic-looking man sitting endlessly in the hotel lobby, and the hall porter with the twitching mouth could all be taken at face value. Now there would be action. Everything else was nugatory—people, places, old ties, a kindness that delayed him even for just mere seconds—everything. "I'm afraid I've got to leave," he said, looking at his wrist watch.

Dinsdale looked crestfallen. "Oh, so soon?" he said. "What a pity."

"We'll get together again."

"Yes, I should hope," Dinsdale said, but he was looking deserted and uncertain. "I say, you're not dashing off like this because of anything I may have said, are you?"

"Nonsense."

"Well, it is rather abrupt of you. And I do sometimes get a bit more searching than perhaps I should."

"Not with me."

"Or anything Lawson may have said?"

Darsoss looked at him, cold and unresponsive.

"Listen, regardless of what you may think, I've simply got to know," Dinsdale said. "Did Miles say anything about me? I can't conceive that he wouldn't have."

"No. And if he had, it would have slipped my mind by now," Darsoss said.

Dinsdale looked frankly into Darsoss' eyes. He seemed to know that in some way he had been short-circuited between the bar and the w.c. He couldn't have dreamed why and how, of course. "I'm sorry, old boy," he said. "Bad form, as they say. Don't know what came over me."

"Forget it," Darsoss said.

He was ready to leave, but Dinsdale took his arm. "Listen,

you will have a free moment, won't you? I mean, we shall meet for drinks when you're not so pressed for time?"

Dinsdale was highly sensitive to Darsoss' sudden disinterest. Darsoss sensed the man was in a shaky state for God knew what personal reasons. It was pathetic, perhaps. But like discarded goods floating by aimlessly in midstream, Dinsdale commanded little attention or effort. "I'll call you, Alex," was the way Darsoss ended it. He patted Dinsdale's arm and walked away.

3

Norma Lawson was a tall woman of thirty with a too-large nose, rosy cheeks, and a pleasant smile. While she cleared away after dinner the next night, Darsoss and Lawson took to the living room of the Lawsons' garden flat.

"Your wife seems on edge," Darsoss said in a guarded tone. "Does she know what's going on?"

"Don't be absurd," Lawson snapped under his breath.

"Then she smells something," Darsoss said. "You keep getting a look in your eyes. I think you're scaring her."

"Don't concern yourself."

Darsoss gave him a look of cold doubt. Then he walked to the window leading to and from a little garden with one small, bare tree and the straggling stalks of vanished flowers, dead with winter. He looked out to the near-darkness, his back to his friend, the hissing of a gas heater suddenly the only sound in the room. They could never be on really good terms after this; they were crippled with the mistrust and suspicion of one for one's own kind, the hostility bred between dogs concerned with the same bone, or the disapproval and indignation one whore feels for another.

"I can't help wondering, frankly," Lawson's voice came, breaking the peace, "just what price you've put on yourself." He spoke somewhat wistfully. "Not money, I'm sure. And it wouldn't be political conviction, would it?"

Darsoss didn't answer, and Lawson said: "No, I'm sure it's not." He paused, then added: "In that much we're in the same bag."

"All that is unimportant," Darsoss said quietly, almost contemptuously.

"Would you say we were both suffering from a dose of acute embarrassment?" Lawson said.

"I'm not suffering from anything," Darsoss said bluntly. "Too bad if you are. To me it couldn't matter less."

Lawson smiled mirthlessly. "I don't believe you, Marco. Isn't that odd?"

"Suit yourself."

The door buzzer sounded at that very instant and closed off further conversation. Lawson was obviously in no rush to admit the visitor. "We're at the Rubicon," he said quietly.

"I think you've crossed it," Darsoss said, then stood there waiting, single-minded, expectant, apart from everyone else. He watched carefully while both Lawsons greeted the arrival of their guests, Mr. and Mrs. Ian Quennel.

"Hello, I hope we're not ahead of time," the man said, pleasant, narrow through the chest, his face tightly fleshed, his mouth thin and serious despite a smile. He was about forty, iron-gray at the temples, and had the look of a man who had never struck a blow in anger.

"Not in the least," Lawson said, and then, after the introductions had taken place: "Put on a pot of coffee, darling, would you?"

"Let me help you, Norma," the woman said in an accent Darsoss recognized as Scandinavian. She was tall and blond and immensely good-looking, her face made for a Steichen photograph—shadow, cheekbone, and eyes that saw through you. Darsoss took it in like a statistic. He was far more interested in the woman's husband.

Ian Quennel gave Darsoss a watery smile of disinterest and moved toward a landscape print over the mantelpiece as if he had never seen it before, not terribly compelled, feeling his hands absently but firmly as a piano virtuoso might, without thinking, and utterly convinced of his own brilliance. They had shaken hands the way people do when they are meeting for no urgent reason.

In a moment or two the women were in the kitchen like obedient supernumeraries, and the three men had developed a conclave in Lawson's small study. "Ian and I were at Trinity together," Lawson said with fake nonchalance. "Now we're in the same spy ring. What a delightful coincidence. Actually, I had always thought of you as mildly loyal, Ian, if certainly not patriotic. It's rather a shock to discover this. Though I suppose life is mostly shocks, isn't it?"

Quennel thought he was joking at first; he smiled, not too amused. Then he could see Lawson was in earnest. "I don't think I follow you, Miles," he said. "You talk as if I hadn't recently made the same discovery about you, leaving out the shock, of course."

"That's because of your pure scientific background," Lawson said. "You're immune to shocks." Then to Darsoss he said: "You're in the same room with one of the A-bomb boys. From Los Alamos to Harwell. Obviously he's the star attraction."

"I assume you're passing some sort of judgment," Quennel said, unruffled.

"We're not here to search our souls," Darsoss said. "So let's cut the shit and get down to business."

"Not polite, but to the point, certainly," Quennel said. "I understand you have a prodigious memory."

"Do you? How?"

"I was told." He paused to make it clear he couldn't be pushed. "I was also told that Miles was to serve as a connection between parallel lines, so to speak; that I was to contact him in a normal manner, as I frequently do, identify myself with a password, and that he would put me in touch with an extraordinary man who turned out to be you."

"What about it?"

"This is what about it," Quennel began. "I have material to transmit—certain scientific data that really cannot be considered the private property of any one nation or single bloc of nations. There are about one hundred pages of rather intricate mathematical and chemical formulas involved. That's a lot to memorize, so I must admit I am a bit skeptical. Or perhaps I should say I'm astonished at the idea. Can you really accomplish such a feat, Mr. Darsoss?"

Darsoss said nothing. The question irritated him.

"Because if you can," Quennel went on, "there is ground for rejoicing. The advantages of carrying this grade of information in one's head are obvious. So much better than transmission by radio, which can be traced with high-powered DF equipment. So much better than a letter to which interception or even loss are ever-present dangers. Or microfilm, which *can* be discovered in transit no matter how cleverly hidden. If you can do it, there are no risks—nothing on paper, nothing on film."

"Someone evidently thinks he can," Lawson said, "or he shouldn't have been sent. You should be a marvelous team. I'm lucky to have such stimulating friends."

Quennel said: "Can you, Mr. Darsoss?"

"You handle your end and don't worry about mine," Darsoss told him.

"I assume that means yes," Quennel said, equable and understanding.

"Are you stationed at the research center in Harwell right now?" Darsoss said.

Quennel answered: "I'm not stationed anywhere. I am no longer employed by the British government. I teach."

"Good God," Lawson muttered. "Is this really happening?"

"Before we go any further," Darsoss said, crushing out a smoked-down cigarette, "what about my guarantee? I don't move without it."

"I'm sorry," Quennel said. "You've the advantage. What guarantee?"

"Go back to whoever tells you things," Darsoss said, "and tell him I have an arrangement that was made on the other end and that he had better verify it. Otherwise it's all off."

"But it may not be that easy," Quennel said with a worried frown. "I can't just make a phone call, you know."

"Whatever you do is your business."

"It might take days."

"Yes, I know. But they've been waiting a long time already," Darsoss said, taking out a cigarette. "So have I," he added, and then struck a match.

"All right," Quennel said. "But agree to a meeting next week. By then there will be word on your arrangement, I'm sure, and we'll have lost no time in getting under way." He seemed suddenly to be guarding a sacred flame, invisible to all but himself, a restrained urgency in his manner. "We can't afford lost time," he added. "Take my word on it."

Darsoss inhaled deeply on his new cigarette. "Where?" he asked.

"Here," Quennel said, and turned to look at Lawson. "We're counting heavily on Miles inviting us."

Lawson flared up. "Why should you, damn it?" he snapped. "I've brought you together, that should be enough."

"But it's not, Miles," Quennel said. "We could have been brought together in any number of ways without you, if that were all there were to it. The real thing, Miles, is that you provide not only a reason for meeting, but a meeting place. Such a combination is nearly impossible to come by; its advantages speak for themselves."

Lawson gave a cry of disgust and rage and Darsoss cut in: "Why the heavy security?"

"Do you know anything about the gaseous diffusion process of separating uranium isotopes?" Quennel asked.

"No," Darsoss answered.

"Well, I do," Quennel told him, feeling his hands as if to be sure they were still there. "I know a great deal about it. And in the name of something called National Security, a number of very suspicious people are aware that I do. They are paid to worry about it, and they do just that. Anything I do, anyone I talk to, is of interest to them. Theoretically. Do you see? They must be lulled."

"I don't need a lecture," Darsoss said, and saw that Quennel smiled indulgently. "I just want to know if anyone is watching you."

"They don't announce themselves," Quennel answered somewhat cryptically. "The point is, if someone is, he must be made to think he is seeing what he is not seeing. Tonight, for example, we have come together under the most normal circumstances. A man has brought two very old friends together in his home. What could be more natural and ordinary? Do you see, Miles?"

"Now, listen to me," Lawson said with the cold anger of an outraged man. "I don't want you to meet here."

Quennel's frown was like a wound. "Miles, we must meet here," he said. "Even if we agreed not to, they would insist on it. You know that."

"Damn it," Lawson snapped. "You can't meet here." He now seemed on the verge of tears. Darsoss hoped such a thing would not occur.

"Miles," came the reasonable and sympathetic voice, the burden of pain for another person heavy enough to touch or to breathe in. "No other place, no other conditions cover and justify meetings between Darsoss and myself, spaced closely enough together to insure the success of what we're trying to do. There is a need for roughly sixteen hours of transmission. For this we cannot meet on street corners; we cannot sit in the park or in a restaurant or in the British Museum; nor can either of us visit the other in any degree of safety without something more substantial than just your mutual friendship to underwrite it. On the other hand, meeting here to play bridge every week or ten days, let us say, is a different matter. Do you see? I hate to keep saying, do you see? But do you?"

"Sixteen hours," Darsoss commented. "How does that break down?"

"Five sessions," Quennel replied, and then looked back at Lawson. "I'm astounded none of this was explained to you in advance, Miles."

Lawson said: "I'd no idea I was any more than an introduction in all of this."

Quennel considered that for a moment and then said: "Well, I'm afraid you are. Unfortunately, against your will. And that is a pity." He seemed to mean every word, his eyes both sympathetic and puzzled. He seemed to be saying that while he felt sorry, deeply sorry for whatever was ailing his friend, nothing was going to stand in the way of what had to be done. Darsoss saw him for a dedicated one, the kind you could grow to dislike very easily. "I implore you to co-operate," he said. "Actually you've no choice, have you?"

"You've touched on an interesting point," Lawson said bitterly. "Though I'm sure you didn't mean to. It must be obvious I'm in all of this against my will. It's almost amusing to see the way you both carefully look the other way."

"Don't tell us about it," Darsoss said in a voice of low-grade pain and disgust.

"But you already know. Oh, not the details. But it must be obvious that I've been promised silence in return for my services, that I'm being blackmailed . . ." Lawson seemed to be dangling now, as if he knew he had told a very bad joke.

Neither of the other two men spoke but simply stared at Lawson as if they couldn't help themselves. Like indecent exposure, it presented nothing new or unexpected but you couldn't ignore it. Lawson seemed to know as much himself and he turned his head and cast his eyes downward.

After a moment or two, Quennel said quietly: "Can we count on next Saturday evening? After dinner, very informal."

Lawson stood there defeated, his conscience exhausted. Darsoss said: "What time?"

Quennel glanced at Lawson and then with apparent small pity said to Darsoss, as if he were empowered to speak for Lawson: "I should think any time between half past eight and nine o'clock."

"All right," Darsoss said.

Then the three men joined the two women in the living room. They exchanged pleasant words, guided by Ian Quennel's restrained bonhomie, as if nothing out of the ordinary had taken place or was ever expected to. Darsoss' impression of Quennel's wife was that she hadn't much to say: the watchfob of the purely scientific man, perhaps his nursemaid and the queen of all his unscientific longings. Darsoss stayed on after the Quennels departed to thank his hostess for her gracious efforts.

"You didn't care terribly for the pudding, did you?" she said regretfully. "Next time I promise you something more continental if I can come by the ingredients."

"I enjoyed every morsel."

"Disa is quite the most exquisite thing, isn't she?"

Darsoss nodded. "Very lovely."

"I hope you liked them. I didn't know they were coming until the last minute. Ian's awfully nice. Though I must say I'm always a bit overpowered by people like him. Perhaps awed is what I mean."

Lawson came in from seeing the Quennels out. "Would you like another cup of coffee?" he said to Darsoss.

"I've got to leave, I'm afraid."

"We must see you again," Norma Lawson said.

"You will," Darsoss told her.

Lawson said: "Let me see you out."

They stood for just a moment or two on the narrow sidewalk, dim lamplight filtered by specks of mist. Lawson was coatless and hatless, a wool knit sweater his only protection from the cold, damp night. He said: "Listen, you're not fooling me."

"What the hell are you talking about?"

"I've been going back and forth on something in my mind right from the start. And now I think I've got it."

"What's that?"

"Do you remember the day we had lunch together? We talked about your wife, and I asked you certain questions. Do you recall I asked you if you were in OSS during the war? You as much as admitted you were." His eyes narrowed with putative wisdom. "It made me think," he said. "And now there's only one logical conclusion."

"Okay. What?"

Lawson answered with an unhappy relish. "You're here to bag all of us, aren't you?" he said. "You're an American counterintelligence agent on detached service to MI5, or something of the kind."

Darsoss didn't answer and Lawson said: "I've hit it, haven't I?"

"You've hit nothing."

"This is not you," Lawson said in an intense low voice just above a whisper. "You're not someone who's willing to commit an act of treachery like this without the slightest concern for consequences. Ian, perhaps. He's always been a bit starko, but not you, Marco."

"It rhymes," Darsoss said. "Good night, Miles."

"You can't be a Russian agent—you can't be. You're going to bag all of us. I don't know whether to laugh or cry . . ."

Darsoss broke Lawson's grip on his coat lapels and tore away from him. "Good night, Miles."

He wished Lawson could be dropped from the whole thing. Excuses were never of any use to the man placed in front of a wall.

4

Three days later, as he walked along Kensington High Street, the sky the color of plums and the air damp with stop-and-start rain, he thought about how he had once admired England in the way Americans often do, even naturalized Americans, for its traditions, its civility, its inns and countryside, its RAF. No longer. It had become a place in which to move with stealth, whose policemen were enemies; where surely, despite assurances to the contrary, there was going to be a fair risk at every turn. He thought of Miles Lawson, of whom one might have said a kind word, but not more, and of whom gross advantage was being taken. Darsoss noted as much without an ounce of passion, without a dram of pity. Nothing was left of friendship. Lawson simply managed to highlight the loopholes, the dangers, the loose ends, the things that could go wrong. Nothing more.

Darsoss entered the lobby of his hotel and the desk man called to him: "You've a telephone message, sir."

Call Maida Vale 2575. "Was this all there was?" he asked.

"That's all I have here, sir."

In his room, Darsoss called for the number, and then waited while the switchboard put him through. He lit a cigarette and in a moment or two was astounded to hear a woman's voice say: "Maida Vale two five seven five . . ."

"Hello, this is Marco Darsoss . . ."

"Oh. This is Disa Quennel . . ."

The accent should have told him immediately. Perhaps it had and he hadn't realized it. "My husband is not here at the moment," she said, and her voice was muffled somewhat. "He asked that I tell you . . . Miles Lawson is dead."

"What?"

A few seconds elapsed; her voice might have broken just a little bit as she said: "He has . . . shot himself . . ."

"Shot himself?"

"I can't say more . . . Just that. Please excuse me . . ."

Darsoss sat with his hand on the phone receiver. The drab winter light of Northern Europe came dying into the room from outside. He smoked his cigarette and didn't know what to think about it at first. Death meant removal, created problems, affected only the living. For some reason he thought about the flattened look of Lawson's overpressed brown suit; he remembered that the jacket cuff had been about to fray.

He telephoned the Lawson flat. There was no answer after six double rings and he hung up. He wondered how this would affect the situation. Lawson had certainly double-crossed them beyond repair. It might otherwise have been the death of someone Darsoss had never seen or heard of until now—the death of a tenth-century mandarin. Things were suddenly not top-hole, were they? All that was left at the moment was the time and place of the funeral; and this he came by through a phone call to Consolidated.

Next day there were a large number of mourners, or at least people tendering respects, in the chapel at the cemetery just beyond St. John's Wood. Darsoss slipped in from the rain and took his place in the back pew on the center aisle. Lawson lay in a plain wooden box on a catafalque in the front of the nave. Darsoss' eyes shifted; this might well have been a hotel lobby or the specially selected spot outside a railway station, the backdrop for a rendezvous or some hushed exchange of contraband; he felt nothing for Lawson; the eyes with the power to penetrate saw nothing, the clever mouth was stilled; Darsoss wanted only a glimpse of Ian Quennel. So far he saw no one he knew.

Undoubtedly Norma Lawson was sitting bereaved in front, close to the remains. The service was being read by a very plain young Anglican clergyman in a dark gray suit—to be brief, obviously, because the idea of a lot of hogwash about the dearly departed didn't suit Lawson. He had caused trouble, but he had certainly proved himself. That he had committed suicide somehow made him more appealing; and now one could think of his virtues, of how he had always been much too steady to have wanted words of praise, and much too enlightened for association with religious cant. Beyond that Darsoss remained unmoved.

Then the service was done. The interment was to be private, for family only. The chapel began to empty slowly, fear and respect freely mingling, the people coming from the pews and into the aisles now. Quennel was nowhere to be seen.

Darsoss moved uncertainly with the people departing the chapel, the scuffle of feet and hushed voices in his ears. It had stopped raining but remained very gray and seemed to have turned colder than when he had arrived. He was not too sure of his next move. Maybe he should simply take the tube back to his hotel and wait, remain in limbo until rescued. Just then a man came alongside of him, trim, taller than Darsoss, even-featured. "Terrible thing, isn't it?" he said in a good accent. "Fine chap like that. Why in the world would he do such a thing?"

He was as faultless as the man who enjoys life in various

luxury advertisements: the special car, the right whiskey, the cigar for those who know the difference. "I should think if given a choice a moment later, people who resort to this would always change their minds."

The mourners were fanning out beyond the chapel parterre; Darsoss and the man were drawing close to the gateway to the street. "There's nothing can't be solved some other way," the man said.

"Did you know him very well?" Darsoss asked as they continued to walk, their words coming out in cold clouds of breath.

"No, just in passing, really," was the answer. "Were you a friend?"

"Yes," Darsoss answered, and said no more.

"Damned shame," the man said. He was genial, relaxed, and decent.

Darsoss peered at him as they came abreast of a parked Humber. The man was fifty, carefully beveled in every way, certain the world was his but willing to share it to a limited extent. You could have confidence in him; he wouldn't crack or funk things. He cupped a flame for Darsoss' cigarette and lit one of his own. Darsoss continued to peer at him. And then he saw it. At close range there was the almost invisible flaw of the brilliant forgery; only the expert or the secretly informed could detect it.

"I'm sure it could have been helped, whatever it was," the man said. Sometimes in a dream the one designated as your father is somehow or other never altogether acceptable as such. He looks and sounds exactly the way your father does, but something is wrong. There is the feeling that he would not cry or care very much if you were killed. "May I offer you a lift . . . Johnson?"

The man had opened the door and was speaking to Darsoss and to no one else, smiling faintly, friendly and confident.

"What makes you think my name is Johnson?" Darsoss said. He was never far off guard; quick shifts and sudden substitutions were always in the offing.

"Because that's the name they gave you in Berlin," the man replied simply. He opened the door wide. "I'm sure we've plenty to talk about," he said.

Darsoss then sat alongside the man, who drove at an even

twenty-five miles an hour from the cemetery toward Baker Street, and was impregnably calm; the kind you would like to watch under fire, Darsoss thought to himself.

"We no longer have a backdrop now poor Lawson is dead," he said with a faint sigh. "So we must provide a new one."

"Let me off at the tube station," Darsoss said, as if the man had not spoken.

The man smiled. "I can see you're not convinced," he said.

"It appears you've made a mistake," Darsoss said. Let him sweat for it; taking chances was only for times when you couldn't play it safe. Let him run up and down the gamut.

"Have I?" the man said. "Then what would you say if I told you that you were supposed to meet with Ian Quennel at Lawson's flat next Saturday, and that now, of course, you won't be able to go through with it?"

"I'd say you'd made a mistake."

"And what would you say if I told you I have information concerning your—guarantee? Yes; that little something you're so very keen on clearing up."

Darsoss crushed out his cigarette in the dashboard ash bowl. The magic words had been spoken.

"What would you say?" the man repeated, as if he were applying a hammer lock and would easily hang onto it until his man gave in.

"I'd say I might like to hear about it," Darsoss said.

"Is that all?"

"What more do you want?"

"I suppose that's good enough, considering that it's *you* who aren't sure of *me* yet, and not the other way round," the man said. "So here you are. There will be three report trips to Berlin." The car came to a stop signal. "They will take place after the second session, after the fourth, and after the fifth and final one. As to your guarantee—I'm told it is built into the structure of the mission. Whatever your perks may be, you're to receive it after the fourth transmission. In short, if you are not satisfied when you arrive in Berlin, you've got it all your own way. There seems to be the strong conviction that there would be no way of forcing you to complete the job. I'm sure I don't know what it's based on, but undoubtedly you do. Perhaps you're a man who can't be punished. There are such.

In any case, that was how it was given me, and I pass it along to you. I hope it suits you. I should think it would."

Darsoss thought it sounded good. "And who are you?" he asked.

The signal went green and the car started off. "Bliss," the man said. "That's all you need to know, except that I'll be issuing your instructions at frequent intervals—to begin with, at least." His tone was peremptory but pleasant, the sign of great skill and vast experience. "As far as that goes, you'll be in touch with no one else." He was surely more than just a spy with a code name, an English traitor with good manners. "I'm sure you can appreciate the problem we're presented with," he went on. "You and Quennel will need protective coloration. You had it with Lawson. Now you don't. We shouldn't have met otherwise."

"Is Quennel being watched?"

"On and off, at the very least. For certain his phone is dekkoed."

"Somebody doesn't trust him."

"It's really not too critical. The real danger exists only during transmission. If, for some reason, you were to be raided while at work, there would be all sorts of evidence of what was taking place. So we must do everything possible to minimize that risk. All moves must appear natural and casual. I've a scheme already, as a matter of fact."

"What kind?" Darsoss asked.

"Not yet. I'll need to think it through a bit further."

"I take it you're the architect," Darsoss said.

Bliss pretended not to have heard and said: "We will need to rendezvous on short notice. That means we will need to maintain a fairly constant contact. We'll do it through chalk signs."

Darsoss looked at his clean, Grecian profile. A Communist spy who could pass for an English aristocrat had to be a great asset to the Russians. "You will be using the High Street station in Kensington frequently," he said. "Whenever you go onto the Piccadilly platform, look carefully at each of the girders with Cadbury dispensers—there aren't many. Should I wish to see you, one of them will be marked. If with a small blue arrow, go to American Express and ask for mail in your name—Darsoss.

67

Time and place will be contained in a letter. If the arrow is white, follow the same procedure at the Cook's office near the Mayfair Hotel. If the mark is a circumscribed cross, go directly to Bethnal Green at three P.M. of that day and station yourself at the pond. It's quite small, you'll be seen. Of course, fair weather, among other things, will govern that one, so it will probably never be used."

Darsoss lit the first cigarette of the second pack of the day.

"The only magic will be between you and me," Bliss said. "We didn't plan on it, but now it can't be helped, I'm afraid."

"If you don't want to attract attention," Darsoss said, "I'd say it's risky."

"Don't worry about it," Bliss said. "It's Quennel who is the target, not you. You're an American journalist with no known Russian or Communist affiliations, don't you see? You're an open book. Even if they did tail you—I'm not Quennel. You could be meeting me quite by accident. I could be selling you pornography. MI5 and Special Branch aren't terribly interested in that. At least, not officially."

"Why wouldn't you attract them? Are you nobody in particular?"

"Altogether."

"Or somebody above suspicion."

"I needn't say it's none of your business, need I?"

"You needn't, but you can if you want to."

"Personally," Bliss said, "I'd sooner we'd never met. But we have. When Lawson shot himself he removed a link. But don't feel at a disadvantage. As far as I'm concerned, you're Johnson. We'll never meet in the open."

"What's next?"

"Tomorrow at about eight P.M., pay your respects to Miles Lawson's widow. The Quennels will be there. It gets you together again. You won't stay longer than half an hour. Quennel will invite you to have a drink. Accept the invitation. That comes under the heading of getting to know each other. We want you seen together in public. That's extremely important."

"Then what?"

"Nothing. Say good night after a bit and go your separate ways. I'll give you the next step when the time comes."

"When do we transmit?"

"When it makes good sense."

68

"When will *that* be?" Darsoss asked, anticipating a long siege of cover-building.

"I'm afraid you must leave that to me," Bliss said. Then he stopped the car. "You'd better get out here and continue on alone." There was a pause; Darsoss turned the door handle without saying anything, and Bliss said: "Good-bye for now, Johnson."

There had been no politics in it. The thing itself was what counted. Bliss was superbly calm and confident of final success if all concerned kept their heads and did what had to be done. England might well have been under enemy occupation, Bliss a loyal Englishman doing no more than his duty, bored by ideology, moved only by a patrician sense of patriotism, modulated but unlimited. Darsoss had no wish to discover the man's real identity. He pulled up his coat collar and began to walk along Bayswater toward Lancaster Gate to cut through the park to High Street. The Russians had themselves one hell of a top agent-in-place.

5

Seven or eight other people were helplessly gathered in the Lawson flat. Darsoss put his hat and coat with some others on the dining-room table. Norma Lawson seemed on an even keel. She was sitting with two older women and all had cups of tea. Again Darsoss' sense of separation was keen; it was like an invisible shield. He said hello to Norma Lawson and gave her a look of sympathy. "So kind of you," she murmured with a thin smile. "This is Miles's mother," she said, and turned slightly and added: "And *my* mother."

An exchange of mumbled words took place. Darsoss then scanned the room. Quennel was not among the people who were both sitting and standing about rather stiffly. One of them, a man, was holding forth in an animated but hushed voice with another man near the garden doors. He was short and bald and vaguely effeminate and very glad it was not he who was being mourned. Death at close range made people uneasy, of course; everyone was ready to be so much nicer than usual.

Darsoss lit a cigarette and sat down near Norma Lawson and

the two older women; he had no choice. "You're an American, are you?" cackled the mother of the widow.

Darsoss looked at her. She was somewhat craggy and simple-looking. "Yes," he said with a polite nod. He looked at Norma and smiled. He was sure she knew nothing.

"Isn't that a Greek name?"

"Yes, it is."

"That's interesting," the mother said. "I was in Canada before the war, you know. But I never quite got to the States. I always meant to. You prefer refrigerated beer, don't you?" Even the presence of death could not still or improve a simple mind. Norma stiffened. "It's a strange custom, don't you think so?"

There was a smile of longing on Mrs. Lawson's thin lips. It was almost as if the liaison between Darsoss and her son had been known to her. Lawson had looked a great deal like her. Darsoss replied to Norma's mother. "Now that you mention it," he said.

Ian Quennel came into the room from the entrance hall, his wife with him, momentarily drawing the attention of all. Quennel was solemn and pinched-looking. The room was not large, and now it seemed crowded.

"I've no words," Quennel said to Norma Lawson. "I hope only that you are well and that you will call on Disa and me for anything we can do."

"Thank you, Ian," she said; and then Disa Quennel leaned in to place her cheek against Norma's.

"Oh, hello," Quennel said, noticing Darsoss. He appeared deeply moved by the moment. Darsoss hoped sentiment wouldn't interfere with the business that had brought them together. He needn't have worried. "Dreadful shock," Quennel said quietly.

"Yes."

They drifted away; Disa Quennel remained with the other women. "It shakes one," Quennel said, his face extraordinarily solemn. "And yet one must get on with it." Perhaps he had sensed Darsoss' doubts and was simply reassuring him. "There can be genuine sympathy, can't there," he said, "and yet the continuing awareness of the day-to-day obligations."

"Anything else is usually not healthy," Darsoss said.

"But it isn't really a question of simply mourning in this case, is it?" Quennel said, very much as if thinking aloud, examining a theory. He concluded in a barely audible voice: "I suppose we drove him to it."

"I think you'd better keep that kind of talk to yourself. Especially when you're in a room with a dozen relatives and friends."

Quennel was silent for a moment or two and then said: "It couldn't have been helped."

They were standing rather far off from the others and there was also a buzz of talk in the room to further protect their softly spoken words. "Does the name Bliss mean anything to you?" Darsoss asked.

Quennel looked at Darsoss. He gave it a moment's thought. "No, I don't think so," he said. "Why do you ask?"

"I was wondering if you were planning on asking me to have a beer with you," Darsoss told him.

"Well, of course."

"Maybe you know Bliss by another name."

"Oh, I see. Well, perhaps so. But that really shouldn't matter to you. It's not terribly essential to compare notes in that way, you know."

"I just want to be sure we're moving in the same direction."

"Of course," Quennel said understandingly. "This has all been rather unsettling." He looked toward the condolence corner where his wife and the others sat with Norma Lawson. "Will you join us at The Red Lion after we leave here?"

"Is it a good thing for your wife to be there?"

"An excellent thing," Quennel said. "What could be more normal and natural? After all, it's all part of establishing some sort of relationship between us, isn't it? I'm sure we'll find things to discuss. We might even actually become fast friends."

The short fat man and a woman, perhaps his wife, were saying good-bye. When they had, Darsoss and the Quennels remained on. Norma's mother had gone to freshen up. Miles Lawson's mother was speaking of her dead son's love of hiking in the Lake Country. "That was where he met Norma," she said. "Wasn't it, my dear?"

"Yes," Norma said.

Darsoss happened to catch sight of Disa Quennel. Every beauty prizes her own good looks, is usually delighted with herself, if only secretly. At a glance Disa Quennel appeared inaccessible, whatever was inside well concealed by an almost cold symmetry. But now there was something showing. In her eyes there were tears; it was unmistakable. She was weeping, for no one's benefit but her own, sitting back as if wishing to remain unnoticed. With as little show as possible she wiped the moisture with an index finger at the lower lid of each eye. Darsoss looked away.

"God in heaven, why should he have . . . ?" Lawson's mother was overcome. Norma sat by her side, their hands touching; Norma's eyes were red from scores of vanished tears. Quennel said quietly: "Had he said anything to you?"

Norma's unhappy mouth tightened. "No. But he . . . wasn't himself. Something was troubling Miles . . . I could feel it." She looked at Darsoss. "Even when you were here to dinner that night . . . Something was not right. Perhaps you weren't aware of it, but I was. You naturally wouldn't notice . . ."

Darsoss said nothing. His silence extended into a cloying yellow fog shortly thereafter as he and the Quennels walked toward The Red Lion. He merely grunted an accord when Quennel said: "Messy driving through this tonight. Or breathing it in, for that matter." Darsoss didn't want to feel sorry for anyone; and after he and the Quennels had arrived in the public bar and ordered their drinks, he sat abstracted by his resentment of the need to extend sympathy or feel pity. Quennel quickly snapped him out of it when he said: "You know, I'm astonished, really, the more I think of it. As a matter of fact, I'm still not convinced that you can actually do what is claimed for you."

It startled Darsoss. "What?" he said, saw that Disa Quennel was not greatly interested, but was obviously privy to the idea.

"Forgive me," Quennel said. "That did sound cheeky. But it is such an awful lot to put in one's head, you know. I assume also you've no training in the field."

Darsoss was astonished and angered. "I thought this was between you and me," he said with subdued force, his lips tight, his eyes narrowed.

Disa Quennel's face whitened. Her eyes were trained on Darsoss for just a moment, then flicked away; they were like ice in a blue light. She might have spoken, but her deference to her husband was unmistakable; he was the one who talked for the family.

"You've nothing to fear," Quennel said. "What can be said in front of me can be said in front of my wife, Darsoss."

"That's touching," Darsoss said. "But I don't like it."

"What difference can it possibly make to you?"

"If I have to explain it, you wouldn't understand."

Disa Quennel rose and said: "Will you excuse me, please?"

The men got up from their seats and Darsoss said: "I'm not rude just to be rude. This is like machinery, no personalities are involved."

She inclined her head in acknowledgment, with what meaning was not clear. Then both men watched her walk away toward the w.c. across the room filled with drinkers, dart-players, and convivial chatter, not unnoticed. "What purpose is there in your wife being in on this?" Darsoss asked.

Quennel took a breath. "The purpose is that she is my wife," he said with scarcely hidden joy in the fact; "that she shares all she is with me, and in turn responds to my beliefs and convictions. She is an integral part of all I am or should ever hope to be . . ."

"Integral," Darsoss said with what he knew to be unnecessary rudeness. "What a word. Sounds as if you work it out on a blackboard."

Quennel tried to remain good-natured. "Does it? All right. Anyhow, you asked, and I'm telling you. There are no gaps between us and no deceptions lurking at every turn. Do you see? Last but not least, I trust her."

"Fine. But I can't say the same, can I?"

"For that matter, you can't even say it of me." Quennel smiled at his conclusive little observation. Darsoss licked his lips and inhaled on his cigarette. "Anyhow," Quennel said, "I'm sure that our first transmission is not far off. Even as we sit here, we draw closer to the moment. The situation is maturing, you see."

"I hadn't noticed anything," Darsoss said.

"Well, it's there. Like grass growing. You can't see it but it's happening." He paused, then said: "Of course, everything is touched with cruelty, isn't it?" His brows furrowed and he seemed to look inward, deeply inward.

Darsoss said nothing and took a big swallow of beer, intense-looking, dark-eyed and somber, but very still at the moment.

He was burning with impatience and felt irritable. He could almost have hated this man before him—Quennel, with that touch of religiosity all compassionate egotists have: the superiority is expressed through self-effacement; life is one long night of St. Bartholomew. "Miles's death grieves me deeply," he was saying. "The news of it very nearly put me in hospital . . . He wanted so much to do what he felt was right—at least not to be a part of what he could not understand. He had no reason other than some dark fear . . ."

"Why talk of it?" Darsoss said with controlled disgust.

"Because my affection for Miles was very deep," Quennel said. "And I can't deny my responsibility in his death. I must look at it squarely, without rationalizations or evasions."

"Can't you do it in private?" Darsoss asked churlishly. "I don't want to hear it."

"The point is," Quennel went on, "I would take the same position again if I were confronted with it. Had I known in advance that his self-destruction would result, I'd have been unable to keep him from it."

"Oh, Christ, why tell me?"

"Because this is a lonely sort of business. I suppose it was simply something I wanted to share with someone who knows the same burden I do. Maybe I had hoped to force you into saying the same thing."

"Listen, friend. I've no burden, and confession has never been my speed," Darsoss said.

Quennel smiled tolerantly. "I suppose I should be grateful that I'm not you," he said. "I just thought it might serve a good purpose to understand what we've done and why each of us has done it. Oh, here's Disa."

"Why don't we break it up?" Darsoss said.

"Oh, give it another beer, it looks more as if we're at least mildly pleased with each other's company." To his wife he said: "Will you have one, dear heart?"

Darsoss glanced at her, a woman who had had tears of tender sympathy flowing beyond her control a little while before and who was also a spy, a willing witness to treason at the very least. "I shall finish this," she said.

"As you like," Quennel said and then ordered two more for Darsoss and himself. "To a world without famine or fear."

"That's a world without people," Darsoss said.

"No. It's a world in which men live together in peace because their wants are satisfied; and they are free to improve their minds and be better equipped to find the verities, and rise above anything they've ever been before."

Disa Quennel raised her glass two inches, her eyes filled with admiration. Just above a whisper she said: "Skål."

They could easily have been three people who had come together simply for ordinary conversation and room-temperature beer, and not because they were engaged in espionage. When Darsoss said good night soon afterward, Quennel's parting words were completely convincing. "Be nice to see you soon again," he said. His wife smiled with dignity and reserve. She probably didn't find Darsoss too appealing. He could see they were a devoted couple. Their righteousness and sincerity brought out the worst in Darsoss. He hated people who thought they had been entrusted with a holy message or a sacred idea—just from nowhere, from the great starry spaces all around, from heaven, irrespective of personal fallibility. To hell with both of them; they were nothing to him. They were simply part of getting the job done. Nothing more, nothing less.

6

"A loyal wife is worth two trained agents who might double-cross you," Bliss said. "And she *is* loyal, you can be sure."

"I don't care what she knows about *him*," Darsoss said. "It's me I'm concerned with. I don't like an audience."

They were sitting in a pub in East Putney to which an American Express letter had directed Darsoss the following day. "I think perhaps you simply didn't like having it sprung on you," Bliss said. "Perhaps I should have told you myself ahead of time. She is certainly not audience. It would be impossible to operate without her knowledge. She's no less trustworthy than anyone you'll ever meet, and more than a match for most."

Darsoss made a characteristic sour mouth. "Okay, it's too late now anyhow."

"Yes, I would say," Bliss said dismissively. "Now, follow this. It will be your schedule for the next week or so." He paused, then continued. "Tomorrow evening at half past seven you will be attending a performance of *The Apple Cart* at the

75

Haymarket. During the first interval, just by the sheerest chance, you'll encounter the Quennels. A very happy accident; especially since none of you has had dinner yet. So what a splendid idea it would be to go on after the theatre to a place in Soho, or perhaps Curzon Street—well known and well patronized."

"How do I get to this performance?"

"I've your ticket. The best stall seat, as a matter of fact."

"Thank you."

"My pleasure. In any case, you'll have your dinner and then again go your separate ways."

"Who pays the check?"

"I'd say you should certainly make an effort in that direction; and you should succeed."

"I ask because this is your show, and I'm not sure what you're after."

"An impression of amiability; an acquaintanceship based upon chance, but supportable through mutual interest and the fact you don't bore each other to death. It's the bricks and mortar for a cover relationship. The link between you must be public and accidental. After that, we shall see. Now, once more, on Thursday evening, you will drop in on Miles Lawson's family and discover the Quennels; the exposure to each other is thus increased through logical circumstances. Do not, however, go anywhere public on that occasion; actually, you should leave and go on to some other engagement. Can you arrange one for Thursday?"

"I think so."

"Good. Now, a week from today, in order to repay you for standing dinner, Disa Quennel will invite you by phone to dinner at the Quennel house. This is a good situation because ten or fifteen others will be there also. The Quennels don't entertain much and about once a year they discharge various obligations to various friends and acquaintances with one all-encompassing dinner party. You'll accept, of course, to the further enlightenment of MI5—or rather, to their confusion, let us hope."

"You're managing my social life brilliantly. I've never been this busy before."

"I know it all sounds rather banal," Bliss said. "All very childish and overelaborate. But they do the same sort of thing on the other side, I can assure you."

Darsoss looked at Bliss and wondered if some great principle really was at stake for him. "I know about the other side," he said, a little sorry he had just as the words were out of his mouth.

"Do you? Then I needn't justify all this, isn't that so?"

"If it doesn't go too far," Darsoss said.

"The idea is that it go just far enough and cover all possible contingencies—or at least as many of them as we are able to imagine; so that later on there's no bitterness or reproach about having done things in a half-arsed fashion."

Darsoss took the theatre ticket when he left Bliss some minutes later, and the next evening had his accidental meeting with the Quennels in the vestibule of the Haymarket, as planned. At dinner they discussed Shaw.

"*The Apple Cart* is one of his less penetrating works, I should think," Quennel said. "Of course, I'm not an authority. But with all his gifts, it seems to me that Shaw lacks humanity, really. He seems to be on the attack simply for its own sake and not out of genuine conviction." Darsoss, dispassionately, defended Shaw as a relatively easy way of passing the time. Disa Quennel obviously knew little of such subjects and beyond appearing very beautiful in a black high-necked dress, contributed nothing to the occasion. The dinner party was a somewhat different matter.

Fifteen other guests came to Quennels' mews house the following Monday. Several fellow physicists and their wives were on hand; also some of Quennel's students at the University: one of them an Indian, one of them a Nigerian, and one of them the son of a Kenya farmer, the last a very polite and intelligent young man who revealed, as the evening progressed, an unmistakable dislike and mistrust of all colored peoples. Some time was devoted by a few of the more articulate guests, in tones of sweet reason for the most part, to disabusing him of his dark views, without success. The young man firmly and smilingly held to his position: enlightenment was needed by others, not himself. Color bias was really not the question, you see. In point of fact, there was nothing wrong with these differences between black and white: for example, they served a quite constructive purpose, after all. The world was divided into two parts—certainly in Kenya: the overseer, and the overseen. That was the only formula for getting things done. Darsoss said nothing, sat smoking and watching. But Disa Quennel, who had not until then spoken beyond basic requirements, said: "When you make such distinctions, you are playing God; and no one has the right to do that . . ."

The topic was unlamentably dead. With a single stroke and no conscious effort, Disa Quennel had managed to make further analysis superfluous. Then, as if confused at having done so, she withdrew into the mysterious quietude that marked her in Darsoss' mind. But his reactions were all faint and perishable; he wanted no diversions.

He took up the subject with Bliss two days later as they sat in a Wandsworth pub, not far from the prison. "How much longer do we have to go on playing Sherlock Holmes meets Alice in Wonderland?" he said in a soft, contemptuous drone.

Bliss was probably not too fond of Darsoss; few people could be. But he held it in check. "It's well worth the effort really," he said, kind and gentlemanly. "We've an excellent situation maturing. Again I must say that nothing could be more valuable than a first-rate cover."

"When does it become first rate enough? After ten years of firmly established friendship?"

"Of course not," Bliss said. He signaled the waitress with an air handed down from the time of the Plantagenets, and ordered a pot of coffee. "Better safe than sorry," he then said to Darsoss. "I've never any objection to preparations for a disaster that doesn't occur, have you?"

Darsoss took a deep breath and said, "Okay."

"There's a good chap. You know, without your astonishing memory this wouldn't be possible. We'd need to work through something less tedious perhaps, but far more dangerous. Tell me, how do you actually go about it? Is there a technique?"

"I can remember anything I look at or listen to," Darsoss replied directly. "Sometimes involuntarily."

"Rather like an irritating jingle running round in your head against your will," Bliss said in a lively, interested tone. "I mean, of course, I realize it's quite a bit more than that. You've about twenty pages of intricate stuff to memorize each time. Will they stick simply because you hear them read aloud to you?"

"No. After I've taken the material in, I write it all down as I remember it, read over what I've written, check with the original source, if possible, and then destroy all my own writing.

By then it has buried itself pretty deeply and I'd need to work very hard to erase it."

Darsoss stopped talking and dragged on his cigarette. Bliss was obviously impressed in his self-contained and imperturbable way. "Well, you're going to be at it by the end of this week—Friday evening, to be exact," he said. "I can promise you that."

Darsoss stirred, his eyes brightened. "Where?" he asked.

"You'll get that in just a moment," Bliss said. "There are one or two intermediate steps."

"What are they?"

Bliss began to drink the coffee just brought to the table. "That's what I wanted to discuss with you," he said. He paused to stir the small sugar ration into his cup, the picture of ease and confidence. "One sloppy move," he said, "or a single tempting short cut could mean farewell. But we now have within our grasp, I believe, the perfect device for putting our theoretical surveillance completely out of kilter."

Bliss paused and Darsoss said: "What might that be?"

"The normal, the natural, the logical—the best of all smokescreens," Bliss answered. "As good, perhaps, as the one Lawson would have provided. No relationship between you and Quennel would ever really be believable—not one that would support the amount of access you must have to each other. Not on such short notice. Men don't make that good friends that quickly. Not unless they're a bit gay." He paused and then said: "But men and *women* do."

Darsoss touched his upper lip with the tip of his tongue, and he narrowed his eyes.

"The groundwork is there for it," Bliss said, as if he assumed that Darsoss had already guessed.

"For what?" Darsoss asked.

"For phase two," Bliss said with faint traces of pride. "For the best diversionary tactic I've ever come upon." He paused, then said: "You're having a sleepless night or two. You've begun to think about Disa Quennel and you can't stop."

"What the hell do you mean?"

"I mean a man and woman can become desperately infatuated with each other at first sight. Anyone will accept that premise, won't they? Of course. Well, you and Mrs. Quennel have seen each other and been in each other's company in one degree or another on five separate occasions. And fate has swept you into . . . an emotional entanglement." He paused to see how Darsoss was taking it and then went on: "What better reason could you have for hanging about and desperately maintaining contact with the two of them?"

Darsoss sat there as if he had just been told the moon was made of cork. "That's very interesting," he muttered.

"You're going to be giving a performance," Bliss said. "Perhaps you will have an audience, perhaps not. We shall go on the assumption that you do. Numerous purposes are served in this way. For one, what better justifies your return from Berlin to London after you've made your first report trip? Nothing I can think of. Think for a moment. I'm sure you'll agree."

Darsoss lit a cigarette and looked at Bliss. "When does the curtain rise?" he said.

"Tomorrow morning. Just after the unsuspecting husband goes off to his job."

CHAPTER THREE

1

Darsoss sat at a small table in a teashop along Church Street and smoked several cigarettes while waiting. "Try not to be seen," Bliss had told him. "But if you are, it's just as well. Especially while trying not to be." The pretense within a pretense, the infinite negative psychology, the ceaseless shifting of perspective, were all there and always advantageous. "Of course," Bliss had added, "if you're not seen, it means they're not watching as closely as they should be, which is all to the good, and nothing is lost. It never does harm to go through the motions. We think of it as cheap insurance." But the phone was supposed to be tapped. If so, then guessing and conjecture were out the window. When Darsoss called he clearly established himself as a man rather interested in another man's wife. She had played her part well enough—not much was required, simply the ultimate accord.

When she arrived, Darsoss stood to greet her, smiled vaguely, and at the last minute took her hand. "Hello," they both said, and sat down. Then there was nothing left to say.

But that was all right; silence was a familiar ingredient in such meetings. All he needed to do was look at her. It would be her option to return the look and then turn away from the intimacy; diffident, uncertain. It was very good from any vantage point, from the point of view of anyone able to appreciate this special vis-à-vis, to find it interesting: the busybodies, the poets; the anguished spinsters or sharp-eyed detectives. Surely it could have been only one thing: a man, dark, unhesitant, dangerous; and a woman, blond, extraordinarily beautiful, quiet and unafraid; on guard, perhaps, but willing; they were together because of the intense curiosity that sparks love affairs. They were content not to speak for long moments at a time. Just to look, and to breathe the same air was enough; to signal with the eyes. They were destined to sleep together if they had not already, perhaps that very afternoon if a place could be had. Otherwise it would not matter; talking and looking would be enough; no disappointments seemed possible. It was in his eyes; unmistakable accord bound them together, perhaps even against their wills. Maybe this was how it appeared to the wispy-looking young man at a nearby table. Maybe he was MI5. Darsoss wondered fleetingly. Then he broke the silence.

"Shall we order tea?" he said.

"It *is* four o'clock," she said. She loosened her cloth coat with its cheap gray fur collar. She wore a tight-fitting black hat, the cloche type. She was formal and slow to decide things. Darsoss sensed deep suspicion in her; stubbornness, too. As she stirred her tea, he looked directly into her pellucid blue eyes and said: "Have you ever done any acting? Perhaps in a play in school?"

"Why do you ask me that?" she asked calmly, but as if sensing a trap.

"Because that's what is required of you now," he said. "And of me." He put a cigarette into his mouth. "Acting is a problem," he said, and lit the cigarette. "I've acted before and I know there is a technique to it. Your pretense must look real to others. Otherwise you are a bad actor. Naturally."

She lowered her head, looked into her teacup, then raised it to her lips. "That is interesting," she said, then blew gently on the steaming surface and sipped from the cup.

"Oh, there's more to it than that," he said. "I can tell you very briefly how it works." What the hell; it was something to talk about. "If you must cry because one of the other actors is pretending to die, you will fail if you try to cry over his pretense."

"What if he is very good and you become convinced?" she said, falling in with it a bit more now.

"You can't count on that," Darsoss said. "So you must be

prepared with the memory of something in your life that caused you pain and tears . . ." His voice trailed off. When Vorst was dead, Anne would not come back to life. The thought came suddenly into his head. It did so from time to time.

Disa Quennel was searching his face. "What is it . . . ?"

He looked at her, her presence immediate once again. "Nothing," he said. "I was remembering a moment in my past. That was what you saw in my eyes."

Her curiosity was latent but unmistakable. She was a complex of checks and controls. "I'll give you an example," he said with a quick change of mood. "If it were up to me all Germans over the age of eighteen months would be dead. I wouldn't shrink from personally doing the job. That should tell you something about my feelings in the matter, shouldn't it?"

She said nothing, but was obviously attentive.

"And yet," he went on, "during the war I was able to pretend that I was one of them. I lived among them for a very long time. They never considered the possibility that I was anything but a loyal German and an ardent Nazi." He paused to see what effect it had had.

"What was the reason for this?" she asked.

"I was a member of American Intelligence," he answered, and saw a touch of surprise on her face. "But that's beside the point. I had very intense feelings about the Krauts; I hated their guts. All I wanted was to kill them." He paused to smoke, then said: "But to them I was just another everyday Nazi monster like themselves, one of the Führer's finest. You see, I'd solved my acting problem. I'd overcome my feelings and was able to create an impression altogether opposite of the truth. Strangely enough, in that particular case, the solution was much more easily arrived at than you might think. Why? Because the pretense was one of ill will toward other people; and hatred; contempt and sadism and cruelty. That's an easy part to play. It has an appeal even for people of extreme good will and compassion. Some of the greatest villains of the stage and screen are known to be very mild or even faint-hearted in private life." He studied her and for some reason he couldn't have fathomed he said: "There's a large reservoir of anger and hatred in all of us."

She didn't like it. "I don't believe that," she said, as if he had trespassed in some way. Her voice was soft but disapproving. Her Scandinavian accent was marked, but she had very evidently learned her English in London.

"Don't you?" he said. "I would say you had a fair sampling of it just the other night in your own home."

She remembered. "The boy from Africa," she said. "He wasn't born that way. Those ideas were given to him."

"They had to begin somewhere. But don't let me disillusion you." He stopped in midstream. It was hard to remain impersonal or disengaged in such a situation. Some sort of conversation, after all, was inevitable and even necessary. How could pretense ever remain merely pretense? It didn't need to take hold of one, as with children, and become reality; but it could spill over if you weren't careful. Darsoss wanted to guard against the incursion as much as possible. "You may be right and I may be wrong," he said. "Anyhow, the demands of pretended affection are very great."

"Fortunately it is not each other we must fool," she said.

He nodded. "We need only to look good from a distance. But even for that you have to have a base on which to operate. You have to appear interested—perhaps even ardent. Otherwise we are liable to give the impression we're planning a robbery or something of the kind."

She said nothing. She was not a person to reply to everything that was said. But there was a faintly offended expression at the corners of her mouth. Darsoss said: "Let me suggest something to you. Think of your husband and how much you care for him, but look as if it's me you're concerned with—not as if your mind is wandering. Do you know what I mean?"

"Yes."

She didn't ask him what device he would use to affect the same impression. He was glad of it and he said: "Good. Outside of that, we can discuss movies or plays or whatever comes to mind. Anything, in fact, except politics." He smiled at her as if she were a warm and trusted friend. "Anyone watching us now would think I was very anxious to win your favors, and that you were seriously thinking it over but hadn't yet made up your mind."

Her smile was somewhat cautious. "Perhaps by next time," she said.

"Yes, perhaps," he said, then sipped his tea.

He watched her while she broke apart a scone, spread jam

on one piece, and began to eat it. He put out one cigarette and lit another. For several minutes they did not speak. Then he said: "Are you Swedish?"

"No, no," she answered quickly. "I'm from Denmark."

"Well, don't be insulted. The outside world doesn't know the difference."

He had allowed himself that much—a rather minor matter, almost in a class with movies and plays.

Not long afterward they parted, a few feet from the teashop door in the cold, clear air. Darsoss held her hand for a moment or two, then turned away and began to walk toward High Street. A doctor was unmoved by the intimate circumstances in examining a female patient; the scientific purpose drained it of color, or feelings of guilt, or uneasiness. And this was the same thing. It was no different from meeting with any other member of the net.

2

A pub in Highgate served as a rendezvous. "All right," Bliss said, and wet his throat with a Pimm's Cup. "It's two nights later," he began as if he were a teacher describing a problem in logic. "Your stolen moments with Mrs. Quennel were all too exciting, as such moments often are. She is all and more than you expected. You can't get her out of your mind; you're positively haunted."

Darsoss sat there, still, his face impassive, as if internal combustion were under discussion.

"She was obviously very receptive to you and yet will not commit herself to seeing you again. She is confused; torn between loyalty to her husband and her attraction to you. It is difficult to negotiate this matter on the telephone, after all." Bliss stopped and his tone took on the quality of a footnote. "You *have* tried, haven't you?"

Darsoss nodded. "Yes, I have. This morning."

"Good. So now you're in a cul-de-sac. If only you could *see* her again. But how? Well, after all, you *do* know the Quennels as a married couple; friend-of-the-family sort of thing. Perhaps you could manage to call on them, impromptu, as it were; you know where they reside and it's altogether possible that you should be passing by sometime. Quennel wouldn't think it so strange, would he? Not really. Oh, perhaps not the best of form—one should telephone in advance—but forgivable and quite reasonable because, after all, you do seem to enjoy each other's conversation." Bliss paused and then said: "This, you understand, is what is going through your head as you wander through the park and do a couple of pubs—say, tomorrow evening at seven o'clock. You'll deliberate long and hard, and by nine o'clock you'll have found yourself at the front door of the Quennel house. Wise or foolish, you'll have made your decision. I'm sure no one is remotely concerned with you for your own sake. But we always operate as if they are, and we never skip even one tiny step in the process."

"You're a most thorough man," Darsoss said.

"I find it very compensating. Whatever is worth doing, is worth doing thoroughly. And this is worth doing. But we shan't discuss that."

"Let's make a pact," Darsoss said but he couldn't help wondering what made Bliss tick. "They're expecting me, of course," Darsoss said.

"Of course," Bliss said. "It's rather good really, isn't it?"

"Maybe. But what about the other transmissions? You can't repeat this device too often, can you?"

"Oh, no," Bliss said. "Something much better will replace it."

"What?"

"We'll discuss it very soon, but not now. Don't want to clutter that marvelous mind of yours."

Darsoss asked no further questions. All the long months and thousands upon thousands of miles were beginning to pay off. Berlin and the struggles with Kalinin and Major Kholenko seemed very far away. Now it was only Bliss and Quennel who mattered. They provided the cold comfort of allies in a fight against the main stream; like men in a small back room planning to reshape the world, plotting against the local post office or police station.

Quennel managed to appear properly surprised when he opened the door to Darsoss' bell-ringing. Disa Quennel was nowhere to be seen and within a moment or two Darsoss and Quennel were alone in Quennel's study. The walls were lined with books, papers strewn everywhere, the room a clutter of disorganized high-mindedness. "There will be altogether about one hundred pages of theoretical mathematics," Quennel said, remaining standing as Darsoss sat down and lit a cigarette, "as well as practical atomic structure and the results of certain nuclear fission experimentations." He went behind his desk and picked up a folder. "We're going to try to get through eighteen pages of this material tonight."

"That's okay."

"You'll be operating solely as a parrot, because none of what I say will make sense to you."

"It doesn't make any difference," Darsoss said. "I'll hold onto anything you recite or give me to read."

Quennel gave him a serious look. "Frankly, that's what we're here to prove or disprove," he said. "Actually, this is a test. I hope you pass it with flying colors."

They began; and by midnight they had done. Darsoss had smoked a full pack of cigarettes, his third of the day, and with a raw throat had managed to recite to Quennel all that had been given to him. The transmission took an hour and a half, repeated once. The playback required less than thirty minutes. Quennel's respect for the feat was unstinting. "I *am* astounded," he said.

Darsoss said nothing, buttoning his shirt collar and sliding the knot of his tie back into place.

"I can tell you now that my skepticism was even greater than I may have indicated," Quennel said. "You've erased all doubts."

"That's fine."

"Brilliant."

"Save it."

Quennel looked hurt but recovered quickly. "A man to whom praise means nothing," he remarked good-naturedly, and got to his feet, stretching his arms and arching his back, as if he were experiencing a satisfying fatigue. "But there must be something." He dug his hands into his pockets with sudden boyish vigor. "You see, I've a feeling of elation about everything," he explained buoyantly. "What we've done tonight pleases me. It must please or satisfy something in you or you wouldn't be a part of it, isn't that so? Something has to have been accomplished for you."

"Something was," Darsoss said, putting on his jacket. "I got that much closer to completing a job I've been employed to do."

"And that is all," Quennel said with irony.

"That is all."

"What a pity."

"Pray for me."

"Perhaps someone should. I personally gave up prayer at the age of five."

"And joined the Communist Party, I suppose."

"I learned at a tender age that popular views were quite comfortable, for the most part, but seldom right."

"Most of us aren't blessed with your insight," Darsoss said, suffering numerous irritations at the moment—his raw throat, his insulted nerves, an indefinable twitch of anger.

"Oh, come now," Quennel said. "Without a goal, without a means—we are nothing. The present circumstances, for example, afford us both." As if it only then had fully occurred to him, he added in a somewhat exultant tone: "By George, I do believe this will work."

"Oh, it'll work, all right," Darsoss said, lighting a cigarette. "Of course it might mean ruining your wife's reputation and making you out the classic blockhead who either doesn't know about his wife or shuts his eyes. But it'll work just fine."

Quennel tried not to appear too shocked. "This problem was considered carefully and over a long period of time," he said, composed and reasonable. "And this was the method decided upon and considered to be the most effective, the one containing almost no risk of detection if all play their parts only reasonably well. Surely if I've no objections, you shouldn't have any."

"I never said I had objections," Darsoss said quietly. "I was just hitting on an interesting sidelight—almost for the sake of conversation, you might say." He shrugged with the studied nonchalance of hurtful intentions. "Well, after all, you won't ever be able to say it was all a gag—that all you did was play a joke on MI5 while committing treason. But of course it's purely academic—not the main point at all, is it?"

There was a great change in Quennel; he suddenly seemed to be trembling inside; his mouth tightened and grew white at the corners. "What sort of person are you?" he said angrily. "What causes your truculence and your childish impatience with other people? The querulous statements you're constantly making. What are you trying to prove?"

"Prove?"

"Yes. What? That I'm a fake? That I'm without motive?

That you are somehow better than I am because you don't share my beliefs?"

Darsoss looked at him. He was a man you would expect to have stomach trouble; you might wonder what a woman like Disa Quennel saw in him, until you stopped to consider that she probably appeared to be a lot more than she actually was. Quennel was a frail but stubborn structure; a commitment flickered in his eyes, one made long ago; and Disa Quennel was gullible enough to be taken in by it.

"Do you have any conception at all of what is happening, of the act to which we are merely instrumental?" Quennel said.

"Yes. But I don't think you do," Darsoss told him. He and Quennel seemed to be sharing a single short temper between them, like the rope dangling from a cliffside, supporting helpless bodies above a chasm.

Quennel's lips thinned out. "Your know-it-all attitude is difficult to ignore: one wants to stick a pin in it."

Disa Quennel managed to knock softly at the door and enter carrying a tray of tea. She was neither seen nor heard until she said: "I knew you were done. I thought you might like this." It was all so cozy.

Quennel gave her a smile. "It might be rather nice, at that," he said. "You will join us, won't you?" He didn't mean it.

"You don't need to be polite with me," Darsoss said. "No one is looking."

"Oh, come now," Quennel said, not quite sure whether to appreciate such candor or not.

Darsoss was putting on his overcoat now. "Come now yourself," he muttered, rude and tired.

Quennel tried to be a benevolent witness and a self-interested petitioner all at the same time. He said in a voice intended to lighten things while it spoke wisely: "Mr. Darsoss is fearful that your reputation will be ruined, dear heart." Quennel looked at his wife, still and as if not breathing, her eyes fixed on Darsoss. "And perhaps it will be."

She spoke quietly but the emotion was fierce. "Nonsense," was all she said. But it was like a fiery projectile aimed between the eyes.

Darsoss looked first at the husband and then at the wife. "I think your husband exaggerates somewhat," he said. "My only concern is the mission, nothing else."

Disa Quennel didn't seem interested in making a reply and Quennel said: "I'm afraid we impress Mr. Darsoss as pompous fools."

"Does it matter—as long as our friends get the bomb?" Darsoss said, buttoning his coat.

"It is not within our power to *give* the bomb, as you call it, to anyone," Quennel said, some of his repressed anger beginning to show on the surface again. "The manufacture of such a thing depends on industrial and technical resources, trained scientists and technicians. The Russians, I can assure you, have these."

"With all the Germans they captured I should think they would."

"The point is, I want to give what is mine to give—the only thing I am capable of giving: scientific knowledge. You see, I happen to believe in Soviet prudence at this moment in history, and the establishment of a true balance of power, one that is absolutely essential to lasting peace—what I would call a *détente atomique*."

"Who are you trying to convince—me or yourself? You don't need to make it slide easy for me, I don't care one way or another."

Quennel's smile was one of angry tolerance. "It is always "Oh, are we having an argument? What's it all about?""

Disa Quennel said: "It *is* rather late."

"I was about to leave," Darsoss said, moving to the study door. "Forgive me for overstaying."

Quennel didn't speak. He could no longer play the selfless missionary or the good host. Once outside Darsoss walked toward the entrance to the mews without remorse. He thought of the narrator in Dostoevsky's *Notes from Underground* who said: "I was rude and took pleasure in being so." More understanding of himself than this he didn't seek at that moment; he knew too much as it was, and the knowledge had not set him free.

3

Bliss was waiting at a table in the rear of a little restaurant in Curzon Street. Darsoss sat down opposite him after they had exchanged a friendly enough greeting. "Rather successful last night, I understand," Bliss said, clean-shaven and self-possessed.

"There was a guy watching the house," Darsoss said.

"Oh, they're watching—at least intermittently. But they're not quite sure what they're looking for. It's our intention to see that they remain puzzled for an indefinite period." Bliss paused, then said: "How do you and Mrs. Quennel get on together, by the way?"

"How are we supposed to get on together?" Darsoss asked.

"Well, you know what I mean," Bliss said, breaking a breadstick in half. "There's no friction, is there? You can be difficult, you know."

"What are you getting at?"

"Nothing, really. Except try to play your part reasonably well."

"I'm pretty good at that," Darsoss said. "Has there been a complaint?" He knew there had been.

"Just makes things easier all around if everyone is compatible," Bliss said. "You're not going to take your next transmission directly from Quennel. You're going to memorize it by reading the written material. You'll do it all by yourself. It won't be as knotty as your first session, and since you came through on that one so well, everyone is quite confident about your capabilities."

"That's nice."

"Do be sweet now," Bliss said.

Darsoss laughed. "I'm very sweet underneath," he said.

"Yes; now listen: Mrs. Quennel is going to deliver the material to you. Do you see?"

"Not altogether."

"She will be acting as a courier on the remaining transmissions," the other went on. "You probably shan't be seeing Quennel again. He'll be putting the material into her handbag. She will then keep a rendezvous with you. You will memorize the material and destroy it."

"Where does all this take place? Hyde Park?"

Bliss looked at the menu. "In a hotel room, of course," he answered. "Where else would two such people go to be alone?"

Darsoss said nothing and Bliss looked up. "Of course you may as well be in Hyde Park to all intents and purposes but those in question. You will work while she sits about and reads or sleeps or stares out of the window or whatever until you are done."

"What are you doing? Cautioning me?"

"Good Lord, don't be so touchy. Of course I'm not cautioning you. I'm merely describing the circumstances. Perhaps now you can see the real value of this arrangement. To a careful observer, something rather suspicious is taking place, to be sure. But of an emotional rather than a political nature."

Darsoss nodded slightly. "It dots the *i*'s and crosses the *t*'s."

"You could say so," Bliss agreed. "By the time the next transmission occurs, there'll be no hint of anything in your relationship to the Quennels but an adulterous love affair. We'll have seen to it. And using her as a courier will entail no risk at all."

The waiter came to the table at that moment. "The scaloppine for me," Bliss said. "And I shall begin with tomato juice."

"And you, sir?"

"Make mine the same," Darsoss said.

"A bottle of chianti with the veal," Bliss said.

"Very good, sir." The waiter departed.

Bliss said: "Tomorrow is Sunday. A day for sleeping in or fidgeting about. As a man entranced by a married woman, under the circumstances, you'd normally do just that. Monday, however, is the day for action. You shall make arrangements, by telephone, for Tuesday morning, at which time you will both be on a train for Brighton. Why? Because very conveniently Quennel is meeting with a group of fellow physicists at Harwell, where he shall remain until the next morning."

"Why Brighton?"

"There's a hotel there you can get into without any bother; I shall fill you in completely on that later. As to your schedule, remain all day and come back to London on whatever the last train is before midnight."

"That's a long time."

"Of course. Isn't that exactly what you would do if this were all on the level—if you and Mrs. Quennel were *not* play-acting?"

Darsoss smoked and sat there without comment.

"We should always adhere strictly to whatever seems logical," Bliss said. "If we do, it will be virtually foolproof. Rather like *The Purloined Letter*. It could have been discovered at any time, really. But people never believe in looking right under their noses."

"I guess that guy wouldn't care if it *were* on the level, as long as the Russians got the bomb," Darsoss said.

"Do you care?" Bliss asked.

"I couldn't care less," Darsoss said. "I'm just commenting."

"Well, it's all a question of viewpoint," Bliss said. "He wants the Russians to get the bomb, as you say, and you want—what? Well, whatever it is, it's why you're in this, isn't it?"

"I couldn't care less," Darsoss said and lit a cigarette just as the tomato juice arrived. It was warm and in no way refreshing.

"Add a small portion of ravioli to my veal, would you," Bliss said to the waiter, who nodded, looked questioningly at an unresponsive Darsoss, and then left. "One thing; we all have our feelings—our various reasons—but we mustn't ever let them get in the way of the business at hand. If this sort of thing is to succeed, people must get along well with each other. The possibilities of friction have to be weeded out."

"You're going at that very hard. What's behind it?"

"I get the feeling you don't like the Quennels very much."

"What of it? Do I have to? Maybe I don't like you either. And I'm damn sure you don't like me."

"Liking or disliking you is very unimportant by itself," Bliss said. "If it's held down, of course."

"Okay."

"Actually one is best off not registering so small an emotion," Bliss said. "It wastes time and dissipates energy; leads to nothing of importance. Deep hatred is the only thing that makes sense; that or perhaps love, if it is obsessive enough."

Darsoss looked a bit more closely at Bliss while the man drank all of his warm tomato juice as if it were cool and delicious. "I'm sure you agree," Bliss said, putting down the empty glass. "And yet you question and carp at every turn."

"You all have the notion you're on a holy mission," Darsoss said. "It gripes you because I don't share it with you."

"Ho-ho. Speak for yourself. I know what I must do for my own reasons, and I never lose sight of it. But that's all. And what you think or feel is of no consequence to me as long as everything runs smoothly."

"It's getting done, isn't it?"

"Yes, but you do give a bad impression sometimes," Bliss said, "and despite your opinion of Quennel, he is not numb to his wife's part in things. Play-acting or not, after all, you are going to be alone together not once but on numerous occasions."

"That's the blueprint," Darsoss said.

"Yes, quite. But a certain amount of intimacy creeps into all of this, you know," Bliss said. "It may come as a surprise to you, but persuading Quennel in this matter was not as easy as you might think."

"What about his wife?" Darsoss asked, remembering not her disdain but her tears.

"That's between them," Bliss said. "Anyhow, do try to get on, won't you? I mean, always be kind to others unless they've hurt you, and the Quennels haven't, have they?" Then: "Ah, here's the scaloppine."

Darsoss sat there surprised at his own anger. He felt it almost in the way a small boy smarts because he has been shown the folly of his wrongdoing. There *was* folly in his manner with the Quennels, and even with Bliss; but he wasn't quite certain yet what it was all about. "Don't worry about anything," he was moved to say to Bliss.

"I'm not worried," Bliss said. "It's my job to manage and to mediate. But don't confuse me with Quennel. Or with anyone else, for that matter. I'm as unsentimental as anyone you've ever known. With secret exceptions, of course."

Darsoss looked at him for a moment as they went on with dinner. Where was the fracture beneath that glassy surface? You had to think there was one when you looked at him: dressed like the leader of the hunt, he was actually engaged in poaching. Darsoss listened to the upper-class tones issuing with ease and nonchalance the particulars of treason, and he thought of a man rowing for Cambridge and deliberately losing to Oxford as if it were the thing to do.

They went over the details of how to negotiate the hotel in Brighton before separating in darkened Curzon Street half an hour later; Darsoss would not remain seated at a dinner table any longer than that, not voluntarily. He was very restless by the time he found himself walking alone in Piccadilly. Bliss had hopped aboard a Number 9 headed toward Hyde Park only because it was the first bus to come along and it served to separate him from Darsoss; it didn't help to ascertain who Bliss was or where he lived. Not that Darsoss cared, of course. He could think of Bliss only in connection with the Quennels now. They all seemed to be sharing a disease in a small ward by themselves, waiting daily to recover, each with a different assessment of what had put him there. It was not unlike quarantine; the world had become very small and strange; the days and nights intense and weird and atmospherically thin.

Darsoss walked along deeply dispirited. Piccadilly swam in hazy light from the signs all around. Saturday night was in full swing, and it reminded him of someone smiling bravely though on crutches. London was a backdrop for cries of murder muffled in the fog, its soft claxons, its hum of voices and occasional shouts, its Bovril and Wrigley's peeking through curtains of mist, all a cover-up for ill will and private acts of treachery. He thought of a middle-aged woman, lacking not charm or beauty but fervor and high hopes, who could, willy-nilly, be raped. He felt engulfed, bad impressions assailing him like ether. He walked along in a secret world, passing by as cab doors opened in front of theatres, as carriage men assisted ladies in and out of cars and taxis to and from the entrances of hotels and restaurants. He walked by, separated from them by his painful knowledge of what was really going on.

He clung perilously to his solitude now. Anne's death became more permanent every day. Perhaps the sight of other women, living, breathing, vibrant and unhurt, made it more forceful. But it was there. The mind could reject it for just so long; the phantasm of reversing events, the taking-back of death, had lingered until now worn through like a shredded garment. There was no going back, he knew, as he strolled through this airless place, and the thought seemed to choke him. He had come all this way as if one could have gone back, as if there had been a chance of reversal if only one would strive to bring it about; more than strive: commit the extraordinary. Each of the invalids doggedly hoped to cure himself, it was true, because he would shrink from nothing regardless of how desperate. But now Darsoss realized fully that there was no cure for him; just the getting in order of certain affairs before losing interest, before the sense of rotting away became too strong.

Tuesday was endless shades of gray, and the temperature was 40 degrees Fahrenheit. About five minutes after the 10:15 A.M. to Brighton left Victoria Station, Darsoss entered a first-class smoking compartment where Disa Quennel waited for him. They were alone and likely to remain that way; December was not the month to holiday in Brighton; train seats were quite accessible.

"Where is it?" Darsoss asked.

"In my suitcase," she answered.

He looked at the small cardboard traveling case on the seat next to her. Could the new balance of power really be inside? It was hard to believe. He looked at her—a beautiful blond spy with moisture on her upper lip: on so cold a day perspiration was like the trickle of blood revealing a small, unfelt wound. She didn't know it was there, her eyes calm, her mouth relaxed. "There's nothing to this," he said to her, for after all, they were pulling the same oar. "The risk is very small."

She looked at him. The cloth coat with its cheap fur collar was tightly buttoned and the same black cloche she had worn on five different occasions clung to her head. "I've no thoughts of risk," she said quietly, as if to say more would have been beyond his understanding.

He knew he had been dismissed. "That's fine," he said pleasantly. "But let me suggest that if anyone walks into this compartment—even a white-haired old lady—you try to look as if we're—how shall I put it?"

She said nothing but was listening.

"We're supposed to be that way," he said. "But if I were a policeman who had started out on that assumption, I'd turn suspicious very quickly. There's something not quite right with those two, I'd say to myself. And if there just happens to be a good one around, he'll spot it if he sees us—here or getting off the train. It shows."

She continued to listen, her expression betraying nothing.

"You see, you don't like me. Oh, don't worry about it, it doesn't matter. But anyone could feel it, even from a distance, it's that thick. It's bad for the show. So overcome it. I gave you a technique, remember?"

She still didn't answer but was obviously riveted to all he was saying.

"Use it," he told her in an even tone. "It's the little things that trip you in this business."

They looked at each other for a few seconds and she said: "Is it any better now?" as if a speck of dirt had been on her chin.

"Yes."

"What shall we . . . talk about?"

"We don't need to talk. Can you remember taking pleasure

you knew was not quite yours to take? Do you remember ever doing something that scared you but was so exciting at the same time it was worth the fright?"

"I'm . . . not sure . . ."

"Too bad if you don't."

"Perhaps as a child . . ."

"Good. Think about it. Not about how much you'd rather not be here with me. There. That's better already. I won't ask you what it was. At least now we don't look like a Levantine white slaver and his latest blond captive."

He patted her hand and then placed himself opposite her, riding backward and smoking and looking out of the window from time to time. The job was what mattered, of course. Not another word was spoken until the train came into Brighton and he said: "We're here."

The hotel, on a side street, was not bad and did have on its sea side a view of the Channel. The man behind the counter was just as Bliss had described him. He nodded and smiled with broken teeth when Darsoss signed "John Richards and wife."

"All right, sir," he said. "Room thirty-two, nice view of the shore. Porter'll take you up."

As soon as they were alone, Disa Quennel unsnapped her small overnight case and took the material from the elastic sling inside. Darsoss looked through it as Disa Quennel stood at the window with her back turned to him. The Channel could have been seen but for the deep fog and low-hanging clouds, winter gloom everywhere. "Only people who want to be alone and care for nothing but each other would come here," she said. It was somehow rhetorical, spoken like a melancholic truth from the Old Testament.

Darsoss glanced up. "Yeah," he muttered. Then he looked at his wrist watch. "It's twelve o'clock," he said. "We can't have lunch until I get this done."

She turned to him and said: "If there's one thing I know about all of this, it is that everything on paper should be destroyed as quickly as possible."

"I trust you'll be able to keep yourself amused while I work," he said.

"I shall think of other times and other places," she said.

"Do that," he said, and then put himself in an easy chair facing the window, his feet up on an ottoman. He lit a cigarette. It was noon.

By three o'clock he knew that he had it and could hang onto it for days without giving it another thought. With a drill now and again it would remain with him indefinitely. He could see the physical placement of the words and phrases: a chemical formula in the middle of one page, a mathematical equation at the top of another. It was easier than the first transmission and quite different. Then he had had to use mixed associations: the sound of Quennel's voice, the inflections, the rises and drops; the enthusiasms, the occasional fatigue, the clearing of his throat. Also there had been Quennel's appearance as he spoke, his posture while sitting at his desk, his decision to rise at a certain point and pause before going on; the deep intake of breath; the distended mouth. The main elements, the facts and figures, the long-dead incident, were always surrounded by secondary details: where a certain table stood, the color of the wallpaper, the flushing of a toilet two rooms away, the pattern of leaves on a tree just outside the window, the crossing and uncrossing of nervous legs—all of this threw the main objective of a recollection into sharp relief. They were like guy wires, or the orchestration behind a melody. The use of them was unconscious; only afterward did they reveal themselves. And now Darsoss had forged the two transmissions together where no one would ever find them, buried and beyond even the slightest suspicion of their existence. Were he to be stripped naked and subjected to the most ruthless search, thirty-eight pages of the most critical state secret of all time would go undetected. Not even a surgeon's scalpel could have dug them out. Yes, he was much better than microfilm or hours of short wave, so vulnerable to direction-finding devices; much better, and worth the bother he was apt to cause.

He lit a cigarette and looked out the window, the day like a vaporous gray dream of profound loneliness, the moment suddenly one of longing and regret. He had almost forgotten about Disa Quennel.

She was seated at the edge of the bed, leaned forward, her hands clasped on her knees, as cool and possessed as a nun. "We can have something to eat as soon as I burn this stuff," he said to her.

She gave him a look of acknowledgment but said nothing and in a few minutes they were descending by lift to the hotel lobby. She seemed to be remembering something suddenly, her mind very far away, but not as part of an exercise in acting. Without conversation they walked outside, a diffident-looking man wearing an overcoat and a golfing cap glancing up from his *Tatler* as they came by, as if he were glad they weren't staying. He could have been a commercial traveler. Darsoss was suspicious of his innocuous appearance and the faint irritation he had managed to affect. This could have been someone there to make sure of things—just for the record.

The weather was still filthy and cold sprays of salt bit their faces as they walked to a restaurant along the promenade facing the Channel, one of the few open during the winter months. It was before the dinner hour and only a solitary lady occupied one of the white-clothed tables. The place was dim because the lights were not yet turned on. A world where there was sunshine, where there was warmth or good feeling, was inconceivable. A waiter with a face the color of zinc was startled to see them but came forward nevertheless. Within a few minutes they were awaiting an order of Dover sole and a mixed grill.

"We're going to stay here until nine-thirty," Darsoss said, lighting a cigarette. "We'll board a ten-o'clock train back to London."

"That long?"

"There was a little man in the lobby," Darsoss said.

"Yes," she said, the corners of her mouth turned down. "I saw him too . . . Do you think he's . . . ?"

"Perhaps."

"Perhaps?"

Darsoss looked at her. The question in her eyes was urgent, her body leaned forward to be closer to the answer. "He has a certain look," Darsoss said. "He thinks he's on the trail of passion. We mustn't disappoint him."

She said nothing; she looked a little bit the blue-eyed queen of a mythical northern kingdom, bedeviled and ignoring her nakedness.

"Between after we eat and train time, we'll remain in the room," Darsoss said. "That should give him plenty to think about."

"Yes, I'm sure it will," she said, her voice low-pitched and acceptant of something unpleasant and irrevocable.

"And they'll stick it in an official report," Darsoss said, dipping an ash. "The information will be evaluated by a higher-up and placed on file. They'll think they know something about your husband's private life he doesn't know. But they'll pass it up because it doesn't pertain directly enough to what they're after—a disloyal act on his part, a false move. So they'll go on watching him and waiting for him to make it; and they'll leave you and me free to blow up Parliament if we want to. It's good at that."

"Please," she implored quietly but suddenly, impatience in her voice. "You needn't talk on and on—like some sort of machine . . ."

"Take it easy, my dear," he said. "I thought you'd tingle at the thought."

"No, it is like the other night when you were so churlish with Ian," she said. "You are always like a powder keg—ready to explode; one can feel it. When you speak—it doesn't matter what you are saying—there is anger in every word." She looked directly into his eyes. "What good does it do to be antagonistic? It doesn't help anything."

Darsoss was put off balance by her unexpected deadly aim. "I had no idea that people in the Party were so sensitive," he said.

"I am not in the Party," she objected quickly.

"Well, then, in the Movement," he said with a gesture of easy concession.

"I am only one person speaking to another," she said, as if she needed no aids or hiding places, her eyes steady and beautiful and undeceived. "Only that."

"Fine. At any rate I don't hesitate to apologize if I have given offense," he said, not quite airily. "If you want an apology, it is yours, madam, without reservations."

"I want nothing of the kind," she said. "I want only that you not hold us responsible for something we know nothing about . . ."

His eyes opened wider than usual. "Where did you ever get an idea like that?" he said.

"From you; only from you . . ." She spoke almost as if bored because the fact was so self-evident.

He said: "Well, you *do* think about things, don't you? Yes, it sounds good, doesn't it? But it happens to be wrong, madam. Dead wrong . . ." He smiled angrily and knew he sounded as hollow as a gourd rattling a few dried-out seeds.

She didn't answer, as if she realized it didn't matter after all, and he said nothing further. Silence was suddenly all that was left to them, both of them finally looking the other way as will people who are annoyed, disenchanted, or momentarily bored with each other but who must remain together nevertheless. They ate their dinners in quietude, lovers who had become familiar to each other, whose longing and unction were no longer constant. The one waiter and the only other diner in the place were probably not taking much notice in any case.

Within the hour they had returned to the hotel room and Darsoss placed himself in back of her to assist her in removing her coat. There was the faint scent of musk, the remains of perfume rising from the nape of her neck, sudden closeness that acts on the senses like magic—all the normal spurs to passion to which he was a sudden witness but not more. The intimacy was inadvertent.

It merely prompted him to say in a quiet, explanatory voice: "Your husband is an opinionated man. So am I." It was as if the conversation in the restaurant were continuing uninterrupted.

"He's not well, you know," she said, taking the coat from his hands and draping it over the front of the bed frame.

"I didn't."

"It's not good for him to be aroused, you see, and it worries me when he is," she said. She began to remove her gloves, her eyes pensive, her mouth serious. "You can't not be cautious about someone you live with . . . a person you're married to . . ."

"He's lucky to have such protection," Darsoss said without any coloration or edge to his voice.

"Let him have his opinions, and you have yours—whatever they may be . . . That's easy enough, isn't it?"

"No question of it. His opinions don't matter to me at all. As a matter of fact, they make me laugh. They're so old and broken-down they went out with Herbert Hoover."

The rueful flicker of a smile crossed her face, and she said: "Can it be the last word on the subject? I wonder." Then she folded her arms across her chest and turned her back to him and walked to the window. She had nothing more to say to him.

"It's the very last word," he told her. "So make yourself at home and pretend I'm not here. Take a nap if you like, we've still got a couple of hours. I'll look the other way."

"Thank you," she said. "I've a book I shall read."

"Good. Go right ahead," he said. "There's nothing like a good book."

Then the wait began, the weird vigil in a vacuum. Darsoss considered briefly Disa Quennel's air of understanding mixed with impatience, a devastating weapon when a woman is unassailably beautiful. But of course it had not affected Darsoss. The sting of anger had been momentary and trivial.

He stood looking out of the window for long stretches of time, and every so often did a turn of the room, smoking almost without letup. Once or twice he elected to open the window to let in the cold night air, the smell of burned-out cigarettes became so intense. To keep them both in some measure of comfort he fed a shilling to the gas meter a couple of times before they were done. For the sake of diversity he sat down from time to time, and once he ran completely through in his head Part Two of the Gaseous Diffusion Process—the differences between U-235 and U-238. And all the while Disa Quennel sat in the *good* chair of the two in the room as if this were the British Museum and her doctorate were at stake. The book she was intensely occupied with was called *English Syntax and Etymology*. The title managed to startle Darsoss. He resisted questioning her about it.

Men had to be attracted to her, he knew, in spite of herself, even at her most forbidding, and perhaps because she appeared unimpressed with herself, almost obstinately unimpressed. What did it matter if one looked like Garbo and Madeleine Carroll? What good was that to anyone compared to a thorough knowledge of English syntax or doing one's best to save the world? Darsoss could see all of that in her, himself securely free from the pull of it, whatever it was—hers or anyone else's. Never once did she look up until the battle with time was finally at an end.

"You might like to freshen up," Darsoss suggested, putting on his jacket.

Wordlessly she left the room. Darsoss waited, smoked a cigarette which, like so many of them by now, tasted foul, and looked around the room with joyless professionalism. Had anything been left to chance? There'd better not have been. The main factors were causality and the full expectation that everyone else was at least as perceptive as Sherlock Holmes, every bit the deductive genius; and that every fine grain of cause and effect would undergo merciless scrutiny. The preponderant probability to the contrary had always to be ignored. Right now something crucial was missing. And it had to be put in.

Darsoss tore back the bedspread, exposing the old patchwork of white tablecloths that currently served for a bedsheet. It was coarse, but innocent and untouched. He regarded it with cold cynicism and then proceeded to rumple the covers and worry the sheets and give it all a used look. Suddenly, at the height of his efforts, Disa Quennel was back. He stopped what he was doing and looked at her. She had come to rest just inside the door, equable but sensitive. Darsoss said: "Just in case. Someone might follow us in and think it looked a bit odd . . . We wouldn't want that, would we, after all our trouble?"

She said nothing and he threw the bolster off the bed. "Nobody would keep that with them very long," he said, reasoning, systematic now. "You have a lipstick with you, don't you?"

"Yes . . ." It was all bloodless and perhaps all the more breath-taking for that, a ticklish moment reached without preparation—like a door opening without warning and revealing all to the wrong eyes.

"Give it here a moment," he said.

Without hesitation she complied. Darsoss extended the waxy pink tip of the cartridge and delicately gave one of the pillows the look of an accidental smear. Then he returned the case to her. "Who wouldn't be convinced now? Shall we leave?" he said.

She looked at him, apt to quiver at a touch suddenly and unable to take her eyes away. Whatever the thought, it had only just occurred to her and it had caused a rush of blood to her cheeks as a seizure might.

"I hope I haven't embarrassed you in any way," Darsoss said, not sure whether he meant it or not.

Without hesitation she said: "Because you've created a clever illusion?" She gave him a superior look. "Do you think I'm made of sugar?"

Darsoss didn't bother to answer an obvious rhetorical question. During the train ride back to London he smoked, of course, and watched her as she alternated between reading her book and looking out of the window. Perhaps she was trying to remember something she had lost. The train proceeded through the night rather than hurtling along. They might have been a compatible but bored married couple, or people who had now been going together for a very long time. Darsoss thought of the emollient glisten he had seen before and wondered where it had come from. They scarcely exchanged a word until the train came into Victoria.

They got out and he walked along with her, among but few other travelers, to the end of the platform. "You needn't come any further," she said. "I shall get the tube here."

"Shouldn't you take a cab?"

"No, no. It's all right."

"Just as you like," he said. He tipped his hat. "I won't see you for a while. That should make you happy."

She showed no emotion. "Good-bye," she said pleasantly enough.

"You'd better let me take your hand," he said, looking right into her eyes.

She got the idea and put her hand in his. "Look at me," he told her, "as if it hurts to part—not overdone, just a little bit. That's it. Say something."

"What shall I say?"

He nodded with a faint smile. "That's good enough," he said, and touched the brim of his hat once again.

"Good-bye," she said again.

Then she was gone, her little overnight case in hand, no longer the threat it had been earlier that day. Darsoss watched her disappear through the gates beyond, as relieved as a school-child let out of the detention room, he was quite sure.

4

In a pub just a few streets away from the Cockfosters station on the Piccadilly line, the first full circle was about to be closed. "Sorry we couldn't have arranged Christmas for you here," Bliss said. "I should think it would be less dreary than in Berlin. But then I'm sure you're not a man to care much for that sort of thing."

"There's always Twelfth Night."

"Yes, of course. You'll return by then." Bliss smiled modestly. "She's by now so much in your blood, that you can't stand to be away from her. So you hop back like a lovesick idiot ten days later. It should be rather apparent by now that you are having a wildly passionate to-do with Ian Quennel's wife. If that hasn't put them off guard, nothing ever could."

"You know, it seems to me that you and I could skip the chalk marks from now on," Darsoss said. "I find it more and more tedious. You can bet we've been seen together over and over again."

"Very likely. But as I've already told you, being seen with me means nothing. You've been seen with a dozen different people besides me. There's no danger in that."

"Then what are you afraid of?"

"You, naturally."

"Oh, I get it. Afraid I'll find out you're the secret head of MI5."

"Let's continue with our complicated and tedious device. It's much simpler that way."

They had a few more drinks, and by the time Bliss said "*Arrivederci*" Darsoss was feeling even more somber than usual. An odd feeling followed him next day, late afternoon, onto BEA Flight 9 to Berlin. Headed toward the North Sea, he felt as if he had left something undone, or that he had lost track of an important thought. It nagged; it nagged desperately, and he smoked cigarettes incessantly, lighting one from another in chains of three and four.

Over the North Sea the soup was dense and threatening; turbulence was marked. The tail of the DC-3 went in all directions as if a great hand were shaking the entire ship. One or two of the passengers became sick. Darsoss stopped smoking and fastened his seat belt as requested by the cabin speaker. He dozed immediately, and in his sleep he realized a terrible loneliness. Suddenly Anne was there with him, speaking to him in French as she often had, acceptant and good-spirited about her own death. There was nothing more clearly defined than simply that much: she was there, alive and light-hearted, yet dead and far away. But had she ever existed? Now, in this very moment, could he have vouched for her as any more than a projection of his own consciousness? Could he now have said that she had had a consciousness of her own? What attested to it? Name? Birthplace? Date? Words on a sheet of paper? Could all of that be trusted at that very moment? She would not, after all, be there when the plane landed; he was not flying toward her, closing a gap between them. Not this time. Not ever.

Darsoss sat up suddenly. He was covered with perspiration. In just a few seconds he came back to the here and now, and he remembered clearly what he had to do. All the instructions were clear. Bliss had said: "Go to Hagenschiedt's Bookshop the first clear chance you have at noon—whatever the day. Wear your hat brim turned up all around and begin to make a list of titles in a small notebook . . ." The usual drill.

It wasn't long before the speaker crackled. "We are coming in for a landing at Tempelhof Airfield within five minutes. Please fasten your seat belts and do not smoke. We trust your journey was not too uncomfortable."

As soon as the plane had parked he lit a cigarette. He went easily enough through customs with his typewriter and Valpak and shortly approached the taxicab rank. Berlin again: a gray and frozen wasteland; "*Hörst du mein Heimliches Rufen,*" a martyred people, victims, ignoramuses, and not a Nazi anywhere; even Vorst was in Russia. At the moment.

He hated this place and the feeling braced him. He sat in the back of a cab transporting him to Frau Nessermann's flat. Hatred kept fear and doubts at a safe distance. It was not easy to live with; like a mysterious trauma it seethed in your veins and along the surface of your skin and made your temples throb; but it kept fear and doubts away. Somewhere within the bowels of Lubyanka Prison lived a man Darsoss was going to kill, a man he needed to kill. Disa Quennel could never have guessed as much, could she? He wouldn't have wanted her to. It was no one's business but his own, after all.

CHAPTER FOUR

1

Major Kholenko proved to be as cool and blunt as ever, as hard as the hairless surface of his skull. Kalinin seemed more in need of a haircut; with his baggy trousers and stringy necktie, he was every inch the man to whom fashion meant less than nothing. "The more elaborate the technique, the better," Kholenko was saying in his British accent. "It's a governing principle. It obfuscates, it confuses, and thereby delays our opponents; most of the time endlessly. I think London has shown great competence. The diversion has worked perfectly."

Darsoss shifted his eyes from the window behind Kholenko's desk, frost on the panes. "Maybe it has," he said. "But it is not letter-perfect."

The two Russians regarded him with mild surprise. Kholenko said: "Is there something you haven't told us?"

"I've told you everything," Darsoss said calmly.

"Then what is this about letter-perfect? They are looking at one thing and seeing something entirely different. What could suit you more?"

"If they weren't looking at all."

Kalinin then spoke. "Oh, come now, my friend. You seem to be going in circles. You've undergone much more in your time, suffered far greater hardships than are present in this situation."

"What exactly," Kholenko asked suspiciously, "is bothering you?"

"My risk is too great," Darsoss said. "Even with only one chance in a thousand of failure."

The two Russians exchanged looks of disbelief. "Are you perfectly serious?" Kholenko said.

"Perfectly." Darsoss disposed of one cigarette and took out another. "What if by some completely insane quirk of fate this thing collapses? Despite the enthusiasm of all concerned, there's always the chance. What will I have gotten out of it?"

Kholenko looked at him with cold obsidian eyes and said: "To the point, please."

Darsoss returned the look and said: "I want you to hand Vorst over to me before I return to London."

"Is that all?"

"That is all."

"So that is it," Kalinin mused, his eyes watery.

"Impossible," Kholenko said coldly. If he was anticipating trouble, he gave no sign of it. "It simply cannot be done. It's absurd of you to suggest it. And we are wasting time. The time has come to turn over the material you've brought with you."

"I don't think it has come quite yet," Darsoss said.

The statement unquestionably chilled the room. Kholenko rose from his chair behind the desk; that much of an emergency was at hand. "Do I understand that you are refusing?" he said.

Darsoss looked up at him. "Life is fraught with dangers," he said. "I could be hit by a tram or a lorry in Trafalgar Square. Suddenly that outweighs the faith I have in your assurances."

"Does it outweigh the value you place on your life?" Kholenko said.

"I'm surprised you would be so crude," Darsoss said.

"Are you? I fear I must suffer your low esteem then. You surely must realize that bargains of this kind are not broken with a shrug of the shoulders. If they were, we would be out of business in short order."

Darsoss had not worn the shirt with the ampule in many weeks, until that morning. He was strangely unfazed by the threat of naked force. Something more potent, more fearful for its presently dim outline, drove him on. "Where would you be if I were dead?" he said.

Kholenko said: "Let me ask you: where would *you* be if you

were dead?" He drew a flat Turish cigarette from a box and clamped it between his teeth, as if the calm and cold people always won out and knew as much beforehand. "*We* would be inconvenienced," he went on, and lit his cigarette. "But we could begin again. You can't say as much, can you?"

Darsoss looked directly into the clinical and unsympathetic eyes. His mouth tightened and he felt, without warning, an attack of terrible rage. He suddenly sprang out of his chair, tense in every muscle, Kholenko facing him like a hated target to be destroyed. "I've had enough," he snapped, his voice raspy, his teeth clenched. "You haven't got one of your cringing little informers in here now, ready to wet his pants every time you curl your lip. So you'd better drop that approach, all it does is irritate me. If you irritate me enough, you might regret it."

Both men looked at him as if he were mad.

"I don't like the terms. I took them on blind faith and now I see it as too one-sided," he went on, the line between the anger of fear and the anger of pure wrath and indignation very thin, either one capable of the blinding pain he now felt above the eyes. "I want a new arrangement," he said, his arm aggressively extended suddenly for emphasis, his thumb doing the pointing. "I want answers. I don't want chess; I don't want threats. None of it will work. I'm a lot older than I'm supposed to be right now anyhow. You think about that, and then either change your tune or kiss my ass, because I'm in no mood to be badgered."

"Such passion, such hate, and so sudden," Kholenko said, coldly impressed but a touch sly.

"Yes, and I follow all of it with my famous disappearing act," Darsoss continued with no less anger but a steadier voice. "I open a door and disappear through it."

An alarmed Kalinin broke in. "This is lunacy, Johnson, I beg of you . . ."

"You can if you want to, comrade," Darsoss told him, seized totally now by a heady desire to put them on the spot in some way, even at the risk of everything. "You can if you want to . . ."

"I do wonder," Kholenko put in, "if you're really quite this mad, or if that is simply what you would like us to think . . . for reasons best known to you . . ."

"Psychology, eh, Major? I'll bet you have all the best books on the subject right at your bedside along with your gun and truncheon . . ."

Kholenko remained undefeated and stock-still, and Kalinin was plunging ahead. "Please, Johnson, don't commit an absurd act for the sake of a momentary and meaningless satisfaction."

"Why not? Maybe it wouldn't be so meaningless at that."

"In the name of sanity, what prompts such a demonstration?"

Darsoss shrugged, the pain still creasing his forehead and forcing him to a sneering smile. "I seem to recall that my life was threatened," he said.

"It was not threatened. Its value was questioned," Kalinin said. "A different matter altogether. After all, to threaten your life would be rather an empty gesture. Major Kholenko was actually in a leisurely and philosophical humor when he mentioned it. Were you not, Major?"

"No, I was not," Kholenko said quietly.

"Of course he wasn't," Darsoss said with a tight grin. "He's a man of action and hasn't the time or taste for academic questions. Isn't that right, comrade?"

Kholenko said: "I believe the threat of death is fearful in most cases and certainly unwelcome, at the very least, to even the most courageous of men—to those who can steel themselves to the thought."

"Okay," Darsoss said. "We're at a fork in the road, comrades . . ."

"There is something, for all your emotion, that I simply don't believe," Kholenko said. "The question of death aside, I find your attack so grossly unwarranted as to be fascinating. I see and hear all of it, but I somehow cannot believe that you actually mistrust us. You see, I don't read books, I read people."

"When you figure it out, let me know," Darsoss said.

Kalinin could stand no more. "Listen to me, Johnson," he said, taking over at the risk of offending Kholenko. "Plans are already made for the means by which Vorst will be given you. They are somewhat elaborate . . ."

"Everything is."

". . . and involve numerous steps and a passage of at least another three weeks."

Darsoss looked at him, some of the emotion so puzzling to

Kholenko beginning to subside. He sensed some sort of headway. "Why?" he asked.

"Why? Because it is not a matter of snapping one's fingers," Kalinin said, cocking his conspiratorial head, his watery eyes now beginning to reflect a certain relish in all of it. "First of all, I can tell you where you will meet: the Baltic town of Perlansk. It is small and depressing and oblivious to the world surrounding it. You will find it most satisfactory, I can assure you."

Kholenko drifted casually back to his position in back of the desk as if order had been restored and one could relax for the moment.

"Two things must happen beforehand, however," Kalinin continued, thoroughly warmed to the images almost certainly conjured up by what he was saying. "One, the charges against him must be dropped. He now languishes, as you know, in Dzerzhinski Street awaiting trial. Believe me, we are not as monolithic as you may think, and the spirit of co-operation between bureaus is not always felicitous; it is often grudging and sometimes not even forthcoming. I will be absolutely candid with you because I strongly feel the occasion calls for it: there is too much fragmentation and dispersal of power in the bureaus and this results in petty jealousies and intense rivalries."

"Don't digress," Kholenko put in evenly.

"I don't," Kalinin said. "I am simply stating important background, if one is to understand. And I think we're all agreed that our friend Johnson is in a very searching mood, whatever his motivations; superficial answers will not satisfy him, so why bother with them? The point is that we must arrange for something at which our judiciary is certain to set up howls of protest. No order can be given to comply with a request such as this because no legal measure can cover it. An extralegal manuever is possible from above, yes; it would be hypocrisy to deny as much. But we cannot ask for it in this case. Responsibility for tactics lies within the individual bureau. We are charged with carrying out strategy; how it is done is our affair. The People's Prosecutor is not interested in our problems out here; he is simply determined to put Otto Vorst on trial and ultimately to bring about his execution. A noble ambition, admittedly. But, as we know, in direct conflict with something much more important and far-reaching. Already I am sure you can see the difficulty. We cannot call upon the internal security forces either, believe me; they are only too pleased to see things prove arduous for us, because they would prefer to control external as well as internal affairs."

"I believe that now you are off on a tangent," Kholenko said. "Your analysis is irrelevant."

"Not at all," Darsoss said, his pain diminished now. "I'm fascinated."

Kalinin shrugged. "It is not my intention to be spellbinding," he said, "but to give you a picture of why your request is inappropriate. The first step, despite the obstacles, will be accomplished in due time. The second step is in the proper approach to Vorst himself. Because when he is clear, we propose to enlist his services again. He is to be persuaded of the fact that he is forever exculpated from any future charges by the Soviet Government; he must be made to feel perfectly safe in that regard. It will facilitate his smooth and safe removal to the—place of his destiny." Kalinin shrugged. "It can be done. But though a vile hyena, he is not stupid, and one must be very cautious and absolutely thorough in dealing with him. He must be put totally off guard, after which he need be given a very convincing assignment and a set of documents and a new identity along with a very believable and urgent reason for proceeding to Perlansk. There must be no struggle in any of this, or all could be ruined." He paused and took stock of what effect his explanation was having. He shook his woolly head as if he were twice his actual age. "It can be done," he said. "But it will be no sooner than three weeks from now that he is processed and ready to be steered toward his just deserts. Surely we cannot wait that long before proceeding with the business at hand, can we?"

Darsoss said nothing.

"He will be under the delusion that he is to keep a rendezvous with someone who will give him instructions concerning a mission in Athens. The rendezvous will be with you, of course. It will take place under a pier in a deserted beach area which I am certain will be to your liking. We shall see to it." He paused, then said: "But *this* is the only means to your end. Your greatest need is for patience and, if I may say, faith. You must take a more optimistic view of things." He looked directly into Darsoss' eyes and added: "A great deal of effort is being exerted in your behalf. One might call it a triumph of the absurd in support of a practical and necessary action."

Darsoss slowly inhaled on his cigarette, his eyes trained on Kalinin. After a moment Kholenko said in his cold way: "May we now proceed with the material from London? I realize it is secondary in importance, but even so."

Kalinin nodded. "Surely you are ready, Johnson," he said.

Darsoss didn't speak, but in a moment was being ushered into a room where two other men were waiting. One was seated on a divan, a notebook in front of him, with a look of scholarly concentration on his face. The other, paying him no heed, stood smoking a cigarette near the window. He was absorbed by the winter scene outside.

Kalinin said: "This is Comrade Vorshov." The scholar didn't bother even to glance up. "He is an authority on the subject at hand." Kalinin then turned to the other man. "Comrade Poskashevolsky," he said, "will translate for both you and Comrade Vorshov." Then, for the benefit of both comrades, Kalinin added: "Comrade Johnson."

Now Comrade Vorshov looked up and regarded Darsoss as if he were to be examined for scientific reasons. Poskashevolsky's manner was common to many translators; he was not directly involved but very cautious and ready for anything. Darsoss gave neither man very much thought. He realized suddenly that something was bothering him, something that would not go away because he would take a drink or light a new cigarette or simply try to think of something else. He did not want to go through with it. That was what everything came down to finally. The realization was like a thunderbolt.

"Poskashevolsky will recite into this apparatus," Kalinin went on, putting his hand on a machine situated on a small table. "It employs spools of tape which run on quite long and can be corrected by erasure at any given point." He added: "It is rather a new tool."

Darsoss gave it a disinterested look. He was astonished by his discovery and his head still ached.

"I am very interested in observing," Kalinin said, "if an audience won't make you nervous."

"Why should it?" Darsoss said.

It was like being mistaken for someone else and forced to

perform as that person would; you've walked into the wrong room but you dare not let anyone know it. A small boy plots and dreams of an audacity; in safety and warmth courage is unbridled and eagerness runs high; the step is taken and its reality is cause for regret. Who hadn't said to himself, What am I doing here? There was always that sickening moment when one knew it was too late to turn back. Darsoss calmly lit a cigarette and felt the profound helplessness of one caught in the vortex of an imprudent decision. If only he had caught up with Vorst on his own.

Kalinin spoke to Comrade Vorshov briefly. Then to Darsoss he said: "We can begin whenever you are ready."

"I'm ready," Darsoss said.

He began to talk. The ampule with its hydrocyanic acid was never more than four inches from his teeth; he could not have bitten into it and let the sleeplessness of a thousand nights and the waking dreams of death and torture go unredeemed. These men would most certainly have replaced him and found another means; he could not have stopped them even if to do so had been his only desire. And it was not. Nor was an act of self-immolation: he was not one for whom a headlong charge to certain death provided meaning. He remembered the face of Luzzi Vorst when he had looked into it and seen the eyes of her subhuman progenitor. And he gave the Russians what he had at that moment to give. Politics was a game in which human beings were used as inanimate objects, governments and ideologies nothing better nor worse than the men who were briefly in charge of them.

But more telling than this, a man had to kill his wife's murderer.

Comrade Poskashevolsky took notes and at intervals recited his translations with great care into the recording machine, assisted from time to time by Kalinin when a phrase or a word was in doubt. Darsoss smoked despite his headache. Comrade Vorshov appeared fascinated, listened, unsmiling and grimly satisfied. It all appeared to make sense. It was five in the afternoon when Kalinin arranged for Darsoss' transportation from Karlshorst to a garage in Charlottenburg from which one could simply emerge on foot without a hint of how he had gotten there.

"You are very impressive," Kalinin said before their parting, the two of them alone in Kalinin's office. "Of course, it must all be analyzed carefully before any judgment can be final."

Darsoss gave Kalinin a baleful look; his nerves were raw, his throat burnt dry by cigarettes and talking. "That's not my worry," he said in his most unpleasant way. "You've got every damned syllable of it as it was given to me."

"I am confident of that."

"And this is final," Darsoss said with the residue of his earlier anger. "I won't deliver the next segment before I get what I'm after. I went through with it today, but that's it."

Kalinin's expression went flat with surprise.

"Oh, I'll pick it up as scheduled," Darsoss was continuing, shooting a cigarette from its pack with a flick of the wrist. "But I'll hold onto it until you come through."

"But I thought I had made you understand," Kalinin said.

"Yes. You live in a bureaucratic jungle with treacherous red tape hanging in your face."

"It is a mistake for you to be this unreasonable," Kalinin said with a coldness in his voice Darsoss had not heard before. "What do you hope to achieve?"

"You're getting all the best of it," Darsoss said, lighting his cigarette. "I never signed a holy writ; I was taking you on consignment. Okay, I don't accept all the clauses; I want an adjustment."

Kalinin shook his head. "You can't do it," he said.

"What's to stop me? Be a realist your*self*."

Kalinin said: "You're convinced there is no way you can be— shall we say, bargained with? Perhaps that is true. And perhaps not. Don't be too sure that you are as free of consequence as you may think. It has been our experience that there is always something one prizes, often without knowing it until the time comes. Of course, you may be the exception. But you may not be. In any case, I strongly urge you to think clearly."

"Speed things up. I won't wait."

"Why? Is it really us you don't trust?" Kalinin said. "Or is it yourself?"

Darsoss looked at Kalinin, who returned the gaze for a moment or two and then turned to look through the window. Snow was falling; it was going to be a very white Christmas.

Darsoss wondered if these men were so sentient that they could see through you or just masters of the educated guess and the shot in the dark. He said: "Tell Kholenko what I've said so that there will be no misunderstandings." He could hardly be bothered to discuss it further. Then he deliberately looked around the room. "Or have we told him everything already?" he said.

Kalinin turned his closely spaced eyes away from the ice-cold view and said: "You are a strange man. You are purposeful; you are nonaligned; you are knowledgeable in certain things; you are, to hear you speak of it, concerned only with objectives: the pragmatist seeking nought but results in a rather special quest. And yet there is that side of you that reminds me of a trapeze artist who is concerned with plaudits, with praise and admiration, and the awe of others; and who, in order to increase this as well as his chances of total annihilation, insists on doing his mad configurations high above a concrete floor without a safety net. Yes, you are a very strange man indeed."

Darsoss made a wry mouth and said: "If you say so, comrade." Then: "Speed things up."

"And if I cannot?"

"I know you can. I have a lot of faith in you."

A moment later Darsoss was on his way to the car pool. By the time he reached the British sector, the snow was falling very heavily; the rubble of Berlin was camouflaged with a white blanket. It was dark when he arrived home. Frau Nessermann was in the front room with several guests, a man and a woman in their fifties, two among the tens of millions who had been against Hitler. "Happy Christmas, Herr Manfred," she said, never having been brought up to date.

Darsoss smiled with lips cracked by the cold, and he wished her the same. One of these days he might take the time to tell her to kiss his ass; or perhaps he wouldn't.

Now as he went to his room he felt no less rotten for having threatened the Russians and behaved with anger and insolence. He wasn't getting enough out of things; there was still too much fury crawling along his spine, as if frustration were mounting instead of leveling off. He thought about it as he sat down on his bed and poured out a half-tumbler of Scotch he had acquired from the PX the day before. His stomach was empty. By ten o'clock he was unable to walk steadily from one side of the room to the other. He had never been so loaded in his entire life.

2

During the next few days he was a free-lance journalist. He walked considerably despite the punishing frost, and visited various points on the intrigue and politics map of the city: a Clay press conference; an Ernst Reuter conference; a Sokolovsky briefing; a displaced persons station; a nightclub in Kronprinzallee he knew to be a black-market exchange: goods acquired by theft, intimidation, and malfeasance were bought with money gained through corruption and murder. First in importance were the overcoats and shoes of the victims; then whatever valuables he or she may implausibly still have possessed. The few scarce marks to buy the even more scarce items of food and fuel came next; the ration stamps so crucial to minute-by-minute living on this vast tundra were last. There were hard and desperate faces everywhere; and there were faces carelessly debauched and pitiless—men, women, children. Through the savage cold air and along the agonized streets Christmas trees were seen being taken home by people who had somehow managed to get hold of them. Frau Nessermann had a small tree; and on her dining room table there was an Adventskranz adorned with blood-red candles. The Communities of the Occupying Powers remained like secure islands in a sea of hunger, displaced persons, children fighting over scraps of bread, and frost-bitten hands and feet. They were concerned quite a lot with venereal disease. Near Frau Nessermann's flat a huge poster stared from a brick wall: VD LURKS IN THE STREETS. Over the legend a voluptuous girl, not well suited to discouraging dangerous appetites, beckoned in such a way that it was somewhat questionable as to whether the message was *for* this thing or against it. It was part of the ambiguity of this shadow world with its ruins, its bleak landscapes everywhere: there were those who were doing better than ever, not in spite of the misery that surrounded them but because of it.

Darsoss watched it all as the man he pretended to be would

have. At best it was voyeurism with which to pass the time and retain an authentic look. He remained in his room several hours a day and went to the hard task of setting down his impressions of this place with its snow beneath a never-melting surface of ice; its corpses, blue, gaunt, and stiff amidst the rubble; its violence motivated by hunger and cold.

On the morning of Christmas Eve he visited with two of the men he knew in the World Dispatch office on Motzstrasse. Downstairs, later, he ran into Vernon, symmetrical and confident. The blue eyes and strong chin seemed imperishable: everything was easy when you knew how. "Let's get a cup of coffee next door," Vernon said.

Darsoss wanted to refuse, of course, but didn't. "Okay," he said.

It was a beer hall and they sat at one end of a long and presently unoccupied table. "Are you still unattached?" Vernon said, going through the ritual of fixing a pipe.

"I've a couple of places that take my stuff," Darsoss said, lighting a cigarette. "But I'm not reporting stories, if that's what you mean. I'm in the think piece business these days."

"Is there money in that?"

Darsoss held his cigarette between his thumb and index finger, as if examining it for flaws. "I don't need money," he said with a smile almost of apology.

"I don't mean to be crass, you understand. I was just wondering."

"The House of Darsossakis always gets by. Money is the cheapest of all commodities."

Vernon struck a wooden match. "Ask the Germans."

"It's food, not money, that's at stake for them. No amount of money can buy something that isn't there, or service that can't be had. What else is on your mind?"

"What kind of think pieces? The war?"

"I don't think about the war if I can help it."

As the waiter set coffee and *Brötchen* before them, Darsoss experienced his familiar edginess. This was the first time he had seen Vernon since he had made his deal with the Russians. When the waiter had left, Vernon drew on his pipe and then put it in an ashtray and picked up his coffee cup. Without ceremony he said: "Would you be interested in running an office—a small news service in Vienna?"

Darsoss said nothing and Vernon added: "We need reports."

"Who?"

"The State Department, roughly speaking."

"Is that what you are now?" Darsoss asked, and dragged on his cigarette.

"Until the new agency is set up, at least," Vernon answered. "We've always been State Department, you just weren't looking."

"I didn't mean that. I thought you were AMG in Berlin."

"Berlin's our nerve center, but the lines are spread out all over Europe. Anyhow, there is this spot in Vienna. The Boss and I have talked about it. Not too tough a job really. Coffee houses, waltzing, turn-of-the-century atmosphere—all it takes is someone who knows the score and has pipelines. Which are built into a news agency, of course."

"Didn't we have this conversation once before?" Darsoss said with a quizzical squint.

"Not exactly. The picture is somewhat different, for one thing, isn't it?"

"What picture?"

"You've had a chance to think about things, I imagine," Vernon said casually and took some coffee. "Everybody changes his outlook after a time, some people more than others. I mean, I see no reason to write you off completely."

"Is it your only ambition in life to make an agent out of me? I don't get you."

"Let me ask you something, Marco," Vernon said without emotion. "You see and hear things, it's inevitable. You know all kinds of people and have entree to various inner circles— just as any journalist might have."

"I've got the ears of all the crowned heads. None of them makes a move without me."

"I'm aware of that. But what I'm getting at is—if you came across something really hot, would you pass it along to us? Would you follow it down as a matter of American security, let's say, or would you first see if it suited your own convenience?"

"Like what?"

Vernon gave a slight shrug and in a not-too-urgent voice said: "A security leak somewhere, let's say in the British War Ministry. Or . . . treason. Somebody selling secrets to the Russians, for example."

119

Darsoss knew that other people are seldom the keen observers guilty men think they are. Yet his heart skipped a beat. "I think you're having daydreams," he said.

With full authority, Vernon said: "People are selling secrets, Marco, make no mistake about it. They're selling them to the Russians, they're selling them to us. For all sorts of reasons."

Darsoss said: "I've no doubt," and at that very moment caught sight of two men entering from the street and realized with some surprise that he knew one of them. It was Alex Dinsdale, whom he had not seen or spoken to since the fateful moments in The Blue Boar. "There's someone I know," Darsoss told Vernon.

"Someone you haven't seen recently?" Vernon prompted with faint pride in his ability to deduce the obvious.

"A British newspaperman," Darsoss said, and continued to look at Dinsdale, who was part of those first few days in London which now seemed more remote than certain events of five years before. "Hello, Alex."

He was at the table. "So this is where you are," Dinsdale said.

"At the moment. How have you been, Alex?"

"Oh, well, you know."

"Yes."

"You never did call me, did you? That's all right, I know how it is."

"I've been very busy, Alex, really."

"You don't look too well, come to think of it. Are you quite done in?"

"No. This is Mr. O'Toole, Alex. Mr. O'Toole, Mr. Dinsdale."

There was a handshake and an exchange of how-do-you-do's. "I don't mean to intrude, of course . . ."

"Not in the least," Vernon said. "We were just idling."

"Are you here for long, Marco?"

"I have no assignment, so it's hard to say. Why don't we have a drink later somewhere."

"Would you have time?"

"The Club around six. Can you make it?"

"Oh, yes."

"Fine."

"You know about Miles, of course," Dinsdale said, his voice unchanged in tone.

It was like a suggestion that he not forget—as one might remind someone who was going on a trip: "You have everything you need, don't you?"

Darsoss wished they had missed each other by a few minutes, that he had missed Vernon, for that matter. He didn't want to look fishy, so he couldn't, in safety, duck anyone. But these obligations were, at the moment, jarring to the nerves. "Yes," Darsoss said. "It was a terrible thing."

"Yes . . ." Dinsdale grew solemn and mysteriously reflective. "Yes, it was dreadful." Then: "Well, until later. Goodbye, Mr. O'Toole."

Vernon broke open the *Brötchen* on his plate. "Something pretty terrible happened to a mutual friend, I take it," he said.

There would be no point in evasions, even though it was Darsoss' instinct to be evasive. It was as if people were standing suddenly on the very spot where one had buried something crucial to one's entire life: they would discover nothing but the proximity was chilling. "Yes," Darsoss said. "He committed suicide."

"Oh," Vernon said. "That's too bad."

"Yes."

"Have you been in London?"

"Yes, as a matter of fact. I'm writing about London in contrast with Berlin."

"You're not interested in Vienna, then."

"Now, did you really think I would be?"

"You never can tell, can you? Anyhow, to round out what we were just talking about . . ."

"Yes, *what* were we talking about?"

"I was telling you that people were selling things. Plenty is going on now, and it will increase more and more as time goes by."

"I'm not interested, Vernon," Darsoss said. "At least not at the present moment."

"People change, Marco."

"I don't have the temperament for that kind of thing," Darsoss said.

"It takes all kinds, Marco," Vernon said. "One thing though;

don't be so neutral and unaligned that you pass up things we can use. Press boys are among our best sources, you know that."

"You have my word on it. Will you give me a lift home? I've got some work to do." He wanted to remain friendly and casual about everything.

"Sure. I'm headed that way."

There was no more to it than that, but Darsoss was left with the impression of a close call. It hadn't been, of course; his grounds were fatigue and strain and a growing uneasiness he only partially understood: it was hard to realize that people weren't looking right through you. Vernon was tricky enough but it was sheer jitters to suppose he knew anything at all.

Dinsdale, blundering, innocent, and aggrieved, was sitting in the bar at the appointed time; few other people were about at the moment. Through a mesh speaker came the voice of Bing Crosby singing "*Adeste Fideles.*" It was Christmas Eve, and the place made an effort to be a little bit like home. Dinsdale had the look of an abandoned bundle. "Do you despise holidays?" he said. "I do."

"I try to ignore them as much as possible," Darsoss said and ordered a double Scotch.

"Christmas cheer is not a natural state of being, of course; but I suppose I envy all the trappings that have been lost to me for so long. That's why I despise it." Dinsdale had some of his drink and then said: "It's a spiteful celebration, because not everyone can share in it. There are such special qualifications. Think of all the Jews and Hindus and such, for example, who are excluded. Poor bastards. All they have is a little unleavened bread and funny hats."

"It's rough."

"Yes. I always have an image of a warmly lit room with a tree in the center, dazzling the eye—fantastic parcels of red and green and silver and gold all about for Boxing Day; a beautiful mother, a handsome father; the exquisite children—two boys, two girls; a marvelous dinner steaming deliciously on the sideboard—all being seen through a window by a couple of tattered and torn urchins shivering in the cold outside."

"They should draw the blinds," Darsoss muttered, then raised his glass and said: "Cheers."

"It would be the considerate thing to do," Dinsdale said. "But then the fun would be spoiled. You see, those scabrous types outside somehow make what's going on inside all the more enjoyable. Can't be any other way, really."

Darsoss lit a cigarette. "No wonder you're alon on Christmas Eve."

"What about yourself?"

"I don't *care*. See?"

Dinsdale's face was touched with a strange smile of doubt. "You know, I would have got in touch with you," he said, "had I known where you were when it happened."

"When what happened?" Darsoss asked.

Dinsdale seemed almost startled. "When Miles did what he did," he replied.

Darsoss inhaled deeply on his cigarette and didn't answer. Dinsdale said: "I wanted very much to talk with you at the time." He gazed reflectively for just a moment into his glass. "It was tragic," he sighed. "But more than one might guess." He smiled faintly. "Talk about the urchins looking in from the outside—I think of Miles that way . . ."

Darsoss narrowed his eyes. "Really? Why?"

Dinsdale waited, then in a modulated tone without theatrics: "Miles didn't commit suicide; he was murdered, really."

Darsoss' heart banged against his ribs. "What are you saying?"

"Oh, I don't mean it in the literal sense," Dinsdale said now that his effect had been had. "No hand but his own actually fired the bullet . . . But it may as well have been another hand. I know it has the ring of a penny dreadful, but there's a sinister force behind poor Miles's death; I'm absolutely certain of it. I have, you can be sure, access to very strong support for it." He looked bitter and calm behind a pained smile based on superior but terrible knowledge. "He was being blackmailed," Dinsdale went on.

Darsoss held his astonishment in check. "How do you know that?" he said, his mind racing. Someone had overlooked something. A man forgets to lock just one of twenty windows in the house, and that is the very one through which a burglar enters. "Did he actually tell you he was being blackmailed?"

"Not in so many words, no. But he didn't need to, it was plain to see what was happening," Dinsdale said. "You see, once we were good friends, Miles and I. Not of late, though. I'm sure you could sense that when we all chanced to be together that day in The Blue Boar. Remember? I'm sure you do."

"Yes," Darsoss said, probing cautiously. "You wanted to know if he had said anything about you."

Dinsdale smiled acceptantly. "So I did. You lowered the portcullis rather quickly, if I remember correctly. Then you more or less vanished. I knew Miles had made some reference to me, he'd had to have done. Oh, that part doesn't matter terribly now, I'm quite sure it was nothing more than general contempt—he did have that. But when he shot himself—just a few days later, wasn't it?—I was very hard hit . . . really . . ." Dinsdale's baggy eyes became recollective and wistful. "I won't go into detail, but I was not myself for days . . ."

Darsoss looked at him. He was still loquacious, still given to flippancy, to clever self-effacements, to chumminess, but he seemed a more sober person than he had ever been. His voice less vibrant than usual, his manner much more deliberate, perhaps for this occasion, he said: "You see, I knew why he had done it."

Darsoss sat there, still as a statue, nothing in motion but the smoke from his cigarette.

Dinsdale said: "Someone had to have been forcing him into something he simply couldn't do with, someone who knew about him . . ."

Darsoss said: "Someone who knew what about him?"

Dinsdale made a rueful mouth. "How is it summed up in just a few words?" he mused. He took a drink and motioned to the bartender for another. "When one doesn't fit the conventional concepts . . . resistance comes rather high in most cases . . ." He looked at Darsoss. "Do you understand? . ."

Darsoss didn't commit himself, waited to hear more.

Dinsdale said: "In England, as everywhere else, people hate what they most fear. The instinct is to kill or to banish . . . Some rather harsh penalties can be imposed upon people for extremely questionable reasons. Prison. Disgrace. All of it. And that's what faced Miles . . . For a crime he had committed? Well, that all depends on how one looks at it. According to English law, it is indeed a crime—perhaps more revolting to society than murder in some instances, more damaging to the public image certainly . . . a terrifying specter to the average Englishman . . . a thing to be exorcised, expunged . . ."

Darsoss by then had the picture; he knew now what it was that had been held over Miles Lawson's head, what had pushed him to the final grievous truth; the problem had become insoluble, hadn't it?

"That's what he faced . . . They will put you in prison for it, actually—strip you of any chance of ever leading a relatively normal life again. It's a marvelous blackmail device. But he fooled them. He didn't do their bidding—whatever that may have been—and . . . he killed himself rather than face either alternative."

"How do you know about this, Alex?" Darsoss asked. "How do you know that Miles was . . . ?"

"Queer?" the other said with the air of someone bearing a lonely and burdensome distinction. "How do you suppose?" Then: "Oh, it's quite all right, I altogether trust you; and anyhow, you would be bound to guess. The point is, someone else knew—found out somehow."

"Who?" Darsoss wanted to know, feeling like someone trying to dodge the sweep of an enemy's searchlight.

"I can't be sure," Dinsdale replied. "But when it came about . . . Miles held me to blame, you see. He felt that the indiscretion was mine, that I had managed to put the person or persons in a position to squeeze him—though he never admitted openly that that's what was happening. It was useless to swear that I hadn't the slightest notion about how or who. These people can find out things without one's telling them; how secret is anything, really? But he accused me and found me guilty. It wasn't until after he killed himself that I began actually to accept the guilt. Oh, not in the sense of having been directly responsible for the exposure; but simply that if it were not for me, perhaps none of it would have happened. Do you see?"

Darsoss said nothing, nodded almost imperceptibly and smoked.

"Oh, it all happened long ago," Dinsdale said. "It was nothing of recent times—Good Lord, before the war. But it had been dredged up—not for use against me, but against him."

"But how can you be sure?" Darsoss said. "You yourself say that Miles never actually said he was being blackmailed or anything of the kind."

"I've told you," Dinsdale replied. "The implications were absolutely clear. True, there was no admission of blackmail. But did there need to be? What does the fact that he killed

125

himself suggest to you? Just three months later, and leaving no note. That he was under no pressure at all? If so, we've a very different set of reasoning powers. I should think at the very least you would grant the existence of a claim."

Darsoss could see all of it meant a great deal to Dinsdale. "All right," he said. "Let's assume you're right. All right, let's say absolutely. What of it *now*?"

"Just this," Dinsdale said. "I believe that Miles was connected through blackmail with some very dangerous people. Aided and abetted by a society clinging to its medieval concepts for dear life, they forced him to suicide." He seemed almost on the verge of tears as he looked directly into Darsoss' eyes. "I can think of nothing more urgent in my life than to discover who they are and what they do to pass the time . . ." He took a drink and then looked back at Darsoss. He said: "Will you join me . . . ?"

"Join you?" Darsoss repeated.

"Yes. You were a friend also. But more than that, you were in close touch with him at the time. Between the two of us, pooling resources, actually, something might be accomplished . . . That's why I'm telling you the part I know . . ."

Darsoss crushed out his cigarette and said nothing.

"Heroic exploits are not my dish," Dinsdale said. "But this is different. As I've said—if it hadn't been for me . . . well, there you have it, basically . . ."

"Yes, I see," Darsoss said quietly. "But I don't know what I could do to . . ."

"Here's a chance to find out," Dinsdale said with a glow of deadly earnest. "Do you know the name Havenhurst?"

"Maybe," Darsoss said and waited for the development.

"The name should be familiar to you," Dinsdale went on. "Charles Havenhurst is highly placed in the War Ministry. Old family, baronet, that sort of thing. During the recent unpleasantness he was Churchill's personal envoy in a score of delicate missions."

"Yes," Darsoss said. "The Viscount Broadsmuir. What about him?"

"Nothing yet," Dinsdale said. "But Miles knew his brother, Arthur Havenhurst. I saw them together on three or four occasions at Havenhurst's club, where I happened to be visiting."

"I see. So what?"

"I think there is a strong connection between the people who were blackmailing Miles and the Havenhursts—that some person or persons wanted to exploit Miles's access to the Havenhursts for reasons unknown—most particularly with the Viscount Broadsmuir."

"You think so?"

"There's little doubt of it in my mind," Dinsdale said. "I'm fairly certain that some sort of espionage was involved . . ."

"Espionage?" Darsoss said, his heart banging that extra strong beat again.

"But what else is there? The loose heading of State Secrets covers plenty, and Viscount Broadsmuir suggests something of the sort to me. And when I think of what cloven hoof could possibly match the one Miles already carried I come up with treason. Because, if my theory is right, espionage for whoever the others were would have been treason for Miles. What else in God's name could have driven him to his death as effectively as such a combination as that?"

Darsoss licked his lips, then finished his drink.

Dinsdale said: "If I'm right, it could make quite a dent somewhere." He added: "It would also make up for things to some degree. Maybe England would be forced to re-examine her manners and mores, and revise some of her idiotic thinking and change her idiotic laws." He was quite impassioned about all of this; as if to somehow temper it, he then said: "It would also be a feather in my cap—and, of course, yours . . ." He smiled vaguely. "I mean, there is that, isn't there?"

"I don't know what I can do to help you," Darsoss said.

"First of all, are you interested in trying to?"

"It would depend on what was needed," Darsoss said.

"It's my opinion that getting next to Viscount Broadsmuir's brother is more than worth a go—getting to know him, that is. *I* can't for several reasons. One, I'm stuck here. For another I have an idea you would be able to gain his confidence more easily than I could."

"To what end?" Darsoss asked.

Dinsdale shrugged. "If I knew that much, I should know all, perhaps."

"I don't know," Darsoss said, tentative, staying with it till the last possible moment.

"You're not on assignment, you say. Well, then. You're

apt to find yourself anywhere, aren't you? London again, possibly?"

"I don't know, Alex."

Dinsdale went inside his breast pocket and removed an oblong wallet. "Here," he said. "This is a *Picture Post* photo of the Viscount and Viscountess at Ascot. And sitting with them is brother Arthur. It's a good likeness . . ."

Darsoss took the creased magazine photograph and looked at it as Dinsdale said: "Arthur is the boy who may have some notion about things. He's at Tootley's. I don't know how you'd go about getting in, but if you're in London you should try." He added: "Unless you're simply not interested, of course."

"I'm not sure yet what my plans are, Alex," Darsoss said as he looked at Viscount Broadsmuir and his wife. They were a handsome couple. But the Viscount was actually not quite as handsome as his brother, Arthur Havenhurst, whom Darsoss had seen many times before and knew as Bliss. "It's possible," Darsoss said, folding the picture and handing it back to Dinsdale. "But I wouldn't want to commit myself totally yet . . ."

"That's your decision, of course. I was hoping you might. But . . . Anyhow . . ." He raised his glass. "Happy yuletide," he said, a trifle thick-tongued suddenly, and visibly deflated. "I've got to go now," he said. "There's a beanfest at the Kammergericht. Will you be there?"

"I don't know for sure . . ."

Dinsdale stood up. "You're rather noncommittal about everything, aren't you?"

Darsoss looked at him without speaking.

"I suppose I counted on you rather too heavily," Dinsdale said. "I shouldn't have. I can handle it alone, of course, but I thought . . ." He broke off with an impatient gesture. "What the hell difference what I thought . . . ?"

Darsoss said: "I'll keep my eyes and ears opened, Alex. You've my word on it."

Dinsdale looked at him with some tolerance. "Can't ask for more than that, I suppose," he said. "All right, old Greek. And —oh, yes; I needn't ask that you not air any of this, need I?"

"You truly needn't," Darsoss said.

When Dinsdale was gone Darsoss sat alone at the bar, one rather tired middle-aged man from a Topeka, Kansas, daily at the other end. Within a few minutes Darsoss walked out, found a restaurant in back of OMGUS that was open to Christmas Eve trade. After he had eaten meagerly he went to his room where he drank heavily, with the expected results.

He fell asleep with the distinct impression that he didn't know who he was or what he was doing in Berlin, and that he was insane. He began to dream that it was visitor's day in the asylum and he was permitted to see Anne. He was the inmate, of course. They sat opposite each other, separated by a glass partitioning, as in prison. But he could not hear her, he could only see her lips moving and her eyes shining, because the partitioning was too thick. She couldn't hear him either. He shouted to be heard but Anne could only smile and shrug her shoulders. Darsoss brought the problem to the attention of a uniformed attendant on his side of the partitioning. "I realize I'm insane," he said reasonably, "but we are unable to hear each other." The attendant was very cordial. "Oh, yes. That's because the partitioning is too thick," he explained. Then he smiled and said no more. When Darsoss looked again, Anne, with her soft brown hair and dark limpid eyes, was gone. Miles Lawson sat in her place, looking into Darsoss' eyes. After a moment he raised a small automatic pistol, its nose pointing directly at Darsoss. Miles Lawson smiled faintly. Then he turned the gun slowly toward himself and with the same faint smile placed it to his temple. Darsoss tried to cry out; he leaped from his seat and pressed his hands against the glass partitioning; he had no voice. Lawson's finger squeezed the trigger. There was no sound but his head snapped to one side under the impact of the presumed bullet and he fell dead from the chair on the other side of the partitioning.

Darsoss awakened, his head throbbing, his stomach violent, his skin dry and hot in that cold room, every pore in his body drained of moisture. Dawn had not arrived and he had begun a hangover in the trembling wake of a blood-spattered nightmare. Now he knew exactly who he was, where he was, and what he was doing. It was a bad hour for such a rude awakening; it was too dark for such a realization; it was an occasion for steel nerves. But all he could do was feel distressed and tell himself that it didn't matter. He had only to locate the importance of his reason, his conviction; they had gotten misplaced in the dark. The dream had been so graphic, so filled with bald accusation and configurations of guilt as to be meaningless.

Miles Lawson's death certainly had not been his responsibility; he had never felt one bit of guilt in the matter. As to the part about Anne: it was simply a cruel reminder, among many, that they could never communicate with each other again. What else? Nothing really. He knew everything else; it was in the marrow, in the nerve ends, in the heart and mind; it had been from the beginning: you didn't need to attach special greatness or superiority to the community you were a part of; but this in no way left you free to deceive, harm, or put yourself above it. Lawson had chosen death to doing so. Darsoss knew it.

He lay there, sick to his stomach and aching in every bone, and waited for daylight. Like a limping man whose every step would cause excruciating pain but whose journey was urgent, he would continue what he had begun.

3

He had begun trying to get out of Berlin the day after Christmas, lousy as he felt, and succeeded only many days later: flights had been grounded, schedules scrapped by ice and snow and zero visibilities. But finally he made it. Rain and sleet obscured the airfield in London. A flare-lined runway aided the landing. London and Berlin seemed to have merged into one great frozen mass. Darsoss had the odd feeling of having traveled endlessly within an ever-expanding sameness of time and space and substance; he would never reach its borders. It was an impoverished place where he was both the ruler and the ruled; a sovereign state with no future and no chance of becoming any better than it was. Darsoss finished quickly with customs, took a taxi to the West End and managed to get back into the same hotel across the street from Kensington Gardens. He was given the same room.

He stood momentarily at the window and smoked and looked out at the weather. Occasional muffled auto horns came up from below; the cars went through the wet streets with incessant hissing sounds. There was slush and rain and it was cold and gray outside. Darsoss remained in the room long enough to hang out his Valpak and remove a pack of cigarettes from inside one of his shoes. Then he left to go about the business of letting Bliss know he had returned to London—Bliss, who was now less of a mystery in some ways and more in others.

Darsoss drew a wavering horizontal pink chalk line along the stone wall outside the Marine Barracks in Church Street. It went about thirty feet like the desultory scrawl of a schoolboy; it couldn't be missed by anyone on the lookout, nor easily noticed by casual passers-by. It went nicely onto the wet surface and didn't wash away in the rain. He pocketed the chalk and entered the nearby red phone booth to call Disa Quennel. From any standpoint this was a logical step.

When she answered his ringing, he thought suddenly of how coldly anxious she had been to separate from him at Victoria Station when they had returned from Brighton. The reminder was inexplicable; any other image might as easily have sprung to mind. "Maida Vale two five seven five . . ."

"Hello . . ."

"Oh . . . it's you . . ."

He tried to match his tone to the words. "I couldn't stay away," he said. "I tried, but I couldn't . . ."

"Yes . . ." She seemed embarrassed.

He had to go a bit further; the drill was the drill. "The thought of seeing you again was all that occupied my mind," he said. Would he have expressed it that way if it had been true? If they had not been two spies in the process of deceiving a possible telephone surveillance? Perhaps he would. It didn't matter. This was certainly good enough as far as it went. "Are you all right?" he asked.

The tone he heard was genuine, truth immediately recognizable. "Me? Nothing can hurt me. I'm like a horse," she told him with regret. "But my husband is in hospital. That is, until I brought him home just this morning . . . He is asleep at the moment." Then: "Just after you left—ten days ago, I should imagine—he collapsed." She said it as if it had been inevitable.

"Collapsed?" Darsoss' eyes stared at the traffic going by outside, the vehicles, the pedestrians with their umbrellas, hunched over and scurrying through the rain, and he associated what he saw with trouble.

"I told you he was not a strong person, if you recall," she said, a reproachful edge to her voice. "He's had a chronic respiratory illness since he was a boy . . ." She stopped as if she suddenly realized that she might be about to say something too far out of character. "It required oxygen to save him," she finished.

Darsoss was stuck for a moment. "I'm sorry about that," he said. "But is there some way I can see you . . . ?"

"Oh, I couldn't leave him . . ."

"Perhaps I could visit . . ."

"I don't think it would be good right now . . ."

"After all, he and I know each other . . ."

She said nothing; her discomfort was discernible in the silence, perhaps more than if she had answered him: everything was veiled—nearby but hidden. Was she the wife whose passion was elsewhere rendering fealty to a husband in need? Or was she simply thwarting the mission with sudden self-accommodation? Was Darsoss hearing true or false or a little bit of each?

"Well, maybe you're right," he said after a moment; this required some thought, a talk with Bliss, who was, after all, their fugleman. "We'll wait and see . . ."

"Yes . . ."

"I missed you terribly . . ."

"I missed you also . . ."

He hung up softly and with the regret of a lover. Inside was the regret of someone who had not foreseen the rigors of a long winter and had grimly to face up to them over and over again. Delay was poison.

Next day he stood on the High Street platform for Piccadilly, his hands dug into his coat pockets, his collar turned up. A small blue arrow was sending him to American Express for a personal letter. For the first time it made no sense; this thing he had done again and again was dismembered in such a way, as he waited in the cold air for the train to arrive, that it was unrecognizable; like saying over and over the name you've carried all of your life until it loses meaning and becomes no more important than the hiss of steam or the tick of a telephone dial. He took a certain numb pleasure in the feeling—one always does—and he knew it would pass. He knew it because something was stronger than all the doubts and misgivings, all the rigors, all the strain. Hate. If you had that you had all you needed. There was no doubt of it.

Within twenty minutes he was sitting inside of a lavatory compartment, so that he could not be seen above the door from the outside. He tore open the envelope addressed to him which he had collected at the mail desk, and he read the typed message: *The Coachman, Middle Street, Streathham, S.W.16.* That was all that was necessary; Bliss had seen his chalk signal and had responded. Darsoss lit a cigarette and set fire to the note and its envelope. In a few seconds he had dropped the flame into the bowl and flushed its charred remains beyond recall.

Once again Bliss had chosen an outlying district—South the River, as Londoners called it. Only the one time when they had had dinner in Curzon Street had Bliss's custom been shunted, probably because he had needed for other reasons to be in the West End and was willing to take what he knew to be a very small risk. He need not have bothered with any of it; he could more easily have met with Darsoss in the foyer of the Ritz and lost nothing. All the caution had been worsted by Alex Dinsdale's guilty commitment to do battle against sinister forces. Bliss couldn't have foreseen or conceived of the meeting in Berlin—of Dinsdale's need for respect, his want of achievement, his desire for expiation. And Darsoss had no intention of enlightening him.

Street lamps were lit and fog was swirling in thick gusts when Darsoss arrived at the appointed place. It was a community of dirty red brick buildings and mean streets writhing in the agony of working-class boredom. The Coachman had just opened its doors to the people of the neighborhood, none of whom could have been expected to know that Bliss was Arthur Havenhurst, or, for that matter, who Arthur Havenhurst was.

The place was dank and very plain. Darsoss ordered a glass of beer and took it to a corner of the room. There was a dart game in progress; someone was pounding on the upright piano in an old-fashioned barroom style. A man and a woman, both in the late twenties, sat lugubriously against the wall near by, glasses before them probably filled with ale because it was the cheapest stuff available. Darsoss watched them covertly, drawn for some reason to their faces, which were marked with a sort of blank dignity; they seemed willing to be together despite contention with circumstances. They watched the room and its occupants with quiet awareness that never quite took them out of themselves, listened to the music, were silent, white-faced, their eyes unblinking. They were two people ranged against the world, preferring harsh union with one another to the smaller demands of easy solitude. They were sitting very close together, their handed-down coats open, their thighs touching.

Darsoss drank his beer, smoked several cigarettes, and read what there was to read in a copy of the *Express*, everything from passing mention of the Zionist movement in Palestine to ice hockey scores. After some time had gone by he looked up. The man and woman were now talking quietly. Their sodality was what seemed to interest Darsoss: the covenant in the uneventful, the ordinary. They had no idea that the real world was one of secret policemen and traitors, of death by torture and sleep haunted with dreams of vengeance; of deceit and treason and official secrets on which their destinies might depend; of ruthless men plotting in back rooms by the sea; of forbidden meetings in hotel lobbies and train stations and whorehouses; of people ready to kill each other for any one of dozens of reasons. No, they had only heard; all the rest was just cinema stuff and Edgar Wallace or Peter Cheyney. Darsoss wondered how they would have reacted had he gone up to them, struck up a conversation and then said: "Listen. I'm a spy helping the Russians to steal British atomic-bomb secrets. A lot of people think it may be a good thing. What is your opinion?" Perhaps there would have been no reaction at all, perhaps their mouths would have dropped open and nothing more; there was always the chance they would simply have wished to be left out of it, whatever it was, not be dragged into anything. People were often like that; they could be galvanized into action only in large groups—something that sometimes worked very well, but as often resulted in disaster.

Suddenly he lost interest in his vagrant thoughts and sizing-up games. Something had gone wrong. Bliss was an hour overdue. Obviously he was not going to make it.

Darsoss was overcome with a sense of foreclosure; this was the first rendezvous Bliss had failed to keep. A grace period of ten to twenty minutes was all you needed to know there was going to be an abort. Darsoss now felt stranded. He got up to leave. He had to keep moving with or without Bliss. He had to make things go with the Quennels on his own initiative. He had no time, above all, to gamble with.

Dian Quennel opened the door of the small Georgian house in the mews and looked at him as if he were someone she couldn't quite place. "Oh . . ." Her mind had been on other things, one could see immediately. "You . . ."

Darsoss stepped inside from the damp night air. "If I had a choice I wouldn't be here," he said.

She looked as if she had been short on sleep in recent nights, pale and drawn, patches of fatigue under her eyes and at the corners of her mouth; she gave the impression that its importance was secondary, at best. "Didn't you understand me?" she demanded, quiet, implacable, angry. "Last week my husband was at death's door . . ."

"Just what is it you think I've come here for, madam?" Darsoss said, vexed but speaking in an even tone of voice. "To push him through?"

"What *have* you come for?"

"I've a very big interest in your husband's health," he said. "I couldn't get much out of you on the phone, and I'd like to know what to expect."

"What to expect? Don't you understand? He cannot be taxed . . ." She shook her head in disbelief at how obtuse he was, and she groped for the words a fool might be able to understand. "Good Lord, can a few extra days or a week make all that great a difference?"

"You never know until they've passed," he said. They were still in the entrance hall, and he hadn't removed his coat. "This is not tiddlywinks."

She said in a reasonable way: "What would you have me do? Drag him from a sickbed?"

He answered just as reasonably. "Maybe British counter-intelligence will do it instead."

Her voice went up half a tone. "What do you mean?"

"I don't know," Darsoss replied. "But today the Resident is missing. The man in charge; the man responsible for everything. He called a rendezvous and didn't keep it." He paused. "It has never happened before," he said. "It is not his pattern."

She said nothing but was sufficiently respectful of the announcement.

"It may mean nothing," Darsoss went on. "It may mean the

end of a beautiful friendship. Or maybe a reunion for all of us at the Old Bailey; it's too early to tell. But it's nothing to rejoice over."

She frowned. "Are you certain there was no misunderstanding of the time and place?"

"It would be nice to think so. But no." He paused. "And now this," he said, bad luck all around him. It could as easily have gone well; but no, it had to sag in the middle like a liana bridge over a ravine in the jungle. He was weary but coldly enraged; he was sick of everything. "Damn the rotten luck."

She sniffed. "Damn *Ian*'s luck," she said, unmistakably indignant. "Think of what it must be like for him."

"You think of it," Darsoss told her. "That's not my department."

"How unfeeling you *are*," she said, as if that finally summed him up.

"Women don't need to make sense, do they?" He couldn't think of a better answer immediately and resorted to a time-tested inanity, pacing away from where he had been standing, then coming back again, drawing his hand across his mouth in perplexity. "We're thieves. There's nothing more than that between your husband and me. What the devil am I supposed to feel?"

"How much you wish to pull him down, to go that far, to call him a thief," she said, a shaky accuser suddenly, azurine flames for eyes. "How can you?"

"Oh, Jesus Christ, madam; who cares?" he moaned, and dug out his cigarettes with exasperation. "We could all be in jail tomorrow, and World War Three could start the day after that."

"God forbid."

"Oh, then that does make some impression on you."

"The thought of war . . . Do you think I am senseless?"

"What about jail? No, never mind," he said. "It's more important to examine the situation as of the moment. Right now we're in limbo. And I don't intend to remain there. I'm here for a reason; to get what your husband has to give—either directly from him or through you, it doesn't matter which now. You say he's too ill to transmit; all right. Then I have to have an alternative." He looked directly into her eyes as she held a position at the foot of the little flight of steps leading to the second floor. "You don't need to defend the staircase, I'm not going to rush it," he said.

"I don't fear that."

Darsoss nodded and stuck a cigarette in his mouth. "I need an answer—nothing vague, a concrete answer," he said.

"My husband is asleep. Lower your voice."

"This is important. Let's not stand here."

Wordlessly she led him to the study where the first transmission had taken place. "Bliss may or may not show up tomorrow," Darsoss said immediately. "I'm going to try to connect with him again; the same rendezvous is still in effect, sometimes people make them at a later date. But in my judgment we've a short-term mission, under the circumstances, not one that calls for endless waiting. And should Bliss remain away, whatever the mysterious reason, I'll consider myself free to make decisions. Actually I'll have no other choice. So the point is, if your husband cannot transmit by day after tomorrow, I'm going to return to Berlin and report on the situation to that effect. I won't hang on here any longer than that with Bliss out of the picture, it's too risky—for me, personally, that is. I've other considerations and I might be placing them in jeopardy if I don't get back to Berlin now. Unless, as I say, the transmissions resume immediately." He paused for breath. "Give your husband that message when he wakes up."

"But is what you're doing safe?" Disa Quennel asked with great uneasiness. "We're supposed to be . . ."

"Yeah. That's right," he said. "But Bliss's absence changes things. He might be under lock and key in the Bow Street Police Station right now, about to start the Crown's case against all of us in return for his own neck."

"Yes, but what if he is not? You said it wasn't certain . . ."

"Nothing is."

"Then shouldn't we go on . . . ?"

"Don't worry about that. We've plenty of latitude with our cover," he said. "Your husband's illness could have dampened your spirits where I am concerned."

"But they still follow, you know. They haven't stopped. They follow and they follow . . ."

Darsoss made a contemptuous mouth. "They've nothing better to do. They know there's something, but they don't have what it takes to come up with it." He had a new feeling of contempt for the British counterintelligence agencies. It was quite sudden but very strong. "From the look of it," he said, "Laurel and Hardy are running the whole thing." He didn't know why he was seized with this spasm of anger until he went on to say: "I hate to think about the innocent people whose well-being and security are in the hands of cretins and boobs posing as public servants."

She said nothing but appeared to be caught by the idea, her eyes suddenly fixed on his face.

"Just as a matter of principle," he added. "But that's someone else's worry. And because of it there's damned little chance of our being caught."

"But you just said . . ."

"It's the things we may not even dream of that concern me: the stupid mishap; someone we don't even know gets into an automobile accident en route with a vital message concerning us; the unbelievable stupidity of a courier or some other small cog; a defector from Russia with a list of names; the hollowed-out coin with microfilm inside that falls through a hole in someone's pocket; a busybody; a would-be detective; an unknown enemy ready to swear to lies about any one of us or even tell what truth he knows; the sudden reversal of sentiment somewhere within our ranks. The betrayal—for whatever the motive. These are the things to keep you awake nights. And the longer things take, the more chances of something of their kind happening." He crushed out his cigarette. "We'll need a code for tomorrow evening, just in case the phone is still tapped."

But her mind had gone off, her arms folded across her chest, her eyes lifted. "Oh, how I wish this were all over and done . . ."

Darsoss was removing a new cigarette from its pack, but stopped what he was doing in mid-air. He studied the face of Disa Quennel very carefully, and with suddenly new eyes. Pain had escaped her like something stolen that falls from its hiding place in one's clothing.

Darsoss said: "So it's that way, is it?" She looked at him blankly and he went on: "Torture, huh?"

She said nothing. She turned her gaze away from his in a way as telling as a signed statement. It was true. Darsoss found the knowledge strangely satisfying. "You're not too happy in this kind of work," he said softly, his eyes reflective, a light smile on his lips. "Maybe I should have guessed . . . But anything for the cause, isn't that right?"

She said nothing. Darsoss looked at her, unable to resist a further step. "Or does that cause get to be a cross sometimes?"

"I don't know what you're talking about," she said.

Darsoss said: "That's strange. I get the impression you do. But then I'm naturally a suspicious man."

"There is nothing to be suspicious of," she said with the barest touch of mockery in her voice. "You are also anxious to be done. Let us do whatever it is we must do and ask no more of each other than that." She looked at him with unwavering eyes. "Please . . ."

"Madam, don't be alarmed," he said. "I was just making conversation—often a bad idea and open to misinterpretation. My chief interest right now is in the signal we use tomorrow night." He put a cigarette in his mouth. "Let's work out something simple." He opened his Zippo and struck a flame. "If I don't connect with the RD tomorrow, I'll telephone you at around seven-thirty and I'll say . . ." He stopped to think of something as he put the lighter to his cigarette. But there was no need to go further with it.

Quennel, wearing robe and slippers, walked into the study at that very instant. He looked old and haggard and the sight of him brought a gasp from Disa Quennel.

"I heard your voices," he said, "luckily. Disa, you'd have sent this gentleman packing; and that would have been quite naughty of you . . ." He went to his desk chair, cold and gray-faced.

"He'd have come back," she said respectfully, but plainly worried.

"Would he?" Quennel said with an air of disbelief, all the more scorching for the mild tone. "Well, perhaps he would have. I assume you're ready to work, Mr. Darsoss."

"If you are."

"I think we've little choice."

"Ian," Disa Quennel began. "You cannot sit here for two, or perhaps three hours . . ."

"It's not on paper, is that it?" Darsoss put in.

"Precisely," Quennel said. "This will need to be a verbal transmission from start to finish."

"You seem to have forgotten," Disa Quennel said, standing

there like the battered conscience of them all, "that just last week you were at the point of death . . ."

"We're all at the point of death, dear heart, more or less, almost as soon as we're born . . ." He smiled the wan smile Darsoss had come to think of as the smile of delicious pain; it was always ready in the face of the doubts and ignorance of others. "Actually, I'm really not badly off," he said. "I'm quite all right, as a matter of fact. Or at least as all right as I shall ever be."

"You think saying it makes it so," Disa Quennel said, as if she had been through it before.

Quennel seemed almost surprised. "There are no guarantees for any of us, dear heart," he said. "The best we can hope for is the chance to make a contribution to the time that is ours . . ."

Disa Quennel was silent and Darsoss smoked, Quennel going back to his smile, this one of hope and understanding. "Sometimes there are holidays . . . such as the one we can look forward to after we've done all that need be done, perhaps in France. You'll like that, won't you? All of this behind us . . ."

She said nothing. Quennel was clearly the head of the household, his frailty notwithstanding; everything, even illness, was a weapon in the right hands. "No opportunity should be allowed to lapse, isn't that right, Darsoss?" Quennel said.

Disa Quennel had withdrawn into herself; a mysterious passivity seemed to overtake her. Darsoss said: "Yes. Let's get on with it."

"You're anxious to be done, aren't you?"

"Why ask?"

"I don't know," the sick man said, as if he did know but wouldn't tell. Darsoss had never seen him in quite this humor before, something untouchable about him, probably the result of severe illness. His nose was faintly beaked by a loss of flesh, and his eyes were incandescent from recent fever and the faraway thoughts a superior person lives with. "I suppose it doesn't matter the motive, after a time, in the doing of certain demanding tasks," he said. "Pressure is pressure, whatever one's beliefs. One man's profit motive may be stronger than another's idealism in the same desperate situation. *There* is a harrowing thought."

"Why don't we get going?" Darsoss said.

"Yes, of course. You won't want to stay for this, I'm sure, Disa."

She stood there for a moment, anxious, reproachful, not at all a part of things, someone whose feelings couldn't be bought or submerged. Darsoss looked at her. She would be a beauty until she was sixty; it was all in the bones and it was there to stay. In a soft tone she said: "Excuse me," and without looking at either of them she left the room. Almost in deference to her there was a moment's silence. Then Darsoss began removing his overcoat and Quennel said: "Did it all go well in Berlin?"

Darsoss inhaled, removed the cigarette and blew huge jets of smoke through tightly pursed lips, his eyes unfriendly and filled with bored contempt. "Swell," he said.

Quennel accepted the caustic tone as altogether normal. "Whom did you see? Vorshov?"

"Yeah, Vorshov," Darsoss said, loosening his tie.

"I thought so. I met him once in Kharkov, at the University, before the war. But I'm sure none of that matters to you."

"How did you guess?"

"You might say I've a sixth sense," Quennel answered.

"That's just swell."

"As a matter of fact, about many things," Quennel said. "For example, I've the distinct impression that you wish to see this mission fail. True or false?"

Darsoss was startled. "Do you read tea leaves too?" he said.

"You were ready to go off to Berlin and leave it in the lurch. Whatever would possess you to do that if not a wish—conscious or otherwise—to see it all go out to sea in a bottle?"

"You had yourself a good listen, didn't you?"

"Not deliberately. It's a small house. And you had quite a lot to say while I was in the process of coming to myself in order to make the journey from my bedroom to the study. I would say you were glad of an excuse to funk things, to go back to Berlin and complain . . ."

"Listen; you were out of action, among other things. That was to be my way of protecting the mission."

"Whatever your reasons, I couldn't help feeling uneasy, and I still do."

"You'll have to solve that problem yourself."

"Oh, there's a good deal more to it than that."

"Oh?"

"The point is, it is one thing to be infected, perhaps through no fault of one's own, with something toxic or crippling. It is quite another to deliberately attempt to infect someone else."

Darsoss' face and voice remained impassive as he said: "What do you mean by that?"

"Well, when you suggest to my wife that she is bearing a cross, and refer to the cause in a mocking tone—wouldn't you say that you were projecting your own feelings, fractious, at the very least?"

"Don't start that kind of thing with me, friend," Darsoss said, covering his uncertainty with an air of confidence. "The people in Berlin couldn't care less about what I think or feel as long as the job gets done."

"But wouldn't you say," Quennel went on, as if Darsoss had denied nothing, "that that sort of talk is always meant to influence the listener? I mean, weren't you in truth attempting to infect my wife with it, inveigh against me, take advantage of her fatigue and the obvious strain of standing vigil to a sick person—in short, get her to think and feel as you think and feel?"

"All you know about what I think and feel would go under your fingernail."

"You're a carrier, Darsoss, that's all one need to know. You carry social and philosophical spirochaete—whether of a defunct fascism or tired liberalism or some shattered theism, I wouldn't know. But it's there, and it accounts for the snarl in your voice, the cover-up of ill-temper, and all the other fits and starts in your personality. You're sick and you're less unhappy about it when others are sick also . . ."

"Is that about all?" Darsoss asked in a steely, calm voice.

"There's still another turn," Quennel said, with no intention of desisting. "I told you once you had a know-it-all attitude one wanted to stick a pin in. What I meant, I see now, was that there was something about you that I, for one, couldn't feel easy with, hard as I would try. You obviously despised me then, and still do—more than ever, undoubtedly—but at last I think I know why." He paused, seemed filled with febrile energy, and then said: "I do, don't I?"

"Yes. You're a bloody saint and I'm just a no-good bastard."

A faded, unappreciative smile crossed Quennel's tabescent

face. "You're in love with my wife," he said without complaint. "The only pretense involved is that you're not." -

"You're insane," Darsoss said in a flat voice. "Completely insane."

"But everything supports it—all the friction between us, all the anger, the effort to incite me about the ruin to her reputation—all of it simple substitutes for direct action, for what you really have felt from the start. It's simple really; think of it. Here you are, an obviously bitter and dissolute person—derelict wouldn't be too strong a term, I think—against everything, in favor of nothing, and most particularly offended, it would follow, by people who have a belief. Through circumstances, you are exposed to the action of just such people, one of them a beautiful and extraordinarily appealing woman—let's be frank. That would be bad enough. But on top of it she is married to an extraordinarily irritating little pedant and pipsqueak with whom she shares the belief. Well. There's no need to embroider, is there? All the subterranean passageways are there, aren't they? Perhaps not so subterranean, at that."

"The only thing subterranean is your mind," Darsoss said.

"Oh, you mustn't misunderstand," Quennel said. "I'm certain nothing has passed between you and that my wife is quite unaware of your feelings. Frankly, I would never have made it a subject except in regard to the mission. It mustn't add to our burdens in any way. If it remains subordinate to what we must do, it needn't matter. So feel and think what you will, but don't expose any of it to my wife or let it in any other way interfere with the performance of your task."

Darsoss felt a strange and deep calmness. "You're a man who hears voices," he said. "No one can argue with that."

Quennel said: "I don't expect you to admit to anything, Darsoss. I am not interested in a victory of some sort where you proclaim guilt or behave abjectly . . ."

"No purge trial? How kind you are . . ."

"I've tried to make clear to you only what I think, with the hope that you will of your own accord exercise caution. That's all that concerns me. Actually, you couldn't contaminate my wife, no matter how you would try . . ."

"Then it's all academic, isn't it?"

"No. Because the wish to tear us down is still there, I believe, and beyond your control," Quennel said with a smile of angry tolerance. He began to fish about for something inside his desk drawer. "Hate draws close to love sometimes, they say—one resents what one can't attain . . ."

"Doctor, my loves and hates never meet."

"If only you could find something that mattered to you, Darsoss . . . Where *is* that key?" His hand fished further, then he arose and closed the drawer. "I mean, you've got to be after something or you'll be drawn into the bottomless uncertainty of our time. And no amount of contempt will keep you from it . . ."

"You know, the more you talk the more I feel like a Jew who is making you uncomfortable because he won't convert."

"Don't flatter yourself," Quennel said with scarcely concealed anger, the corners of his mouth going white. "You know very well what the source of all this is—the attempt to achieve confederacy with my wife . . ."

"Confederacy." Darsoss laughed. "You do find words."

"The appeal was obvious—perhaps even to her," Quennel went on, his hands going into the pockets of his robe like nervously searching hooks, a man capable of separated and simultaneous actions. "She asked that you do nothing more than what is expected of you. But you've more than that inside of you, you're not that uncomplicated, are you?"

"The more you talk . . ."

"And the more you protest . . ."

"You're the protester, Quennel."

"Can anything compare with your bitterness about how stupid the security men were proving to be? Laurel and Hardy, I think you said. Almost as if you were disappointed they hadn't discovered what we are doing . . ."

"Don't ever think that," Darsoss said, an angry heat in his face.

"Of course all people have a touch of that in them," Quennel continued, glad to have drawn blood. "That desire to be punished for something they themselves cannot deal with on a conscious level. Haven't they?"

"Don't ever mistake me for anyone like that," Darsoss said.

"I think it was confirmation that you wanted of her," Quennel said, "driven by the feelings we've already discussed."

"The only affection I could possibly feel about your wife,

Quennel, is sympathy," Darsoss said. "Deep sympathy." He crushed out his cigarette. "Now, why don't we do the job?"

"I'm sure that's exactly what she would return to you," Quennel said. "And we'll begin as soon as I locate the key to that file drawer . . . I've left it upstairs apparently, I'll need to go for it."

"Go right ahead."

"But I hope it's all quite clear to you," Quennel said, looking at Darsoss with an imperious stare. "I don't expect a change of heart or remorse from you, or anything of the kind; and, of course, I'm not in the least bit interested. All of this has been merely to say that if you're as keen on ending this association as I am, you'll go through the motions rather like an automaton and contain everything else."

"Why don't you shut up? I'm getting sick of listening to you," Darsoss said, as if he were completely bored.

Quennel gave him a superior look. "I'm sure," he said. Then, after a moment of silence, he walked as swiftly as he dared to the door and left the room.

Darsoss sat there smoking, hearing Quennel ascend the staircase just outside. The place was deathly still; the light was dim and the floor heater was giving off a rancid smell as if it were newly bought and not yet burned in. It was a smug room, books lining the walls and suffocating one with implied prestige and eminence; it was part of what had enslaved Disa Quennel: presumptive superiority. But few women were scientists or theoreticians; they had a generic incapacity, if not distaste, for abstract ideas; a so-called cause paled next to the need for a muffler and galoshes when it rained. It had enraged Quennel, driven him to accusations, visions of betrayal, fear of weak links around him; to the absurdity of the suggested passion—as if it were *he* who had been swept up in the pretense and lost to reality; surely the others hadn't been. Darsoss had but one passion, after all. Quennel, like all saints and Messiahs, was quite out of his mind. If he was not, how riddled with uncertainty he himself had to have been.

Darsoss inhaled on his cigarette and walked nervously to the door. There was a sound on the staircase. Quennel was returning with the file drawer key that was apparently so important to the proceedings.

Darsoss paced away from the door, on edge and mistrustful. Even his fine, vortical hatred caused him anxiety. You had to get something like this done before things got to be too hard, or a moment's cowardice ruined everything. The changes in people were treacherous, he knew. Few things were more frail than the strongest of men, the deepest of convictions. A blow on the head could rob a priest of his faith, destroy a lifetime's acquisition of scientific knowledge. And death needed no analysis. It came to call again and again, and each time it did, plans were canceled, dreams were ended, the survivors were left to clean up the mess. Even as the sound of the slippered feet stopped, became claudicant, and then dragged, Darsoss knew that Quennel was going to die. And when the sound of the falling body came, Darsoss knew the full impact of the fear of time and events.

He raced from the study to the hallway with its fine oak planks and wooden pegs. Quennel was on the floor, crumpled, still as the wood, the attitude of death conspicuous and incontestable. But Darsoss turned the still pliable body and leaned in to listen for life, for refutation; but there was none.

Disa Quennel came from a stock-still position in a rear doorway, her eyes frozen with the sight, with a strange scissoring step, swift but somehow unsure, as if part of her didn't want to be there. She sank to her knees and put her hand on her husband's arm with silent horror. Then she saw. "He's dead," she exclaimed, her voice strangled. "He's dead . . ." Her eyes filled with tears. "Oh, no . . ."

Darsoss didn't know what to do or say. He could only think of how once again things were being ruined. Surely she had to have expected this one day. Now it was here. He didn't know whether to reach out to her or not. He did nothing, watched, waited. She cried without sound, but her voice was thick with suspiration when she said: "It's not easy to play God . . . is it . . . ?"

It was a curious thing to say, an odd way to put it at that moment. Yet Darsoss, without fully understanding it, found it telling. "You should telephone your doctor," he said. "Or tell me and I'll do it for you . . ."

"I shall . . . You had better leave . . ."

"No. I'd better stay. The friend who happened to be in the neighborhood and just dropped in . . ."

They looked at each other in undefinable silence, as if taking charge of madness that was not their own, a box with deadly contents that someone had left with them: a severed head, a poisonous snake, a petri dish of the world's vilest disease; they didn't dare let go of it just yet. "All right," she said. "I shall ring him . . ." She seemed dried-out suddenly; as if, without warning, nothing was left inside.

CHAPTER FIVE

1

He drank two double whiskeys in The Coachman. Several of
the regular patrons eyed him; this was the second night in
succession that a stranger had appeared in their midst. The
piano reverberated with an old-fashioned song or two; the dart-
players were in full swing; the unhappy couple sat in the same
seats as the night before. Darsoss sat against the wall, a gouged
and ring-stained table before him, smoked cigarettes and drank,
and thought about the absurdity of human endeavor—the good,
the bad, the failed but well-intentioned. He thought about Disa
Quennel, alone in the house in the mews, so much in the dark
and listening for guiding voices coming from nowhere, respond-
ing as best she could to circumstances she really hadn't made.
He felt sorry for her. He found that Quennel was repellent to
him even in memoriam.

He realized too that he didn't like Bliss much either; he had
never had any strong feelings before. But now, as Bliss appeared
and sat down next to him, an obvious toff to attract the glances
of Coachman regulars, Darsoss thought of him as an opponent.

"Sorry about yesterday," Bliss said with no indication he
would go any further.

"I was ready to go back to Berlin," Darsoss told him. "This
was the last try I was going to make."

"Unavoidable, I can assure you. Everything go all right?"

Darsoss nodded. "Up until now."

"Yes. We do have a spot of bother. A series of stalls, rather like Burma during the war."

"It's not my problem, you understand," Darsoss pointed out.

"Well, you're not responsible, of course. If one were religious, one might call it the hand of God."

Darsoss recalled Disa Quennel's allusion. "Whoever's hand it is, I'm back to Berlin."

"Are you?" Bliss remained composed.

"I am. We had a special arrangement."

"I recall."

"This wasn't accounted for in the original agreement."

"The hand of God never is."

"They would love that description. You must be in this for the sport."

"Listen, old boy. You've a funny notion of how this business works. Your job is far from done. We all take the same setbacks, you know."

"Oh, I'm not resigning, just protecting myself with the management."

"I *am* the management, Johnson."

"You're the shop foreman, Bliss. This is between me and Berlin. I'm on a very special arrangement."

"Yes, I know all of that. But you've in no way fulfilled your part of it. The mission is still in effect and everything that concerns you still comes through me." The slightest irritation showed through but the tone was still one of gentlemanly composure. "You can't simply walk out because it suits your mood."

"New terms are all that suit my mood. Quennel is no longer with us, or hadn't you heard?"

"Yes, and he undoubtedly left valuable material among his personal effects. That's our immediate concern, nothing else."

"You're off the track. You realize I was there when he died, don't you?"

"No," Bliss said. "It comes as a surprise."

"He was going to transmit to me directly."

"You more or less took over for the one day I was out."

"I'm not a mechanical doll. When I come to a corner I turn. It was a question of meeting with him or going into cold storage until he was up and around and able to type the stuff himself. It was his idea. But it didn't work out too well."

"You got nothing, then."

"We never got started."

"You mean he died right before your eyes?"

"More or less."

"Quite something. Health wasn't his strong point. How did his wife take it?"

Darsoss dragged on his cigarette, then said: "Quietly." He thought about what had happened, about Disa Quennel's eyes red and puffed after tears had ceased to flow—the moments after the ambulance and the doctor had come and gone. "She can swallow a lot," he said.

"I imagine this is rather more than the normal dose."

Darsoss licked his dry lips. "Anyhow, that's how I know Quennel had nothing on paper," he said.

"Then you can be sure he was going to work from rather detailed notes."

"What of it?"

"They do exist, I know for a fact. There is someone who can make sense of them to a large extent—at least to get us a step further along until we can work out something new." He paused to light a cigarette, then went on: "Do you remember Brian Mornier?"

Darsoss did remember immediately. "A student of Quennel," he said.

"Very good. He was at the dinner party you attended."

"Yes. Had some interesting racial theories; made the evening, as I recall."

"Ah, yes. He's quite good. Son of a Kenya farmer and all of that."

"You mean he's in the network? That's pretty rich."

"He's a brilliant student; Quennel's very best. Rather convenient. Anyhow, he will be able to do something with whatever is there. Your job is to get it from Mrs. Quennel."

"*My* job?"

"Can you think of someone else better suited to it? You *are* inside, so to speak. The cover is still working, by the way. It might draw attention if you cut it dead suddenly."

"That's what you think," Darsoss said. "It was fine to begin with. But nobody's really keeping track. I went out and came in and didn't even have my suitcase opened."

"Even so."

"It was good, but there's not much call for it now Quennel's dead."

"That's all right. We don't simply drop things just like that. It's a bad, sloppy habit. You still have entree; you'll use it to get what we're after. I'm sure you can without much difficulty."

"What if nothing is there?"

"Most unlikely. But you can't wait until his belongings are gone through or destroyed, you have to move with some alacrity."

"You do something for me, Bliss. Contact Berlin and tell them to have my payoff ready immediately—not three weeks from now, but by the time I arrive on the weekend."

"I can't tell Berlin anything, old fellow. I can only tell you."

"Then I'll tell them myself. As soon as I get this other thing out of the way."

"You'd better not linger; and I'd forget about any unscheduled trips if I were you."

"There's a funeral tomorrow. I know it's sentimental of me, but why don't we wait until it's over?"

"She'll give you what you're after, I'm sure," Bliss said, stubbing out his cigarette casually. "She'd be afraid not to, she's gone this far."

2

Between that evening and the following afternoon, Darsoss took to haunting the lobby of his hotel much in the way of old people who have nothing else to do and nowhere to go. They fix on the comings and goings of others, read their newspapers and wait for death in the impersonal atmosphere of a public place. Darsoss could see what was behind it: whatever the fight, it was badly waged in the baneful solitude of a small hotel room; whatever the fear, it was harder to face. As Quennel's funeral took place, he realized that if he were to die suddenly he would have very few mourners; he had lost contact with so many people.

A sizable number of Quennel's students now sat in the chapel where Miles Lawson's body had lain some weeks before, a few of whom Darsoss remembered from Disa Quennel's dinner party, and also numerous colleagues. Brian Mornier was among them; tall, blond, and with a face cheerfully cruel the way handsome faces can sometimes be. Darsoss wondered whether he was a Communist or just someone whose chief interest was adventure; he was not the type one associated with either scholarship or social reform. Odd types abounded in this game, and for odd reasons.

Disa Quennel wore black, her face veiled, and she was flanked on one side by a woman Darsoss had never seen before and on the other by Norma Lawson, another victim of arcanal warfare, tenderly returning a favor. Disa Quennel saw him, he could tell; through the veil came a look of recognition, perhaps even an appeal. Or was that seeing too much?

The ceremony was secular and coldly unsentimental despite God, whom Disa Quennel knew to be stern and implacable. A fellow physicist spoke of Quennel's indomitable spirit and his love of mankind; of his great gifts as a scientist and as a teacher of science. An announcement was made: "Mrs. Quennel requests that no condolence visitations be made so that her mourning may remain private." Then it was done and the chapel was emptying. Darsoss heard someone say, "He's being cremated, you know. I suppose that part is private." Someone replied, "I should certainly hope so."

Just a few minutes later Darsoss had got on a bus at Swiss Cottage and sat down on the top tier. For some reason, undoubtedly unimportant, he realized that a new year had begun without his notice. He gave it no greater attention than that and then was conscious of someone sitting down next to him. It was Brian Mornier, callow when seen closely, perhaps because a touch of acne lingered and there were pits in the skin. "Hello, remember me?" he said good-humoredly.

"Sure. What do you want?"

"Just a footnote. What you're looking for is in a locked file drawer in a ledger marked Proverbs. You can't miss it."

"How do you know?" Darsoss said.

"Does that matter? I saw it put there, for one thing."

"Is that all?"

"Actually," the other replied.

Darsoss nodded.

"Now, I suggest you get to this as quickly as possible."

"Don't worry about it," Darsoss said, adding this one to the list of people he didn't like very much. He was precocious and full of the joy of being a key figure in juicy circumstances; Darsoss suspected the nature of the cause didn't matter very much. "Everything will work out just fine."

"Yes, it had better. When can we expect to hear from you?"

"When you do," Darsoss said.

"You shouldn't put on airs with me, I'm not a lad running messages."

Darsoss made a wry mouth, half a grin forming. "You'll get your recognition, just be patient."

The young man smiled as if he knew he was being dismissed. "You know, I really believe that I could get this done more easily than you could," he said. "Mrs. Quennel knows me as one of his students. It's not far-fetched that something of academic value to me should be in the locked drawer. She wouldn't actually know the difference. The earnest young chap who admired the GOM."

"Forget that. I'll take care of it."

"You see, that puts her in the position of continued complicity. She may not wish to go on with it now her husband is dead. Frankly, I don't think there's anything in it for her any longer. Coming from me, you see, the request has a certain innocence. From you it's more of the same."

"Look, son, don't get too astute or you're liable to botch everything."

"If you don't mind, don't call me son," the young man said.

"How did you happen to become a physicist, a type like you?" Darsoss said, taking sudden pleasure in the chance to jeer.

"What is that supposed to mean?" Mornier said.

"You have the look of an outdoor man, not someone who's stuck away in classrooms and laboratories."

"Really? That's very unscientific of you."

"I know. But I'm rather disappointed. You see, I believed you that night."

"Oh? Well, you were meant to."

"The British Empire in Kenya; kicking niggers in the ass when they needed it; yes, I'm really disappointed."

"I'm terribly sorry. Perhaps someday you'll meet my father. He's the real thing."

Darsoss looked at the young man, the glimmer of a knowing

smile on his face. "Yes, that would be swell," Darsoss said. "Maybe someday you can tell him all about this. I guess you'd like that, wouldn't you?"

"It has a certain appeal," Mornier said. "Don't nag me too much," he added as one might say: "Please pass the salt." Then he went further. "I've had it done by the best in the field."

"Stay out of my way and it's a deal," Darsoss said.

Mornier looked at Darsoss the way he might have at the obviously abhorrent father in Kenya, and said: "Sure," in the tone one uses when he means: "I can wait until later to give you what's coming to you." It is a face-saving technique: you're impotent at the moment so you pretend you're merely very patient. Mornier had probably used it often.

When he saluted airily and departed a minute or two later, Darsoss was glad to see him go. The meeting impelled Darsoss to act more quickly than he might otherwise have. He hadn't been altogether sure of how to approach Disa Quennel, but now he was moved to choose the straight line. Everything considered, it was the safest way.

When he arrived at the house in the mews it was dark and only a dim light showed through the vestibule window from somewhere within, probably the study. He rang the doorbell, glanced over his shoulder, and waited for her to answer.

She opened the door and looked at him in surprise. She wore black but didn't appear bereft or inconsolable. There had been tears in cold solitude, surely, and memories whispering in every corner of all the rooms; but ultimately she seemed weary and merely disenfranchised, the victim of a dispossess notice or an unfair court verdict.

"May I come in?" he ventured to say.

"I thought I'd seen the last of you," she said, undecided but faintly impatient. "I thought I'd seen and heard the last of all of it . . ."

It took him aback. He closed the door behind him as if to shield her from prying eyes. "You'll be fine," he said stupidly. "I mean to say, you're a young woman, and your chances are far from used up . . ."

"That's terribly nice," she said, a rictus forming but not a smile. "How stupid of me not to have realized that myself . . ."

What a botch he was making of things with that sort of bunk; he didn't in the least believe it anyhow. But he wanted to find some way of smoothing things out, finding out what was there and acknowledging it. "Would you rather I said nothing at all?" he said quietly.

"It doesn't matter," she said. "That's the way life is." She turned toward the living room and Darsoss followed her without invitation as she said reflectively: "It could have been uneventful and dull. Once the war ended, I thought it would be. Simply a matter of knowing where you stand day after day, ordinary and boring . . . and wonderful. Except one doesn't realize it at the time . . ." She stopped for a moment, stood still in the center of the room, her hands clasped in front of her, then said: "All the while it was something quite the opposite . . ." It was deep regret and pity rather than the grief that strangles a surviving lover. "But now . . . it's finished—the sneaking back and forth, and living a lie; and what is left? A cold, empty house, and ashes in an urn, and things to be forgotten as soon as possible. That is what is left. Nothing I'd care to preserve." She paused. "And you," she added, and then turned to look at him across the room where he stood just inside the entrance way. "What could be left here for you, now Ian is gone . . . ?"

Darsoss took a deep breath. "There is one loose end," he said. "Let's get it out of the way and then you won't see me again."

"What is it?" she asked.

"There are notes," he said, moving toward her, his overcoat unbuttoned but unremoved—a mandatory formality. "The other people are anxious to get hold of them. They're in the locked file in the study. Do you have the key? He left me to go fetch it the other night."

"So that's why you've come," she said. "More of the same. The game goes on . . ."

This was the opening. "And you don't want it to," he said.

She looked at him curiously and said nothing.

"Am I right?" he said.

She was on guard and very edgy. "Right? Right about what?"

"That whatever your feelings about your husband were, this whole thing had you by the throat, didn't it? You weren't in it the same way he was, were you?"

"What are you trying to make me say?"

"Nothing," he replied with a touch of triumph and a tight smile. "I think perhaps it's already said." He narrowed his eyes and drew closer to her. "You were doing it against your will, weren't you? Like eating worms. You'd deny it otherwise, and you're not denying it, are you? You didn't deny it the other day. I saw signs of it then. All you did was pull back when I got nosy about it."

"What of it?" she said, subdued but defiant. "What is it you want of me?"

He paused, appraised the inroad, and then in a more relaxed tone he said: "I'll be more than glad to tell you." He quickly lit a cigarette that had been waiting for about a minute between his fingers. He said: "There's a ledger marked Proverbs in that file drawer—which I want to destroy . . ."

Her eyes widened. "Destroy?"

"Yes, destroy. Burn every page while you watch."

"Pages of formulas . . . ?"

"That's my intention, so that I can safely tell them the cupboard was bare. They'll take my word for it, they don't know I'm ready to lie to them, they've no reason even to suspect. That's bringing the game to an end—at least your part in it. The curtain will come down and the performance will be over. I tell you that because I know it's exactly what you want, and I can take the chance of telling you the truth."

"But why should you . . . ?"

"Why? Because without those notes, the mission is stalled and I've grounds for complaint; I can't be held too tightly to certain terms. It's not easy to explain but I have a private matter—a personal interest that is best served by what I want to do . . ."

"I don't understand . . ."

Why should she have? What could she have known of his restrictions, of his commitments, his pledges; the labyrinth in which he lived? "It would take a long time to clear it up for you," he said, "and it really wouldn't matter to you in the long run. Just take my word, it works out that way."

"Does it?" She was openly skeptical now, perhaps even bitter, all of her grievances converging on this single point.

"What reason would I have to lie about it?"

"To make it all simpler," she answered. "You were right. You were able to see how I felt about it. You thought perhaps that I would not go on with any of it now . . . that I would not co-operate . . ."

"Yes. That's logical," he granted, trying to sound as reasonable as possible. "But it happens not to be the case."

"How can I know that?"

"Damn it, madam," he exploded. "Don't you have any instinct for what's true and what's false? Can't you tell when you're being lied to?"

"Not always," she said, sincere, shaken by his tone.

"Well, what does it take?" he went on with violent impatience. "A ouija board? A sign from heaven? Or how about a trial by poison?"

"Please. You must understand . . ."

"Yes, and you must understand too," he said, pacing two steps away and then back. "The ledger could be taken forcibly. Doesn't that occur to you?"

"By you?"

"By anyone. Think it through. Why would I need to say any of this if it weren't true?" He dragged ferociously on his cigarette. "In plain words, I see a way of double-crossing them, and that's what I want to do . . ."

She now believed him, her manner less guarded, her eyes softer and more acceptant. "But I'm astonished," she said quietly.

He said: "I was never their man—the way your husband was; you could see that much yourself. But I had what they were after and they knew my price—oh, not money, something else —and only they could pay it. It's something I must have; so I made my bargain. But honor and faith are irrelevant, if not laughable, in this sort of an arrangement. I have grounds for demanding payment ahead of time, because the mission has broken down. I'm sure you see the point. I can't be expected to wait indefinitely while they replace your husband or work out a new plan. Simple psychology."

"You mean that you wouldn't then continue to serve them?"

"Not once I had what I've been promised."

"But . . . surely you couldn't succeed in such a thing."

"I've a good case."

"I mean—afterwards . . . They would kill you. You must know that."

He had never given it too much thought; he had never thought beyond getting Vorst in the water and drowning him slowly and painfully; he didn't care about anything beyond that. But the suggestion of his death now embarrassed him because it

157

had been spoken aloud by another person—by this person in particular, with whom he had traveled in both estrangement and intimacy; it was like the sudden revelation of an embarrassing ailment one has always kept to oneself. It would never be the same casual and private matter again. "My God," she said, elevating the idea. "They would kill you."

"Do you have the key?"

"If you're going to quit them, quit them and run away, don't expose yourself further . . ."

"That's logical if all you want is safety."

She was appalled at the thought of his death; but more appalled as it came home to her that he too was aware of the possibility and didn't seem to care. "Do you want to die?" she asked.

"Now, listen to me," he said, and then had nothing more to say. But he went on feebly: "I'm not your worry."

"No," she granted with some embarrassment. "I suppose you would go on with it in order to get whatever it is you're after if there were no other way . . ." She spoke almost as if a hope had been dashed.

Darsoss said: "What if your husband hadn't died? What would you be doing? Quitting—or going on with it?"

She said nothing and Darsoss then made his point. "Something was stronger than the guilt and the panic you may have felt," he said. "Otherwise you'd have been out of it. But you went on with it out of—what? Love? Respect? Devotion? Gratitude? Fear? What's the difference?"

"Not fear . . ."

"All right, not fear," he said, as if it didn't matter anyway.

"Ian was never anything but gentle and kind," she said.

"What about the key to that drawer?" he said quietly.

She was indecisive, and he said: "It destroys your last link with the network. Bear that in mind."

Almost immediately she said: "I'll get the key."

The ledger was where Mornier had said it would be, its pages filled with a partial accounting of the world's new perils. A cold, unused fireplace in the living room served as its place of destruction. "The binding is too thick to burn," Darsoss said as they both watched the consumption of the torn-out pages. "I'll get rid of it later." Then they were silent until the flames vanished. "From these ashes," Darsoss said, turning to look at her, "I hope your fiery phoenix will arise . . ." He smiled. "Or just one with a quiet, uneventful future . . ."

She looked at him, clearly ready to trust him, her suspicions gone. "Let me fix you a cup of tea or coffee before you leave," she said unexpectedly. "It would be no bother . . ."

She lowered her eyes, seemed embarrassed. Darsoss hesitated; he didn't know how he felt about the invitation; comfort meant nothing to him; it could compromise one, and he almost reveled in its absence; in the cold, the rain, the barren rooms he lived in, so much the Spartan with the fox under his tunic. But he said: "All right."

They sat in the tiny kitchen while the tea steeped some minutes later, at first in silence while Disa Quennel stared thoughtfully into space, and Darsoss smoked, strangely relieved. Part of the burden was gone. He looked at her. She seemed tired and thinner than she had ever been. In her eyes was that indefinable look of profit through sorrow.

"I would try to get as much sleep as possible, if I were you," he said.

"And once I'd got it," she said, "what then?"

"I wouldn't stay on alone here too long," he said.

"Perhaps not," she said, and then considered her next thought for a moment before saying: "And if I were you . . . I shouldn't try what you have in mind . . ."

Darsoss didn't answer her.

She said: "You see? It's futile, isn't it? No one is anyone else . . ."

He dipped his cigarette ash. "What you're really saying is, break the bargain but don't try to collect on it—as if that would make the difference. But it wouldn't. Just breaking the bargain is enough to put them in a furor; you don't need to do any more than that."

"You seem almost light-hearted about it," she said.

"I like a good joke now and then," he said.

"Yes. But who has the joke? You? No. In Danish we have a word—*vanvid*. You could translate it to mean 'gallows humor.' "

Darsoss smiled. "Don't worry about it. Nothing will happen anyway," he said.

"I think if someone plays the Russians false, the one thing to do is run far away and hide," she said with undeniable wisdom.

"Now, listen. It's too bad you know anything about it at all. I only wanted to tell you something you could understand, so that you would trust me and be convinced that we were on the same side and that you were safe. But not out of kindness. You had to know what I was doing if I was to feel safe myself, in case they decided to check up on me. Do you see?"

"Yes . . ."

"So don't give me credit for generosity. I don't deserve it, I don't want it. And I don't want your concern or fear. I am acting purely in self-interest. You should never worry about people who do that. They bring things on themselves. Anyhow, I'm not worried; I see light at the end of a dark tunnel, that's all that counts."

"Yes . . . You're different now than before . . ."

Darsoss inhaled deeply on his cigarette and then gazed at the coal end as he exhaled. He said: "The world is an asinine place; and I don't look for absolutes, and I've no allegiances, no devotions, no political beliefs. But nothing has ever gone more against my grain than acting as an agent for the Russians . . ." He trailed off, torn between a growing impulse to confess, a new sensation, and his adherence to the idea of never explaining anything to anyone.

She said: "There is something within us, something far beneath the surface, that says: 'Yes, this is right; no, that is wrong; and here is something else—both right *and* wrong.' "

Darsoss looked at her and she returned the look. They had gone from one conspiracy into still another; it had drawn them into the intimacy of people trapped together underground or in an elevator between floors. She drew a breath. "I think that is what God is—perhaps that and nothing more . . ."

He said nothing, and she then looked at the tea, saw that it was ready, and began, in silence, to pour. She sat stirring slowly for a moment or two and then said: "Ian didn't know how I felt about . . . what we were doing . . ."

After a brief pause, Darsoss said: "Didn't he?"

"No," she said. "Otherwise he would not have allowed me to be a part of it . . ."

Darsoss didn't for a moment believe it, but it was obviously important to her to be able to think so, or, at least, to say as much to Darsoss. It got under his skin, but all he said was: "Should you have told him?"

"I couldn't have—oh, there were so many reasons . . ." She looked directly at Darsoss and said quietly: "You mustn't think that you saw all sides . . . I didn't believe in communism; but I believed in Ian's wish to do what was right . . ." She paused and then recalled: "Do you remember how he once made a toast to a world without famine or fear?" Her face, which had become chalk-white in recent days, flushed a little with the thought. "He meant that; that was what he wanted . . ."

Darsoss didn't want to upset or irritate her and he could not allow himself to react honestly. "Yes, I remember," he said.

"It all sounded fine," she said sadly. "But there was something wrong . . ."

Darsoss could see that she wanted to talk and he was more than willing to let her.

She looked into her teacup and said: "It all seems so very long ago when we met—London during the blitz . . ." She thought back to it. Darsoss watched her steadily. "I was attending school; I wanted to become a translator; I was studying; I had no money. I secured a permit to work as a housemaid, I wasn't allowed anything else . . . I was *very* poor . . ." She smiled faintly to think of it. "I possessed one pair of stockings. I never wore them in the street when I had to go anywhere— I needed to walk everywhere, I couldn't afford bus or tube. I would put my stockings in my purse and then take them out and put them on when I got to wherever I was going—classroom or wherever it may have been . . . It preserved the stockings but my legs were always blue, because it was wintertime . . ." She looked at Darsoss, who was listening intently. "I was huddled in a bomb shelter during an alert when Ian appeared. No other person was there. It was almost the sort of meeting one expects to see in the cinema. Nothing else about it was like that . . ." She paused, thoughtful, and determined to put things in the right way, and then said: "The key to Ian's nature was immediately apparent to me: his satisfaction came through giving of himself, toward helping others. I was in such dreadful difficulty at that moment, I shan't go into it . . . But he knew . . . He arranged for my tuition, which I did not ask him to do, so that I was able to make ends meet—a loan, he called it, until I completed my studies and secured employment as a translator. He said nothing of love, nothing of passion—until he asked me to marry him. And little then; Ian wasn't intense in that way—

he gave a different sort of love and got a different sort of love in return—something decidedly not like anything in the cinema." She stopped as if she had said too much and yet not enough all at the same time. "He'd never been well, of course. Perhaps that was the answer to many things. Perhaps his own hardship made him so keen to the hardships of others . . ."

Darsoss thought back to the night he had met Quennel and how his charitable nature had been able to withstand the hardship of Miles Lawson. He wanted to tell her she was the victim of a hoax. He merely waited.

"He brought my mother out of Denmark through Sweden," she went on, "and arranged for her to live out of London so she wouldn't be subjected to the raids. He needn't have . . ."

"Perhaps he wanted it that way," Darsoss ventured.

"She lived with us here until her death."

"Do you think it was against his will?"

She shook her head. "No . . . But I owed him so very much. More than that—it seemed as if one would be safe and right to do anything he would ask . . ."

Darsoss said carefully and with great restraint: "But it wasn't . . ."

"Not unless you felt as he did," she said. "You can't force that, I discovered."

"What do you think he felt?" Darsoss asked.

"He wanted a better world," she answered in an almost questioning tone. She added sagely: "As he saw it . . ."

"Yes," Darsoss said, holding back with difficulty, he so much hated everything Quennel had stood for, more at this moment than ever before. "Yes, as he saw it."

"But one can't take the action of God . . . even with the best of intentions . . . I think that was what was wrong . . ."

She was trying to find an answer to whatever it was that she now felt; Darsoss was moved to guide her. "Was there no more than that?" he queried in a cautious tone of reason.

"I don't know," she said. "But of the three of us, he was the one who believed—you didn't, and neither did I. That makes him different . . . He could perhaps condemn us for it with more justice than we could claim for ourselves . . . I don't know . . ."

Darsoss, fully realizing it was none of his business, had to voice his opinion. "Listen," he said gently. "His convictions were less than he told you they were."

"But he was sincere in what he believed . . ."

Darsoss crushed out his cigarette and looked at Disa Quennel's searching eyes. It was Quennel's very sincerity that most offended him, because it was a form of his supreme egotism, his ability to place himself above his community—faulty and corrupt, yes, but not worse than any other, and, since it was not founded on three-in-the-morning intrusions by secret police, and extralegal acts of confiscation, incarceration, and execution, better than most. "I think Marxism-Leninism as practiced by Stalin may have withered for him long ago," Darsoss had to say, "but not whatever it was that first drove him into communism . . . Hatred for his governess, perhaps . . ."

"Do you really think that?"

"Yes. He seethed with hatred," Darsoss said, ready, once begun, to continue on to the end of it. "I know. I've had the experience myself."

"Hatred? Ian?"

"A smile doesn't hide it," Darsoss persisted as calmly and quietly as he could. "What he did was an act of hatred. That's why he did it easily. He hated England; he had to have. No man betrays his own society out of love; it has to have given him some reason for deep anger and grievance, real or imagined. He couldn't do it otherwise; he would wind up like you—in agony every step of the way; or like poor Miles Lawson . . ."

Tears had sprung to her eyes; nothing else moved, but her eyes were filled, one tear welling up and spilling through the lower lashes and onto her cheek.

Darsoss had sudden and deep regrets. "I know this was not the best time to say that sort of thing," he told her, looking right at her. "But I think it is urgent that you realize something, and I think that if you let this particular time pass without doing so—you may never. And I think that would be . . . unfortunate." He paused, then said: "Whatever debt you may have had—you've more than paid it."

There was silence. She brought out a handkerchief and used it quickly and as if trying not to be noticed.

"But who am I to tell you that?" Darsoss said quietly.

She looked at him but didn't answer and he grew desperately

uncomfortable. She looked away and they sat in silence for long moments. Darsoss sipped some of the tea and then said: "Perhaps I'd better leave now. Don't bother to see me out. Goodbye . . ."

He left her sitting there alone in the kitchen. She hadn't even turned to watch him leave, hadn't tried to stop him, and a chill of astonishment pursued him into the street and through the misty night. It was just right for entertaining any lugubrious thoughts you might have had—all of your misgivings and longings. Darsoss walked along in battle with unanswered questions and all the doubts that grew in near-silence and fog.

That Quennel was not yet cold in his grave—more exactly, that his ashes were not yet cold—had seemed insufficient reason to remain silent and tolerate the vestiges of an old misconception. But what right had *he*, Darsoss? Had he something better with which to replace an old misconception? The question remained there in the middle of nowhere as he continued to walk along, smoking, his feelings as clouded as the night itself.

3

He awakened after five hours of fitful sleep. When the phone rang he knew it was she. "Good morning," she said, as if she had just come out of a trance.

He sat on the edge of his bed with a sense of loss he resented, with desire that seemed remote, which he also resented. "Good morning," he said.

Her voice was a little diffident and strained. "I've never called you on the phone before. But I wanted to say—good-bye. I hope you don't mind . . ."

"Not in the least," he said, not sure whether he minded or not. "How are you?"

"I don't know altogether . . . It's stupid of me; I'm such a fool, I finally realize. I've always suspected it, I suppose . . ."

Darsoss felt a sudden twitch of the nerve endings. "Are you at home?" he asked.

"No. A public phone. Did I awaken you?"

"No. I've been up for hours; out and back already."

"Stupid of me . . ."

"Why do you keep saying that?" he said.

"I don't know. I suppose I'm nervous . . ."

"Are you?"

"Somewhat. The weather is foul, isn't it?"

"Isn't it always?" He was beginning to grow impatient; his detachment wasn't complete enough; it had been just the day before.

"I was afraid you would go away and we wouldn't say good-bye . . . It's unorthodox, I know, to be concerned about that at this time. But then life hasn't been . . . well, you know . . ."

"Yes," he helped her. She was a woman alone, calling a friend, the brand-new widow from a marriage in which paternalism had been dominant and duty exceeded passion. "It needs no explanation."

"Eyebrows would arch, wouldn't they?"

"Arched eyebrows are woefully ignorant as a rule," he said. "They arch when they should remain straight; they furrow when they should arch."

"Yes . . ."

"What will you do now?" he asked because he could think of nothing else and it seemed a respectable and conventional thing to say. "Do you have family? You do, of course."

"They've their own lives; why disrupt them? I shall be quite all right; it's very nice of you to think of that . . ."

"Not really."

"It is . . . Could we meet? Or is that brazen?"

"Brazen? There's nothing new in our meeting . . ."

"Yes, but not without . . ."

"Don't go into that on the phone—even a public one," he said evenly. "The point is, I'm busy. I don't know when I'll get free."

"Of course. I understand."

"I'm telling you the truth," he said. "But there's an inn in Datchet. It's a long way out, before you get to Windsor. You would need to take the Green bus, but I don't think we should meet any closer in, and it would be better if I didn't come to your house."

"All right . . ."

"I'll get there some time just after five o'clock."

"Yes . . . That's all right . . ."

Then they were finished and Darsoss sat there in silence that seemed to mock him. He felt threatened from within. Why had he agreed to see her again? No one was watching any longer; and even if they were, how light the consequences had proved to be—the menace of a bronze lion, or the gargoyles that overlook European cities: they are there and easily grown accustomed to. Then why? He didn't want a woman or a friendship; he wanted his hatred, whole and untouched. He wanted nothing else. It required all of his attention. Extinction threatened fires that weren't stoked. He realized that he should never have given his opinion; he should have left her to make her own inventory in her own way; if the poison roots of a hoax remained in the soil, so should it have been. There was more of which to be wary than a moment's cowardice or a blow on the head or death itself.

Now he went about a certain step in the process to which he hoped to devote only a little time. At three-thirty that afternoon, he came out of a sharp wind that would have taken his hat but for a quick save, and into the vestibule of an apartment building in Shepherd Market. He knocked on the door of flat Number 3 and was admitted by Brian Mornier.

"Come in, old boy. Bliss should be along in just a moment or two. I trust you've had success."

"This your flat, son?" Darsoss asked, strolling past him to a living room alive with Ashanti wood carvings and Masai ceremonial masks, spears and swords on the walls. "It's dazzling."

The tall, blond boy, whose looks were marred by childhood pockmarks, smiled. "Helps me to look my part, you know," he said, brushing off the assault. "Actually I do like this sort of thing, strangely enough. It's a part of my background I can't quite bury. Ambivalence, you know."

"Yes, there are contradictions in all of us," Darsoss said. "I guess your Dad takes care of all this, doesn't he?" For some reason he had zeroed in on this young man; it was perverse, but he had no desire to quit.

"I've an income," the other said with equanimity. He was hopeful of striking back sometime in the future.

"Just ragging you a bit, Brian," Darsoss said with a smile. Now that he had double-crossed them he was feeling somewhat expansive; the sense of growing control was responsible. He knew something they did not know. "Just kidding."

"That's perfectly all right. What about the ledger?"

There was a knock at the door. With an air of annoyance Mornier went to let Bliss in.

"I see we're meeting right in the heart of Mayfair," Darsoss said with a kind of fake pleasantry.

Bliss rubbed his hands together to kindle some warmth. "Do you find it chic?" he said with a smile of mistrust and innate dislike.

"Convenient, anyway," Darsoss said. "I was getting pretty tired of chasing out to East Putney and Shooter's Hill."

"So sorry," Bliss said. "But as long as we're not in public it doesn't matter."

"I should have thought of that myself. But then that's why you're the RD and I'm just a drone."

"Do you have the notes?"

"I've already asked that question," Mornier said, standing in back of Bliss like a gifted apprentice. "And I've the strangest feeling the answer is no."

"You're absolutely correct," Darsoss said, stationed near the bookshelves under a painting of a white hunter carrying an elephant gun. "There was nothing in the file of that description," he said, his hands in his coat pockets, his hat unremoved. "Or anywhere else among Quennel's belongings in that house."

Bliss's cheeks were pinched with cold. His face was otherwise marked with patience but some disbelief. "Are you sure?" he said. "Did you search thoroughly?"

"I just said so," Darsoss said, looking at Mornier's doubting eyes.

"Sometimes one overlooks something," Bliss said. "You received complete co-operation, I trust." He seemed unruffled by the report. "No resistance. The woman is in mourning, of course."

"Complete co-operation."

"I can't understand it," Mornier said. "I know that ledger was there. You couldn't have looked in that drawer."

"All right, Brian," Bliss cautioned.

"He put it there in my presence," Mornier insisted.

Darsoss shrugged and pulled out his cigarettes. "Maybe he put it somewhere else afterwards," he said casually, and then began to light up.

"Where? Nothing was better than that locked file drawer."

"Maybe he shoved it up his ass before he died," Darsoss said. "In that case, it's gone up in smoke."

Mornier's face froze. "You could go up in smoke yourself," he said.

Darsoss said: "Just looking for an answer that'll satisfy you, son."

"Let's stop the bickering and come up with an answer that satisfies us all," Bliss said. "Obviously we need to think of something else."

"While you're thinking, I'll be in Berlin," Darsoss said.

Bliss looked at him sharply. "I shouldn't, if I were you," he said like a friend giving advice.

"Well, you're not. But thanks." Darsoss then felt the need for some prudence. "I'll start back the moment I've concluded my business with the Bureau," he said. "By then you may be off the ground with everything."

"Just a moment," Bliss said. "There's a small but important matter to consider, if you can spare a moment of your precious time."

By now Darsoss had moved to the living-room entrance abutting on a darkened foyer. He turned and looked at Bliss, who said: "A discussion of Mrs. Quennel is in order. I don't think she can be completely overlooked. While perhaps she is now obsolete as an active part of this mission, she is not divorced from it; she knows what there is to know. I think that factor requires some evaluating, don't you, Johnson?"

Darsoss frowned a little and fluttered a hand noncommittally. "In what sense?" he managed to say casually.

Bliss, his coat and hat removed, his arms folded in front of him, paced a few feet back and forth in the center of the room. Mornier's eyes followed him and shifted to Darsoss when a reply was in order. "What do you think of her?" Bliss said. "Would you trust her?"

Darsoss' heart skipped a beat; he was not sure why. "You yourself said she was as reliable as hell," he pointed out as if they were discussing an automobile engine. "Better than two trained agents, who might double-cross you, I believe was the way you put it."

"Yes, that's right. But that was when Quennel was alive. Now she hasn't the same incentive, has she? Remember this is academic for the moment; it's simply the sort of thing men in our position should do as a matter of routine."

"I agree." Darsoss shrugged, dragged on his cigarette, and said: "I see no reason not to trust Mrs. Quennel, if that's what you want to know."

"Aha. That's fine. As I recall, you were very leery of her when you discovered she was in the game. I had to talk my lungs out to convince you she was safe." He smiled in reflection. "What happened to change your mind?"

Darsoss was afraid to shrug again; a show of indifference went just so far before it boomeranged. "How do I know?" he said, mildly testy, maybe a touch bored. "I suppose you were convincing."

"Is that all?"

"She did her job, that's the main thing, and she caused no fuss," Darsoss said.

"Yes."

"It's my opinion that she wants nothing except to be left alone," Darsoss said. Then he did shrug. "I'd say she was basically a person who lives inside of herself—someone who can spend a lot of time alone."

"A recluse?"

"No, not that extreme. But someone who enjoys solitude. A quiet, unobtrusive existence."

"Hmm. I mean, you must remember that she knows who you are," Bliss said, his hands tightly clasped, his two index fingers steepled into a tight point. "The hazard is all the greater for being sketchy sometimes. While it's hard to see in exactly what way that could work against you, there's no denying it would be better if she didn't know you."

Darsoss suspected a possible trap somewhere; something went along the surface of his skin, then was gone. "What are you getting at?"

"What I'm getting at simply is that you are a part of this network," Bliss said, looking right at him. "If you are in jeopardy, so are the rest of us. If Mrs. Quennel knows you, we are all only that little bit more safe than you are should she not be as reliable as you're so sure she is."

"I've told you what I think."

"Would you feel better if she were—shall we say, neutralized?

Don't misunderstand me; I mean taken somewhere in the country and well cared for—a protective custody, you could say."

Darsoss was afraid to clear his throat. Bliss went on: "Of course, that does have its drawbacks. Once you circumscribe someone in that way you build his own sense of jeopardy. He becomes defensive and as a result more dangerous than he may have been to begin with. I mean, where does it end? So actually you're left with a choice of either leaving well enough alone or—going all the way, I suppose."

"Why don't you dig into her background and get something on her?" Darsoss said with raspy contempt. "Maybe she'll commit suicide and save you all this brainwork."

Darsoss then wondered if he hadn't gone too far as Bliss went a shade white and said: "You really should learn to censor some of the things that pop into your head, Johnson. One day someone who doesn't know you quite so well is likely to misunderstand your particular brand of charm." He was always able to fall back on the control bred through generations of dealing with tenant farmers at home and excitable colored peoples abroad.

Darsoss was neither. He said: "Well, then, stop talking like a Bulgarian spy with a knife up his sleeve. For you *are* an English*man*."

Bliss smiled. "But like all, eccentric. Perhaps some day you'll sing that all the way through for us."

"When I'm in good voice," Darsoss replied, ready to walk out.

There was a moment's silence and then Bliss said, "Goodbye, Johnson," with an unexpected ring of finality in his voice, and then turned his back and walked to the bookshelves. He may have wished to give the impression he had washed his hands of dealing directly with Darsoss and would exercise a more effective method of getting things done from then on.

Darsoss was unmoved, but as a parting gesture that cost him nothing, he said: "Think of it as compassionate leave. It won't take long. Just a few days. What's a few days more or less in an epoch like the one that's just begun? Right? Right. Well . . . cheerio, gentlemen."

And as Darsoss was closing the foyer door behind him, he could hear Mornier saying: "I'd like to conduct my own search for that ledger. Nothing less would satisfy me."

Darsoss nearly brought himself to turn back and say: "Stay

clear of Mrs. Quennel," but thought better of it. They were no danger to her; she would be safe, he was sure. That would have to be the forecast from any logical point of view.

4

The inn at Datchet was half-timbered and charming and easily attained because it was along the Green Line route to Windsor. That was why he had selected it; it was out of London, yet accessible without an automobile, and Darsoss was able with little difficulty to deposit his Valpak and typewriter at the airport en route.

Disa Quennel was sitting in the lounge, wearing the coat with the cheap fur collar; a woman not new to anything but better for it, awaiting an important arrival and unmindful of the scrutinies of strangers, the attention of some of the local bloods, the vagrant thoughts, the wandering eyes.

"I couldn't sleep last night," she began immediately. "And after you'd made such a point of my getting as much sleep as possible."

They sat side by side on a cushioned wooden bench in a room with a low beamed ceiling, a crackling fire, and a stone floor covered by hooked rugs.

"Forget anything I may have said yesterday," he said. "Anything and everything."

"You think you hurt me," she said knowingly. "But you didn't . . . After you left I couldn't get any of it out of my mind—all that had happened to the three of us, and what it meant, what the survivors were left with . . ."

The landlady came over and asked: "Will you have something from the bar?"

"Sherry for me, please."

"A double whiskey."

"Thank you."

Darsoss smoked and dipped an ash. Disa Quennel said: "I don't know what we are to each other, it would be very difficult to describe . . . It's as if we haven't caught up to whatever it is . . . But I want to say something to you—because soon we shall say good-bye and that will be the end of it . . ."

"Yes, that's right. That should make it easier."

"It doesn't."

Darsoss looked at her and knew he was drawn to her; whether as an object of sympathy—someone in need of protection, a woman alone against all odds—or out of his own loneliness, he could not say. Perhaps both. The thought of Bliss and Mornier ran nervously through his mind. "Then maybe you'd better think twice before you try," he said.

"Don't be afraid," she told him, as if she would never do anything to make things difficult. "It's a question. And, of course, you don't need to answer . . ."

"All right."

She waited just a moment or two. Then she said: "Why do you want to kill yourself?"

Darsoss said: "What makes you think I do?"

"It's very plain," she said, her voice soft and tragic. "Isn't it plain to you? . . . It must be."

"Maybe it appears that way, but it's not true. There is something I must do. You know that. There are risks in doing it, that's right. But if anything happens to me, it will happen incidentally, not through forethought on my part. The French say, *en passant*. And that's the way it is."

"Is it that unchangeable, this thing?"

"Listen," he said in a kind and confidential tone. "I've crossed a line I can never really recross. No country, no soul, and even your employer holds you in contempt. I couldn't let all of that stand for nothing . . ."

She said: "Yes, and I am the same."

"No, you can truly say that you were used. I can't. But it doesn't matter now. That's the price. Right or wrong, I've paid it."

"For this thing . . ."

"Yes."

"What is it?"

He knew she had approached it breathlessly and with great effort. He gave her an almost avuncular look. "Would you really want to know?" he said, shaking his head up and down with foregone certainty. "You really wouldn't, now, would you?"

She said: "I really would"—she looked down—"if you would tell me . . ."

"Afterwards, you'd be sorry," he said.

"But I would know."

"Is that so important to you?"

"It seems to be, doesn't it?" There was a note of surprise in her voice, and a hint of embarrassment. "But I don't mean to . . . pester . . ."

"Listen; people are always sure they can stand anything you have to say before they hear what it is. Then you tell them your secret and they're appalled."

"Would it appall me?"

"I think there's little doubt of it."

"Perhaps I would appall you as much . . ."

"You? How?"

"With something of my own."

She looked at him, soft but somehow challenging, and he said: "I don't think so. But only because nothing appalls me. That doesn't mean I would advise you to try."

"You don't want to hear anything, you mean . . ."

"I'll hear anything you might wish to say. But you might be sorry once you had said it, do you see?"

"Perhaps . . ."

"You can't share some things with anyone. Oh, you can give them facts and figures. But that's not enough. They would need to share your consciousness, and that's still quite a trick, isn't it?"

"Is it? I don't know . . ."

"Certain things are not transferable—certain emotions, certain thoughts. We're all as black as the devil inside, in one way or another. I don't mean evil, necessarily, but beyond understanding . . ."

"Yes . . . That's me, I think—black as the devil . . . Ian is dead less than a week, and I have no feeling about it—no sense of responsibility to him . . ."

Darsoe said nothing, and Disa Quennel looked at him. "Are you appalled?" she asked.

"No," he said evenly. "How can you be responsible to a dead man?"

The landlady came to them with the drinks. "There you are," she said, and her good spirits were jarring. "Just signal for more; I'll see you."

She left them, and Disa Quennel said: "But there's no feeling, you see. All the feeling I had at first was for myself . . . Now that's gone and I am left with no feeling."

He had not trespassed, he had not affronted or scathed her the night before; he had opened wide the door to this very moment. Surely he couldn't have wanted to.

"It sounds very cold and callous when one puts it into words, doesn't it?" she said.

Darsoss took a deep breath, gazing at her with a growing sense of association through affliction. He thought fleetingly of those two happily wretched people with their look of drudgery whom he had seen in The Coachman in Streatham. He said: "You and I know your life was hell because of him. What is there to mourn?"

Then she said nothing and they sat there in silence, without looking at each other, as if something further had to come about of its own accord before they could say anything more to each other.

"Mourning is a fake thing most of the time," Darsoss finally went on. "People put on the show that's expected of them."

"I couldn't mourn," she said simply. "I was surprised to discover how it really is with Ian dead. At first there was shock. Then a sense of relief. Then guilt. Now there is nothing. There is so much the feeling of Ian's never having been." She paused, then said: "Do you see why I must be as black as the devil?"

"Do you want me to say you are?"

"Am I?"

"I've already said you've nothing to mourn, in my judgment," Darsoss said. "It's what *you* feel that matters."

"When my father died, my mother cried for days."

"I saw you cry, if that's important to you."

"For myself . . ."

"How do you know why she was crying?"

"I know."

"All right. Death isn't enough. You and Quennel had no marriage. You were Trilby, and now you've awakened." He paused, knew she needed an acquittal, and then said: "What astounds me is how a woman can live with a man five years—no matter how exalted his worldly status—and never question his divinity in all that time, and think when her decent impulses asserted themselves that she was warped for having them."

"It wasn't that, just that he was good and kind."

"As one is to an inferior."

"He was brilliant and . . ."

"And he had you bamboozled with guilt and inferiority and eternal gratitude and it worked just beautifully for him."

"He was not so bad a person as that," she said dispassionately. "And he knew so much. Who was I?"

"He used the toilet just like anyone else . . ."

She said nothing. Darsoss wanted no further discussion of Quennel and he suspected she had gotten all she needed by now. "So you feel nothing," he said. "We won't tell the neighbors . . ."

"You mustn't be that irreverent. Neither of us should."

"Sorry. It seems to come out that way."

"Last night, after you had left," she said, looking right at him, "I thought not about Ian, but about you; because it was too late to think about him, but not too late to think about you. I couldn't help myself; I didn't set out to think about you. But I did . . ."

Darsoss cleared his throat nervously, but said nothing.

"I thought about what you had done, and what you were going to do—that you would be dead, perhaps, in a matter of days . . . That's the point of it all, the thing I can recognize in you. You don't care, and that is a type of suicide . . ."

"Now, look . . ."

"In Denmark suicide is . . . frequent," she said. "My father . . . died from his own hand." She paused and said: "Last night you mentioned Miles Lawson's name and what he had done. I think of my father when I think of Miles. I suppose I was feeling very low and so I . . . well, you saw for yourself."

"I'm sorry," Darsoss said.

"My father was a sensitive man," she said. "He felt everything very deeply. He could not earn enough to support my mother and us children. It was too much for him. He grew more and more depressed . . ."

"I'm sorry," Darsoss said.

"He was good and he was intelligent and honest . . . My mother and my brothers and I could have stood for anything but what he did . . . Just as Norma Lawson could have . . ."

"Now, listen to me," he said. "You have the wrong idea and you seem to want to cling to it . . ."

She had stopped talking and it was clear that she would probably not go further with it. But the intimacy had become a foregone conclusion, and Darsoss felt it necessary to say: "And even if you were right about that part, I would never leave a close survivor to fend for herself . . ."

Now she was saying nothing and Darsoss found that he was going forward. "I think that's what counts the most—whether you risk your life or deliberately set out to end it: who is left behind? In my case, there is no one . . . Anyhow, I think you make more of it than it's worth. You're kind and sweet to do so. But don't . . ."

"You have no relatives . . . or friends?"

"Do they matter?"

She didn't answer and he said: "I was married," and realized that he wanted to let her know that much. "My wife is dead."

She looked as if she had been stuck with a pin but held the pain down and uttered no sound. "I am sorry . . ."

Darsoss licked his lips, made an ineffectual little gesture with his hands and brought his cigarette to his lips. "So am I," he said softly and wearily. Then he looked into the fire. "She was murdered by the Germans."

Now her tears appeared. Darsoss both loved and hated the sight of them. "I see," she murmured, looking into his eyes as if all had been revealed to her, as if all of his heart and soul were suddenly captured in just a single snatch of conversation, a fragment of his thoughts. "I see . . ." It came from deep inside of her.

"Nothing is ever any good after such a thing," he said. "All you want is revenge . . ." He swallowed nearly all of his drink.

"Revenge?" she repeated. "Against whom?"

"Against whom do you think?" he said. "The murderer."

She didn't answer. He looked away, tossed his cigarette into the fire, wondered about all of it for a moment, then said: "That's what has kept me alive until now."

"Is there a *single* murderer?"

"I know his name," Darsoss assured her quietly. "I know where he is. Oh, yes, there is a single murderer."

She was silent for a moment and then said: "I remember when we were alone in the teashop the first time," she said, "you were talking about how to create illusions of emotion. You said that one used a memory in order to act out a role . . . You were suddenly lost in a state of terrible longing and there was a look of deep sorrow in your eyes. You said you were

176

remembering a moment in your past . . . I didn't think to ask then what it was, it was none of my concern . . ."

"Well, now you know."

"And somehow it's the reason for everything else, isn't it?" Her voice grew hushed and guarded.

He was surprised at first but then he realized he had told her as surely as if he had made a direct statement. She was a sentient person in so many ways—she couldn't have missed it.

"Yes," he said. "It is."

"You talked of revenge," she said very cautiously.

"I prefer the word justice," he said, sensing a touch of pleasure at the thought of telling her all about it.

5

It assumed new proportions, and became more immediate, like the revival of a well-remembered play: the starkness remained; it wore well; and the same sense of dejection finally took hold, the futility and the anguish. Tears appeared in Disa Quennel's eyes, but she had said little. The landlady had brought Darsoss two more drinks—singles—within an hour; it had taken that long to tell Disa Quennel the essentials, to hand into her keeping a part of himself.

They sat silently for several moments, the fire burning down to where it would soon need a log, Darsoss finishing his drink and smoking his cigarette. Then Disa Quennel said: "Now I know you."

"Yes, I'm afraid you do," he said.

She said: "You asked just a while ago, how can one be responsible to someone who is dead? Well, one can . . . One definitely can . . ."

She sipped some of her sherry and Darsoss sat there without moving.

"She would hate what you are doing . . ."

"I was insane to tell you," Darsoss said quietly.

"Do you expect to achieve peace when you"—she lowered her voice to a whisper—"kill this man?" She drank some more of her sherry—still her first—and then raked her upper lip with her teeth. "Do you think you will die happy because of it?"

"No one dies happy," he said.

"One should," she said.

"You're right," he said. "One should."

The trace of a hopeless smile was on her face as she looked into her glass. Darsoss found himself appraising her suddenly. Something had evolved between them without notice, like a thing that has its genesis at night while one sleeps: a bud that is fully open to the morning light, sudden and unseen in its growth; or a field of frost arriving in the dark and surprising the early riser at dawn. He was conscious of curiosity he had not felt in long, cold eons of winter: an image of passion crossed his mind, a sexual posture in which this woman was his partner. It took him by surprise; excitement struck a light, maddening blow at all the right nerves and then danced away, leaving him mortified. "But you shouldn't try to save me," he said, a little hazily, looking at her lips wet from the sherry, her eyes frank and critical but sympathetic. "You might succeed and then you would probably regret it." He wanted to save himself from the dangers of the deception they had wandered into, two people alone and searching and not quite responsible for their actions. "Finish your drink, and we'll have dinner here, if you like," he said, taking out his cigarettes.

She said: "When you do it . . . after it's done—what then?"

He said: "The first impression you make is one of a far-off, distant creature of unshakable calm—cold-nerved and tranquil—much too beautiful to be believed. Finally, all that's left of that first impression is that you are much too beautiful to be believed."

She wasn't interested. "Have you ever thought beyond that?" she said.

"Right now, I don't want to think any further ahead than dinner," he said. He tossed his cigarette in the fire and took her hand. "Come. Take along your sherry."

The landlady seated them in an oak-paneled dining room not too far from the window with its umbral scape of trees and winter night. A few other people were seated elsewhere. Darsoss sat opposite Disa Quennel just the way a soldier might when taking the last desperate moments of his leave with a rueful lover or wife before going off to the front or on some exceedingly harrowing mission; spurious gaiety fared badly against the reality of the moment. The man always attempts to cushion things by acting unafraid and even nonchalant. This wasn't anything like that, of course.

"Shall we have wine?" he said, looking at her beautiful but cheerless face. "A Bordeaux, if they have one?"

He looked around to find the waitress. "Maybe we can get a bottle of Château Latour or Haut-Brion. They can make what we're eating less noticeable." He couldn't locate the waitress. "I once concerned myself with that sort of thing from time to time." He smiled. "Not lately, though."

"It seems mad being here this way," she said in a low voice, as if to thwart an eavesdropper. "Suddenly."

"Does it?"

"Like the unexpected sight of yourself in a mirror after you've had an accident . . ."

"Why do you say that?"

"There's death just in back of us," she said. "Death fresh in your heart and soul . . . murder your immediate objective"—her voice sank to a whisper—"crimes against the state . . . And here we sit eating and talking of whether or not to order wine with our dinners."

"I must admit you have a way of putting it," he said casually.

"Doesn't that strike you as mad?" she asked.

"I wouldn't know what sanity is," he replied calmly. "After a time you grow accustomed to almost anything."

"With each moment that passes I find it more and more difficult to imagine that I am sitting here with you in what has turned into a farewell dinner with wine and everything just before you leave to kill someone and then perhaps be killed in turn . . ." She shook her flaxen head, the consternation seething behind now steady eyes. "I'm a widow of five days sitting here with a man . . . And I want to be, that's the worst part of it . . ."

"Why not just forget everything else?" he said in the platonic way of someone trying to cajole a woman into letting her guard down, his reasons quite the opposite of the usual ones. "We've had our share of sweat, don't you think so?"

"All right," she said. "We're like two people who are getting ready to go to a Black Mass . . . But please, no wine . . ."

At that moment the waitress came over. "Did you want something, sir?" she asked.

"Coffee, I think."

"For two?"

"Yes."

"With sugar?"

"If possible."

The waitress walked off and Darsoss gave Disa Quennel his undivided attention. Women were women under all circumstances: they wanted to prevent or avoid violence; they wanted to save men from themselves; they wanted peace and security. "Listen, I don't know how anything will be afterwards," he said. Then he could find nothing more to say. They drank their coffee in silence. Darsoss was feeling somewhat leaden. Within a short time they left the inn.

The Green bus went along the Bath Road to London through the dark, strong winds sweeping in from the Salisbury Plain. They sat side by side over the right rear wheel. "I hope you'll be all right," he said feebly.

"Of course I shall."

"Listen . . ."

"Yes?"

Darsoss took a breath. "In case anyone should pay you a visit, don't let them know either in word or deed that you disapprove or that you're against them. Do you see what I mean?"

She needed no explanations. "The others . . ."

"Yes. It's all right as long as you do nothing to frighten them—to make them think you're cause for alarm. Don't express an opinion or make any sudden moves."

"I know."

"Brian Mornier is a member, by the way. Did you know?"

"No."

"Are you astounded?"

"I suppose I am."

"Just so you know about it. Do you know Arthur Havenhurst?"

"No."

"He's the man I know as Bliss. He's the head man, as far as I can determine. He's about fifty. Charm and good manners; the best of backgrounds, it sticks out all over. Those are the only two, I think. Chances are you'll never hear from them. But it's just as well that you're aware of them."

"All right."

"You'll be fine," he said stupidly, his eyes going anxiously toward the darkness marked with lights and dim silhouettes passing backward into the night.

"I'm not afraid . . ."

"Of course not—why should you be?" he said. But he was not altogether at ease at the thought of Bliss and Mornier. Of course he was sure that they had no logical reason to bother her unless she gave them cause. This she wouldn't do; soon she would probably be forgotten by the network of which she had so improbably been a part.

Darsoss looked at his watch. There was plenty of time. The airport was not too far ahead on the right. He said: "There's a chance that if I had been quicker or smarter or given more of myself than I gave—I could have saved her . . ." He looked directly at her. "I've never gotten that thought out of my mind. I live with it. Somehow it may have been because of me that she died."

"But how?"

"I'm not sure," Darsoss replied, and then said with low-keyed urgency: "You asked: 'What then?' I can only say, maybe that feeling will be gone. And that will be quite enough."

The conductor announced to the few passengers: "London Air Terminal."

Darsoss began to arise and Disa Quennel said: "But does someone who has died come back to life. . . ?"

"I get off here."

"What if the feeling doesn't go away?" she begged of him.

"Good-bye . . . Disa . . ."

She took his hand. "Do you wipe out the original crime?" she said in a hoarse whisper, her eyes pleading for logic and sanity; they were there for the taking.

"Good-bye . . ." He withdrew his hand as the bus began to draw to a halt a hundred yards or so before reaching the gateway to the airport. "Take care . . ."

"God bless . . ." She murmured the words and watched help-lessly as he departed.

Darsoss stood on the road after alighting till the bus had rolled by him on its way to London. Her face behind the window slipped away quickly and vanished, the eyes half afraid but eager for a chance, the mouth questing. Darsoss turned and walked toward the administrative and passenger structures far off in the distance. He walked alone and with unalterable purpose, cold and full of familiar poison. Nothing could wash *that* out of him.

He waited one hour in the passenger building before his plane departed. He smoked incessantly and tried not to think of Disa Quennel. But his sense of detail was pitiless; the last glimpse of her wouldn't let him rest. How much of themselves people leave behind; and how little they realize it. And the dead never know.

He paced slowly back and forth an untraceable journey in the large and coldly indifferent room. He smoked and considered his own damnation. It seemed wrong to seek any alternative to it. In a few minutes he would fly into the night, wintry and lonely as his soul, and that would be that. If all went well, within days Otto Vorst, who had undoubtedly enjoyed the task of slowly killing Anne Levi Darsoss, would be in his hands. He was sure nothing else mattered.

6

Hot or cold, Kholenko's manner never changed. He was the perfect state tool; he had an uncomplicated devotion to the denial of all requests and the single-minded unco-operativeness of a chess opponent. "Very simply, you had no warrant to come here," he said in a British accent sometimes heard on stage and in the movies. "The mission is still in effect. You've enormous gall."

Darsoss sat there, smoking as usual. It was the next day and he was trying to gather his scattered thoughts and figure out his best move without the knowledge of the two men he now faced, one of them a person he had never seen before, not Kalinin. "Do we have to talk in the presence of others?" he said, as if it were a breach of etiquette to do so.

"He understands no English," Kholenko said. "And his intelligence is that of a moron. You may speak freely, whatever it is."

"That's very interesting," Darsoss said. "Why is he here?"

"He's a useful person," Kholenko said cryptically.

Darsoss looked at the new man. His eyes were like the eyes

of anyone willing to kill a total stranger at the behest of others. He looked at Darsoss without special interest, his face the shape of an elongated egg, his lower lip tucked in stupidly, subhuman and bored. "If I told him to do so, he would put a bullet through your head—or the head of anyone else, for that matter," Kholenko said, no small flicker of amusement visible. "Since you're interested, there is only so much he is capable of. He is never sent anywhere by himself. But he has one rather captivating specialty. He seems to prefer firing into the ear. He carries a Luger because the nose can be easily inserted." Kholenko paused in his humorless recitation. "There seems to be some margin concerning the course of the bullet: through the middle-ear area and out the back of the skull; down through the roof of the mouth; out through the epiglottis, or perhaps the top of the head. It evidently varies from time to time, and death is not always instant. It seems to absorb his interest."

"I'm impressed," Darsoss said, stifling a simulated yawn. Then: "I don't trust the London network."

"What do you mean by that?"

"Oh, it's not a question of loyalty; it's just that now with Quennel dead, they're floundering."

"You mean Michael. That's the code name."

"No one ever told me. Anyhow, that's why I came to Berlin on my own. I wanted to discuss it with you and get a new set of instructions directly from you."

"That's the business of the network," Kholenko said. "You surely don't expect Berlin to plan and conduct tactical operations going on six hundred miles away, do you?"

Darsoss inhaled deeply on his cigarette and said: "You miss the point. There are no operations. I don't want to wait forever for them to get a bright idea. And I don't intend to . . ."

"Threats again."

"I just thought you should know; don't take the unfriendly view of everything, it's bad for your digestion. Bliss wouldn't tell you himself, but he's empty-handed. And my specialty is useless right now; there's no one there to talk, so there's nothing for me to memorize."

"Is that all?"

Darsoss didn't answer immediately. Had he left out anything? "No," he said. "What about Vorst?"

"Ah, I wondered when you would bring that up. I'd almost given up hope."

"Had you? You should know better. The fact is, I'm getting very sick of all this."

"Yes, but you seem more reasonable than ever before. I like that."

"Well, I'm getting older. There's no point in wasting energy needlessly. You know how I feel. I don't need to do a hopak about it every time I come in here. You people are on notice and you know it."

"The hopak is a very demanding dance," Kholenko remarked dryly. "Return to London. Your specialty shan't go to waste."

Darsoss looked at the murderer who stood off from Kholenko's desk, the apex of a triangle with the other two men who were seated. At times killing was probably a humdrum affair; but on other occasions there was fun to be had, undoubtedly. Darsoss said: "It'll go to waste if you try to screw me."

"Screw you?" Kholenko repeated for verification.

"You know."

"Oh, yes. But why would we?"

Darsoss shrugged ever so slightly. "You'd better not."

"Don't be difficult. We've been very patient with you."

"Stop it before I cry." Darsoss got up to leave. "I won't wait forever."

"You won't need to."

"Okay. I'll probably hang around about a week before I leave Berlin," Darsoss said. "So don't get nervous."

"Just behave normally, as always."

Darsoss snorted and walked to the door. "Where is my friend, by the way?" he said. "Or is that a state secret?"

Kholenko didn't answer immediately. "I'll convey your regards," he said, then pressed a button for Darsoss' escort.

As he was being driven through the falling snow to the garage in Charlottenburg, Darsoss sat thinking and looking as deeply into himself as he dared. The cruelties of a *déjà vu* were many and great—that instant when one can smell, taste, and feel the past, a particular moment of either bliss or agony that returns to torment one. The dank smell of the cellar of a farmhouse in Châteauneuf came back again and again like recurrent fever. It had been a Maquis base; the place of hope where the final words were exchanged, the promise of freedom given, where Darsoss had last looked into Anne's face, trusting but wise, a flicker of doubt in her soft, candid eyes, an air about her of preparation for the worst. Perhaps she had known in some mysterious way what her place was in this time of hatred and madness, that everything could not have come out well, after all. Darsoss became conscious of this only after he had parted from her to arrange for transportation to the pickup point outside Orléans; they could have been safe in London that very night. Her arrest took place just minutes before his return; his entire life was changed only minutes later. The incitement had endured from that day to this. Perhaps she *would* have hated what he was doing and what he had done; but that hadn't mattered, he had never even considered it. Somehow he had been less than he should have been—in wisdom, in courage, in the strength of his love. And he had known immediately what he must do, once the worst had been confirmed—not by the standards of anyone else, not through consultation or advice, nor in the face of community demands, but on the urgings of his own hatred and a septic desire for vengeance. Someone had sportively tortured the tender soul of the woman he had sworn to love and protect, taken her life slowly and harrowingly. That was what had led Darsoss to the very moment, to these thoughts and considerations, here on this hellish blue-cold day in this hellish blue-cold place. Nothing else. But now there was something from still another source—new and undeniable. Disa Quennel had asked him two mercilessly logical questions. Does someone who has died come back to life? Can the original crime ever be wiped out? They were logical, yes; but weren't the sentiments wishfully simple and naïve? Of course. The obvious concepts are the first to come to mind with the bare hope for bare guidelines; and how often they disappoint the best of people.

It was three in the afternoon when Darsoss reached the Club and went into the bar. Two or three people greeted him. "How's the book coming, Marco?" the CBS radio man asked.

"It blows the lid off everything," Darsoss said, and walked with a double Scotch to the telephone room, a flutter of excitement in the pit of his stomach.

As he took up one of the phones in the bank near the windows looking out to the furry snowfall, he hoped Kholenko hadn't noticed too much or attached great significance to whatever he had noticed. And a moment later he had managed to engage the English-speaking operator.

"I want to place a call," he said, "to Mrs. Disa Quennel in London; Maida Vale two five seven five . . ."

By the time he had come into Kholenko's presence, he had almost forgotten why he had made the trip. Something had happened: the embarrassing loss of an obsession had taken place. The fever of a crippling rage had subsided by itself: Vorst's life or death—the very thing that had governed his every waking moment and some while he slept—seemed secondary all of a sudden. Or at least there was room for something else, for the eagerness he now felt as he waited for the response to his call, for the sound of her voice.

"It's you," she said, a breath of joy escaping her. "Where are you?"

"Berlin," he said, trying to remember the details of what she looked like, and now, for the first time, he could not do so. "As soon as I got here . . . I began to miss you—much too much. Are you all right?"

"Yes . . . I can hardly believe it's you . . ."

"It's me, all right. Listen . . ."

"Yes . . ."

"Do you want to meet me somewhere? I know that's not the best way to put things, but—you understand, don't you?"

"Yes, yes. Where? Berlin?"

"No. And not London. The best thing would be somewhere like Amsterdam or Copenhagen, if you like . . ."

"Yes . . . But there are some difficulties . . ."

"Answer yes or no. The relatives in London?"

"Yes."

"Concerned about you, are they?"

"Somewhat . . . I mean, they seem concerned with—"

"With your future plans?"

"Yes . . ."

"Understandable. They mean well, of course. But don't worry about that. It will work out. How soon could you be ready to fly to—say, Copenhagen?"

"Not Copenhagen."

"Amsterdam, then. How soon?"

"A day. But how can I secure a travel permit? And . . . the relatives might be . . ."

"It will all be taken care of. Be ready and then wait for my call. Probably tomorrow afternoon. All right?"

"Yes . . ."

The hellish passion was cold and couldn't be rekindled; but something had taken its place. If only he could grab hold of it.

CHAPTER SIX

1

"At the present time there are an estimated ten thousand spies in Berlin," Vernon said with a faint air of amusement. "More than half of them are Russian, of course; the rest Western, some both Russian and Western."

He sat at a table in Pommler's with Darsoss, the place bulging with GI's, *Schatzis*, and miscellany, the three-piece band playing "Chattanooga Choo Choo" and giving the impression of an effort to curry favor. "There are reports made every sixty seconds," Vernon went on like a man who knew and enjoyed his subject despite its seriousness. "There isn't an item under the sun that isn't being reported on or lied about. Some of it is garden fresh. But most of it wilts. It's becoming a highly competitive field—information. Get it, sell it. If none is available, make it up." Vernon shook his head and drew on his pipe. "There've been drastic changes since our day," he said. "The emphasis is on the everyday, seemingly meaningless fragment. And that's what is swelling the ranks. How many pencils are sharpened each day at OMGUS? How many erasers are used? How many phone calls? How much toilet paper? If you can't steal a big secret, pile up enough peripheral facts and you might stumble on half a secret worth passing on." He looked around the room and said: "Out of fifty or seventy-five civilians in this place, fifty or seventy-five are either looking for information, trying to sell it, or willing to consider it."

Darsoss dipped his cigarette ash. "It always was a nice little town," he said.

"One of the best. Actually, it's too bad we have to use these people this way. It's bad for them and it could be bad for us. But that's not our fault. The Russians started it. So what could we do?"

"And there are plenty of people roaming loose who shouldn't be," Darsoss said. "Some of them pretty bad ones. But then we know that, don't we?"

"Well, not too bad, if we can help it—not on our side."

"Oh, I'm not criticizing, just remarking," Darsoss assured him lightly. "I mean, that's the way you have to play—if you're going to play at all. What else?"

Vernon said. "You know, the more we talk, the less casual the conversation sounds."

"You think so?"

"At first," Vernon said, "I had an idea that you might want to talk about that thing in Vienna. Remember? The news agency."

"Haven't you filled that yet?"

"It takes the right party. But I can see you're still something less than interested. Now, why do I get the feeling that you've a point to make?"

"Well, maybe because I've already made it," Darsoss said. "But there is something else, as a matter of fact. As you said not long ago, I see and hear things. You were wondering how I would handle it if I ever came across anything important. Now you're about to find out." By this time the band was playing "Deep in the Heart of Texas" and the revelers were doing the hand-clapping thing at the appropriate point.

Vernon said: "I think we ought to get out of here." He spoke in an unornamented tone, cold and direct. "To a room I *know* isn't wired," he added under his breath.

Through rain and sleet, through a brumous atmosphere tingling with cold, they went by taxicab toward Grunewald. Dim street lighting pointed to power shortages. A small car came suddenly out of a cross street as Darsoss and Vernon were being transported silently along Clay Allee, and their driver swerved to miss it. "*Himmel,*" he exploded, the cab losing traction, Darsoss tensing as a prolonged skid took place. "*Verfault verdammt geistesschwach!*" The collision was averted, the skid ended, and the journey continued, the driver muttering various epithets a moment or two longer. Darsoss relaxed; a man with responsibility was always more wary and anxious than a man who had none; he felt a heavy one now. Vernon looked at him and said nothing. The silence continued until the cab reached its destination.

It was a church, untouched by war, its cusp edged with ice, its large front doors closed, the sidewalk before it a sea of brown slush. The nave was large, the rows of pews broken by three aisles, and the altar was lit and watched over by a smooth stone Christ. One elderly woman in black was kneeling in the front row. Darsoss and Vernon sat down next to a pillar in the rear. "Is this your clearing house?" Darsoss said.

"I never feel safer anywhere," Vernon said, glanced toward the altar and added: "Go ahead."

"Can you arrange transportation for a civilian from London to—say, Amsterdam?" Darsoss said.

"You mean a travel priority? Why? That's loosening up now, anybody can get passage almost anywhere with very little delay."

"But not on short notice—say, a day or two."

"Is that all you want?" Vernon asked.

"There are complications. There could be an attempt to arrest the departure of this person."

"What does that mean?"

"That means the person will need protection."

Vernon said: "ABC. Who is this civilian? Why does he need protection? And what is your interest in him?"

Darsoss took a deep breath and said: "Did you have to pick this place? Now I can't smoke."

"Then talk fast and we'll get out of here."

Darsoss said: "Don't break in with questions and I'll give you what I know. MI5 have been running a half-assed surveillance on a British atomic scientist whom they suspect of being in contact with Soviet agents or their cutouts—that is, they were until last week, because the scientist in question died on them. He left a widow. She's the civilian to be gotten out of London. Her passage would need to be arranged and her protection would be against what is left of the London network. She knows nothing, but she might be making them nervous; and I think any move on her part to leave London right now would bring them in on her—that is, if she tried it on her own."

"When can I break in with questions?"

"If I can hand you part of the net—maybe all of what remains of it—my request would be more than justified, wouldn't it?"

"In other words, the atom scientist was guilty of whatever it was, and you know this to be a fact even though MI5 does not. Also this request is personal. Is that about it?"

"What I'm getting at is that if you see this woman safely onto a plane for Amsterdam, you'll automatically be saving her life and breaking the back of a Soviet spy ring in one stroke."

"But no names yet."

"But eventually."

"What does the woman have to do with it? Mrs. Atom Scientist. What is she to you?"

Darsoss licked his lips and frowned at the Virgin on the pillar next to him; he hadn't noticed her before. "Somebody I'd like to save a few bruises," he said.

"She knows nothing, but you know everything, is that it?"

"I was tracking a story. I came across it accidentally."

"Why didn't you hand it over to MI5? They're obviously not as bright as you are."

"This is cleaner."

"I think you're ad-libbing, Marco," Vernon said. "Otherwise you'd let me know how you know what you know."

"What kind of a deal can I get, Vernon?" Darsoss asked directly.

"I don't know what kind of a deal you're trying to make," Vernon said. "But I know you're trying to make some kind of a deal. Otherwise you'd have gone straight to the British with whatever you have. Or even the Boss—not me."

"The Boss isn't in Berlin, I've already checked."

Vernon nodded. "Care to wait for him?"

"No, I'd rather work it out with you first."

"Okay. Now let's not kid; it's about the woman, nothing else. She's under the gun in some way and you're disturbed by it. You are willing to trade whatever it is you know for a clean bill of health for her. I'd have to be dumber than I look not to see that."

Darsoss waited for several moments before saying: "There are a lot of bad numbers floating around, aren't there?"

Then there was silence; it seemed to stifle the nave, broken by the far-off shuffle of slippered feet somewhere in back of the altar. The woman in front rose, went to the altar, lit a candle, and crossed herself. Darsoss sat there, almost ready to move another step along.

"I'm getting at something with all this, Marco," Vernon said, looking at him. "Whatever it is you know—and I've an idea it's pretty high grade—the woman told you, didn't she? All right. I don't need an answer. I'm going to assume it's true; and with that in mind I can tell you that you'd be surprised how many Communist spies are married to each other, and work together as teams. Ideology and sex seem to go hand in hand in the brave new world."

Darsoss said: "Do you want to make a deal or not?"

"Sure. Once I know what kind of deal it is."

"Get her out of London. We can iron out the particulars later, for Christ's sake . . ."

Both men glanced toward the altar. "Careful, you'll be over-heard."

"What about it? Do you only make deals with ex-Nazis?"

"Take it easy."

"I can give you two important members of a network operating against British and American atomic weapons interests—both Englishmen, one highly placed in the Establishment. Say you're interested in the deal before you start demanding documentation."

"I just want to know it's there, Marco."

"It's there."

"Was the husband passing secrets?"

"Yes."

"To the people you're talking about?"

"Yes."

"And the wife wasn't in on it?" Vernon said, lightly incredulous. "You can't mean that, Marco."

"The woman knows nothing," Darsoss said. "I would know if she did, believe me."

"Maybe you do," Vernon said, tauntingly casual.

Darsoss gave Vernon a quick, contemptuous look.

"You might know all about it—or enough to be interesting,"

Vernon said. "Men in love—real or imagined—have been known to do all sorts of things. You could easily be protecting her, now, couldn't you? You are in love with her, aren't you?"

"What are you trying to do, Vernon?" Darsoss said in an angry whisper.

"What are *you* trying to do? No, don't tell me. I'll tell you. You're yelling stop thief; and while everyone is running on past you, you're letting one of the crooks hide in back of you."

"I'm bored, Vernon. And I need a cigarette."

"You don't look bored, Marco."

Both men rose automatically and began walking toward the entrance doors. Once outside they stood under the vaulting doorway arch, specks of snow eddying like dust as the fall subsided. Darsoss was smoking immediately. "I don't need to draw pictures for you, Marco," Vernon said. "You know damn well that if you were Security and knew who this woman was you'd go after her like a shot. You'd put her in a web and watch her struggle and when the right time came you'd devour her. And you know it. Be fair. Be objective. A man can't do what you're referring to without his wife's knowledge."

Darsoss was silent; a feeling of fatigue weighed heavily on him as they stood there in the cold and damp night, an empty Catholic church in back of them, as sacred as the whorehouse in Pankow where he had met with Kalinin so long ago, and just as passionless; this was hard, tedious work, but it had to be done.

Vernon said: "But . . . trades are possible if they're good enough. Why? Because at least half the time, people aren't nearly as important as things. People sitting in prison are of no earthly good to us if we lose something tangible by their doing so."

Darsoss glanced at Vernon, who went on: "The point is, if she's not in too deep—and *if* the exchange makes sense, something might be arranged." He paused. "But one thing I'd need 1to know. How much does she mean to you?"

"Why the hell would you need to know that?" Darsoss snapped.

"So that I would have some idea of what I was trying to turn the section upside down for. And if this thing is what it looks like, that's probably exactly what would need to be done—not to mention meddling in the affairs of the United Kingdom. There's a cab." He whistled shrilly. "Come on, let's grab it."

Vernon began to move out toward the street and Darsoss said: "You grab it. I'll walk a little bit."

"Walk? Are you nuts?"

"Yeah. Maybe I am."

2

Darsoss sat in the bar of the Club drinking Scotch and smoking, unperturbed in the realization that he was making a mess of his liver and his lungs. More and more he depended on cigarettes, and his whiskey intake had increased perceptibly in recent months. He couldn't conceive of a long life anyhow, so it didn't worry him at all. He looked at it the same way a man might look at his inability to scale a sheer wall as a trained climber might, or to run a mile in four minutes and ten seconds: the limitation was inescapable but not of great urgency. More important than anything was getting a good *quid pro quo* out of the tugging back and forth that obviously was now going on. The bargaining was part of the childish game—perhaps the biggest part; the value seemed often to be in how it was all done, like a game of poker played for matchsticks.

But something more was at stake for Darsoss now—more than the impersonal gains of the professional spy, or the avocational intriguer. He saw himself as a figure of *Weltschmerz*, unhampered by sentiment certainly; but like a cracked earthenware jug that can get to and from the well if the trip is swift enough, he still had something left in him. That was why he now sat there drinking and smoking and waiting eagerly for whatever came next so that he might see Disa Quennel again.

Vernon slipped in alongside of him, presenting no surprise or need for explanation. "Marco, if these guys are British, treason is involved, and the British can't be by-passed in this thing. They'll need to be in on it."

Darsoss shrugged. "It's up to you to convince the British that it's in their best interest to co-operate with you. It shouldn't be hard; we worked with SOE and MI6 all during the war; they know us. If that's not enough, you can let them know it's the only way they can duck the egg that's about to hit them in the nose. In other words, make them know this is a chance to keep

194

it all in the family; you're doing *them* a favor, not the other way around."

"That's *your* say-so."

"No. It'll be yours and the Boss's. Because by the time we're done you'll know it in all its terrible beauty—the whole thing. You know me better than to think I would kid you about that, Vernon."

Vernon lifted his chin and tilted his head, his eyes beaming thoughtfully to a corner of the ceiling. Then he looked at Darsoss. "Okay. What's in it for us?"

"That's easy. It puts you one ahead of them, and gives you a chance for more control in joint atomic research matters where it is desperately needed. The man I'm talking about was at Los Alamos, and until not long ago at the British research center in Harwell. That's what you'll get out of it. Not to mention breaking a Russian spy ring—and, brother, a damned important one. What more do you want? A case of champagne?"

"A weekend with Rita Hayworth."

"Why? She have some information you're after?" Vernon laughed and Darsoss inhaled quickly and fiercely on his cigarette. "As long as the woman is safely out of it, I don't care how you handle it," he said. "Except that I would like to see those other guys wrapped up anyhow."

Vernon nodded sharply, and his eyes took on the glow of interest of a player who was coming into possession of the ball. "Okay, kiddo. Now, let's get to the guts of it. Number one: as of this moment, you're trying to hide the truth about the woman—you and I both know it, and so does the Boss; you're trying to sneak her through before you admit it—make us buy as blind as you can; you're rattling the box and asking us to bid ahead of time or not at all. Because if you're on the level about this stuff—and no doubt you are—you're going to have to admit it eventually to substantiate your story. Come on. She is implicated, isn't she?"

"I'm not your witness, Vernon."

"Don't snow me, Marco. Remember, this isn't a courtroom; you're talking to me, and you can take it all back later anyhow. But wasn't this woman in on whatever her husband was doing? And hasn't she reformed, ready to go straight?—just to put things in a loose but graspable form. And aren't you in love with her—or let's say, deeply involved—and thereby committed, shall we say, to her extrication from a bog of espionage and treason? And isn't that how you happen to know as much about it as you do? You've got to tell me that much if you want to get a happy ending out of it."

Darsoss sat stonily, Vernon's eyes fixing him sincerely and knowingly. This was not yet the moment to concede the point. Vernon had to want the fantasy desperately, had to be hungry enough for the intrigue, enough to turn his back on Disa's complicity. Once that feeling was in the air the complicity itself could be granted; it would then be a point of negotiation; the Boss would go along, barter the very basis for all that was going on these days.

"You love her, don't you?" Vernon said in a suddenly hushed voice, not characteristic of him. "All the other poison is past, isn't it? What's dead is dead, isn't it?"

Darsoss had never seen Vernon like this before. "If I'm going to do anything about this, it's got to make sense to me," Vernon said.

Darsoss was about to leave him—to end the phase—when Vernon put a hand on his arm. He glanced quickly to a table, perhaps too close for comfort, but then relaxed when he heard the babble it was setting up as three men and a woman sat with their drinks and opinions. Vernon was satisfied, and looked at Darsoss. "The Boss will make the thing work—square Whitehall and all of that—if she will just give us all she knows, nothing more, nothing less."

Darsoss waited; maybe they were getting closer to the finish line.

"Is she a hard-line Red? If she isn't, we're more than halfway. From what I can guess at, you and this woman are more than just friends. That suggests that she was not ideally happy in her marriage. All she'd need to do, in that case, is say she performed under duress—if she did indeed do anything—and tell whatever she knows. Her position can be that of an informant with immunity. Whatever she tells us, we'll build the brief for ourselves. She'll never need to appear in court."

"How can you guarantee so much just like that?" Darsoss asked.

"Because we've made a deal or two before," Vernon said.

Darsoss nodded. "I just wanted to hear you say it."

"Accessory raps can be squared. If that's all it is . . . It is just that much, isn't it?"

Darsoss gave him a smile that was like a twitch. "The word for you is disarming," he said.

"How about names and addresses?"

Darsoss waited, then said: "Let me think about it."

"Look, don't get too grabby," Vernon said, a little annoyed.

"I want to make sure we understand each other," Darsoss said, his eyes catching the lady correspondent at the other table, good-looking in a square-jawed way. "I'm not admitting to any of your fanciful conjecture," Darsoss went on, shocked to find the lady smiling at him suddenly, his eyes shifting quickly back to Vernon's face. "I'm offering you two good names in return for preferred passage between London and Amsterdam . . ."

"No, Berlin. It's got to be Berlin. Sorry I neglected to mention that."

Darsoss kept cool. "Why Berlin? You said yourself there are ten thousand spies in Berlin . . ."

"No danger there. The whole thing would be accomplished with minimum breeze," Vernon assured him. "You could act as emissary once she reaches Tempelhof, we wouldn't do anything to make you unhappy. But we'd need to talk to her, just to be on the safe side. MI5 isn't going to be exactly overjoyed by foreign intervention, and we should take the feeling of hijack out of it as much as possible. One way of doing this is to make a full report on what we've done, making it look like joint action. That would absolutely include an interview with the woman. The Boss, you can bet, won't have it any other way, it would give him the feeling that he wasn't really running things. You know." He shrugged. "What the hell, that's the least of it."

Darsoss crushed out his cigarette and took the last of his drink. Maybe it was just as well; once she was by his side and out of the reach of Bliss and Mornier, the whole thing could be denied anyhow. They were a long way from court; Vernon had pointed this out himself. "But no escort," Darsoss said. "No guards. All you do is make certain she gets on that plane unmolested; and that I meet her alone. No cops, no State Department. Are we in sync?"

"Almost," Vernon said. "What kind of proof do you have concerning these two big fish? The woman's word?"

"No. She doesn't even know them." He paused. "It's the testimony of one of the members."

"I see. Is that all?"

"No. He'll need a deal in return."

"Aha."

"Yes, exactly. And it's a must."

Vernon shook his head a little. "I can't guarantee that. The British Government can be pushed just so far, chum."

"This character is not British. Would that matter?"

"You know better than that. Of course not. He's a spy, not a traitor. The charges are worded differently, that's all."

"He might not like that."

Vernon's eyes narrowed. "Who is this guy?"

"An American. What can he get if he's instrumental in blowing this network? That's got to be worth something."

Careful, cautious, Vernon said: "It's possible. Just possible."

"Can you say there would be an effort in this regard if the information is top grade?"

Vernon waited, glanced at the entrance to the room where two men were entering and scanning the room for familiar faces—an INS man and the *New York Journal-American* guy; Darsoss knew them both very well. "I think we should get out of here," Vernon said.

"Not yet. What about that part? Can you?"

"That much—yes," Vernon answered quickly and uncomfortably.

"Okay. You'll get enough to make it stick."

Vernon's eyes grew disbelieving. "What the hell are you getting at?" he said.

Darsoss said: "I was in on it . . ."

Vernon was shocked.

"I had my reasons . . ."

"You, Marco? Jesus Christ . . ."

"You never know about anybody, Vernon—not even yourself. But that's something for another time. Right now I figure I'm worth something." He paused and said pointedly: "Both the British and the Americans have made deals with grade-A Nazis. Remember, we were talking about that earlier, weren't we? And this was after we had them over the fire—not because they had come in on their own, but because they were nailed, nailed with blood on their hands going back twelve years . . ."

"Yeah," Vernon answered, recovering slowly. "I remember how smoothly you brought up the subject. You've a good forensic mind, Marco . . ."

"Sure. And if them—why not me?"

Vernon said quietly, almost awed at the thought: "You must be nuts about this woman . . ."

Darsoss closed his eyes for an instant, as if to shut off the analysis. "Remember what I'm telling you, Vernon," he said. "I won't go over for it—I'm not in the mood."

"We should get out of here. No, sit still. Here comes Jack Devlin. I'll shove off. You know the World Dispatch office. Right upstairs is the Monschau Electronics Company. That's ours. Meet me there at midnight—that's about an hour from now . . ."

"Gentlemen," said the visitor, "I hope I'm not intruding. We're looking for a couple hands of five-card stud. O'Toole, what about you?"

"Tomorrow. I'd love it tomorrow." He got up to leave.

"Can I interest you, Mr. Darsossakis? Say, where the hell have you been?"

"See you chaps," Vernon said, patting Jack Devlin's arm and departing.

"So long, O'Toole."

Devlin plunked himself down next to Darsoss, glanced over his shoulder at the figure of Vernon going through to the outer foyer, and then turned to Darsoss with a frown of prune-like intensity. "Say, what the hell does O'Toole do for a living?" he said.

Darsoss lit a cigarette, snapped his Zippo shut and blew out several jets of smoke. "Why don't you ask him sometime?" he said.

Devlin said: "Okay, okay. What about sitting in, give us a chance to cover our soaring expenses in style, at least?"

"If I can get out after an hour."

"Better not. You'd walk away winning and you'd just make everybody sore." Devlin got up. "Let's have a drink sometime."

"Love to."

After a while you go through all of the outlandish drill, as Bliss would call it, as if it were commonplace. The shock was that it did become so. People in concentration camps, for as long as they survived, must have found it hard to conceive of life without brutal beatings and bestiality and ritual indignity; one might almost have grown accustomed to such things, if not completely inured. Darsoss wondered if he could live without the constant presence of conspiracy, without hatred, without tension from minute to minute. Could he come out of all of this without too much forfeit? He wanted to discover as much for himself; that was why he had been willing to go as far as he had with Vernon—he would not have secured the opportunity otherwise; he could not have made the necessary arrangements without a spectacular amount of currency. And gall. There might still be some difficult checkpoints; but at least there was the sensation of flight. And now, as a first big result of the quick and daring shows of faith and the willingness to gamble, Darsoss awaited the arrival of Disa Quennel. That much had to be in the works; the night before in the offices of the Monschau Electronics Company, he had told Vernon all that was needed for that purpose.

Next day at lunch time in a café near the Zoo station, Vernon joined Darsoss at one of the tables. Suddenly he inspired confidence. He had the face of an American who never lost games, who never worried, and who could get things done. "Seven o'clock tonight. BEA Flight nine into Templehof. Fast work, if I say so myself."

Darsoss had to smile. "Good," he said with restraint but feeling satisfied.

"Have you spoken to her?"

"I called about an hour ago and alerted her. She's ready."

Vernon gave him a look of solicitude. "I would call this the back door to redemption," he said. "I'm still trying to make up my mind about you. I guess I never did know you, did I?"

Darsoss said: "Did you get a vet on Mornier and Havenhurst?"

"Don't worry about them for now," Vernon said. "As long as we know who and where they are, Mrs. Q. won't be bothered."

Darsoss drank some of the erzatz coffee and said nothing.

"Vorst doesn't matter any more, does he?" Vernon said thoughtfully.

Darsoss said: "I don't know . . ."

"But it doesn't burn, does it? It couldn't. You couldn't have quit if it still did."

Darsoss conceded the point with an upturned palm. "Maybe I've lost my guts."

Vernon knew better. "Afraid I'll think you're sentimental? Don't worry, I won't. But you're not exactly cold and unemotional either."

"A man should kill his wife's murderer."

"Unless it gets too costly."

"What would too costly be?"

"Didn't you find out?"

"I told you, maybe I lost my guts."

Vernon paused before saying: "MGB isn't going to be happy with you."

"That's their lookout." Darsoss looked directly into Vernon's blue eyes. "But you be damned sure they don't know Mrs. Quennel is here to talk to you. The way you do that is to take her deposition fast—it concerns only me and her husband—and then get her out with a personal release from the Boss in writing."

"I told you her status will be that of an informant."

"No slip-ups, please."

Vernon smiled faintly and said: "Marco, the U.S. Government isn't going to double-cross you—rest assured."

"Unless there's a good reason."

"You're getting a deal, Marco," Vernon said. "There may be a few scars, but nothing to what it could have been . . . You walked on some pretty thin ice . . ." Then, with his hand on Darsoss' shoulder, he said: "The Boss wants to see you at ten o'clock tomorrow morning, by the way. There's an art gallery on Paulsenstrasse; it's called Krosza. Ask for Charles and say you're Baker." Then: "See you later." And he left Darsoss sitting by himself.

Darsoss remained there long enough to drink a second cup of coffee and smoke another cigarette. Then as he walked along swiftly in the bright, clear cold, he felt a curious combination of elation and anxiety. Two huge snowplows were grinding back and forth in the square and traffic was more dense than usual, perhaps because of the momentary clemency of the weather. He wanted to walk away the next few hours. He felt a strong push from events but also the uncertainty that accompanies a new and unplanned move; there is always the sense of wonder and caution about entering an uncharted place, a tough neighborhood where the alleyways are unknown and the doorways are dark and unfriendly. It struck him that what people considered the right thing to do could carry its guilts and fears with devastating illogic and fearful inconsistency. He had changed sides twice; he was defying a system, a faceless piece of machinery, an implacable enemy. Not only was he leaving the network flat, he was blowing the whistle on it. This was the big burden. Krivitsky had come over and talked, hadn't he? And hadn't they got to him finally, just a few years before, during the war, in Washington. Not Berlin, Paris, or Shanghai, but Washington, D.C. Of course Krivitsky was a Russian. It was of small comfort; and he found himself vaguely pondering the possibility of revisiting abandoned places and the forsaken haunts of other times before any of it caught up with him. And he knew that Disa Quennel was responsible for it. He could have almost resented her for it; but he didn't.

He threw his cigarette down in the brown mangle of ice and snow and stood at the curb along the broad Bismarckstrasse. Then he signaled a cab which took him to Frau Nessermann's flat. The lady, heavy and desperate, was carrying a basin of water she had boiled on the kitchen stove toward the far end of the sprawling apartment. "Will you want to use the bathroom, Herr Manfred?" she said.

"No. Go right ahead, *gnädige Frau*."

"Thank you. One must try to remain clean in spite of the hardships."

There was a point somewhere, Darsoss felt. He said: "We must never lose heart," and continued down the hall to the door of his room.

But he didn't go in right away. The tip-off nail had fallen from the overhead molding. Someone was inside. He had ceased to carry the gun weeks before so he was left with only his wits, a defensive weapon at best. But he wasn't too concerned. He turned the doorknob and pushed the door in fully, but remained just outside the room. Kalinin was his visitor.

"Your charming landlady let me in," Kalinin explained, standing near the window, the gutted hulk of a building fifty yards behind him.

"She neglected to tell me," Darsoss said, startled but behaving as if this were exactly what he had expected. "Or did you frighten her into silence?"

"Not deliberately."

"Not that it isn't nice to see you," Darsoss said, tossing his hat on the table and taking off his coat.

Kalinin had the look of a man who had a duty to perform. "Did you know you were being followed?" he said evenly.

Darsoss' heart skipped a beat. "Followed? Is that so? By you?"

"By Kholenko. He's having you watched." There was a surprising and inexplicable sardonic quality to Kalinin's voice, a fierce resentment in his tone: the implied criticism was immediately visible and Darsoss felt a cold hand clutch at his insides. "You have joined the ranks of those who warrant special attention, my friend," Kalinin said with a smile of experience, his motives not yet discernible, the next moves uncertain.

"How flattering," Darsoss managed to say calmly.

"You are very interesting to me, Johnson," Kalinin said with flat sincerity. "There is always the badinage intended to counteract an urgent atmosphere. But it never makes me laugh."

"I didn't see you at the meeting," Darsoss said.

"Aren't you concerned about being placed under observation? You must be. I wouldn't believe anything else possible. Don't be afraid to express it to me. I am, you might say, somewhat in sympathy with you. For the moment."

Darsoss looked at Kalinin with new interest. "What is this all about? Are you trying to trap me into a confession of some kind? Is this a security check?"

"Your caution is understandable. But none of the conventions apply in this case. No, my friend, I am only trying to tell you certain things . . ." His voice grew wispy in its strange candor, as if he were casting back to some other time and place for his guidance. "Why?" He shrugged slightly, Slavic and wistful. "Reasons of the heart . . . *Force majeure* . . ." He looked once more to the street below and then turned his watery eyes on Darsoss. "I undoubtedly sound somewhat mysterious to you . . . if not altogether insane . . ." He smiled. Darsoss couldn't tell whether his eyes were simply moist, as they normally were, or if he had run to such a fit of inexplicable sentiment that these were tears. "My compulsion is irresistible . . ."

Darsoss waited for more and Kalinin said: "Be careful of your movements from now on . . ."

"Such as?"

"Kholenko is a Georgian and he lived abroad in the chilly atmosphere of England for quite some time," Kalinin said with strange discursive ease. "The combination was devastating." He shook his head. "What women and wine are to most men, secrecy and interrogation are to him. His passion is confined to the dossier and the police blotter. That's a very bad person to have as a foe." He paused. "I happen to be from Rostov," he said. "I don't suggest that this answers everything, but it may have some relevance."

Darsoss thought Kalinin had lost his mind. "In any case, you are suspected of . . . something," Kalinin said. "I tell you because . . . Kholenko and I are different people. Let that suffice for the time being."

"Why should I believe you?" Darsoss asked logically.

"Because you are a spiritual Rostovik. I don't know. Perhaps you shouldn't."

"I might. But why should I?"

"Let me tell you *why* you are suspected of something," Kalinin said. "Kholenko has enormous cunning—a nose like a timber wolf. And the teeth. And the heart . . ."

How much he did, though never with venom beyond his words, disdain Major Kholenko. "He found no trace of what he called the old madness in you when he just saw you; the anger, the obsessiveness that once marked you were missing. The absence of the poisonous gleam in your eyes was most suspicious. Just that much. And now you are being watched."

Darsoss said nothing, realized just how perceptive Kholenko was, beyond even Kalinin's estimate. He smoked his cigarette.

"Last evening you were seen with an agent of the CIG," Kalinin went on. "I was able to discover the substance of the report."

"He's an old friend," Darsoss said. "I was on their side once."

"Do you usually go to church together?" Kalinin said. "But

even that doesn't matter much. They are aware of your former associations."

"They?"

Kalinin smiled. "Kholenko."

"Is someone following me now?"

"At the present moment, no. I saw to that myself."

"And now we're simply passing the time of day, just like old friends who know they are surrounded by second-rate policemen, and timber wolves who have no appreciation of the better things in life."

Kalinin smiled. "You are still skeptical, but less so than a moment ago," he observed.

"Shouldn't I be? What would you say if you were me?"

Kalinin was pale and sad and there was no smile; the cheerful gargoyle seemed to have discovered a flaw in the joke—perhaps that it was on him. "I would say nothing," he said. "I would simply listen. Of course that is an easy assumption for me to make in your behalf, since I already know what I have to say." He raised a hand of denial. "No, no, before you even think it—I have not gone over to the other side. But I must tell you this if anything is to make sense to either of us . . ." His voice seemed to crack, and Darsoss could hear the faint click of swallowing away an obstacle in his throat. "I wouldn't be here now," Kalinin said, "but that I think of that morning when you were dispatched to London. I know that will sound like more bilious nonsense, the nauseous green excrement of a feverish mind possessed of demons and trolls. But it is true; I have never been unconscious of that moment when I found out about your own demons . . . your own sick heart and tormented brain—that essence of you which Kholenko saw was absent now; I never dismissed it, not even when you came with your arrogance and belligerent insults only last week; inside of you was a woman whom you loved even in death and for whose memory alone you would consign yourself to hell—if there were such a thing. You may recall that when you talked, even briefly to me that time, I was . . . chilled to think of it. For not two rooms away, asleep and unsuspecting, was my own wife—my Natasha, mother of my son, Nikolai. It is sometimes easy to imagine another person's position if one has the same weakness, the same vital interest. It is much less for your sake than my own that I tell you all of this . . ." He shook his head. "I am an Official; but the Official clashes with other things inside of one; I've control over bourgeois sentiment, yet cannot misinterpret feelings that are hatred and feelings that are love. We Russians more than any other people have unmatched restraint; but sometimes merely to touch fingertips with a woman causes a rush of uncontrolled emotion; and to know that special heart, the look in certain eyes with their depth of feeling, is to be enslaved forever . . . And to be separated from such enslavement is to hate whatever it was that caused the separation. And to feel pain. In this case, I feel not only my own pain but yours as well; and since mine is quite enough, I can lighten my burden only by doing what I am doing. The Soviet Union will endure . . ."

"Something has happened to your wife?" Darsoss ventured.

Kalinin said: "The Center issued a directive recalling her to Moscow three days ago; my mission in Berlin is to continue for an indefinite period . . ." He didn't look at Darsoss as he said: "We are separated . . ." He blinked his moist eyes. "My incentive is . . . lessened, to say the least. The post had advantages; any post would if I could have Natasha and Nikolai with me . . ."

Darsoss took a deep breath. "Yes," was all he said.

"I hardly know you; yet there is no other person I could safely tell this to. Besides, there is no one else who would stand to benefit by it. It is ironic."

"Yes, it is."

"Oh, there is more. Much more."

Darsoss didn't like the role of surrogate priest or psychoanalyst. "Well, at least your wife is . . . alive and well."

"There is more than that. For one thing, the action is a manifestation of bureaucratic indifference which disappoints me as a Marxist; for another, it shows personal animosity and mistrust which embitters me as both a worker for the State and the head of a family under a socialist government. Kholenko arranged it"—he waved his hand again—"but that is secondary."

"Is it?"

"Yes. It pertains to personal differences, the details of which are unimportant," Kalinin said.

"He got your wife recalled to Moscow," Darsoss pointed out,

watching the other man carefully for a misstep. "That doesn't sound very secondary to me. I'd say you'd like to set him back for it, maybe dim his star a little bit . . ."

Kalinin looked at Darsoss ironically. The two men were on opposite sides of the small room, Darsoss standing with his hands dug into his pockets, frankly doubtful. "I can appreciate the whole thing," Darsoss assured him, granting a whit of personal sympathy. "I don't have to tell you that. But that's why I can see what it is you're after. If you can ruin this operation through me, Kholenko has got to suffer by it . . ." He paced a few feet and stopped abruptly. "If I'm convinced I'm being watched I might get scared enough or angry enough to botch the entire thing. You could always start over again, but in the meantime Kholenko has got to go down while perhaps you're going straight up. And when you get to where you're going, just by the way, all the old arrangements would naturally come in for some rearranging. Discredit Kholenko and you have it all in the bag. Theoretically, of course."

Kalinin said: "How very uncomplicated you make it."

"Don't get me wrong," Darsoss said, sitting down, "I wouldn't blame you. But I have a stake, remember, and I need to be very careful about things like this—about people who give me information—of any kind."

"Listen," Kalinin said, coming forward. "Perhaps there is the dim hope for what you so astutely suggest. But it is very dim—secondary, as I have said."

"What else is there?" Darsoss said with more skepticism than he actually entertained.

Kalinin gave him a look of all-encompassing wisdom encircled with hopelessness. "I foresee the possibility of long winter nights," he said, then turned away to gaze through the window to the invisible future, his voice carrying his thoughts with woeful acceptance. "How many—I can only guess . . . But I do not want your face in my mind on those nights—be they one or one thousand . . . I don't wish to see it in the dark . . ." He faced Darsoss again. "And I very well might . . ."

Smoke spilled slowly from Darsoss' mouth, his eyes narrow; his breathing stopped, his heart stilled. "*My* face? . . . What do you mean by that?"

"Only that much as I fight against it, I cannot overcome a certain feeling which I can neither resolve nor even explain through a dialectic; and since I am an atheist I've no recourse to God. Yet I must do something . . ." He shook his head and seemed almost befuddled, showing a side of himself that was totally new to Darsoss. "Everything seems to have crowded in suddenly," he said with unexpected vagueness.

Darsoss got up from his chair and said: "Why should it be *my* face you expect to see in the dark?"

Kalinin said: "Perhaps one or two others also . . ."

"Yes, but we're talking about mine," Darsoss said, in pursuit, steely-voiced, not to be denied. "Why my face in the dark?"

"Because of my part in what has been done to you . . ."

Darsoss was brought up sharp and he stared deeply into the seed-like eyes of the man before him. "What do you mean by that?" he asked.

"You have been deceived, my friend," Kalinin said. "When I knew it at first, I tell you frankly it didn't matter to me in the slightest . . ."

Darsoss waited with a sense of the ground slipping away under him.

"When, however, I learned of your emotion on that cold, misbegotten morning, my knowledge of what was going on grew less supportable. Though in my allegiance to all I hold dear, I pushed aside my distaste. But now . . ."

"Now?" Darsoss intoned.

"Otto Vorst is not in prison; he never has been, so far as any of us know. He could be anywhere in the world at this moment. We never arrested him . . . You were the victim of a hoax—because of our interest in your gift of total recall."

Darsoss was flabbergasted. He couldn't believe it.

"It was all carefully engineered," Kalinin said with a sigh, as if he were actually beginning to experience relief after an emetic.

"But I got to his daughter," Darsoss exclaimed, peering with maddened disbelief into Kalinin's face. "I traced her; I saw the letter to her—she couldn't have anticipated—this is crazy. I checked and cross-checked . . ."

"Did you? Not really. You could only operate on probability and that left a great deal of hidden territory. The girl was not Vorst's daughter; she was part of the deception—a little Hitler

Youth whore selling services to save her miserable life. The letter was written by MGB. The letter written to Vorst's brother in Madrid—also an MGB inspiration. The photograph—likewise, a forgery. In fact, everything that led you to our first meeting was synthetic. It was all based on information about your circumstances . . . Oh, it took a lot of doing. The good thing was that there was margin for error, despite everything; because so much in life is conjectural, such a great deal do we depend on assumptions built through recurrence of the casual, the unavoidable restatement that *causes* these natural assumptions. Well, since the assumptions themselves are often incorrect, why could not their causes be contrived to begin with? Statement and restatement—completely false—lead to assumption, also false. Do you see? By the time you got to Bureau Number One, you were so certain of Vorst's existence and of Soviet desire to conceal it, that you asked for no final proof of what we wanted you to believe. Do you see? Manifestly ingenious, really; your entire line of attack was based not on verification, but on striking as good a bargain as you could. Ours at first was to withdraw, to appear disturbed by your discovery. We had set a pattern of reluctance; we had allowed your pursuit to go on so very long, each scrap of information to be come by only through great effort—carefully guided, of course—so that by the time you reached our doorstep, there was no doubt in your mind of Vorst's existence and whereabouts. You had been conditioned. Tracing him was a long and difficult matter; your mind demanded a reward for your efforts. Had we approached you directly, of course, the situation would have been much different. You would have been skeptical. You would have demanded full authentication. Since we did not have Vorst in our possession, we couldn't afford such an approach . . . You had to come to us. And you did . . . It took more than a year from the time of your first inquiry, but you did come . . ." His voice shook a little bit now, and he was smiling and weeping at the same time. "Well—now you know . . ."

"Yes," Darsoss murmured. "Now I know . . ."

"How you deal with it is your own affair . . ."

"What would you do?" Darsoss asked flatly, still not sure of how to assess what was going on inside of Kalinin.

The other man grew strangely aloof. In a voice that put some distance between him and Darsoss, he said: "I am not here to plot against the Soviet Union," his head drawn back indignantly. "Don't misunderstand anything."

With some sarcasm Darsoss said: "How could I?"

Kalinin said: "I had a devil to exorcise, so to say. And I have done just that." And then he was ready to depart.

"One question," Darsoss petitioned him. "Just one."

Kalinin, his hand on the doorknob, regarded Darsoss now as he might have a stranger, as if they were all done and no reason for candor or amiability was left. "What is it?" he said.

Darsoss said: "What about the guarantee of delivery before the fifth transmission?"

Kalinin answered: "There was to be no fifth transmission." He then walked out and left Darsoss alone in the room.

4

At seven o'clock Darsoss phoned Tempelhof from the Club. "Is Flight nine from London on time?" he asked and was told the plane was coming in right at that very moment. He said: "Thank you," and went back to the bar.

Dinsdale was there with three or four other newsmen. "Hullo," he said cheerily enough. "Still on the book?"

"Yeah, you could say that," Darsoss answered curtly, glancing at his wrist watch and ordering a double shot of Scotch.

"Stick to it, laddie."

Darsoss said nothing, was feeling very edgy, very short-tempered; it was as if without warning lack of sleep had caught up with him. But it was more than that, much more. They had used him and abused him beyond his wildest dreams, and even the great idealist, Quennel, had to have been in on it to the extent of lying about how many transmissions there were to be.

"Let me ask you something, Alex," he said. "Do you remember when we talked about my wife?" He took a drink and watched Dinsdale closely.

"Yes, of course," was the reply. "I remember vividly."

"Was that the first you'd heard of it?" It was important to know, to document his folly and the ruthlessness of others.

Dinsdale, fatter and more aggrieved than ever, gave him a quizzical look. "Why do you ask that?"

"Just wondering."

"As a matter of fact, I had heard about it before that," Dinsdale said. "The Mordrams had somehow or other learned of it."

"The Mordrams? I haven't seen them in years."

"Well, you needn't have. But Jack did know. He was in one of the hush-hush outfits during the war. Maybe that was how he came across it, German records, probably intact with the whole thing . . ." He seemed suddenly squeamish. "Why go into it?"

"Had he told you much?"

"Oh good Lord, I don't know," Dinsdale said impatiently. "He told me the essentials, I suppose. What difference can that make now? I mean, it must be terribly painful—it is to me."

Darsoss gave him a mean look. "Did you tell Miles what you knew?"

"I don't recall. I may've."

Darsoss continued on like a cross-examiner, slowly, relentlessly. "Do you know if Mordram saw much of Miles? I mean, I wonder if he could have passed along what he knew to Miles."

Dinsdale said: "Well, you can ask him, if it's that important to you."

"Maybe I will," Darsoss said and drank nearly all of what was in his glass.

Dinsdale, after a brief wait, said: "I have the damnedest feeling that everything is going to blow up in our faces one of these days. Right here in Berlin."

"Think so?" Darsoss said, his mind elsewhere.

"The trouble is basic. The Communists can't seem to win elections. They can't be expected to be graceful losers. It would be just like expecting Stalin to wear a dinner jacket. Oh? Are you off? Just as I was getting to some of my more fascinating theories."

"Yeah. See you later."

"Everything all right?"

Darsoss looked at him. "Why do you ask that?"

"You seem very jumpy."

"Forget it."

"And frankly, you look awful, old boy. Why did you ask about Miles and all of that just now? Do you know something?"

"About what?" Darsoss said.

"About Miles's death," Dinsdale said, lowering his voice.

"Just what you told me. I'll see you later, Alex."

He walked out to the street, and walked two blocks before he picked up a cab. "Hotel Graff Hirshorn," he told the driver, then sat back to think some more.

Jack Mordram. Darsoss hadn't thought about him more than fleetingly for quite a long time. His assignment to a British Intelligence unit would have explained it, of course; an MI6 major had been Darsoss' original source after the war; Mordram could easily have been a part of the same group. And perhaps now, he was even a member of the network—a contact of Bliss. Between what Mordram knew about Anne's death and the information the Russians themselves had about Darsoss' unflagging pursuit and relentless inquiries concerning Otto Vorst, the entire scheme could have been hatched. A case could certainly be made. Miles Lawson's innocence was manifest; he had died half convinced that Darsoss was a counterintelligence agent for the British. He had been a victim of crossfire. His death had been an inconvenience to them; just as Anne's death had been a boon, something for which they had to have been grateful. For the first time Darsoss felt an urge to hurt them in some way.

He got out of the cab in the British sector and made all of his movements casual and unconcerned: he paid the driver unhurriedly, took back his change, searched for the proper gratuity, and then lit a cigarette as if he either didn't know he was being watched or didn't care; the way things were arranged there would be nothing overt to report concerning his comings and goings of the next few hours; and by the time an evaluation would be made, the whole thing would be over and done. That was to say, barring the unforeseen, the mishap that was unexpected but took place, nevertheless, at least half the time.

Darsoss clicked his lighter shut and crossed the sidewalk, cleared of the snow for the moment, and entered the Graff Hirshorn. It was a moderate to high-priced hotel with a large lobby and a clacking marble floor and numerous arrivals and departures. That was why he had picked it for her; she could slip in and out without too much notice. "Has Mrs. Quennel arrived?" he asked the desk clerk.

"No, she hasn't," he was told after a quick glance at the register.

Darsoss looked at his wrist watch. It was eight-fifteen. Certainly there had been plenty of time to arrive from Tempelhof, even allowing for delays in customs and passport inspection. No immediate possibility came to mind.

"Are you sure?" he asked, knowing the question was futile.

"Yes, I am. I have a reservation but it has not been called for."

Darsoss went to the phone booths near the entrance to the bar. All were occupied and he began secretly to twitch, his face betraying nothing. He smoked nonchalantly while he waited. Within a few seconds a phone was free. He called Tempelhof. "Flight nine from London arrived at nineteen hundred hours," the information girl told him in a British accent.

"Could you check the passenger list? Was there a Mrs. Quennel on board? Q-u-e-n-n-e-l."

After a moment's silence, the voice said: "I am sorry. I show no one of that name."

"You show no one of that name," he repeated hollowly.

"Perhaps she is on Flight ten, scheduled to land at twenty-two hundred hours."

At the desk, Darsoss approached the same unyielding, untouched desk clerk. "Should Mrs. Quennel arrive sometime later tonight or tomorrow morning, see that she gets this immediately." He handed the man an envelope containing his address at Frau Nessermann's and the Club telephone number.

"Yes, of course."

His next move was in the balance. There were too many people at the Club he might have to be civil to, and he didn't know if he could carry it off. He considered a vigil in the hotel lobby as he paced slowly and thoughtfully toward the wall of glass-paneled entry doors. He stood looking out to the wintry street, half-heartedly lit, people passing back and forth on the sidewalk, bundled up if they were lucky enough to have coats, the traffic mostly British military. The distance between London and Berlin seemed epic suddenly, dark and cavernous and impossible to cross.

Still trying to think things through, Darsoss lit a cigarette and turned around without purpose, indeliberate. He looked across the expanse of marble to a chair with its back placed flush against a wooden column in the lounge area. Vernon was sitting there reading a copy of *Tageblatt*, absorbed but obviously awaiting Disa Quennel.

"What are you trying to pull?" Darsoss said.

"Marco, hi, chum," Vernon greeted him, good-willed, sincere, putting aside the newspaper. "I'm not trying to pull anything. Here, let's sit on the divan."

"Then what the hell are you doing here?" Darsoss asked as they placed themselves side by side. "You were going to stay clear until tomorrow. What happened? Somebody get nervous?"

"No, no. Nothing like that. Don't get upset."

"I'm not upset. But I think your guys on the other end may have slipped up. She wasn't on that plane."

Vernon shook his head. "They didn't slip up," he said confidently. "Everything went fine. She got here all right."

"What are you talking about? I just checked both here and at Tempelhof."

"Oh, not this hotel. And not that plane. She came in a little later on another one."

"What do you mean?" Darsoss said, after a moment's pause.

"Just that," Vernon replied matter-of-factly. "It all went off beautifully."

Darsoss was going to wait until he was sure of what faced him and he let Vernon go on. "You're a sentimental man, Marco," Vernon said. "Or maybe romantic is more the word for you. Either way, you're not lucky. It's a terrible combination."

Darsoss knew what it was now as he looked at the tan and intrepid face next to him. A small, knowing grin announced defeat and conceded betrayal; it was an absurd world in which Darsoss was the loser.

"What kind of a double-cross is this?" was all Darsoss could find to express his feelings of shock and frustration.

"It's not a double-cross, Marco. Your pass was intercepted, that's all. But that's part of the game. It's called International Football. That's what we're playing. Of course I have one advantage over you. I'm on both teams . . . Johnson."

5

"I never expected us to meet this way," Vernon said, already looking like someone Darsoss only vaguely recognized. Then he stopped. He was not going to say anything more on the subject, two English WAACs entering the area for social purposes and plunking down in chairs only feet away.

"Have you known Dal very long?" one said. "Only since his posting to the motor pool," was the answer. Their voices were contained, but the merest tick self-conscious; American civilians brought that out in one. "Are we on time?" "More or less." "Perhaps we should leave and come back. It might be a good thing to keep them waiting." "Oh, really, Mary. Want to give a bad impression?" They were quite silly, of course.

Vernon smiled with faint amusement and warm understanding of younger people. Darsoss twitched and stood up and sauntered a few feet away as if nothing very pressing was on his mind. In a moment Vernon was by his side. "The mezzanine's a good spot," he said.

Darsoss opened and closed his hands with angry strength. He looked up toward the open corridor suspended halfway between the lobby floor and the ceiling. "What for?" he said with scarcely moving lips.

"We can talk. It's Grand Central Station down here."

"Listen, you bastard . . ."

Vernon calmly turned away and after a moment's hesitation Darsoss followed him. They ascended the staircase on the right, near the elevators at the rear of the lobby, thick chenille carpeting still there from the good old days. The mezzanine itself was semi-darkened and ignored at the moment because it contained access, one could tell immediately, to nothing more than two rooms for public hire—banquets and conventions, mainly—both of which were silent and obviously not in use.

"Life is a bag of strange beans," Vernon remarked with what seemed like deliberate inanity. He said no more until they had sat down on a divan near the marble balustrade, so chic and French, overlooking whatever went on below—exits and entrances, the signs of boredom, the looks of expectation, and perhaps meetings between spies—yet far removed from the crisscross. After a quick, token glance behind him, Vernon said: "I thought it might go all the way without a hitch. But we haven't had that kind of mission right from the start, have we? All the nut-house things that have happened, all the unforeseen circumstances: Lawson's Dutch act; the new cover—Bliss's idea, of course; then Quennel's health . . . Incredible. The hard part was getting you in the first place. After that everything should have been smooth as silk; there was nothing in the way; nothing except people—and their individual breaking points—the little things you never count on—the dumb, simple-minded things that can overturn the most elaborate arrangements and make jerks out of geniuses . . . We all know about that, don't we?"

Darsoss' astonishment ebbed slowly. "Where is she?" he demanded gutturally, ready to spring.

"I welcomed her at the airport personally. She's safe and comfortable," Vernon answered. "If you want her to stay that way, you'll call off the double-cross and face life as it is, Marco. You're in it, and you're going to stay in it. You don't have a choice unless you don't care what happens to Mrs. Quennel."

"But nothing is left now that Quennel is dead. What good am I?"

"Let us worry about that. Besides, you're a little bit dangerous now. You were ready to blow the London network. It took too long to put it together. You need a cooling-off period. After that we can think about the next move."

Darsoss said: "What pest hole did you crawl out of?"

"Stick it in your nose," Vernon said, smiling. "Who are you? Nathan Hale?"

Darsoss didn't answer. There seemed to be no end to that burned-out feeling, the angry inner weeping.

"You screwed up my timetable and put us in the hostage business," Vernon said. "Nobody likes that."

"Feel double-crossed, eh? Well, that still leaves you one ahead of me, doesn't it? I know there's no Vorst anywhere, that you rigged the whole thing, that there was a bullet or a knife or a glass of thalium waiting for me at the end of it . . ."

Vernon's jaw muscles flexed and he went a little white under his mysterious suntan. "What do you mean by that?"

"Go to hell," Darsoss said, shaking inside with fear and rage, so often hand in hand.

"I don't think you figured it out this fast," Vernon said. "You would have, I know. But it sounds like someone told you ahead of time." He could see a stool pigeon in the ranks. "Who was it?"

Darsoss looked at him. "The *Blitzmädel*," he said. He felt bound to protect Kalinin. "She has a big mouth if you twist her arm hard enough. Very interesting, maybe sheer genius. You started out with one ready-made factor: Quennel and I had a mutual friend who was open to blackmail. From there on you put it together like a cuckoo clock. It *was* you, wasn't it? That part, naturally, she didn't know."

Vernon said in a quiet voice: "The need arose for a very good agent with his own legal means of moving freely in the West. The Center called for it and Berlin was charged with putting it together. It fell to me because my network is London based. You had everything, Marco—everything we needed. No one was aware of that to the extent that I was, of course. Normally there would have been as much chance of recruiting you as Bill Donovan. But Vorst made the difference. I was able to steer you to Madrid because Vorst's brother *had* been there, and it presented the perfect chance for the letter with the photograph and the Dahlem validation."

"And then you let me chase myself in circles until that exact right minute, when you simply steered the girl into Pommler's while I was sitting and waiting for just that to miraculously happen. Good actress. Who coached her? She was especially great in the indignation scene after discovering I had stolen the letter from her dear old dad."

Vernon gave Darsoss a coldly friendly look to accompany a truthful but cruel assessment. "You had sunk into madness, Marco, and it was made to order for people who know about such things."

Darsoss said nothing but looked at Vernon, who now began to fiddle with his pipe and tobacco pouch. "But you're wrong about the other part of things. We weren't planning anything nasty. What for? We would have told you Vorst was dead and we were ready to prove it with all the very trimmings we'd used up till then. We would have wrung Luzzi in on you again. You'd have accidentally run into her in Pommler's or some other place. She would have pulled a small scene with you, asked you in a bitter tone if you were satisfied now that her father was dead. I would have corroborated it." He smiled with one corner of his mouth. "Do you recall how I would come to you with a vet on everything K and K would feed you? If they told you Vorst was working for them, I would give you a variation on the same item; if they said Vorst was under arrest, I would back it up with approximately the same thing, only later and not as full."

"Yes, yes, yes, you're a genius . . ."

"The same thing would have held again. You'd have bought it, Marco . . . You'd have had to; you couldn't have lived with yourself otherwise—knowing what you'd done. You'd have needed the justification of having been told the truth to begin with."

"Freud and Tallyrand all rolled into one . . ."

There was a moment's silence and Darsoss pulled ferociously on his cigarette and emitted jets of smoke meant to kill. Vernon lit his pipe and seemed calm about the whole thing. "The world is a place in which to make out; nothing else," Vernon said. "In law school I found that what I was learning was a matter of tricks, of watching for the mistakes of others and capitalizing on them. And in trying cases, that everything was based on saying one thing and meaning another—that all attorneys, as a matter of course, tried to fool each other; that both plaintiff and defendant were engaged in matching wits, irrespective of justice; and that ultimately there was no such thing as justice by strict definition. With that in mind, I can assure you that nothing in my trial experience compares with my time in OSS. And the idea of returning to a civil practice was a pale prospect for me. That's part one. Part two—I now have an account in a Swiss bank that just reached six figures. It's the best of two worlds, you have to admit." He sucked on the stem of his pipe. "It sounds venal; but it isn't, because it's preceded by a certain attitude—a philosophy, in fact. I begin everything I do with a total realization of the elusiveness of so-called right and wrong. There's no sacrifice of principles involved."

"Don't explain," Darsoss said.

"It's life-size chess, Marco. The pieces feel joy and pain and fear, but it's chess. You, for example, tried to castle and left your queen vulnerable." He lifted his chin recollectively. "You know who Bliss is, of course. But you don't know *why* he is *what* he is. Well, for Bliss—or Arthur Havenhurst, if you prefer, brother of the Viscount Broadsmuir—the two most important pieces on the board are queen and castle; and he plays a very unorthodox game in their behalf. Actually I'm getting away from chess and into symbols. But Bliss pursues just one end. To keep his castle and his queen inviolable. In short, Bliss couldn't possibly make the freight on his country house—one of England's stately homes—without resorting to some rather filthy habits like opening up to the public a few times a week, a device that would exempt him from property tax, among other things. As impoverished gentry—unlike his illustrious brother—he had no other choice, not one that he could have made publicly, anyhow. In any case, he escaped the dreadful fate I just described. As a well-paid Communist agent, he maintains a high standard of living and is saved from contact with the unwashed masses. The socialist movement is damned unpredictable, isn't it? Except that politics are really beside the point."

"What is the point?" Darsoss said, interested despite his other problems.

"To achieve the human touch—I mean, to make you see that we're all frail and doing our best to get by." He smiled.

Darsoss didn't say anything for a moment or two. Then: "Listen, Vernon: let her go; she has family in Copenhagen. I'll stick. But don't make her take this rap. She went all the way down the line for Quennel; all she wants is to be left alone. You have my word I'll stick . . ."

"Marco . . . I can't afford to be romantic, not even if I wanted to be." He flexed his strong, clean-looking hands. "Why don't we go down to the bar for a drink?"

Darsoss crushed out his cigarette. "Me? Drink with you? You think I want the plague?"

"You see? This is what I mean, Marco. You can't be trusted. You bear out how wise it is to use pressure in dealing with you. For all your knowledge and experience, you're very artless and unsophisticated. I'd mark that a handicap for the moment."

Vernon was no longer Darsoss' old comrade in arms; he was just a man as heartless and perfect as carefully conditioned mahogany. Human relationships complicated nothing for him; he hadn't even the task of hardening himself against them. He had been born with all the advantages required for the game of life-size chess. "We were lucky at that," he mused, ignoring the contempt of his asinine prisoner. "If the Boss had been in town, it might all have been different." He shook his head. "The little things—the stupid little things will kill you every time, won't they, Marco?"

Faces swam before Darsoss' eyes, people coming in and out of the lobby below, more than half of them Allied military personnel, mostly British. At least a few assignations were taking place at that very instant. The feeling of being condemned just inches from the freedom and unawareness of others was

219

acute; secret damnation burned in the breast so much more intensely than if it were a matter of public record. Vernon was saying: "A courier gets hit on the head—not by the opposition, but by some cheap crook who never saw him before and is just after his wallet." He flexed his mouth with a connoisseur's deep but safely distant appreciation. "The goods you're waiting for never gets there and a whole mission is screwed."

Darsoss stirred in his seat, then stood up suddenly, his hands thrust within the folds of his unbuttoned overcoat and into his back pockets, a picture of anger and revulsion. "I've met the whole crowd," he said with open disgust. "You're the worst of them."

Vernon stood up and with a look of clean living in his eyes he said: "Sorry you feel that way."

"What did you expect? Where have you got her?" Darsoss said, staring into the other man's pale eyes. "What assurances do I have that she's all right? And when does she go free? You don't expect me to go on while you keep her captive indefinitely, do you?"

"We'll need to take that part as it comes," Vernon said simply. "In the meantime you'll stay in Berlin until Bliss can arrange things on the other end. It will be based upon a request from GRU which I imagine their boy Vorshov will draft. You met him, of course. It might take months . . ."

"Months. . . ?" Darsoss dragged fiercely on his cigarette. "Why don't you make it years?"

"You've been making too many short jumps anyway, so it's an opportunity to stay put for a while. It'll look better." Vernon paused, then said: "Don't make it rough on yourself, Marco."

They might have been two men in any ordinary business discussing the problem of shortages or bad distribution—not life and death; not casual double-dealing and everyday treachery. Darsoss looked at Vernon with contempt and disbelief, as if Vernon were Hitler explaining his Jewish policy. "I mean, it's this way for now," Vernon went on. "Try to take it more in stride. Nothing can change it—unless you do something rash." He paused. "And if you do, I can promise you that Mrs. Quennel will be killed on the spot. Plain enough?"

Without waiting for a response Vernon turned away from the balustrade, almost as if to insure against being pushed over. The move had no such purpose and he wheeled back almost immediately to where Darsoss stood, motionless and on the short end of everything. "But that's not going to happen," he said like a good friend giving encouragement, "because it would be stupid and useless and totally unnecessary."

Darsoss didn't answer and Vernon said: "I leave you with this: Mrs. Quennel will be living in great comfort, if not luxury—not as a prisoner, but as a guest, really; circumscribed, naturally, but in a manner hardly visible to the naked eye."

"It sounds terrific," Darsoss said with a sneer, but feeling despair.

Vernon abandoned completely the pretense at conviviality, his face fixing with a bland smile of pleasurable anger. Without a trace of love he said: "Be nasty and see what it gets you." He continued to look into Darsoss' eyes for a moment or two before adding: "You've got a bad set of defenses. All it takes is the right dame and you're a dish of cream. And remember—I know it."

Vernon moved away in a desultory fashion, as if he was in the process of a long, fragmented good-bye, ready to turn back several times with afterthoughts before final departure. Darsoss remained where he was; he didn't want to leave the mezzanine with Vernon. He watched, and said nothing, but in a moment was alerted to a change in Vernon, a loss of the usual ease. His back turned, Vernon appeared suddenly rigid, standing not more than ten feet away from Darsoss along the balustrade. His eyes were trained on the foyer below; on something or someone that had riveted him to the spot. Darsoss looked toward the lobby entrance and couldn't believe what he saw. No wonder Vernon had turned to stone.

Disa Quennel had come in from the street—uncertain, searching, ready to take refuge or run from attack. She moved to the reception desk where several other people were engaged, and she seemed very far away. She had on the flat-soled shoes sensible women are said to wear for traveling, walking, and running.

Vernon made half a decision; his hand went inside his coat at the hip but no further, the situation broken into crystals of choice, numerous wrong moves among them. He never made his turn. Darsoss had landed on his back with ferocity born of a single choice, not many—a lame choice and a final one.

The impact was great, Darsoss having used the arm of the

divan to leap from for the extra power he badly needed to try such a thing, but Vernon remained on his feet.

Darsoss wrapped his left forearm under Vernon's chin, grasped the crook of his right elbow to lock it, and worked his right hand to the back of Vernon's neck—pushing forward from the rear and pressing backward from the front. It was a hold meant to strangle while bearing the victim to the ground under you. In the lobby below two British Army sergeants had joined the two WAACs; Darsoss had a clear but disinterested look at them. He drove Vernon far back from the balustrade to keep them from possible exposure to eyes that might casually drift upward from the lounge; the privacy was thin here but he wanted to protect it.

Vernon gasped for breath and clutched wildly at Darsoss' left arm and the locking hand while he kept his feet with Darsoss riding him like a harnessed beast. The difference in size and strength was immediately apparent to Darsoss, who needed this ruthless advantage if he was to survive. He used every muscle in his body, keeping his full weight off the ground, straining to cut off Vernon's air and bring him down. He knew he was not meant for this fight; he could finish it only if he never lost position and hung on endlessly. It was like trying to contain an enormous steel coil and if he failed he was as good as dead. Vernon staggered about in the dimly lit and empty corridor with Darsoss on his back, his shoes sinking into the opulent carpeting that had managed to survive World War Two, the breaths of both men coming in painful doses. Darsoss tried to bear his victim forward, his face debased by strain and savagery, by the pain of struggling to kill someone; no one could look that way at any other time, all the restraints and controls gone.

At the doors of one of the darkened reception rooms, Vernon caved in under him, face down, the thud a final sound after the tentative scuffling and the searching for breath and the escaping gasps that no one could have heard even ten yards away. And now it seemed to have run its brief and violent course.

Darsoss waited. Vernon was alive but made no sound. Quickly Darsoss' right hand went inside the overcoat, his left arm keeping its position around Vernon's throat. The yield was a .38 automatic with appendage for a silencer. The Maxim silencer was tucked into a specially sewn carrier on the inside panel of the suit jacket. Darsoss' examination was perfunctory. He stuck the silencer attachment into Vernon's coat pocket, Vernon silent under his straddle. The idea of killing him was hard to swallow, and Darsoss wondered very fleetingly if an escape could be made without Vernon's death. But was that the objective? He didn't know, his muscles fluttering from the strain of the fight, his ability to think clearly not quite at its peak, and he couldn't stop to think it through. He had to get to Disa . . .

Vernon's hand snaked around Darsoss' wrist and pulled. The sudden jerk tore Darsoss forward. Before he knew what had happened he was on his back and he was looking up to see a white face through the tan, and ice-cold hate directly above him. He was no match for Vernon and never had been. But he had weakened Vernon enough to be able to slip out and get off the floor. Vernon was up right after him and in a moment had him caught against the doors of the reception room. "Marco . . . you bastard . . ."

The blows were mostly the flat-side hand chops that tear at the nerves when they land correctly. Vernon knew how to use them and Darsoss felt them pouring in, his forearms blocking some, missing others, one catching him across the bridge of the nose. A groan came up from the bottom of him, the very soul of him crying out, surely loud enough to attract attention. The doors at his back buckled inward and gave him egress, the darkened room a ghost-like configuration of white-clothed banquet tables bordered by empty chairs, the phasm of Nazi heydays everywhere. The smell of it was vivid and it caused him to buck forward as if all of it were still there to be fought and shattered. The hatred felt useful, if not satisfying. Vernon became the target, a surrogate for Otto Vorst—perhaps the very man who had tortured Anne, who had not let her die until life was a mere technicality. Darsoss wanted to shatter Vernon, pound him until nothing was left of hatred and all the things that had caused it—a naive concept when you are outweighed by forty pounds. He got nowhere.

Vernon swung him around with his back to the open doorway giving onto the mezzanine, grabbed his coat sleeve and jerked him forward and sank a fist with the drive of a piston shaft into Darsoss' belly. Darsoss' belly was not tough enough for such a blow. He felt as if his entire intestinal tract had been mashed, as if his eyeballs would fall out of their sockets. He grunted and moaned and was nearly sick right then in the middle of the dance floor. Vernon seemed to stand back and survey the damage. The brief moment gave Darsoss the avenue he needed to follow his instinct, and he whirled away as fast as he could out of the grand room to the mezzanine where it had all begun. He caught only a glimpse of Disa Quennel, at the reception desk so far away. That and no more. Suddenly, limp and defenseless, he was dangling in midair. Vernon had caught up with him quickly enough, had lifted him from the floor and was heaving his body into space—not over the balustrade, as Darsoss' first sickening instinct had told him, but in the other direction: Vernon also wanted privacy, now that it had come to this. It was the convenient way to end things. It would be done secretly. There would be no penalties; only a mystery would be left behind. Darsoss knew all of this even as he went through the air.

He had never been handled this way by anyone before; when he fell to the floor, his pain overrode his sense of humiliation. He knew he was finished and could only barely move, his eyes upward, a blurred image of the salon doorway his only impression. In seconds Vernon would crack his epiglottis; it was the thing to do. He could have cracked Vernon's had he moved with less hesitation just a minute or two before. Why hadn't he? It was hardly worth a thought now; he was a goner. He waited. But nothing happened. He could hear the distant hum of the foyer and the whirring of the elevator shaft; and the opening and closing of a cage door—perhaps on the mezzanine itself. Was there also, within those few eternal seconds, the sound of frantic search, the hard breathing and scurry of a man looking desperately for something in a very small area. For something. But what?

Darsoss' head rolled to one side; he thought perhaps it was the automatic pistol not twelve inches away from him that the other man was searching for.

He reached for it. His hand went around the grip, his thumb flipping the safety catch, his finger into the trigger guard. He raised his head; Vernon had made the same discovery and was coming at him in a leap with the single intention of killing him as quickly and ruthlessly as one crushes out a cigarette or snaps a stick in two. Darsoss could only squeeze the trigger and roll away into the banquet room. The shot rang out and shook the place with unexpected violence. Vernon fell fast, not flat but in a crumple. The muzzle velocity was not as great as that of certain other hand weapons, and the bore was smaller; the victim wasn't torn apart and felled like a dropped log. But a shot through the head killed him, and Vernon was surely dead, just as Darsoss had wanted him right from the beginning. A philosophical point was implicit, but Darsoss was all for skipping it, which he did. Instead he considered fleetingly the accuracy of the gun at short range and tossed it a couple of feet away from him. The acrid smell of cordite was unmistakable.

Now there were the voices of excited and startled people who had heard the shot ring out. Within seconds curiosity would overcome the shock and the initial sense of caution that a nearby gunshot causes; the scene of the crime would be swarming; like a player who couldn't think of an answer in the allotted time, Darsoss would be out of the game. He had to get out of there. Numb in some places, throbbing with pain in others, he got to his feet as quickly as his shaky state would allow.

The expeditionary force went forth from the lobby: the reception clerk, the porter and the elevator man, and a couple of British soldiers. As they ascended on one side of the mezzanine, Darsoss went down the other, his hands in his pockets, an insane ease in his movements. You needed a certain amount of arrogance at a time like this to keep from crumbling.

Disa stood near the reception desk—a lost madonna surviving a world of harlots and corrupt policemen and cold hotel lobbies in the middle of a dead continent; the sight of her sent a thrill into him, taking him quite by surprise. She had to know that something was wrong and that it concerned them, and he gave her an almost imperceptible nod of confirmation of the need for caution. Sensitive, willing her fears inside, she waited to be controlled and commanded.

The eight or ten people on hand were drawn like lobby moths to the flame of commotion, a single man of enormous sang-froid continuing to read his newspaper in spite of all. On signal Disa crossed the lobby and went to the phone bank, substantially removed from the focus of turmoil and out of the full sweep of things. Darsoss took her hand, icy through the thin glove she wore, affirmation in her touch, promise in her eyes, caution and pain colliding. "Your face . . . Oh, my God . . ."

"Don't waste time over that," he said, dabbing the traces of blood at his nostrils, feeling a twinge of pain. "Are you all right? I know you were abducted. How did you get away?"

"You know? But how. . . ?"

"You were to be a hostage, but never mind that now—we must talk fast. Is anyone following you?"

"I don't know for certain," she answered, excited and breathless.

"What happened?"

"I don't know that either," she said with a shake of her head. "Three men stopped me at the aerodrome. I knew you couldn't have sent them, as they tried to make me believe, because I was to meet you here . . ."

"Yes, yes . . ." His eyes flicked toward the possible approach of an enemy and then back to her face. "Then what?"

"One was an American who left me shortly with the other two, who were Germans. Suddenly, as they were forcing me toward an automobile, both of them ran off and two other men were chasing after them. One turned and came toward me—a large man in a bowler hat, not German, I don't think . . ."

"Yes, yes, never mind that. What happened then?"

"I ran off in between the other automobiles and lorries—it was rather like a maze, you know, and it gave me an awfully good chance to escape to the w.c. where I hid until I thought it might be safe to come out and take a chance . . . But when I did, the man in the bowler hat was still in the neighborhood—still looking about . . ."

"But he didn't see you?" Darsoss prompted.

"No. Luck was with me, because there's no mistake it was me he was after," she said. "But I got away in a cab," she added with a glimmer of terrible enjoyment.

"And you'd never seen any of them before?"

"No." She shrugged quickly, Darsoss noting her somewhat mussed look, the flush of excitement in her face. "I suppose I shall never see my belongings again. I had to leave them . . ."

"Never mind that."

"But you. What's happened here?"

"We'll talk of that later."

"But—"

"Not now, for Christ's sake. Go back to the reception desk and ask to be escorted to your room. Wait until I contact you.

It won't be long. But go quickly now, and don't look in my direction when I walk out of the hotel."

"But   "

He couldn't resist that perfect mouth and those eternal eyes, that subject look of trust. "But what?" he said. "Come on, be quick about it."

She looked directly at him. "Are you glad I've come?" she asked, as if she weren't sure.

He threw a quick and anxious look toward the lounge. He said: "I'd have been very lonely if you hadn't. Now for heaven's sake, go. I don't want us seen together . . ."

"Yes," she said in an obedient whisper, intense satisfaction and no shame in it, but hardly able to tear herself away.

He smoothed his hair down quickly, his hat missing, ready to depart. "Go, go, go," he said in a soft tone of commandment.

She had returned to the desk when the manager and two others came down from the mezzanine after their shocking discovery. The reception clerk swept quickly to the entrance doors, the managerish-looking guy fleeing to an office in back of the registration counter. A third white-collar type, somewhat less simmering, came up to Disa, nodded acquiescently, hit the call bell, and signaled for an escort. Though she had not even a suitcase, she might well have been accompanied by twenty separate pieces of matched luggage; her fears and self-doubts simply didn't show. A bent-over man of seventy in somewhat tattered livery and carrying a large ring of keys began leading her toward the elevators as if she were the prima ballerina of the Berlin State Opera, right past a group of people milling about at the foot of the mezzanine stairs.

Darsoss smoothed down his hair once again, buttoned his coat, dug his hands into his pockets, and walked out into the main arena, across the lounge carpeting toward the vestibule marble, unnoticed. Unnoticed until the feverish reception clerk appeared in front with two British MPs. The three of them were placed without warning just inside the doors leading to the sidewalk, directly in line with his route of march.

The clerk had obviously just summoned the two soldiers from the street, and he was startled by the sight of Darsoss. Recognition and alarm flooded his face like a blush which he promptly conveyed to the two policemen with him. The three conferred briefly, keeping Darsoss in sight every second. Darsoss tried the nonchalant and unconcerned approach to escape from a red-handed situation: you try to stroll by as if you don't even know anyone is there; it is about as effective as wearing a sign that says, It's not me you're after.

"This is the man," the clerk said.

"I beg your pardon . . ."

One of the British MPs said: "Understand there's a dead man somewhere on the premises . . ."

"On the mezzanine," the clerk said in English, with a pronunciation of the sibilant word that put one in mind of Weber and Fields.

"This chap says you were here with the dead man just a few minutes ago," the MP said. "Your nose looks as if it's been bashed recently. Here now, it's bleeding, isn't it?"

"It's an allergy," Darsoss said. "I think you have the wrong man. If you'll excuse me . . ."

"I think you'd better not leave yet, sir."

"This was the man . . ."

"Are you an American, sir?"

"Yes."

"Well, we can contact your chaps after a bit . . ."

"Tried and convicted already, am I?"

"No one said that . . ."

"The body is on the mezzanine."

"You've the wrong man, corporal," Darsoss said, able to see that Disa had safely disappeared from the scene. "Now, if you'll excuse me . . ."

"How do you know he's dead?" the second MP asked.

"You can tell easily," the clerk insisted. "We've all seen dead people before . . ."

"Has a doctor had a look at him?"

The clerk said: "There is the doctor at this moment." A bald and angry man with a pince-nez and a satchel was on his way to the staircase. "They must have got him away from his dinner . . ."

Darsoss grew uncomfortably conscious of the attention they were attracting. He felt marked for life.

"Let me see your identification, please," the first MP said. "Quinn, you go with this bloke and see what's going on. I'll be along in a minute."

"Right this way—to the mezzanine," the clerk said, leading the second MP away.

"Your papers, please—whatever you've got: passport or ID card . . ."

"You can't ask me for that," Darsoss said.

"In this sector I can," the MP said. "All police matters are British Army business . . ."

Darsoss had not gone this far just so he could meekly surrender to an MP who could as easily have been around the corner as right outside the door; there were better ways to pay the piper than that.

"You seem to have a split lip, too," the MP observed, and observed no more. Darsoss in the next instant had sent him sprawling backward over a suddenly extended foot to the marble floor, a cry of surprise and anger splitting the air. "Bloody son of a bitch—"

Darsoss fled into the cold night, the beating he had had nagging him as he ran along but not slowing him down to any extent. Snow and ice made the turns difficult, the corners rougher to negotiate than they would have been normally. He ran until he felt a cutting and spiteful stitch in his side. At that point he walked along swiftly for a block or so, hardly noticed or cared about by anyone because of the bitter cold, and soon he was certain he had either eluded pursuit or hadn't been pursued at all. That he was clearly marked was certain, however, and he could obviously never return to that hotel again or, for that matter, to the British sector of Berlin. Not that this was cause for concern in and of itself; it wasn't. It merely supported a feeling of leakage—a narrowing-down of what margin there had been. It couldn't be ignored or neglected.

He turned into a crowded club on Kliest Strasse, just a few streets outside of the British sector. There was a tremendous din set up by the occupying soldiers, their dames, and the people who had made their deals. Darsoss sat at the bar, unapproachable and unapproached, and waited for a thought to come into his head. One did. Who was the man in the bowler hat?— remote and hazy, a large dim figure of untold influence, yet without a face or a name. He couldn't fail to matter; he had reversed everything simply because he was unable to finish what he had begun. Could he have known as much, whoever he was;

229

could he have had any idea? Darsoss sat there thinking deeply about the power of the unforeseen, and he made a small grimace of understanding and satisfaction at the idea of stupid little cogs who foul big wheels and jam large machines. But was this that sort of thing? Not likely. Yet it revealed nothing on direct examination; it held no solution, offered no key to tomorrow's locked door. These would need to come from elsewhere, Darsoss knew. He still had his next move to map.

He sat and drank and listened to the music and thought about Disa with marked longing. And after a short time he realized that his best answer—his only answer—was the Boss. It would be an extension of the original plan, actually. There were certainly no guarantees attached to it, but it was worth the chance.

6

An anonymous house in the country was essential to all Central Intelligence Services—the Headquarters people, the ones who plan, who require privacy, whose life blood is secrecy. The salient demand of such a place was that it afford total protection from unauthorized eyes and ears. In the spacious study of just such a place, west of Dahlem and north of Zehlendorf, on the afternoon of the following day Darsoss sat, having talked and having smoked cigarettes for hours. No one had seen him or heard him but General Thaddeus J. Malone—the Boss to all and sundry in his section.

He was a beefy man of fifty, left with faint traces of the Irish good looks of a vanished youth. His eyes were bloodshot blue, his hair an authoritative white, his jawline still strong, his smile engaging and effortless and there as if to warn you he was a step or two ahead of you. Darsoss suspected him of being brilliant, an organizational genius, perhaps. A huge Second Empire desk separated the two of them, great windows behind the Boss's chair giving onto an expanse of lawn and trees dressed in white, earth and tree bark showing through here and there.

"Okay," the Boss said, lighting a cigarette. "Now let's look for the holes. Why didn't you keep going? You could've gotten out of Berlin. With O'Toole dead and the woman basically out of anybody's reach, you had an almost clear shot at the moon. I doubt the Russians have any idea about this; and you were

230

going to double-cross them and take your chances anyway. So what really stopped you?"

"Easy," Darsoss said. "The threat of future prosecution. For myself, yes. But more for Mrs. Quennel, who of anyone I've ever known least deserves punishment. With Bliss and Mornier still loose, she could never be free from the possibility of being hauled into a British court and sent to prison. They would pull both of us in, as a matter of fact. This beats them to the punch— just in case they were ever to be nailed for this little monkey-shine."

"Uh-huh."

"Point two—the British MPs and a dozen people in the hotel got a good look at me. I'm not exactly unknown, so I wouldn't make a good fugitive. Even if I could, I wouldn't. That's not for me. Or for Mrs. Quennel. I want to preclude the possibility of any future catastrophes; I don't like the idea of all those loose ends waiting to reach out and strangle us someday when we would least expect it; I want it off the books. To get it that way I'm making the same offer I made to Vernon."

"Exculpation."

"Yes, that's right."

"Except that it's not exactly the same offer."

"It certainly is. You've got my method of recruitment," Darsoss said, using his right-hand middle finger to enumerate each item on the fingers of the left hand. "The techniques they use; *my* personal motives; the MGB personnel involved; the code names and descriptions of various couriers and cutouts; points of rendezvous and habitation—the house in Pankow, for example; the amount and exact nature of the material I transmitted; the source of the material itself; *and*—the star attraction— the jolly old London network, its most important members, without doubt; with a chance to bag even more, who knows? But that's not all. You know what else you've got? British Security right by the balls."

"Yes, but it's still not the same offer."

"What in the world do you mean?"

"I mean it sat a little too long out of the icebox and the taste is off; it's gathered a slight mold, like quinine water will if you let it stand a couple of days without a cork." The Boss drew on his cigarette. "The big thing is the RD in this particular case. And he *is* dead; so the network is dead automatically, without any further ado. So you're left with footnotes. Assuming, of course, Vernon *was* the RD."

"Well, I can't *prove* that. But it's a little premature, isn't it, to wonder about it before you go into all this other stuff?"

"That was just my little aside. Skip it. Frankly, Vernon looks right for it—and based on more than just what you're telling me."

"He claimed he had six figures in a Swiss bank. That was part of his case. You might check it."

"Lots of people do. Even if we located the right bank, half those accounts are under code numbers or phony names. Forget it. The point is, I see it all just as you're telling it to me."

"Well?"

"Well what?"

"You don't really want to send us over, do you?"

"Me, young feller? Who do you think I am? The Ruler of the Universe? The Jewish God of Vengeance? No, I'm just not sure you can expect too much, looking at it very realistically."

Darsoss' heart jumped and his stomach tightened and he dragged on his cigarette. A calculated risk was always just that and nothing more; yet people treated it like a sure thing gone wrong when failure resulted. "You see," the Boss began, "these two jokers in London are really of use to nobody now. Professor Quennel is dead, so they're without a source. You're out of it, so they're without a courier; Vernon's death leaves them with nowhere to go and nothing to do."

"Berlin could find something for them to do."

"No, they couldn't. Berlin is concerned with Berlin. Berlin is a pickup and a dispatch point because of its peculiar geopolitical placement. But it's the Central Directorate that sets up the different operations all over the globe—GRU. And London's connection to GRU, in this case, you can bet was through its Resident Director, not MGB. And MGB in Berlin operates on directive from GRU. If Vernon *was* the Resident Director— and I pretty well buy that—it's dollars to doughnuts that your friends in Karlshorst haven't the slightest knowledge of it."

"Then where does it begin, and how did MGB get to me on Vernon's blueprint?"

"On a relay system. I'd say that a courier connected Vernon with the Center or GRU, and that Major Kholenko operated on instructions relayed from Moscow and never had any contact with Vernon at all."

"He knew Bliss."

"Only the code name Bliss. Not more, I can underwrite it. As to these other items—the *Blitzmädel* and the goons who picked up Mrs. Quennel at the airport—Vernon could safely expose himself to them, they wouldn't especially understand or care what was going on. Although MGB could have arranged for the *Blitzmädel* on instructions from a cutout—it's possible."

The Boss crushed out his cigarette. "The whole business is getting sticky," he said. "Hard and fast standards are out the window. I'll tell you it was a shock to learn about Vernon last night. It was before I talked to you, and I didn't know this part of it—but I got a bad feeling about it. I couldn't think of any reason why he would be murdered if his nose was clean. He wasn't in anything that big or rough—that is, that we knew about."

"Then you take my word."

"That part is immaterial." The Boss liked to keep people off balance; he probably thought he needed to. "You could have been wrong," he went on. "*He* could have been lying. But when I got the call from Winters saying you had come in looking like that"—he gave a nod of acknowledgement to a blue welt along Darsoss' jawline, and the slightly puffed and split lip— "I started to hear voices . . . the built-in radar . . ." He tapped his chest to show where the radar was.

"Listen, you can't say I don't have an offer; you really can't."

"I didn't say you don't have an offer. I'm just questioning its power to wipe out what amounts to an act of treason on your part—mitigating factors notwithstanding. Let me have some coffee brought in." He spoke into the box on his desk. "Lauralee, get some coffee in here, will you? Don't mix it, bring us the cream and sugar, we'll do it ourselves." He smiled at Darsoss like a priest who understood you better than you did yourself. "Not everybody approves of peacetime Intelligence activity, but they're going to damn soon. The days of black and white are gone, if they ever existed at all." The Boss was given to meandering abstractions; through devastating sleight of hand they always seemed to end in a point to dig your eye out. "For example, do you think it's wrong, in your heart of hearts, to lie, steal, and double-cross? Sure you do. But under all circumstances? Well . . . obviously not . . . But there I am—answering for you."

Darsoss wanted to hide his growing consternation. "That's okay," he said. "It's the way to get the answer you're after."

The Boss was unfazed, smiled and said, "That's right." He lit another cigarette, as heavy a smoker as Darsoss. "I'll let you in on something," he said. "I was about to get out of all this and go back to New York, back to my practice. There are some people who want me to run for the Senate, and that's what I'd like to do. But something stopped me. I've held off resigning because of it." A sense of personal destiny and importance was modestly entertained, but certainly taken for granted.

Darsoss took a deep breath, waited. He didn't get the explanation; he hadn't expected it. "You know, nothing is a simple matter," he said. "We're surrounded by semantic hoaxes. Terms like loyalty, and free choice, and immorality. There isn't one of them that doesn't beg all questions."

The coffee, cream, and sugar arrived on a tray, carried by Lauralee—a tall, beautiful auburn-haired girl with a somewhat spectacular figure and an unexpectedly graceful and intelligent air. "Many thanks, Lauralee," the Boss said. And when she had walked out he said: "You saw my secretary? She is admittedly enough to knock the spots off a leopard, no room for argument."

Darsoss knew him well enough to know he hadn't taken leave of his senses. "Sure," he said, and waited.

The Boss nodded with an air of someone who never depended fully on another opinion before making up his own mind. "To be sure," he said. "And I can tell you that the idea of congress with her is not unappealing to me. I don't want to appear coarse or improper, but I believe such a thing might be effected if I were to give it some effort. Yet I haven't, nor do I have future plans in its regard. Why? Because I might easily compromise myself, and what is more important, the United States. So I've put it out of my mind. A moral position? No. Sheer pragmatism. Such a situation would constitute second-degree immorality at worst—a mere technicality. But it would be stupidity in the first degree; because my risk would obviously be far greater than anything a man of my age would have the capacity to gain

from taking it. See? Everything is governed by circumstance."
He took a sip of coffee. Darsoss shifted in his chair.

"You might think," the Boss resumed, "that a man who
sleeps with another man's wife is a rat. But look closer. Maybe
he isn't. You might go along with Secretary Stimson that gentlemen don't read other gentlemen's mail. But maybe they do—
and must. As to whether they remain gentlemen—that's another
one of the semantic hoaxes."

"Not many people of your eminence would admit as much,"
Darsoss said.

"Am I what you'd call eminent?" the Boss said with a seraphic
smile of self-depreciation leavened by satisfaction. "I suppose
I am. Anyhow, you don't admit that kind of thing publicly—
only the poets and philosophers can afford to. But that's what
I'm getting at. I've been given all the verities, beginning at my
mother's knee and continuing on to the heads of the Jesuit
fathers; managing to stay out of jail, acquiring a law degree
from a top university, becoming a U.S. Army general . . . But
I read other gentlemen's mail." He shrugged. "I suppose it's
oversimple to say it's that kind of a world—but it's true, I'm
afraid."

Darsoss watched the Boss sip his coffee, and hoping he didn't
sound desperate he said: "Yes, that's right. As you say, the
days of black and white are gone. Compromise and individual
value assessments are in—for better or worse. But here is a case
of better—right here in this room, in your hands and mine.
And we have the chance to make something out of it—something that will give us the best possible balance . . ."

"You mean your proposal? The state's evidence gambit."

"Yes. Buy it."

"I can't," the Boss replied bluntly.

"You can't?" Darsoss repeated, shocked, and got out of his
chair. "But why? What value can there be in the imprisonment
of two people who saw their mistake and voluntarily tried to
make amends . . . and got into this kind of a jam for their
trouble?"

"What do you think I can do?"

"Act on the information I'm giving you. Make Mrs. Quennel
an informant and me a witness for the Crown. You can do it,
and make the British like it."

"On the contrary; it's my implicit obligation to contact BMG directly and defer to whatever action they would want to take. You must think of me as Malone the Omnipotent."

"No, I don't. I think your next step in this thing is optional. You can push, pull, or let go if you want to, and we both know it." Darsoss ran his hand tightly over his hair as if groping for his next thought.

"Logic, not emotion," the Boss cautioned.

"At least give Mrs. Quennel a break. She deserves it. Squash that part of it. Send me over alone, if that's what you feel you absolutely have to do."

"That's still emotion talking, Marco," the Boss said. "It doesn't tell me *why* I should act on what you're saying."

"Doesn't it?" Darsoss' rage partially eclipsed the object of his petitioning. He paced away and wheeled around suddenly. "How about because you've made deals with Nazis?" he shot back. "If you've been able to override the verities, as you call it, in that regard, one more time won't matter. I don't think your verities would even notice at this point."

The Boss may have been seething underneath, but he gave Darsoss a wise look and part of a smile. "Listen to me, Marco," he said. "Up till now I've tipped my hat to women and given my seat to old ladies in the subway. But I'd kick them into the gutter and break their ribs if it would keep us a jump ahead of the Russians. Because that in my judgment is the only way a just and lasting peace is even possible. Maybe we won't get it, but then every game starts out without a winner." He grew the slightest bit more intense as he continued: "I'm not some flag-waving son of a bitch with the stars and stripes sticking up his ass and out of his ears; but I do believe sincerely and whole-heartedly that we are more responsible and less uncivilized than they are; and we've got a long way to go."

"So what?" Darsoss snapped in disgust now, his hand dug into his pants pocket.

"Just this. If deals are made, as you just stated—and I'm not going to get into that very complex area with you now—they may have been made painfully." He stood up now. "Any amnesties or clemency was hard won, I can assure you. And the return on them was service . . ."

Darsoss looked at him and said nothing.

"Service we couldn't duplicate anywhere else in this muddy

236

war we're already fighting. You yourself just talked about individual value assessments, remember? Well, we do make them."

"Fine. But I'm talking about one of the most extraordinarily kind and decent human beings you'll ever meet—herself a victim, torn apart in something she could scarcely understand but always instinctively hated and suffered in the process of. Make your deals with Nazis till hell freezes over, but why stop short with her?"

"Because there's no *quid pro quo* here," the Boss answered directly. "You're having a fantasy. We have other sources for most of that material anyway. Don't you see? It's not that good—not now."

"Then what would be?" Darsoss asked, his voice reduced suddenly.

"That's a big question," the Boss said, lighting a cigarette, and strolled from his desk to place himself near a pull-down map of Europe. He shrugged. "A return on your investment that makes sense, that could justify an action as distasteful and critical as bringing pressure on the closest ally . . ." He shook his head. "You don't have that."

Darsoss said: "Don't I?"

"No, you don't," the Boss answered. "All *you* have," he went on, "is the ability to speak four languages; the gift of eidetic imagery; an understanding of politics; credentials as a journalist; and training and experience as an intelligence agent." He paused. "And what good would that be to anyone?"

Darsoss exhaled smoke in slow half-surprise, his eyes narrow and turned sly and perhaps derisive. "So that's it," he said softly. He knew the Boss's use of the thin veil; the trick of pretending to give the ball a fling into space but actually dropping it over the shoulder, he had seen all the tactics before. "Service . . ."

"Service?" the Boss echoed. "Did I say anything about that?"

"Not in English, no."

The Boss grinned a wistful, sentimental grin. "Are you applying for a job?" And then, as if it had been the slightest of casual asides, a wisp of nonsense to go unnoticed, he went on immediately to something else. "Anyhow, I think you see what I mean," he said.

"You mean a lot of things," Darsoss said. "Which of them are we talking about?"

"The spot you're in," the Boss said with an elusive edge of satisfaction in his voice. "I mean, don't get the idea I'm not tuned in; I am, believe me. Oh, I think you've been a madman and a horse's ass; but I must admit privately that the extenuating circumstances are more than anyone could fail to be moved by and understand." He began to stroll. "When all is said and done, you didn't do what you did for money; you didn't do it for ideological reasons or, as in the case of Vernon, for whatever warped pleasure such things render. As a matter of fact, you say you were revolted by your action—and all your subsequent behavior points to the truth of that; you could almost plead temporary insanity in all of it—almost, though not quite. But one could safely say this thing was an aberration, not your pattern or inclination, not characteristic of you, God knows." He inhaled and shrugged. "From that point of view, you're as trustworthy to this day as anyone I know—no more apt to blow his gaff than the Joint Chiefs of Staff. But the Law is a demanding mistress and position is all. So you fall short of the mark, with everyone clucking their tongues and saying how ironic it all is."

But Darsoss knew this was not all. "I guess I was mistaken," he said, making a countermove clearly meant to force a certain response one knew was there but couldn't prove. "It sounded almost as if . . ." He shrugged it away. "But no."

"As if what?" the Boss said innocently.

"As if you were about to make a proposition . . ."

The Boss said: "Proposition?" He smiled. "That's a funny idea, at that," he said as though it had just occurred to him. "Think of it. You're blown for both sides on the face of it. Nobody in their right minds—not even the Russians—would suspect that we would employ you, under the circumstances." He nodded appreciatively. "But if you were to get an acquittal, let's say—just to see how really funny this is—on insufficient evidence, or even a pre-trial dismissal, you would, theoretically, be perfect for a spot that has to be filled in Vienna. The cover is a news agency." He stopped, then said: "Really very funny."

"So that's it," Darsoss said again.

The Boss went on as if he hadn't spoken. "A perfect setup," he said musingly. "The Russians don't know you double-crossed them; they would think you were nabbed. You would be almost above suspicion."

238

Darsoss shook his head knowingly. "This has been it from the minute I gave you the story, hasn't it?"

"Now we're coming to something else," the Boss said. "You haven't given me as much as you think—not nearly. And I can back that up," he said, sitting down again at his desk and then holding up a folder like an exhibit to be recorded in a courtroom. "When this came to my attention," he began, "I postponed my plans and set aside certain personal ambitions. I had to. It's an MI5 report. It's in my possession by sheer accident. I was having dinner with someone in London one night about two weeks ago. He described the curious details of a surveillance they were running on a British atomic scientist. I was intrigued and asked to look at the file. Your name was in it, as we both know."

Darsoss drew cautiously on his cigarette, as if it might be deadly, and waited to hear more.

"The ironic thing, of course, was that the British had no idea that you once worked for me," the Boss went on. "And I didn't tell them. I didn't tell anyone; and I had no intentions of telling anyone. I wanted you accountable to no one but me."

"Accountable to you?" Darsoss said, puzzled only momentarily. "Oh, aha. Yes, I get it . . ."

"Of course," the Boss said. "I believed the whole thing just as the British did. There it was: the disloyal wife of a suspected Communist spy and traitor—bound to be in on her husband's activities; or at least close enough to find out about them. And who is her *inamorata*? Only a former OSS man. And who knows that? Only me. If Mrs. Goering had been one of our agents during the war we'd have had a promising situation. This looked almost as good in its own way. Nobody doubted that you were a love thief for one minute, Marco." He pushed the folder toward Darsoss. "You can look it over if you like."

Darsoss said: "What for? To prove you knew the joke all the time?"

"I was about to contact you when Quennel died," the Boss said, calm and unstoppable. "I thought we might have a talk. In my judgment you were in a perfect position to perform a crucial act of counterespionage. I thought I would begin by appealing to your patriotism."

"I'm glad I saved you the bother," Darsoss said.

"Don't be *too* mad at me," the Boss said. "You're here now instead of in Vernon's vest pocket because of what happened.

239

I didn't just drop the whole thing after Quennel's death, I sat right on top of it. That was why I knew Mrs. Quennel got on a plane in London this afternoon, even though I didn't know why, or who had arranged it. And that was why her arrival at Tempelhof was covered. It is also why your story about Vernon holds up so well: his mysterious presence at the airport was duly noted at the same time . . ."

Darsoss saw the light. "Then it was you . . . That was how . . ."

"The bowler hat you talked about belongs to one of our lads," the Boss said.

"*Your* guys," Darsoss said with open surprise.

The Boss nodded. "They fouled the operation a little bit; the idea was surveillance alone. But someone got overanxious and in the ensuing melee, the lady turned out to have excellent reflexes."

"So *that* was it," Darsoss intoned, still somewhat astonished.

"Yes," the Boss said. "Now let's see how good *your* reflexes are. What were we talking about? The Russians, weren't we? And Vienna, that's right. Do you waltz, Marco?"

"You can do better than that, Boss."

"All right, I'll try," the Boss said. "You've committed a certain act for which, isolated and of itself, amnesty is unheard of and clemency almost as rare. But a man's good record doesn't go entirely to waste *all* the time. Not just for one slip. Not if he hits a long enough ball." The Boss paused, looked at Darsoss, and poked his index finger at an invisible set of conditions. "There," he said, "is your *quid pro quo*." And then he added with twinkling eyes and in a solemn voice: "There is no other."

Darsoss didn't answer.

"You can think about it, of course. But not for too long. These things don't wait."

Darsoss said quietly: "Yeah, I'm aware of that. What if I refused?"

"I would wish you luck," the Boss said. "I don't want to see you languishing in a British prison—or this woman, for that matter. Of course she would be free from all further attachments or liability to prosecution, if I had the power to intercede in such a situation. Right now I don't, as you can see. After all, you are a private citizen of the United States who helped citizens of Great Britain to violate the Official Secrets Act of their country. I mean, that is your status as of this moment, isn't it?"

Darsoss said: "There's a word for this, isn't there?"

The Boss smiled indulgently. "There's a word for everything," he said. "We can't always achieve subtlety and finesse, much as we might like to. I believe there's a war to the death going on."

"What if I came up with nothing?" Darsoss said. "What if I went back to the Russians?"

The Boss said with unbeatable simplicity: "Why would you do that?"

Darsoss couldn't think of a reason.

"Besides, they wouldn't have you now. If you made an overture it would only arouse their suspicion. Remember they know you too."

Then there was silence for several moments, Darsoss looking at the Boss, whom he knew to be anything but a good loser. The Irish charm, the virile smile—all of it—could sink behind a looming black sulk, silent and threatening as storm clouds. He never smiled good-naturedly in the face of failure or defeat. And he was amiable and good-natured right now. As if he knew he had Darsoss. "No, you could do us a lot of good in Vienna," he said. "Nobody'll gain a thing if you're sitting in the pokey. And there you will sit . . ."

The door opened and Lauralee came just inside. "Winters is here with a lady," she said.

"Send the lady in," the Boss said, "but not Winters."

Darsoss stiffened a little bit, lit a new cigarette, and both men waited in silence for Disa to enter the room. When she did she gave Darsoss a smile of allegiance, almost secret, one of the few he had ever seen from her, like a presage of better days to come. "This is Mrs. Quennel," Darsoss said, looking at her with a sense of possession. "General Malone."

"How do you do," the Boss said, gesturing her to a chair, rising himself. "Won't you sit down."

"Thank you."

"General Malone knows all there is to know," Darsoss said to her and then sat down on the arm of the chair a few feet away from her own, leaned toward her. "I've been trying to reach an agreement with him—on several different grounds . . ."

The Boss gave no sign of his thoughts at the moment.

"I have tried to tell him you were *used* right from the start . . ."

"Why should you?" she said, almost in disappointment.

"Because I can think of nothing more pointless and wasteful than for you to spend two to five years of your life in prison—nothing more unjust . . ." He went on: "The point is, we've committed an act for which we can easily be charged and punished. But we can go scot-free in the full sense of the term; we can be free from charges—technically, legally—and no one could ever bother us about any of it again. What do you think that's worth?"

"What is being asked?" she said, almost as if she were not quite sure of him.

"In your case, Mrs. Quennel," the Boss said, "simply cognizance. That is, a deposition concerning your own part in the things that took place—under duress, of course—so that you are purely an informant. After that—your everlasting silence."

"That is all?" she said, a hint of skepticism in her voice.

"Basically, Mrs. Quennel, that is all," the Boss replied.

"I can't believe it," she said.

"Can't you? Why not?" the Boss asked.

She answered: "Does anything ever go that way?"

"There is one other thing," Darsoss said. "A need for my service . . ." She didn't seem to connect immediately with what he was trying to tell her, and he added: "In exchange for this complete clearance we're being granted, I would need to do certain work for the Government . . ."

"I didn't think you'd raise that subject, Darsoss," the Boss said, impatience in his tone.

"But I must," Darsoss said. "She has to know why we're going to Vienna, doesn't she? Oh, I could tell her I was running the news agency, but she'd never swallow that—she's been lied to by experts." He looked directly at Disa and said: "I'm of use to them, you see . . ."

"As an agent," she said.

"Yes . . ."

"And otherwise?"

"Otherwise . . ." He left it there.

"Prison," she said.

"Yes."

"Darsoss, you're way out of line," the Boss said.

"Look, be practical," Darsoss told the Boss earnestly, turning to lean over his desk for just a moment. "We got here together, Mrs. Quennel and I; we're in this thing together; the medium of exchange concerns both of us or neither one. If we go to Vienna, she's in on it. It's better as a team."

"This is the craziest thing I've seen yet," the Boss said calmly.

Darsoss looked at him pointedly. "You want it to work, don't you? What could be better than if she's part of the cover? That's one they'd *really* never dream of."

"To be an agent," Disa said to herself sadly.

"On the other side this time," Darsoss said, turning to her. "Bear that in mind."

"Why should you think even for a moment that I would agree to such a thing?" she said, looking right into his eyes. "Do you think my skin is that precious to me?"

"It is to me," he said with tremendous candor that came from the fever of the moment, as if the other man weren't there. "Your skin is very precious as far as I am concerned. I think it's cheap at the price . . ."

She was touched, perhaps even a little breathless. But she said: "You think I am so frail, so vain and selfish that I could agree?"

"Does prison appeal to you?"

"No," she said. "But the thought doesn't make me cower. There are worse things . . . Losing heart . . . losing faith . . . having no food . . ."

"Listen," Darsoss said. "You'll not only go to prison; you'll be stripped of your British citizenship, and then you'll be deported . . ."

"All right—but don't you see?" she said imploringly, her eyes trying to show him her very insides. "What happened before to both of us is what brought us to this point . . . here and now. And it would never end; and we could never come to terms with it—we didn't before, why should we this time? Do you see? It begets itself . . . it doesn't matter which side— the politics are not important. What is important is being forced to do something that goes against the heart and mind . . . But it is what *you* feel that counts; I can't decide for you . . ."

"But you know what will happen to you . . ."

"Yes. But there will be an end to it one day. And perhaps everything will be washed away by then—everything that isn't quite gone yet . . ."

Darsoss said: "And then what?" He looked deeply into her eyes, swept with the feeling of love for another person once again.

She said: "I would want us . . ." She stopped, her eyes lowered, the awareness of time and place suddenly very keen.

Darsoss gazed at her, wanted her answer desperately. "Go ahead," he coaxed gently. "Say it. It's all right . . ."

She said: "I would wait for you; and I hope you would wait for me . . . I know that's not all there is to it . . . But it's how I feel . . ."

There was a moment's silence and then Darsoss turned to the Boss and said: "You heard the lady."

The Boss said: "Yes, I did." He put his hand on the phone. "I hate to make this call," he said.

But he made it, and they watched a few seconds while he waited for a response. Then they looked at each other with the knowledge between them that no human arrangement is perfect. Or any good at all, perhaps. At the moment it didn't seem to matter. There may even have been a measure of joy in it.

ABOUT THE AUTHOR

Elliot West was born, raised, and educated in Brooklyn. He is the author of *Man Running, These Lonely Victories*, and *The Killing Kind*. He lives in Vermont.

James McClure

"A distinguished crime novelist who has created in his Africaner Tromp Kramer and Bantu Sergeant Zondi two detectives who are as far from stereotypes as any in the genre."
— P.D. James, *New York Times Book Review*

The Blood of an Englishman	71019	$2.95
The Caterpillar Cop	71058	$2.95
The Gooseberry Fool	71059	$2.95
Snake	72304	$2.95
The Sunday Hangman	72992	$2.95
The Steam Pig	71021	$2.95

William McIlvanney

Laidlaw   73338 $2.95

"I have seldom been so taken by a character as I was by the angry and compassionate Glasgow detective, Laidlaw. McIlvanney is to be congratulated."
— Ross MacDonald

The Papers of Tony Veitch   73486 $2.95

Poul Ørum

Scapegoat   71335 $2.95

"Not only a very good mystery, but also a highly literate novel."
— Maj Sjöwall

Martin Page

The Man Who Stole the Mona Lisa   74098 $3.50

"Page is full of life and good humor, and ingenuity, and his novel is a delight."
— *New Yorker*

Julian Rathbone

The Euro-Killers   71061 $2.95

"Well-written....the ending is sharp and bitter."
— *New York Times*

A Spy of the Old School   72276 $2.95

"This deserves consideration right up there with Le Carré and company."
— *Publishers Weekly*

Vassilis Vassilikos

Z   72990 $3.95

"A fascinating novel."
— *Atlantic*

Per Wahlöö

Murder on the Thirty-First Floor   70840 $2.95

"Something quite special and fascinating." — *New York Times Book Review*

Elliot West

The Night Is a Time for Listening   74099 $3.95

"The major spy novel of the year."
— *New York Times*

Look for the Pantheon International Crime series at your local bookstore or use the coupon below to order. Prices shown are publisher's suggested retail price. Any reseller is free to charge whatever price he wishes for books listed. Prices are subject to change without notice.

Quantity	Catalog #	Price
_____	_____	_____
_____	_____	_____
_____	_____	_____
_____	_____	_____
_____	_____	_____
_____	_____	_____
_____	_____	_____
_____	_____	_____
_____	_____	_____
_____	_____	_____
_____	_____	_____

$1.00 basic charge for postage and handling $1.00 _____

25¢ charge per additional book   _____

Please include applicable sales tax   _____

Total   [   ]

Send orders to: Pantheon Books, PIC 28-2, 201 East 50th St., New York, NY 10022.

Please send me the books I have listed above. I am enclosing $_____ which includes a postage and handling charge of $1.00 for the first book and 25¢ for each additional book, plus applicable sales tax. Please send check or money order in U.S. dollars only. No cash or C.O.D.'s accepted. Orders delivered in U.S. only. Please allow 4 weeks for delivery. This offer expires 4/30/86.

Name _____

Address _____

City _____ State _____ Zip _____